The Night They Vanished

Also by Vanessa Savage

The Woman in the Dark
The Woods

The Night They Vanished

VANESSA SAVAGE

GRAND CENTRAL
PUBLISHING

NEW YORK BOSTON

Copyright © 2022 by Vanessa Savage

Cover design by Faceout Studios. Cover photo © Silas Manhood/Trevillion Images. Cover copyright © 2022 by Hachette Book Group, Inc.

Grand Central Publishing
Hachette Book Group
1290 Avenue of the Americas, New York, NY 10104
grandcentralpublishing.com
twitter.com/grandcentralpub

First published in Great Britain in 2022 by Sphere.
First U.S. Edition: May 2022

Grand Central Publishing is a division of Hachette Book Group, Inc. The Grand Central Publishing name and logo is a trademark of Hachette Book Group, Inc.

The publisher is not responsible for websites (or their content) that are not owned by the publisher.

The Hachette Speakers Bureau provides a wide range of authors for speaking events. To find out more, go to www.hachettespeakersbureau.com or call (866) 376-6591.

Library of Congress Control Number: 2021952130

ISBNs: 9781538708231 (trade pbk.), 9781538708248 (ebook)

Printed in the United States of America

LSC-C

Printing 1, 2022

This book is dedicated to Tim, Jess, and Georgia

The Night They Vanished

<Update: NewUser1 has added one new listing...>

Want to know what really happened the night they vanished? This perfect family—the successful business manager, the happy housewife, the straight-A student, gone in a heartbeat... Why? What could possibly have happened?

Dig deeper, though, and things look different. A failed academic. A lonely wife. A teenager with dark secrets. Dig deeper and you see what's missing from that perfect picture of a perfect family. And you see who is missing. And you start to wonder—did they vanish or is there a darker crime to discover?

So... Want to know what really happened the night they vanished?

You do, don't you?

Then <click here>

Welcome to *The Dark Tourist*, a website where you can explore the darkest places in Britain, the sites of some of the most notorious crimes the UK has ever seen...and some that are hidden, secret, only whispered about after dark, only known by a few...

And now you.

Free access to over one hundred notorious sites...

Search by location, crime or date...

For only £9.99, **exclusive membership** to more hidden sites—

Maps, background history of the crimes, insight into the murderers and their victims, guides to the surrounding areas—all can be yours for only £9.99...

Sign up here:

Chapter 1

dark tourism
noun
noun: **dark tourism**
  1. tourism that involves traveling to places associated with death and suffering.

HANNA—Wednesday 7 p.m.

The unopened Christmas card watches me from the shelf. It does that a lot, sometimes shouting for attention, sometimes calling coyly. I should put the thing away in a drawer. Or burn it. Or maybe I should actually open it. It probably just says "Merry Christmas." Or it'll be one of those round-robin cards, detailing everything my family has been up to over the year, a bragging list of their achievements, a hollow reminder of all the things I haven't been there for— *Look at what you're missing!*

Or—and this is why I still haven't opened it—it could be a personal message: *Why haven't you...? When will you...? I wish you'd...* Or, if it's written by my dad rather than my stepmother (highly unlikely but...), it'll be: *How dare you? I should have known you'd... Typical behavior from you... I should never have expected more...*

Why on earth should I subject myself to that? Bland

message, round robin, screaming accusations—it'll hurt whatever it is, so the bloody thing can shout all it wants, I will *not* open it. But my resolve wavers as it always does when I go to grab it, to bin it, to hide it, my hand hovering in mid-air, like I think I'll be punished for daring to throw it away unopened.

My phone buzzes and I glance at it. It's Dee being telepathic again. *Okay?* the message says.

Am I? Another buzz—*I know what today is. We can rain check if you like.*

Not telepathic then, she doesn't know about the card. She's just noted the date. The irony is I'd forgotten. Haunted by a damned unopened Christmas card rather than the things I should really be haunted by. I catch sight of the tattoo I got last year—it's not like I could forget for long now that I have that permanent reminder.

I turn my back on the card and tap out a reply to Dee. I won't cancel our night out, not because of a card *or* a date.

The sky is ominously dark when I step outside, so I head for my car even though the pub is only ten minutes away. To be honest, I probably would have taken the car even if the sky were clear. The quickest way to the pub skirts the park, along a quiet road popular with joggers. But it's also popular with joyriders, because it's long and straight with no speed bumps, and there was a nasty hit-and-run less than two minutes from my house a few months ago. The police sign appealing for witnesses is still there, but as far as I know, no one has come forward. Like I said, the road is creepily quiet. So, car it is, even though the one-way system means it'll take just as long to drive as it would to walk.

But I freeze, keys in hand, when I get to my car—my

front tire is flat. I could cry, I really could. Why do I bother? I should take this as the sign it obviously is, let today's date envelop me and coat me in a layer of darkness, go back in, cancel Dee, stuff myself with cake, and cry myself to sleep.

I crouch to look closer—the tire is not just flat, it's shredded. No way is this a puncture: it's been slashed. The urge to cry fades as I straighten up and the first drops of rain fall heavy on my head. Clutching my car key so tight it digs into my palm, I storm back into my house, swearing under my breath as I chuck the keys down and get out my phone.

"Liam—you fucker," I say as soon as he answers.

There's a pause. "Hanna?"

"You slashed my tire, you shit, you absolute *shit*."

Another pause. I hear muffled voices, hear him moving, a door closing. "What the hell are you on about?" he says when he comes back on the line.

"My car—my tire slashed to ribbons. Ringing any bells?" I say it through clenched teeth.

"Are you insane? Why the hell would I slash your tires? Jesus, Hanna, you need to get a life and leave me alone. I've told you this before. If this is some crazy cry for help, I'm—"

"Oh, don't give me that shit. What is this, some kind of revenge? For all the delusional paranoid crap you spouted at me just because you saw me near your flat? I told you I had nothing to do with what happened."

He snorts down the phone. "Yeah—you keep telling yourself that, why don't you? Look, I haven't been near your car, or your house, or you. I'm with my girlfriend; I've been with her all evening. I've moved on—hell, I'd moved on before we broke up. You need to let it go and stop calling me." He pauses. "Or I really will go to the police."

I'm squeezing the phone so hard I'm amazed I haven't

crushed it to dust. "Oh...fuck off," I say and stab at the screen to end the call, wishing I still had a bloody land line so I could slam the receiver down.

I hate, hate, *hate* that he can still do this to me two months after we've broken up: make me so angry I'm shaking. He is such a bastard—I can't even go to the police because he'll no doubt get his new *girlfriend* to lie and say he hasn't left her side, that it's me harassing him and not the other way around...

It had to be him, right?

Oh God, have I just made a total fool of myself? I take a breath, try to let out the anger. It could have been kids, it could have been anyone. I can feel my cheeks reddening. Oh God, Liam is going to think I'm crazy.

No. No—I won't do this to myself. It's his own fault my mind automatically went to him, if he weren't such a idiot I never would have assumed...

I cringe again, remembering my rant. I'll delete his number—delete all his bloody contacts off my phone. I'll get the tire fixed and that'll be it.

I'm horribly late and of course the rain has gotten heavier since I came back in. I take another deep breath. No—no excuses. I'm going out. The walk to the pub will be good and perfectly safe—that rain will cool me off and I can forget all about it—the car, the unopened card, today's date—before I meet my friends.

Wednesday night and our neighborhood pub is not busy. To be fair, though, it never is—that's why we like it. We're always guaranteed a table—like a bunch of nans, we can't be doing with standing all night, shouting to be heard. Yes, we're still just about in our twenties, but I did my partying years starting at fourteen, sneaking out through my bedroom window, plastered in makeup with bad fake ID. Jaded and cynical before my fifteenth birthday, the year everything turned to shit. Dee and Seb have been coupled up since sixth-form college so they're as nan-ish as me when it comes to a social life, more keen on dinner parties and the kind of parties with quiet background music and lots of comfy chairs rather than clubs. Five minutes here and I'm already feeling soothed, Dee and Seb's presence like a warm blanket and a mug of hot tea. I don't mention the slashed tire or my angry fit at Liam when I walk in half an hour late and soaking wet, just mutter I had a flat battery so had to walk.

Dee frowns, passing me her dry cardigan from the back of her chair to put on, while she sends Seb to the bar to ask for a pot of tea. Literally a hot blanket and a drink to go with their presence. "You walked the park road?" she says.

I smile. "Dee—the hit-and-run car isn't Christine. There isn't a possessed Plymouth Fury lurking around every corner waiting for unaccompanied women to flatten."

"It's not funny," Dee says. "I heard it was no accident. That the driver deliberately mounted the pavement and hit her at sixty miles an hour."

I wince and then shiver as someone opens the door to the bar and lets in a blast of cold air. "No, of course it's not funny, but my point stays the same—whoever did it is not still lurking around, are they? I promise to always cross the road safely, Mother Hen."

Dee glances round to check if Seb is still at the bar. "Changing to a nicer subject—what are you doing on Friday night?"

I shrug. "Well, not going out walking, obviously…Netflix? Possibly a pizza if I'm feeling daring. Why, did you have a better offer for me?"

"I might. How does a date sound?"

"You want to take me on a date? Dee, I'm flattered, but what about Seb?"

"Oh, ha ha, *very* funny. It's one of Seb's friends—Adam? I'm not sure if you've met him, but he's been at parties we've all been at, so you may have run into him."

"A blind date? Oh God, Dee—really?"

"What's wrong with a blind date? He's nice—really nice. Fairly recently single, I think. He and Seb were at university together. He moved to Wales a few months ago to work with Seb so he's employed." She pauses and grins. "Better than your last few boyfriends already, right?"

I pull a face. "Come on, Dee. Me and a nice, employed, solvent man? That's never going to work, is it? Besides, I'm *awful* at first dates. You've seen me if someone tries to chat me up—"

"Stop it," she says gently.

"Stop what? He wouldn't be interested—unless you've told lies about me." I smile. "Which you probably have because if you gave him the real lowdown, he'd never—"

"Stop it," she interrupts, less gently this time. "Stop punishing yourself, stop running yourself down. You do deserve a nice date, a nice boyfriend—someone sexy but decent who won't cheat on you or try to swindle you or treat you like shit."

Tell that to the Christmas card on my shelf, I want to say but I keep quiet—one more negative comment and Dee will get really mad.

"Come on," she coaxes. "I saw you flinch at the word 'date.' You can't let your dad do this to you. It's like he's permanently sitting on your shoulder, putting you down."

I don't know whether to shudder or laugh at the image of

my dad in miniature form sitting on my shoulder, but Dee's right. He is always there.

"And," Dee continues, "you can't let Liam the loser do this to you either. He's gone, over, out of your life. Forget him and move on. Forget both of them."

I look down at the table, picture myself telling Dee about the tire, about my phone call to Liam, about that ridiculous night outside his flat. Would she believe it was him? Or is she going to think as he did—as I'm beginning to worry myself—that I'm so screwed up I was just looking for a reason to ring him and torture myself all over again? Oh, fuck it—maybe Dee's right. I should forget I ever met Liam and wasted six months of my life on him. Maybe I'll go home, chuck the Christmas card in the bin unopened, and say yes to the blind date. Maybe Seb's friend Adam likes prickly women who socialize like his nan.

"What are you thinking—can I set it up?" she asks, as Seb returns with our drinks and I take a grateful sip of tea, warming my hands on the cup.

"I was thinking about Christmas cards, actually."

"*Christmas* cards? Hanna—It's *February*. Are you sure that's just tea you're drinking?"

I don't agree to the date, not even when Seb joins in with Dee's coaxing, painting Adam as the perfect date. Dee frowns at my protest that me and perfect are not a good mix, but she lets it go after I promise to think about it.

And I do, I think about it the whole taxi ride home, indulging my imagination in a scenario of me and the perfect Adam hitting it off, falling in love, living a fictional happy-ever-after.

I laugh to myself as I unlock my front door because even

solely in my imagination I can't do it. Even in my imagination, the perfect scenario won't play out—the happy-ever-after is flimsy, a cardboard cut-out I can't make real.

What is real is the reminder of that Christmas card—the reminder of who I am and what I've done and why I don't deserve any better than a man like Liam. I think that's why the Christmas card is still there, why I go through the almost daily ritual of should I open it, should I throw it away—and end up doing nothing at all. It's a reminder, and a warning, and a way to punish myself.

There's an envelope on the mat when I get in—a yellow Post-it note stuck to it: *Sorry—this was delivered to mine by mistake!* The note is from Ben, my half-house neighbor. The postal mix-up happens quite often because of the oddness of our flat layouts. It was what attracted me when I was viewing flats: after traipsing round a dozen identical uninspiring box flats in Cardiff Bay, this place was a breath of fresh air. It was more central, close to the park, and, for some reason, instead of splitting the house into floors, the developer had divided it into two flats vertically to create two maisonettes, both with a living room and kitchenette downstairs and one bedroom and a bathroom upstairs. It was like owning my own mini house with a one-bed flat price and it meant both Ben and I had a narrow strip of garden out the back. The two identical front doors, despite being labeled 27A and 27B, seemed to confuse the postman regularly.

I peel off the yellow sticky label and look at the envelope. My name and address are written on the front in a neat but unfamiliar hand, but the size and weight of the white envelope are so similar to the unopened Christmas card that I shiver, for a moment convinced that the card has found its way back out into the world to be re-delivered. Especially when I walk into the living room and the Christmas card isn't on the shelf where I left it propped up. I almost throw the newly delivered post across the room before I spot the missing card, the envelope face down on the floor. The wind, that's all—the wind blew it off when I opened the front door.

I pick it up and try to calm myself down. Of course it's not the same card. This isn't Harry Potter with dozens of cards about to fly down the chimney until I open one. I rip open the new envelope and immediately wish I hadn't. It's a sympathy card. *Sorry for your loss*, it says on the front in swirly text above a picture of some lilies. I open the card with a shaking hand, but there's nothing written inside. It's not coincidental or accidental, the arrival of this card. Someone knows the significance of today's date. And the only person I can think of who knows the date Jacob died, and would send this card to me, is my father. But would he really be so breathtakingly cruel?

Of course he would. I blink tears from my eyes. It's stupid, so bloody stupid. Dee is right—I've let that Christmas card sit unopened on the shelf for over two months, allowing it to torture me daily, and in the end, it didn't matter— my father got in a sneak attack, swept aside all my defenses with this new card.

I rip up the sympathy card, tear it into tiny pieces, crumple the envelope up into a ball. I reach for the Christmas card to do the same, but hesitate. My dad isn't in that envelope— it's just me, punishing myself, exactly as Dee said, but I'm not ready to open that one, or tear it up. I grab the card, open a drawer in the dresser, and shove it inside, right to the back. I won't give it another thought, even if I'm too cowardly to actually either open or bin the bloody thing.

I double-check all the doors and windows are locked

before heading up to take a bath, still twitchy about my poor car. Now that I'm calm, I really don't think Liam had anything to do with it. Furtive tire slashing is not his style, but the thought that my ex is enough of a shit that my mind immediately turned to him is depressing.

Before I switch off the light to go to bed, I send a text to Dee, typing quickly and pressing send before I can start prevaricating: *Okay—set me up with a nice solvent non-cheating non-toxic man.*

Chapter 2

thedarktourist.com

    \<Suspicious login alert\>

    2019-02-17 login failed: incorrect authentication data—6 attempts

    2019-02-18 login failed: incorrect authentication data—24 attempts

    2019-02-19 login failed: incorrect authentication data—9 attempts

    2019-02-20 login failed: incorrect authentication data—35 attempts

    2019-02-21 login failed: incorrect authentication data—38 attempts

    2019-02-22 login failed: incorrect authentication data—12 attempts

    . . .

    2019-02-23 login successful: access granted

Friday 7 p.m.

Jeans or a dress? I hover in front of the mirror, a pair of skinny jeans in one hand, a patterned wrap dress in the other. Oh, for God's sake, we're only going to the pub. I chuck the dress onto the bed and pull on the jeans. Only the pub, but maybe a nicer top than the plain black jumper I'm currently wearing—it is a date after all.

"Oh, for God's sake." I mutter it out loud this time and sink on to the bed, shoving aside the pile of clothes I dumped there as I dithered over what to wear. A date. And not just a date—a blind date. I pick up my phone and call Dee.

"Remind me why I'm doing this again?" I put her on speaker while I take off the black jumper and replace it with the dark green velvet-edged top Dee bought me for Christmas.

"Because you haven't been out with anyone since Liam the loser and I'm fed up with seeing your miserable face and hearing you moan about it?"

"Not making me feel any better." I go over to my dressing table and hook in my silver earrings.

"Okay—because Adam is nice, and I think you two will really hit it off?"

"Nice—is there a worse word to describe someone than *nice*?" I hesitate as I reach for my makeup bag. Will the red lipstick be wasted on someone so *nice*?

"There's nothing wrong with nice. It doesn't mean boring. It means *decent*. It means he won't be shagging two other women at the same time as you and always accidentally forget his wallet every time you go out."

I wince. Ah, yes, Liam. Maybe I'll stop regretting my meltdown at him on the phone—he might not have slashed my tire, but he was still a shit. I put the red lipstick away. I wore it on my first date with Liam and he ended up wearing more of it than me after a teen-style kissing marathon outside the pub. I go with a berry lip-stain instead. More durable. Although Mr. Blind Date doesn't sound likely to ruin my makeup. Too *nice*.

"But a blind date, Dee? It's just so... desperate."

"It's not really a blind date, though. You two have actually been in the same room together although you didn't technically meet."

I have vague memories of Dee pointing out a tall bloke with black hair at one of her parties. But as he had his back to us at the time and was on his way out of the door, that's all I have. Tall, black hair.

That's Adam, she'd said. *He was Seb's best mate at uni.*

So now Dee is trying to set up her best mate from school with her boyfriend's best mate from university so we could be a cozy foursome, having cozy dinner parties forever more and living happily ever after, blah blah blah.

The thought makes my throat go tight. However many warm cardigans and hot drinks Dee wraps me in, I am never going to be the cozy dinner party type. Never ever.

I wonder how Seb pitched me to Adam—did he describe me as *nice*?

Ha. Doubt it. I love Seb because Dee does, but our relationship has always been a bit... wary? Is that the word? Of course, he met me at my rock-bottom worst—when I was more feral monster than best friend to Dee—so it's understandable a hint of that original wariness is still there. To be fair, if it wasn't, I'd think less of him.

I sigh and glance down at my phone to check the time.

"I'd better go if I'm going." I pick up my bag, check for keys, money.

I pull a face at myself in the mirror. It's my dad's face in feminine form that looks back at me. I hate that I got none of my mum, that I look so much like him. It's why I tried so hard as a teenager to change how I looked—bleaching my hair, plastering on the makeup, piercing my nose. Bonus points for me how insane it made him. I've stopped doing that now, but maybe I should start again. Blue hair could be nice to match my eyes.

"Do you think I'd look good with blue hair?" I ask Dee.

"Hell, yes, I think you'd look shit hot with blue hair." She pauses. "Please, Hanna, let yourself enjoy tonight. Remember you *are* worth it. You are worthy of a *nice* man, a *good* man. You have to stop hating yourself."

They're the words she's been saying to me for nearly a decade. I look down at the tattoo on my wrist. "Thank you, Dee, but I'm okay, I'm *good*—I don't need another intervention. Save the motivational speak for your clients. I'll call you tomorrow, let you know how it went."

He's late. Only five minutes, but as I ended up being fifteen minutes early, I've now had twenty minutes of jumping every time the door opened, every time I saw someone tall or someone with black hair. He's late and now I'm pissed off and self-consciously aware that everyone in the pub—with their sideway glances at the table I'm hogging, the spare chair I've refused to give up five times now—thinks I've been stood up.

I'm extra antsy because this bar reminds me of the one where I met Liam, where he "accidentally" spilled my drink and flirted as he bought me another one. Three months in and I caught him "accidentally" spilling another woman's drink in another bar like this one when he didn't realize I was there. The fact that I carried on seeing him for another three months after that doesn't make me feel any better about being here.

It means when Adam finally appears, six minutes and twelve seconds late, I greet him with a scowl instead of a smile and am already wondering how long before I can make my escape. My shoulders are hunched, and I can almost feel the hostile prickles becoming real all over my skin. I'm like a curled-up, scowling porcupine. A curled-up, scowling porcupine nan wishing she'd stuck with the Netflix and pizza plan.

"Hanna?" He raises his eyebrows as he speaks and despite the scowl on my face, I grudgingly acknowledge he has a good smile. He looks nice, like Dee said. I force myself to smile and stand up to greet him.

"Hi, Adam."

"Sorry I'm late," he says. "Can I get you a drink?"

"Um—just a Coke, please."

"You're driving?"

I shake my head. "I don't drink."

There's a short, awkward silence and I wonder if he's evaluating the situation, wondering how much fun a date in a pub with a non-drinker could possibly be.

The awkward silence gets longer when he returns from the bar with my Coke and a pint for himself and even though I hate myself for it, I find myself again comparing it to my first date with Liam, the one that ended with a lipstick-sharing kiss that invited catcalls from passing strangers.

Dee's plea to give this a chance echoes in my head. "I'm sorry," I say. "Dee didn't actually tell me much about you other than how nice you were."

"Nice?" Adam winces. "Thanks, Dee. She couldn't have said sexy or funny or...dangerously brooding? Anything but *nice*?"

I laugh. "So that's the real you, is it? Sexily funny yet dangerously brooding?"

He grins. "Or dangerously funny?"

There's another silence but it's a warmer one, and I remember that although there were no silences on that first date with Liam, it was purely because he didn't let me get a word in. He monopolized the conversation for the entire six months I knew him. And Adam maintains eye contact the whole time we're talking. Liam was always looking away, looking to see who'd walked in, who'd walked out. Adam looks at me like we're the only people in the bar. The attention makes my cheeks burn and something—only a tiny something, but *something*—flutters in my stomach.

"I'm almost scared to ask what Dee said about me to get you to agree to this," I say.

He smiles. "All good things, I promise. She said you were smart and pretty. Quiet but only until you got to know someone."

"But not *nice*?"

"Oh, definitely not nice, she said."

I laugh and raise my glass. "To Dee and her terrible match-making sales pitch. We must both be desperate if we agreed after that."

He hesitates, opens his mouth, closes it, clears his throat before speaking. "Actually, I asked about you first. A while ago now—I saw you at a party, so I already knew about the pretty part of her pitch. I talked to Seb about you, but he said you were seeing someone."

I'm flustered, wrong-footed. I didn't, I don't...I'm not the girl someone notices across a crowded room. Men tend to come across me by accident, surprised to find me in a quiet corner. He asked about me? When? Why didn't Dee mention it?

I lean back in my seat. I need to get this back on standard first-date track. "So, dangerously nice Adam—you work with Seb?"

It's an awkward segue but other than a slight hesitation

before he answers, he goes with it. "Yeah—I'm freelance, but I do a fair bit of work for his company."

"You're a web developer?"

He nods. "I know—it sounds pretty boring. Code and PHP and WordPress. But I design as well. What about you?"

I shrug one shoulder. "Nothing exciting. I work in admin."

"But at a magazine, right? Seb told me."

"Yeah…and I do some writing. Freelance as well, but I've sold a few articles."

"So, is that what you'd like to do full time?"

I hesitate. "Not really—I mean, yes, I'd like to write full time, but not in a nine-to-five. I'd have to move to London to get a decent writing job. I'd rather stay here and free-lance. The joys of a city, but I like being able to get to the sea in under an hour."

He smiles. "Yeah, me too. I'm originally from some suburban commuter town no one's ever heard of a million miles from the coast. I came here for college and although I've done my stint in London, it was like coming home when I moved back here."

"When I was a kid, all I wanted to do was leave Wales. I wanted to move away, deny my roots, drop the Welsh accent. London was the intoxicating dream destination I spent my teen years yearning for…" I pause, shrug, write off five or six years in that one shrug, before continuing. "Then after a while, I worked out I didn't have to run that far. I stopped, took a breath, and realized I *like* living in Wales. It was the small-town life I needed to get away from, not the country itself."

I make the decision as I get up to buy another round of drinks that this will be the last one. He is nice, as Dee said, and funny, but with no hint of any sexy or brooding, it's fairly obvious there's no spark. I'll drink my second Coke, make sure it's been an hour, and come up with some polite excuse.

He's rolled up his shirtsleeves by the time I get back to the table and he runs his hand through his hair, leaving it a bit messed-up. It makes me pause—I've got a thing for a good forearm, I can't lie, and the sexy bed-head thing is a definite improvement on the Mr. Clean Cut who walked through the door. Okay, so possibly some sexy to add to the nice and funny.

He's leaning back in his chair, looking more relaxed as he starts his second pint, and as I sit opposite him, still stiff and awkward, I wish, for the millionth time since I stopped, that I still drank. I used to like it—not getting drunk necessarily, but the slow mellowing, the warm fuzziness. I was never very good at stopping at the warm fuzzy stage, that was the problem.

"So, Seb said you and Dee grew up together?" he asks, back to the first-date script, but distracting me by leaning forward and resting his delicious forearms on the table, one of his hands brushing mine.

"That's right, in some minute village you definitely won't have heard of. Littledean—a diminutive of the almost as small West Dean, about forty minutes down the coast." I pause and smile. "West Dean has pubs, a few shops, and a school. Littledean is tucked on the end, about twenty houses, one village shop, and a bus stop. Oh, and a holiday park. Me and Dee were the only kids of the same age who lived there permanently—we had to end up as either best friends or mortal enemies. But it is near the sea. We pretty much grew up on the beach."

"It sounds idyllic."

I snort. "Hardly. I spent all my time on the beach to get away from my house."

"Ah, sorry. I didn't mean..."

"It's okay. Ignore me. I didn't get on so well with my dad growing up—I spent more time with Dee than I did at home. She's my real family."

He runs his hand through his hair again and I get a definite surge of the warm and fuzzies. Maybe the barman sneaked vodka into my Coke. Then Adam leans forward and smiles and I'm—Woah. *Really* good smile. Maybe I'll stay for one more Coke after all.

"West Dean...Littledean...Actually, I have heard of it."

"Really?"

"Yeah, I stayed with Seb's family a couple of times when we were at university, and we visited a few places I was interested in..."

"In Littledean and West Dean? Seriously?"

He opens his mouth, closes it again, then laughs. "Okay— I promised Seb I wouldn't mention this on a first date..."

"You're married? A serial killer? A priest? Is this where the dangerous you mentioned comes in?"

"I built this website...it makes me a bit of extra cash. It's called The Dark Tourist."

I look back at him blankly.

"Dark tourism—you know, where people do tours of notorious historic crime scenes?"

"What—like the Jack the Ripper tour?"

"Something like that—but my website specializes in under-the-radar sites. People pay a subscription and get access to the stories and locations. I got interested in it back in uni when I stayed with Seb and his family. Such a small, close-knit community and there are all these places with

such sad histories that no one from outside knows about."
He pauses and shoots a glance at me, his cheeks looking a
little red. Is this where he tells me he's got a voyeuristic kink
for old murder scenes?

I pull a face. "That sounds...really creepy. Who would
be interested in *that*? What about the poor people who still
live there?"

"You'd be surprised—it's a genuine thing. There are
loads of other websites dedicated to it. But what mine
offers is like...say if you went to London to do the Jack the
Ripper tour, you could go on my website and get a list of
another ten crime sites you might not have heard of."

The wannabe journalist in me feels a little tug of curiosity—
it would actually make a pretty good story to find some of
the people who do this for fun. "So is that what you're into,
then?" I ask. "Lurking round murder sites on your day off?"

He smiles again. "Not exactly. I did a lot of photography
at uni as part of my course and I got into urban exploring—
you know, where you explore abandoned buildings? I found
it fascinating. Some of the places I went to—whole lives just
abandoned. The whole Dark Tourist thing started from there.
One of the abandoned houses I checked out...I looked into
the history of it and it was pretty gruesome, not a serial-
killer house or anything—nothing that would make the
nationals, but for people into dark tourism..." He stops.
"It does all sound pretty creepy, doesn't it? Now I get why
Seb suggested I don't mention it on a first date."

"And it might explain why Dee went no further than
nice in her description of you—nice but with creepy, ghoul-
ish hobbies?"

"Mmm, maybe rewind and pretend I never mentioned
it?" He pauses. "Maybe save it for the second date?"

It's an invitation of sorts—we've both finished our drinks and it feels like this date is over. I'm surprised to see we've been here over an hour and a half. Longer than I'd planned. And I'm not sure anymore that I want the date to be over. His hobbies might be a bit off, but he's actually...I like him. I like his hair and his smile and his arms. Oh, his arms...

But do I like him enough? Enough to accept a second date, enough to hesitate in some doorway and wait for a kiss? See how durable the berry lip-stain is? After Liam, I'm not sure if I can be bothered. If I like him enough to bother.

"Listen," he says, leaning forward, giving me that smile again. (Maybe I do—if he keeps smiling that smile, maybe I do like him enough.) "Do you want to see something?"

A surprised burst of laughter escapes me. "Do I want to see something? What—your penis?" I clap my hand over my mouth—did I really say that out loud?

His smile freezes, then widens. "Well, I wasn't offering that quite yet," he says. "I was going to suggest dinner before a full frontal." He hesitates long enough for me to die of embarrassment, to pull off my burning skin and bury myself in the ground.

"I was actually going to show you a building."

"A building?"

"An abandoned one. I found it a while ago—it's not far from here."

"So, on our first date—when we're essentially strangers—you want to take me to an abandoned building..."

He laughs. "Dangerously brooding, remember? But I'm not planning to murder you, I promise."

"Oh, that's reassuring. Because of course if you were planning to murder me, you'd tell me up front."

23

"Well—how about I don't actually take you *into* the abandoned building—we just look through the window? It's...it might explain better why I'm into the whole urban exploring thing. And maybe it could be something you write about? I'm always looking for features for my website if you can't sell it elsewhere."

I could just go home now. Pick up that pizza, watch some crap TV, call Dee and hear the disappointment in her voice when I tell her the date was over in under two hours.

Or... "Sure," I say. "Why not? But no murdering, okay?"

The conversation flows more easily as we stroll along the brightly lit streets. He tells me about his younger brother and his parents, his friends and his job. I tell him very little, skating over the subject of family but telling him more about the writing I've done, how I dream of earning a full-time living from freelance writing. He seems genuinely interested in my little life: the home, the career, the friendships I'm so proud of building. Perhaps we should have done the date this way round—met somewhere a mile from the pub, talked our way there.

The streets get less well lit as we walk away from the center of town and despite my earlier joking, I do begin to feel a little on edge. I know he's a friend of Seb's, but to me he's a stranger and no one has a clue where I am. My imagination paints a picture of me never making it home, of Dee calling, worried, of Adam acting surprised and pretending we parted ways at the pub while wiping my blood from his hands and stuffing my body in the freezer.

"This is it," he says, making me jump, interrupting my macabre thoughts.

It's obvious the house is abandoned—no secret urban

explorers' code needed—the windows are boarded up. It's a small Victorian end-of-terrace on a quiet, badly lit street. Half the houses seem empty: they look neglected and overgrown.

"I'm not sure about this," I say, looking back toward the brighter, busier streets.

"Come on," he says, walking up the path and round the side of the house.

I hesitate, then follow, cursing as I almost trip over a large stone. The garden is a jungle and I have to push aside overgrown plants to catch him up. He's in the back garden. The boards from the window here are lying on the floor, the glass in the window is smashed.

"Did you do this?" I speak softly. It's dark and quiet and even though I know the house is empty, this feels too much like breaking and entering. I don't want someone hearing us and calling the police.

"No—squatters or kids, I don't know. There's nothing worth stealing inside."

I join him at the window. He pulls out his phone and switches on the torch app, shining it into the house.

It's a dining room—the table still in place, two chairs, one lying on its side on the floor. There's a vase of dead flowers in the middle of the table, a bowl and a plate, everything thick with dust. It's weird and creepy and somehow sad and the back of my neck prickles.

"I wonder what happened," Adam says, his voice as quiet as mine. "Who lived here? Where did they go? It's like they just disappeared halfway through a meal."

"Maybe the owner died and didn't have a family to clear the house for them." The earlier pang of sadness I felt grows.

"Yeah…" He sighs. Then he turns to me the same moment I turn to him and we're both leaning in and then we're kissing in the garden of an abandoned house. I shiver as he pulls me closer.

How very un-nanish. Fifteen-year-old me would have been proud.

And that's the thought that makes me pull away.

Chapter 3

SASHA—November, three months earlier

"Mum says she's going to go down the pub with Steve and I can have up to twenty people over."

Expand and simplify 3(h + 2)−4

How the hell am I meant to concentrate on algebra with Carly and Seren's nonstop whispering?

"She said I can have a bigger party next year for my six- teenth, but she'll buy some drinks."

"Who's coming?"

Shut. Up. For. God's. Sake. Shut. Up. I want to turn and stab them both with the pen clenched in my hand.

3(h + 2)−4 = 3h + 2, I write, my pen nearly going through the paper.

"Tyler, of course."

A dick.

"And Dylan."

A moron.

"Nathan and Finn."

Both moronic dickheads.

"Ewan because he can get weed."

I roll my eyes and turn the page.

"I wish Mum would hire somewhere, then I could invite the Year Elevens as well."

Ah—Year Eleven. Even more brain-dead idiots than in Year Ten.

"But where? The holiday park?" Carly and Seren both giggle.

My shoulders are so stiff now they're actually aching.

"Oh yeah, and then I'd have to invite never-been-kissed, never-been-pissed Sasha Carter and have her pervy creep of a dad slathering over us. Urgh—can you even imagine?"

Do they not realize I can hear every word? My desk is literally a foot away from them.

More giggles.

Of course they realize.

Not that I care. It's just annoying having to listen to their pathetic inanity during a math lesson; *that's* the only reason my shoulders are so tense.

Two more years. Two more years and then Carly and Seren will be gone, sweeping hair off the floor of Classy Cuts, passing the time until Dylan or Tyler or Finn gets them pregnant and they can raise a whole new generation of inane, black-eyebrowed, bleach-haired, orange-faced morons. And then I'll finish high school, then university, then gone, gone, gone, over the hills and far away...

But in the meantime—Seren is poking me in the back with her pen. I glance back at her.

"What's the answer to number three?" she hisses.

I ignore her and turn back to my work.

"Bitch," she mutters. Then I'm forgotten as she goes back to whispering with Carly, arguing about whether Sourz or WKD gets you drunk quicker or whether they should just go for neat vodka.

Thank God math is last lesson. I swear I'd have to kill myself if I had to listen to anymore plans for the precious party.

The Night They Vanished

Emma catches up with me in the bottleneck outside the main doors where everyone waits for rides or busses. She's in top set for math while I am, shamefully, only set two. She doesn't have to put up with any idiots like Carly and Seren and I'm working desperately hard to get moved up.

"Are you coming into town? Latte and a steak bake from Greggs?" she asks, getting her phone out of her bag. Everyone around us also has their phone out. Every single person, I swear. Except for me. Everyone goes to Greggs after school as well. Everyone except for me.

"I can't," I answer, like I always do. "I have to get home."

"Cool," she says, already wandering off, not looking up from her phone. "See you tomorrow."

"Yeah," I say to empty air. "Tomorrow."

I call Emma my best friend. I don't think she'd say the same about me. I watch her now, catching up with a crowd of other girls, walking off toward town with them, talking and laughing.

I call her my best friend because she's the only girl I hang out with, mostly in lessons when we have to do partner work, but if you asked her, what would she call me?

Dad doesn't like me getting the school bus. Instead, he collects me every day from outside the train station because it gets too busy on the school road. So, every day I get to follow everyone as they head up to town to Greggs or the Spar or the chip shop and I get into the car with my dad and spend the five-mile drive home sharing every second of every lesson but not getting asked a single question about anything non-academic. I'm the great hope for the Carter family. Dad's ashamed of being nothing more than the manager of a holiday park because his academic work doesn't pay, Mum doesn't work, and Hanna—well, no one ever talks about Hanna. Hanna *non grata* I call her. But not out loud.

But me—everything Mum and Dad perceive they did wrong with her, they've corrected when it comes to me. So, Hanna got to have her friends over, she got to go out with her friends, she got to go out full stop. Not me. I get to go to school, then I get picked up and I go home. That is it. My life. It's for my own good, they say. Look at what happened to your sister, they say. Only I can't, can I? Because Hanna buggered off before I ever got to know her and barely bothers with me when she does come back to visit.

I used to wonder if it was because we were only half sisters. Her mum died years before I was born, when Hanna was younger than I am now. Then Dad met my mum, and along I came. Hanna must have been jealous, must have felt left out. It could be my fault she went off the rails the way she did. That's what I used to think, anyway, until Dad set me straight, always reminding me of the reasons I have to be the good girl, the rules girl, the girl who brings glory instead of shame to the family name.

I hate Hanna now. For leaving. For leaving me. For not thinking about the repercussions of her behavior, for being a Carly or a Seren, for the knowledge that a fourteen-year-old Hanna would think fourteen-year-old Sasha was a total loser. For getting away. For having her own home, friends, a job. For having a *life* that never includes me. I hate her.

I expect Dad to be waiting, leaning against his car in the station car park, all swept-back hair and scowl, arms folded, dressed up in a suit like he always is. He usually stands there, not looking for me, but frowning at groups of kids like Carly and Seren and their gang, really scowling at them, so I get why they find him creepy. But there's nothing pervy in his attention, he's just disgusted watching them in their skirts so short they're barely visible under their school jumpers, listening to them shriek and swear. I know it's disgust because I regularly get to listen to him ranting about them on journeys home as I sit next to him with my below-the-knee skirt and makeup-free face.

Today is different, though, because he's not there. I stop in surprise. I scan the car park again—no, definitely no sign of his car. Has he ever not been there waiting for me? Once, I remember, when Mum was really poorly, and he was looking after her. I feel a twinge of alarm—what if something's wrong? See—*this* is why I need a phone. I hover for ages, totally at a loss. I can't start walking—it's five miles home.

I glance across the road toward the high street. Emma and her friends are probably still hanging around by Greggs. Possibly even still in the queue because it's always mad busy after school. I tense up—could I? I could, couldn't I? I could go over there, hang out, lurk outside the shops in a dodgy manner like a *proper* teenager. Dad couldn't exactly shout at me for it, when he wasn't here to pick me up...

I don't even manage a single step in the end (although I like to pretend I would have taken that step), because Dad pulls up next to me, looking well pissed off, even though *he's* the one nearly half an hour late.

"Where *were* you?" I ask as I get in and do up my seat belt. "I was starting to worry."

"Nowhere. It doesn't matter. I had to take the car to the garage. It took longer than expected."

I raise my eyebrows, but keep my face averted. I don't want him to think I'm giving sass, but he sounds...agitated.

He's silent after that, for the entire journey home, not

even asking me about school. He's driving faster than usual, as well, like he's trying to make up the time. Yeah, definitely more weird non-Dad behavior. He went away for two days last week and has been jumping on the phone every time it rings, diving for the post ever since. I hope he hasn't applied for another academic job. He does it at least once a year—usually at the end of a summer season—and never gets them. He has no teaching experience, so the universities don't want him, and he's never had anything original published in academic journals. You'd think at fifty-six he'd give up and just coast until retirement. Rent a cottage in the village with Mum—I'll be gone by then, they won't need anything big.

"Listen," he says, "can you not mention me being late to your mother?"

Oh God, he *has* applied for another job, hasn't he? That's where he's been today, at some stupid interview. I look at the clock on the dashboard. His speedy driving hasn't made any difference.

"We're nearly half an hour late—she's going to know."

He's quiet for a minute. "Tell her you had an after-school meeting."

"But—"

"It's not a request, Sasha."

Oh. Right. Yeah, definitely another interview for a job he won't get, and he doesn't want the humiliation of sharing that with me or Mum.

The roads get narrower as we drive toward the holiday camp, winding down toward the coast, getting darker as the trees lining the lane crowd in, arching up and over the car. It's a good thing I'm not claustrophobic.

The sign for the holiday park is faded and peeling. The owners paint it every March in readiness for the season, but now, in November, the perky spring chicken in his blue coat looks sad and jaded, an unfortunate bit of peeling paint making it look like Charlie Chicken's had his eye gouged out. His coat is all rags and someone (probably Tyler or Ewan or Finn) has graffitied over the *Charlie Chicken Welcomes You To West Dean Family Fun Park* sign, "hilariously" changing the N in "fun" to a CK.

Ha. The F-word is probably more accurate than Fun. I've overheard the kids in school talking about what they get up to here. They don't come to the discos anymore—dancing the Macarena with poor Ross dressed as Charlie Chicken is hardly cool. But they come up on weekends in the summer with their illicit bottles, eyeing up the visiting tourists, pretending to their parents that they are coming to the discos, so they can get rides, climbing over the fence to gather at the bottom of the kids' playground, which is hidden from the main site, especially after dark, leaving broken glass and used condoms everywhere.

But not now, not in November. Post September, it's just us here full time: me, Mum, and Dad. No lights from the caravans or the clubhouse. No lights anywhere except our house, with the security light at the front gate unnerving us by coming on sometimes at four in the morning, bright as a UFO landing. Dad goes storming out when that happens, me and Mum huddled together, scared to death that someone's breaking in, but there's never anyone there. The motion detector is too sensitive, that's all, picking up a creeping fox or badger. And the silence. God. I complain about the noise all through the summer season, kept awake until two in the morning, but in the winter the silence is absolute, only broken on stormy nights by the wind moaning through the trees.

33

This is my home, has always been my home—kids' discos and bingo I never went to, a swimming pool I'm not allowed to use, a playground I was scared to go on because older kids would take over and bully the little ones.

Sometimes, during the season, Dad used to send me over to the clubhouse with messages and I'd linger, watching city kids down for a week in a caravan doing the Charlie Chicken dance while their parents drank cheap lager and spritzers. I'd walk past the swimming pool, breathing in the steamy chlorinated air, watching teenagers fly down the water slide.

Dad never sends me anymore. I think he worries I'll get corrupted like Hanna and go off the rails. That one sneaky dance at the kids' disco will have me dyeing my hair and starting smoking and drinking. Running off and leaving them like she did at sixteen.

He'd kill me if he knew I sometimes walk around the grounds, following Owen and Ethan, the two men he hired part time to keep the site from going full-on wild. I don't think he sees them as a threat because they're older and they never come to the house. Bet he wouldn't think that if he knew how often they skived off to smoke behind the caravans, if he heard the things they say when they have spotted me.

The holiday park used to be an old manor house and grounds a billion years ago. All gone now except for the crumbling coach house, which is where we live. Such a contrast to the concrete main block and the rows and rows of static caravans. I think the house is why Dad took the job—you can't see the gaudiness of the rest of the site from the front windows and I think he likes to pretend we're

Georgian coach-house types instead of the weirdos who run the holiday park up the hill.

My room's at the back, which is a nightmare in the summer because everyone walks past, drunk and singing at the end of the night as they head back to their caravans. But I like it better than my old room at the front, which barely fit my bed in it. My new room used to be Hanna's, big enough for a desk and single wardrobe.

We get back and Dad disappears into his office. Mum's in the kitchen, preparing a casserole and listening to Radio 4.

"Hello, darling. How was your day?" She moves her Nigella cookbook and sits with me at the table, asking all the questions Dad forgot to ask about school. I play the game, the Nigella-Radio-4-Georgian-Coach-House game, and pretend West Dean High has intellectual discussion sessions, that Emma and I spent our lunch hour talking about the unseen poetry module in English. I'm never entirely sure if Mum gets that it is a game. She doesn't have anything to do with the holiday park and she's always much happier when the park is closed so it's easier to pretend. She cooks Nigella and River Cottage, listens to Radio 4, does the flowers for church, goes to a book club, and likes to wear dresses. I think sometimes she's fallen so far into the pretense, no one, including Mum herself, can remember what she was like before we began this game. She glances at the clock on the wall. "You're a little late, aren't you?"

Dad's in his office, but I bet he'll be able to sense it if I told Mum he was the one who was late. "One of the teachers kept a few of us back," I say instead. "To talk about how well we're doing, not like a detention or anything."

She smiles. "I didn't for a second think it was a detention; I was just wondering where you'd both got to." She gets up and reaches into the fridge to pull out a carton of mushrooms. "But as it was just a school meeting, I needn't have worried."

"Mum?" I wait to ask until she's gone back to her casserole, finely chopping onions and mushrooms. "Did you ask Dad about me maybe getting a phone for Christmas?"

She pauses and sighs. "Sasha, we've discussed this. What do you need a mobile phone for? Your father says—and I do agree—they're a distraction. We don't want you getting into social media or stupid games. When you're eighteen, you can buy one yourself, but until then…"

I wilt, even though I didn't expect anything different. "Okay. I'm going upstairs to do my homework."

I don't tell her I've already completed all my homework for the week—if I did that, she'd find chores for me to do, or call Dad out of his office to set me extra study tasks.

I get all my books out of my bag, opening one at random so I won't be caught if either of them comes to check on me. Making sure the door is closed, I crouch down and reach under the bed for a wooden box.

I found the photos in the box two years ago when I moved into this room. Hanna had hidden them under a loose floorboard, which is a total cliché when it comes to hiding places, but I guess it worked because no one had found them. We don't have any photos of Hanna in the house, but I'd never really thought about it until then. She is Hanna *non grata* after all: never mentioned, no reminders left around.

But when she used to visit, she must have found it weird—all those silver-framed photos on the mantelpiece of Mum and Dad and me and not one of her. God, those horrible, awkward visits—Dad and Hanna silent and scowly, Mum fluttering around bringing tea, sandwiches, biscuits, jumping up every five minutes to bring something else no one wanted. I used to try, but my big, grown-up sister made me so much shyer, she was so cool and brave, a different hair color every time, sometimes with a stud in her nose, once with her nails painted black, and the last time, with an *actual tattoo*. I wonder if she did all that just to wind Dad up, or if she dressed like that in her other life?

I used to try to talk to her, but she'd barely look at me, caught up in her silent scowling battle with Dad. The visits always ended up in an argument—either Dad would say something horrible or she would. They'd shout and she'd leave. And we'd all sigh and relax and she'd be Hanna *non grata* again for another six months, sometimes longer.

But the photos I found…they'd never be silver-frame worthy. She must have been my age in them and the first time I saw them, I got goosebumps all over. I flick through them now, sitting on the bed. Who was this girl with bleached-blond hair and too much black eyeliner? She's laughing in all of them, hanging on to a different boy or girl from a crowd of strangers. They look older than her, the boys dressed in black with hair hanging over their faces, some of them with as much eyeliner as Hanna. There's a girl with red hair, one with black. They're all in ripped jeans and T-shirts—they look like a rock band. I kept trying to pick out Dee when I first found them—Hanna once told me they've been best friends since they were five, but she's not there.

I hear a creak on the stairs and throw the photos back in the box, shoving it under the bed and diving to my desk. Just in time because it's Dad who comes in.

"I'm sorry I didn't ask you about your day earlier."

I close my book, so he doesn't notice I haven't written anything in it. "It's okay—it was a pretty boring day."

He sighs. "That's not the right attitude, Sasha. No day in school should be boring when there's so much to learn."

"I'm sorry."

There's a pause and I'm wondering if I've forgotten something I'm meant to have done. If he's going to ask me to lie a bit more for him.

"I received a letter today," he says eventually.

My heart gives a little flutter. "A letter?" I repeat.

"It's an offer of another job."

Oh. But I thought... "You found an academic job? In a university or..."

He shakes his head. "No, no. It's another holiday park. In West Wales. Somewhere nicer than this. There's a very good school close to it. Excellent results with an outstanding sixth form."

I drop the pen I've been holding. "We're moving?"

"Yes. Things have been... difficult here recently so it's a relief. I need to give three months' notice, so we'll be moving early next year. It will give us time to settle into our new home before the summer season begins. It's a larger park, but with a bigger and better staff, not so reliant on me doing everything. My job there will be more hands-off managerial."

I don't know how to react, how to feel. I'm not sad to be leaving my current school—how can I be? But a whole new town, a whole new school halfway through Year Ten? And why was he being all weird about being late if it wasn't a secret job interview?

"I'll leave you to process the information," Dad says, moving toward the door. "I don't want to see a dip in your marks, so I expect you to talk to your mother or myself if you have any questions."

"Wait," I say as he steps on to the landing. "What about Hanna? West Wales is so far away..."

"I believe Hanna has made it quite clear she has no interest in this family. I expect she'll be happy to be relieved of the expectation to visit."

"But...have you even told her?"

"I don't wish to talk about Hanna." He pauses. "And please do not try to contact her."

I rip a piece of paper out of my notebook after he leaves and write *Dear Hanna* across the top. I feel a sick-making mix of fear and defiance as I do it. Dad told me not to contact her, but it doesn't feel right, like not telling her we're leaving is a punishment too far for her lack of visits. I hesitate, my pen held over the paper. It would be much easier if I had a phone and could just send a text. What am I meant to say in a letter? *Hi, haven't spoken to you in months but by the way we're moving to the other end of the country and Dad didn't want you to know?* And I don't actually know her address by heart. I don't think addressing it to *Hanna Carter, Cardiff* is going to work. I drop the pen and stare at the blank letter. Should I even bother? She doesn't, does she? I'd have to ask Mum or Dad for her address when Dad's just told me *not* to contact her and I'd have to look up her phone number because I've never actually called her. Dad's right, she's made it perfectly clear she's not bothered. I screw up the piece of paper and drop it in my bin.

The girl in those photos, the woman who visits so rarely and briefly, is a stranger. I bite my lip. My question now—in the next couple of months before we leave—is do I do as Dad wants and just let her go from my life completely or do I try one last time to make her less of a stranger?

Chapter 4

I can't settle to anything after Dad leaves, so I put my shoes back on and go downstairs. I hesitate in the hallway—Dad's office door is closed, and I can still hear Radio 4 from the kitchen. It's already getting dark outside but it's only four thirty. I'm probably safe until at least six. Even though I'm not banned from going outside, I make sure I'm quiet as a mouse opening and closing the front door. I'm not banned, but Dad doesn't like me going out.

I don't know why he worries, though. What does he think I'm going to get up to in a closed holiday park in November, when we're miles from the nearest house? At least in summer I can ease the boredom by watching the tourists, envying the really happy ones, getting a shocked kind of thrill from listening in on the really sweary, shouty ones. Out of season, all I can do is watch Owen or Ethan, listen in on their banter as they prune shrubs or trim borders. It's not exactly a scintillating hobby, but God—these winter nights last an eternity, and sometimes I think I'll go completely insane if I don't leave the house.

I head up toward the caravans and am rewarded by the sight of Ethan trimming the weeds around one of the vans. I prefer Ethan to Owen. I don't like the way Owen stares at us—Mum and Dad as well, not just me—when he thinks we're not looking. He's all smiles when Dad's giving him work but the smile vanishes the moment Dad looks away. I see it, even if Mum and Dad think he's perfectly polite and charming.

Ethan is younger and quieter and doesn't smile much at all, but he seems less fake. It's funny because it should be Ethan who gives me the creeps because he's the one who just got out of prison. Dad doesn't know I know this, but I listened in when Owen came to talk to Dad about the new part-time worker he wanted to bring in, telling Dad how reliable Ethan was, how he made a mistake and wasn't at all dangerous, and how Owen wanted to give him a chance...

I'm dying to ask what he did, but of course I'm not supposed to speak to either of them. I can't even imagine Dad's reaction if he *caught* me talking to one of them. I'm guessing it might be a spectacular enough misdemeanor to rival one of Hanna's from her mysteriously shady past. So, of course, I'm extra careful to only ever go near them when I know Dad is either out or safely tucked away in his office. I'm hovering now, out of sight behind another caravan, watching Ethan. I wonder what they'll do when we move? I know Owen has other work—he runs his own business and has other properties and gardens he maintains—but Ethan seems to be here almost full time. Will Owen have enough work for him if the new managers don't keep him on? I don't like the thought of him reoffending because we moved and he lost his job. Like it would be in some tiny way my fault.

I step out from behind the caravan and instantly regret it because Owen walks into view as I step out and it's too late to duck back out of sight—Ethan has seen me, and he switches off the Weedwacker.

"Oh, look—you made it home. Did your dad sort out

his car trouble?" Owen asks, and he's grinning as he says it, laughter in his voice. Ethan frowns but doesn't say anything. "Did he go and see my mate like I suggested? Tricky spot to break down, that was."

I've no idea what he's talking about, but I don't like the way he seems to be laughing—at me or Dad, I don't know which—so I ignore him and speak to Ethan.

"We're moving soon. We're leaving." I don't know why I blurt it out, why I think he might possibly care.

It's Ethan I speak to, but it's Owen who answers, as he sits on the caravan step and picks up a bottle of Coke. "Yeah, they're shutting the place down."

"What?"

"I've just been out front, putting up the For Sale board."

"I…I didn't know they were selling it." I thought the decision was Dad's, not something forced on him because they're selling the place.

Owen takes a swig of Coke and holds it toward me, still with that grin on his face. I take it and almost choke as I take a huge swig.

"What *is* that?" I ask, eyes streaming.

He laughs. "Just a touch of vodka to keep me warm."

"You bring vodka to work?" God, I sound like a disapproving vicar.

"Our little secret, yeah? You don't tell on me and I won't tell your dad you're out here drinking vodka with us. I don't think he'd be too impressed, would he?" He stands up and takes a step toward me.

"Leave her alone, Owen."

Ethan says it so quietly it takes me a second to register his words and register the fact that he said them to Owen— his *boss*, someone older and *much* bigger. With my cheeks totally on fire, I walk away from both of them as Owen turns to face Ethan, full-on hostile with his arms folded.

All flustered, I forget to check the coast is clear and burst through the front door just as Dad comes out of his office. I press my lips tight shut. Oh God, oh God, will he be able to smell alcohol on my breath?

"Where have you been?"

"Just out for a bit of fresh air. I had a headache."

He frowns. "Have you finished all your homework?"

I nod, keeping my mouth shut.

"Okay. Well, dinner's almost ready. Go and wash your hands and change out of your uniform before we eat."

I run upstairs to look out of my window. I can see the caravans on the hill from here. Ethan and Owen are still there, and it looks as if they're arguing.

I go into the bathroom and brush my teeth twice, even scrubbing my tongue with my toothbrush until it stings. I stare at myself in the mirror, my guilt over that stupid single swig making me paranoid that it will be obvious. But I look exactly the same.

I lie in bed waiting for Mum and Dad to come up, listening for the telltale creak of the floorboards, the soft murmur of voices, the click of the landing light going off. I hear their door close and wait, counting down the minutes. Twenty minutes minimum. I worked this out after a heart-failing near miss when I tiptoed out after ten minutes only to meet Dad heading for the bathroom. Too much longer than twenty and I run the risk of falling asleep and missing my shot. I glance over at my alarm clock. Twenty-two minutes. That'll do.

Up, dressing gown on, socks on my feet—slippers are

43

too noisy. Tiptoe out, breath held as I pass Mum and Dad's door, with a pause to check no sound comes from inside. I grin as I hear a gentle snore. Like clockwork. The snore means I don't have to be as careful going downstairs as I usually am, but I still step over the creaky boards I know are there.

It's when I get downstairs that I start taking the real risks—even more than that illicit swig of vodka. Up until then, if caught, I could say I was getting some water or a book I'd forgotten, but the moment I open Dad's office door, I'm stepping into forbidden territory. But it's become a temptation I can't resist and it's now almost a nightly thing, me sneaking down here—because Dad has a computer. A computer with broadband. The only computer access I get is in school and even the argument that it might be detrimental to my studies won't make Dad relent and let me use the one at home.

Not that I would in front of him, anyway. Because I'm not sneaking down at midnight to type up a quick essay, am I? The computer comes on and I log into Facebook. Everyone at school is on Snapchat or Instagram, or sharing TikToks. I avoid those for that very reason. The last thing I want is to share more time with the idiots from school. Facebook, though—it was so easy to set up a fake account. Quick Gmail setup, fake photo furtively scanned in at school one lunchtime, fake name, and I was away. I could be whoever I wanted—and it's amazing how many people will just accept a random friend request from a total stranger.

I went on first looking for Hanna, wanting to find out more about her life, but I couldn't find her anywhere. I asked her, all casual, on her last visit and she said she doesn't do social media. Who doesn't do social media? Even

The Night They Vanished

I do social media and I don't have a phone or a computer. Well, Julia Collins does—a random name I picked out of a newspaper. I thought it could have been a good way to keep in touch with my sister, but no. Still, it has been a good way of stalking my sister, because I know who Hanna spends time with and some of the stupid people who randomly accepted my friend request included both Dee and her boyfriend. They haven't even noticed that my fake photo is a scan of one of the old snapshots of Hanna I found, with her front and center, grinning away with her bleached hair and nose ring. That fake me didn't really look like a Julia, so I changed it to Jules, made fake me eighteen and at college. I accept all friend requests that come my way, including the lonely American soldiers, the shirtless men looking for love, everyone. I post fake statuses about the fantasy life I've created for fun-loving Jules, off living her best life at college.

And when I get bored of that, I scour through Dee's timeline, looking for Hanna. She's easy to find; she seems to be at every social thing Dee does. I've even learned to pick out Hanna from Dee's statuses—when she mentions a *friend* and doesn't name or tag them, it's fairly obvious she's talking about Hanna. So, I knew when my sister bought her flat because Dee talked about her friend's housewarming. I knew when she lost her job, when she found a new one, when she got a boyfriend...It doesn't really make Hanna less of a stranger, because we don't interact, but at least I know a bit more.

There's nothing new on Dee's timeline tonight, though, so I amuse myself posting jokey responses from fake Jules on to the timelines of her "friends." I'm about to close down when a private message pops up in the corner of the screen—it's one of my shirtless wonders, with a photo that's obviously as fake as mine. I'm smiling as I pull up the message, but the smile disappears as I read it.

Sasha Carter. Fourteen, Yr 10 at West Dean High.
Tut tut—what would your daddy say?

Heart galloping, I lean over and yank the plug out of the wall, like that immediate shutdown will make the message disappear. But it doesn't matter that the computer screen is now blank, that fudging message is burnt on my retinas. And oh God—I'm going to have to turn the computer back on, aren't I? Otherwise Dad will know I've been using it. That stupid Facebook page might still be cozily sitting there when he switches it on next.

But the wire looks like a snake, the plug like its head and teeth, and I'm sure it'll bite me if I go to touch it. Sitting there dithering, I become aware that the curtains aren't properly closed. There's a six-inch gap where the black night stares in, watching me.

Who did this? Who sent that message? Are they watching me now? No, that's stupid. It has to be someone from school, but how on earth would they have figured out it was me? Yes, I've sneakily logged in a couple of times from school, but only ever when I'm alone in the computer room, pretending I'm doing work in lunch hours. None of the teachers ever say no to me. It's almost disheartening that they trust me so completely not to abuse the privilege. No one else gets to go on the computers at lunchtime, but I can, because I've never once been in trouble, never once sassed any teachers or been late or failed to hand in homework. I'm such a damned goody-goody they even make exceptions for me when they do whole class punishments. *You can all stay in at break-time—but you can be excused, Sasha. I know you weren't part of this.*

Stupid teachers. Thinking they were rewarding me for my good behavior—do they never think how bad it will be for me later as I walk out of the classroom and everyone else has to stay behind?

I shake my head. This is not the teachers' fault, is it? I'm the one stupid enough to have either left evidence after using the computers or been blind enough not to notice the most likely answer—someone must have been spying on me on those sneaky lunchtime sessions.

Chapter 5

thedarktourist.com
    <Update: NewUser1 has added two new listings...>

HANNA—Saturday 9 a.m.

"So how *was* it? I was hoping you'd call me last night..."

I sit up in bed and glance at the clock. Dee lasted until nine fifteen before calling—I'm impressed by her restraint. "Well... he took me to a creepy abandoned house on an even creepier street."

"He took you to an abandoned house? I thought you were meeting him in the pub?"

I smile and put her on speaker so I can haul my laptop toward me and type in a URL. And there it is—Adam's dark tourism website.

"It's what he's into—taking girls to old murder sites or abandoned houses full of ghosts."

"Right..."

"Yeah—apparently Seb advised him not to mention it on a first date but he couldn't control his abandoned murder site urges."

"Okay—you're freaking me out a bit now. I know Adam and he's really—"

"Nice? Yeah, you said that."

There's a pause. "Are you okay? He didn't...?"

I laugh and let her off the hook. "I'm fine. He was funny, and he *was* nice. I thought at first a bit too nice? Boring? But he got more...interesting."

"You mean you fancied him?"

"God, have you seen his arms? And his smile?"

"*Yes*. I *knew* it. So...did you? Do the deed in some dirty abandoned murder house?"

"Ew—*no*." I hesitate and lower my voice. "But we did kiss. In the garden of a dirty abandoned *not* murder house." I pause, and shiver again at the memory. It was a *very* good kiss.

"Double *yes*. Did you take him home? Have nice, decent sex and exorcise Liam forever?"

"Actually, he kissed me, and I freaked out and ran away."

"Oh, Hanna..."

I sigh. "I know. But I'm hoping he'll think I was creeped out by the abandoned house thing rather than that I'm a total idiot."

"You mean you want to see him again?"

"Maybe..."

"YES! Woohoo—that's it, I'm buying a hat!"

"Oh, shut up. I'm looking at his website now, actually. That's the main thing that's a bit off. I want to do some digging—see if his weird hobby is a deal-breaker or not." I click on new listings, looking for the house he told me about last night. I scroll down and gasp.

"Hanna? What's wrong?"

"What did you tell him about me?" I whisper.

"What?"

"*What did you tell him about me?*"

"Where you worked—that we grew up together, that you're amazing. Hanna, what—"

"Did you tell him about my family? The holiday park?" My mind frantically replays our entire conversation from last night. I told him where I grew up, but nothing else...I think of that sympathy card that arrived the other day, the unfamiliar handwriting. "Did you tell him about Jacob?"

"Of course not. Jesus, why would you think I would—"

"Shit. Fuck. I've...Dee, I've got to go. Text me Adam's address, will you? I need to make a surprise visit." I end the call and drop the phone back on the bed, zooming in on the newest listing on Adam's website. I click on the button to find more details, but it takes me to a login page. I must be mistaken, I must have...

Oh God—the total *shit*. He was supposed to be nice, he was supposed to be *decent*.

I jump out of bed and pull on my jeans, grabbing a jacket to put on over the T-shirt I wore to bed.

I don't stop to wash or brush my hair. As soon as Dee texts the address through, I'm marching out of the flat and half-running down the street. Adam doesn't live far from me and there's no way I'm doing this over the phone.

It's still only nine thirty on a Saturday morning, but I don't care if I wake him up. God, I can't believe I fell for it, that I let him kiss me outside some creepy abandoned house, thinking he was *nice*, thinking he was *funny* and *sexy*, thinking he was the opposite of Liam.

I catch the front door of his building as someone comes out. Good, now I don't have to give him warning I'm on my way up. I'm too impatient to wait for the lift, so I jog up three flights of stairs, pausing at the top to get my breath back before knocking on his door. Actually, I don't knock, I bloody pound on his door. I don't care if half the floor comes out to see what the racket is. I hear movement inside his flat and bang on the door again.

The door flies open. He looks like he just woke up, hair all over the place, stubble on his chin. He's dressed—a faded T-shirt and jeans—but his feet are bare.

The scowl on his face gives way to a half smile, half look of confusion when he sees me. "Hanna? Hey, what's up? I thought...Um...did we arrange something for this morning?"

"Is it some kind of sick joke?"

His smile disappears. "What? What are you talking about? And what are you doing here?"

"I'm talking about your website—my house on your fucking website." I'm shouting and I don't care.

"I have no idea what you're talking about, but will you come in before my neighbors call the police?" He opens the door wider and I shove past him, going over to where his computer is.

"Get your website up."

"Hanna, for Christ's sake, will you just tell me what the hell is wrong?"

"*This*," I say, clicking on the new listings page of his Dark Tourist site. "*This* is what's wrong. Why did you do it? I don't get it..."

He leans in to look at the screen, frowning, zooming in like I did to read the details.

"I didn't do this," he says, stepping back. "I didn't put this up. I haven't updated the site in the last month." He's still frowning. "You say this is your house?"

My heart is still racing, but I'm wrong-footed. He sounds genuinely confused. "It's my family's house. It's where my dad and stepmother and my sister live. It wouldn't let me go any further without logging in." I feel sick as I look again at the words under the grainy photo of my family home.

Welcome to The Dark Tourist
New Listing:
Site of a *terrible tragedy* in small coastal village.

This, coming so soon after that horrible sympathy card… That's what sent me racing here. Someone knows about Jacob. Someone wants to bring it all up again. I wanted… I wanted to come here and make Adam delete it all before anyone else gets the chance to rake through my past.

But when Adam goes through the login process and another page loads—it's not about Jacob at all. There are more pictures of the house, details about my family. The main photo is of my dad, Jen, and Sasha. And when I read the text I feel faint. It's… That's not what I expected.

New Listing:
EXCLUSIVE IMAGES from the site of a gruesome triple murder—Two adults, one child, *brutally killed* in small coastal village.
Sign up NOW for more information—exclusive crime-scene photos, background information on the murder victims, maps and more!

"The site must have been hacked," Adam says, sitting at the desk, tapping his way into the back end of the site. "Shit. I'm locked out." He shakes his head. "Don't worry— I'll get this sorted. I'll get this taken down."

I stare at the back of his head. *I don't know him*, my

mind keeps repeating. This man—this man who kissed me in the grounds of an abandoned house, who runs a website about murder sites for fun—is a stranger. Hacked? How can his website have been hacked and my family home put on there—we went on a date last night; it's hardly coincidence, is it? My brain is scrabbling to catch up.

"Why would a hacker put *my* family up there? We never met before last night—and the details...That's my house, their names and ages—a *photo*, for fuck's sake."

"Hanna, I swear I didn't do this. How could I? I don't know your family."

"But you know where I used to live, where me and Dee grew up. I told you last night. And you knew anyway, didn't you? When you stayed with Seb when you were at university—you said you'd heard of the village. Did you go there? What else did he tell you?"

"But why would I? Even if I knew all about you before our date—why the hell would I do that?"

I shiver. Yes, why would he? I step back, glancing toward the flat door, stepping away from Adam, and wishing I'd asked Dee to come with me. I'll leave now, call her back, and—

"Don't look at me like that," Adam says and there's a plea in his voice. "Don't look at me like I'm some kind of monster. I didn't *do* this."

"Then who *did*?"

He shakes his head. He does look genuinely distraught and it eases some of my fear. He can't be that good an actor, can he? And he's Seb's friend—they've been friends for years...

I bite my lip. What if he's telling the truth—that his site

got hacked? But even so—who makes a website like this anyway? One that revels in murder? I hover, my hand on the door. But if not him, then who and...?

"The date," I mutter, stopping and turning back to Adam, still hunched over his computer. "On the site—the date of the 'gruesome triple murder'—it's today's date."

He looks back at me. "But you've spoken to them, right? Your family? I mean, I've no idea what's going on, I swear, but it's not real, it's just the site's been hacked."

I freeze. Shit. I didn't...I haven't...I didn't even think of calling them, because I thought it would be about Jacob when he logged in. I thought it was going to be about *me*. I fumble my phone out of my pocket and call my dad's mobile, then Jen's. They both go straight to voicemail.

"No answer from either my dad or stepmother," I say and there's a wobble in my voice.

"Your sister?" he says. "She's a teenager, right? All teenagers are glued to their phones, aren't they?"

I chew on my lip. "Sasha's not allowed to have a phone. My dad's really strict." I pause. "But she has a secret pay-as-you-go one..."

"You got your sister a burner phone?"

"I didn't get it for her." Actually, I've never stopped to wonder who *did* get it for her. I wince as I bite my lip too hard and taste blood. "I don't want to get her in trouble by calling."

Adam stares at me. "I think this might warrant a call."

I pray she has the phone on silent as I call, but like Dad and Jen, my call goes straight to voicemail. I look at Adam and shake my head.

"Landline? Work numbers? Could your dad or stepmother be in work on a Saturday?"

I nod, already scrolling through my contacts for Dad's office number. I frown and lower the phone. "Disconnected number. How can it be disconnected? It's the number for the holiday camp. It's their main landline."

Did Dad mention a change of telephone numbers last time I visited? I don't think so, but that visit was cut short, I remember, when I rolled up my sleeves and he saw my tattoo. I ended up walking out after another fight about how I was ruining my life, like getting a tattoo was the ultimate sin.

I don't know the names of any of Sasha's friends. God, how crap is that? There are no close neighbors to the holiday park to call and I have no idea who my stepmother is friends with. My dad never really invited friendships. I look at Adam. I'm lost. I don't know what to do.

"When's the last time you spoke to them?"

"I don't know…before Christmas?"

"Before Christmas? Hanna—it's nearly the end of February. You haven't spoken to your family in almost three months?"

I don't tell him I didn't actually speak to them at Christmas either. I timed my call for when I knew they'd be out and left a message. My family isn't like most families—regular Sunday lunches, shopping days with my mum. My family is…well, I don't really think of them as my family anymore. My mother is dead; I've never got on with my stepmother. And my dad is…it doesn't matter. Dee is my family. Dee and Seb and Mari, Evan, and Jo. They're the ones who are here for me. They're the ones who stuck by me and helped me make my shit life a lot less shit. Not my parents or Sasha. And that's fine. I like that, I'm happy with that. But Adam's disbelief at the fact I haven't spoken to my family in months makes my cheeks burn with shame.

"We're not exactly on speaking terms," I say. "I left home when I was sixteen and they were quite happy about that."

Well, my dad certainly was.

I look at the computer screen again, that fucking listing. *Gruesome triple murder.*

"Do you think I should call the police?"

Hope

thedarktourist.com
   <Update: Find out more about the murder victims:>
   the FAILED academic,
   the LONELY wife,
   the teenager with DARK SECRETS...
   <click here >

Saturday 11 a.m.

We're waiting at the local police station. Adam insisted on coming with me, his laptop in a bag with him. He took a screenshot of the listing in case the hacker takes it down before we get to show anyone, and we appear more ridiculous than we already do. I haven't had chance to call Dee for reassurance that Adam really is the nice, decent man she promised...I want to believe he had nothing to do with this, but my mind keeps poking at the nagging worry. And none of it is helped by being here, in a police station: somewhere I swore when I got my life back on track that I'd never visit again. I try taking deep breaths, but it doesn't help the incipient panic. It's Dee I want next to me, holding my hand, not Adam.

   The woman behind the desk looked bemused as I attempted to stumble through an explanation of why we were there.

But I don't care—I just want someone to take me seriously enough to check on my family and confirm they're actually alive. I keep trying their numbers while we wait; Adam keeps tapping on his keyboard, a frown on his face.

A door to the right of us opens and a uniformed officer pops his head through. "Do you want to follow me?" he says.

No, I don't. I haven't been in this particular police station before, but with its tiled floors and disinfectant smell, it reminds me unpleasantly of the one I spent too much time in as a teenager. I found myself sweating when I gave my information to the woman at the desk—like there'd be some alert coming up when she tapped in my name, like I'd been some master criminal rather than a wayward teenager pulled in for minor offenses back then. They wouldn't have instant access to a juvenile record, would they?

My fear levels ratchet up a little higher at the thought of the police officer hauling out my records and listing all my possession and drunk-and-disorderly cautions in front of Adam.

"Come in; have a seat," he says. "I'm PC Barker."

We sit opposite him in a small room with claustrophobic dark green walls. I wonder if this is where they bring suspects, but he doesn't show any signs of taping our conversation, or even making notes. He looks bored, or tired, or both, a man in his late twenties at either the beginning or the end of a long shift.

"Do you want to tell me what this is about?" he says, leaning forward.

Adam and I look at each other and I wait as Adam opens his laptop and turns the screen to face the police constable.

"I'm a web developer," Adam says. "My site got hacked—I

don't know when. I haven't checked it in a couple of weeks, and I didn't see any alerts."

"It's my family's home—the latest listing on his site. It's my family's home and it says they've been murdered. Today." I talk over Adam, so our words merge together in a jumble.

"Okay—one at a time, please..." PC Barker says, and I pause to take a deep breath, trying to explain in a calmer tone. Adam completes the story, taking the officer through the website and what it does.

"And what's your relationship to one another?" PC Barker asks, looking from me to Adam.

I glance at Adam, but he doesn't say anything, so I answer. "We met yesterday," I say. "Last night—we had a date, a blind date arranged by mutual friends."

He asks for Dee and Seb's details and it makes me twitchy as I watch him scribble down names and numbers. "They don't have anything to do with this—it's wasting time."

PC Barker shakes his head. "If you two only met last night and Mr. Webster is correct that someone has hacked his website, then what we have here is, at the very least, a malicious prank that's targeted at *you*. As you are essentially strangers, if Mr. Webster wants to find out who has hacked his website and why they've targeted you, he needs to look at the people who knew you two were meeting last night—beginning with your friends." He pauses. "If it turns out to be something more than a prank, then that is also where any official investigation will start: finding the connection."

The words *malicious prank* spark in my head. "Wait—someone slashed my car tire the other night. I assumed that was just a *prank*. But it's not the first time my car's been damaged... And there was a card from my family. I hadn't opened it, but when I got home that same night, the envelope was on the floor..." I let my voice trail off. I don't mention the sympathy card because then I'd have to explain why it was sent.

"Do you have any idea who might have slashed your tire?" The PC ignores my rambling about the envelope.

"I thought at first it might have been my ex..."

"His name?"

"Liam Harrison."

"And does this ex know his way around computers?"

"What—can he hack into websites? Not as far as I know." I pause. "But I don't think it'll be him. He's got a new girlfriend, he's hardly still interested in me or who I'm dating. I don't think he was that interested when he was with me, to be honest." I can feel myself blushing as I say it, the burn of humiliation as I admit the truth—that Liam was bored of me within weeks of us meeting, that I would buy all the drinks, the dinners, pay for all the nights out, and that was why he stuck around.

"But you thought it might have been him damaging your car?"

"I...I think I was mistaken. I was angry. I'm still angry at him. I rang him and I think when he answered that for a second he didn't have a clue who I was. He's forgotten about me."

I refuse to look at Adam as I say this.

"Did he know your family? Did you ever talk to him about where they lived? Did he know your friends—the ones that set you two up?"

"No. No to all of it. It was never that kind of relationship— it was surface, superficial. He met Dee and Seb a few times, we hung out at the same places where everyone vaguely knows everyone else, but they all blatantly disliked each other. Like I said—he's forgotten about me. And even if he hadn't, he's way too lazy to go to this much trouble. Slashing a car tire is a bit different from hacking into a website. This is not him."

"Can you think of anyone else who might target you or your family?"

I shake my head. "I left home when I was sixteen; I don't even see my family anymore. I—"

He interrupts me to move on to Adam. "And you, Mr. Webster? Any ideas who might have hacked your site?"

Adam shakes his head. "No idea—but like you said, this is too specific to be a random hacker. This is targeted at Hanna."

"Adam knew where I grew up. He even knows all the crimes that have happened in my home town. He knew where my family lives." I blurt this out and feel Adam stiffen next to me. "I told him last night—it would have been easy to google my family, wouldn't it? I'm from a very small village..." Maybe I had started to believe Adam's complete innocence in all this—but talking about Liam has made me realize how blind I usually am when it comes to spotting trouble.

PC Barker looks puzzled. "I thought you came in together to report this? Are you changing the nature of your complaint? Do we need to speak to the two of you separately?"

"No, that's not...It just seems far-fetched, that's all. That for some reason, I've been targeted by a hacker who somehow found Adam's site on the same night I was having a blind date with him and decided to put my family up there? And the information—who would know my dad's a failed academic? He doesn't work in an academic field—he manages a holiday park. They'd really have to dig to find out his background. But that doesn't make sense either because the rest is rubbish. Why go to the trouble of finding out my dad's academic history and then just make up a load of nonsense about the others: Jen isn't *lonely*, and Sasha doesn't have *dark secrets*. She's an open book, the perfect child."

There's a pause. "Yes, the whole thing seems pretty far-fetched, if I'm honest." PC Barker sighs and leans back. "I can check out your family—I'll speak to someone at their local station, get someone to swing by the house and do a welfare check. And the website—are there any other hacked listings?"

Adam scrolls through to check and freezes. "Christ, there's another one—this one." He points to his screen and PC Barker nods.

"Okay. I'll print these listings out and show them to one of my colleagues in CID. I'll also ask our Digital Investigations Unit to take a look at the site. I'm sure it's nothing—some hacker's idea of a joke—but we'll check it out."

"But how can it be a random *joke*?" I burst out. "I only met Adam last night—how would they have found my family? And why?"

The police officer's sideways look at Adam and his flushed-face response give me my answer. He doesn't think the site's been hacked at all. For whatever reason, he believes Adam put my home on the site. I'm reminded again of my earlier frisson of fear. Adam is a stranger—a stranger who gets his kicks exploring abandoned buildings and investigating murder sites.

*

62

There's an awkward silence as we stand outside the police station, sent on our way with reassurances that we'd hear from PC Barker soon.

"It wasn't me," Adam says again as I pause on the cusp of walking away. "I didn't put your house up, I swear. Why would I do that? Christ, Hanna—I had a great time last night. I liked you. A lot. I thought you . . . Why would I do that?"

"Why would *anyone* do that? If not you, it has to be someone who knows you—or me. Someone who knows we were together last night." I shake my head. "Dee only set this up three days ago."

He frowns. "Actually . . . she's been trying to set it up since New Year."

"What?"

He shrugs. "She knew I was interested and said—through Seb—that she wanted to set us up as soon as you and your ex split."

"So, what—you've been hovering and watching and waiting for two months?"

"Jesus—*no*. I made a passing comment about you that Dee latched on to. *She's* the one who's been hovering and hinting ever since." He runs a hand through his hair and sighs. I can see the frustration on his face. "I'll speak to Seb. And I'll see if I can trace anything back to whoever hacked the site. I'll close it down. But it'll be okay. It's like the officer said, a prank—horrible but just some malicious hacker. They'll speak to your family and I'll take the site down and this will be over."

God, I want that to be true. I want the next call I get to be some irritated one from my dad in response to my frantic messages. And it has to be true, doesn't it? It's a sick joke, that's all.

But who hates me that much—to do such a horrible thing?

"I need to go," I say, edging away.

"Hanna, please. We were going to go out again. Can I—"

"Mr. Webster!"

We're interrupted by PC Barker calling after us, jogging down the steps. He reaches us and grabs Adam's arm. "Mr. Webster, can you come back inside, please? You too," he adds to me, tugging on Adam's arm.

"What's this about?" Adam says, not moving.

"Can you just come inside, please? CID need a word."

I can hear sirens as PC Barker leads Adam back into the police station and I shiver as I hurry after them, throat tightening in sudden panic. Have they found my family?

Chapter 7

SASHA—November, three months earlier

School next day is a particular kind of torture. I'm convinced every whisper, every giggle, is aimed at me. I didn't sleep at all last night, even though I was careful not to look at Facebook again after I plugged the computer back in. I just shut everything down and went to bed. But it was like my eyes were wired open. Every time I tried to close them, they'd snap back open. Consequently, today, everything is coated in a layer of fuzz and my eyelids droop in every lesson. I literally have to keep pinching myself to stay awake in Religious Studies, which is quite amusing as Miss is talking about self-flagellation in religion. Maybe it was nothing to do with atonement or punishment, maybe they used to whip themselves to stay awake in really boring religious services.

I'm not hungry when lunchtime finally rolls around. In fact, I feel sick and have to hold my breath against the cooking smells wafting from the canteen as I walk past, head down, jostled by idiots desperate to stuff themselves with pizza and chips.

The computer room beckons me, the door enticingly ajar, blinds half down to reduce glare on the screens. It's empty, as usual. Mr. Harris pokes his head out of his office as I walk past, but he smiles and waves me on when he sees it's me.

"Mr. Harris?" I call, before he disappears. "Has anyone else been using the computers at lunchtime?"

He shakes his head. "Not recently. As you know, we only let students in at lunchtime under exceptional circumstances." He pauses. "Most pupils have computers at home."

Jeez, it's worse than I thought. I smile and walk on into the computer room. I thought they were letting me in because I'm such a good student, but it's actually because they feel sorry for me. Dad, at parents' evenings, is always quite upfront about letting teachers know I have no access to computers, a mobile phone, or the internet. At the last one he even tried to argue technology wasn't needed for my education in front of the IT teacher.

I decided, around four in the morning, as I was lying awake, staring at the ceiling, to just go ahead and delete my Facebook account. I'll miss the fake me but it's the best thing. Delete it, pretend it never existed. I can always rejoin someday.

But when I log in on the school computer, after first making sure the door is closed and there's no one hiding in the big cupboards (yes, I really did check), there's another private message.

Don't think about deleting the account Sasha
    I'll tell your dad if you do
    I'll tell him you sneak downstairs in your flowery pajamas
and use his computer

The end-of-lunch buzzer breaks my paralysis. I close down the computer and leave the room, bouncing off other kids as I head blindly for math. I know it's paranoia, but it seems like every one of them is staring at me, like every single one of them is in on the joke and knows about the Facebook messages. I know it's paranoia because in reality I bet three-quarters of my own year, let alone the rest of the school, would be hard pressed to pick me out of a lineup if you asked them. Wasn't that part of the reason for my fake Facebook account in the first place: to be *visible* for once, even if it was all a lie?

Is it my imagination, then, the hush as I walk into the classroom and take my seat? I sit near the front—I always take a seat near the front—and for the first time I regret it. I can't see without turning if any of them are really looking at me, or talking about me. Mrs. Roberts comes in and I try to pay attention to the questions she puts up on the whiteboard, staring down at a blank page in my book.

I can hear them whispering behind me, punctuated by the odd snort of laughter or high-pitched giggle from one of the girls. I'm so tense my hunched shoulders are aching and I've barely taken in a word Mrs. Roberts has said all lesson. The whispering started as soon as I sat down, and I know they're talking about me. It must have been Seren or one of the other girls who found my fake account on Facebook and sent that message. How did I give myself away? I know I used Hanna's photo, but it's a fifteen-year-old photograph. There's some similarity in the shape of our faces, our smiles, but her eyes are blue, her hair dark and wavy. I'm...bleh. Straight mousy hair, boring sludgy eyes. You'd really have to look close to see any of me in that old photo of Hanna. Maybe I forgot to log off one lunchtime, or I logged out but left Facebook up with my timeline.

The temptation, as soon as I saw the new message, was to just do as I'd planned and delete the account. Well, the temptation was to delete the account and then throw the computer out the window, but I managed to resist that panicked urge. I was going to delete it, I was, but then I thought, What if that makes whoever sent the message so angry they really *do* tell my dad? What if they've taken screenshots of some of the stuff I've posted? God, I'd be totally screwed if Dad saw any of it. It's not like I've been sending nudes or anything stupid, but caught up in the high of doing something so verboten, I might have said some stuff to my "friends"—particularly those fake shirtless American GI Joes...

I switch between going hot and cold as I think of the flirty messages I received as "Jules," the smutty innuendos and outright dirty messages I got in response to the profile photo. I didn't say anything rude back, but I clicked *like* on those messages because I did *like*—I liked being Jules for those few minutes, even if it was all fake. Oh God, oh God, it seemed like silly fun at the time, but the thought of *Dad* reading them? I feel sick.

I glance up at the clock on the wall. Ten minutes of the lesson to go. There's a knock at the classroom door and someone calls Mrs. Roberts out into the corridor. The moment the door closes behind her, the noise level in the classroom rises, more laughter, thirty teenagers no longer bothering to whisper. Some of the boys start chucking screwed-up balls of paper at each other. I keep my head down, trying to ignore them and finish the questions on the board. But then a ball of paper hits the back of my head and it seems like the whole class erupts into laughter as I jump and then spin round to see who threw it.

Half the boys are in hysterics and Seren's holding up her phone, facing me. Is she *filming* me? Anger fuels my imagination—I can so imagine Seren sending those messages, egged on by her moronic gang of minions. I reach over and snatch the phone out of her hand, jumping up, sending my chair clattering to the floor. I'm about to chuck the phone down to join it when Seren lurches over and grabs my arm. The boys start up a chant of *fight fight fight*, even though we're just struggling for possession of an iPhone, and then the classroom door slams and Mrs. Roberts' outraged voice shuts everyone up.

"Seren! Sasha! What on *earth* is going on? Both of you—the office. *Now.*"

I'm hot with shame and mortification as I sit outside the Head of Year's office. I've never been sent to the office, never been sent out of class, never had a detention or anything. I can hear Seren's raised voice inside the office, telling her side of the story, all outraged anger. She's spent plenty of time here, so I'm not surprised Miss Jennings assumed she started it.

Oh, Christ almighty, if they call Dad over this, it would be worse than him finding out about the Facebook account. Then I think of all the stuff I've posted on there. Maybe it wouldn't.

Seren stalks out of the office, pausing to scowl at me and mouth *you're dead* before marching off down the corridor. Ah, great. Absolutely wonderful. Miss Jennings pokes her head round the door of her office. "Come on in, Sasha."

Chapter 8

HANNA—Saturday 1 p.m.

I'm taken back to the same room and offered a cup of tea. This time, the wait is longer and this time, Adam isn't with me. He was escorted down the corridor to a different room. My hands are shaking as I sip the weak tea they bring me. I can't even call Dee or keep trying my family as they asked if they could check my phone—for what, I don't know. Should I have said no? I don't know my rights; I don't even know why I'm back in here. I feel sick at the thought that something's happened to my family, that's why they've dragged us back in. But they'd tell me, wouldn't they?

Every word of that website listing keeps replaying in my mind over and over—*gruesome triple murder, two adults, one child, brutally killed*. That can't be it, though; they'd have people in, grave faces as they broke the news...and they wouldn't have found anything so quickly, would they?

Unless...unless...How long has that listing been on Adam's site? He was saying to the officer before that he hasn't checked it in a while—I'd assumed it was recent, because we only met last night, and there was no connection between us before then. Well, that was what I *thought*. I was going to have to have a word with Dee about that... But the date—the date on the website: today's date.

Dee must have been planning this for a while. Must have agreed with Adam when they were going to set it up...Did they do that planning in a public place? Somewhere someone was listening, so they'd know when and where we were going to go for our date?

And that stuff on the website about the family—Sasha's secrets and Jen being lonely—that has to just be clickbait, the kind of tabloid sub-heading that would have you clicking through to rummage through someone's dirty laundry. Sasha's fourteen—what dark secrets could a fourteen-year-old have? My mind leaps to the secrets *I* had at fourteen and I feel a little sick. No. Not Sasha. You couldn't find anyone more different to the girl I once was.

Without my phone, I have no idea what the time is, no idea how much more of today is left. But it's not real, not real, I tell myself. It's ridiculous—my family is fine. This is some weird, sick joke that the police will get to the bottom of. They'll let me go with reassurances my family is fine, I'll call Dee and find out from Seb what the hell is up with Adam and—

The door opens and I jump, spilling lukewarm tea all over the table.

It's not PC Barker, it's a plainclothes officer ten years older, carrying a folder and his own cup of tea.

"Miss Carter? DC Norton, sorry it's taken so long to get to you."

"It's Ashton. Sorry, legally I'm Carter, but I prefer to go by my mother's maiden name. Ashton. Hanna Ashton, but you can just call me Hanna. And I don't understand...Is this about my family?" I can hear my voice wobble and I hate it.

"Sorry," the detective says again. "I should have said right away—we haven't found out anything about your

71

family yet, but I promise local officers are checking it out as a matter of urgency."

"Then what *is* this about? I don't understand what I'm doing here. And where's Adam?"

"I wanted to ask if you know a Gemma and Katie Bentley?"

I stare at him blankly. "What? Who? What has this got to do with anything?"

"Do you know the names? Gemma and Katie Bentley?" he asks again.

I shake my head. "I don't think so."

"They're sisters—sharing a house on Meadow Close. Gemma's twenty-four, Katie's thirty-one." He's looking at me expectantly and I try to process the names, where they live—Meadow Close isn't far from me. Wait...Gemma Bentley...

"It's not the girl from the hit-and-run, is it? The one before Christmas on the park road?"

"And Katie Bentley?" he asks, not answering my question.

"I'm sorry, no. I definitely don't know either of them— Gemma Bentley's name is vaguely familiar, but only from reports about the hit-and-run, I think, because it was just around the corner from my house."

He sighs and scribbles something on a piece of paper.

"Can I ask what this is about? Why you're asking me about two complete strangers?"

He looks up at me, face blank. "I'm sorry—it's part of an ongoing investigation. I'm afraid I can't share any details with you."

"*What* ongoing investigation? How can a hit-and-run from months ago be relevant? I came here because I was worried about my family and now you're asking me about two women I've never heard of, but you won't tell me *anything*."

"As I said—we're tracing your family as a matter of urgency, but I can assure you anything we ask is not designed to waste your time." He pauses. "Can you run me through your movements last night? From leaving the house, to meeting Mr. Webster, to what time you got home again."

He keeps interrupting my account with questions I can't answer properly: Did anyone see me walking to the pub? How late was Adam? Did he give any explanation as to why he was late? Could anyone vouch for the time we arrived and left the pub? And then as I talk about after we left the pub, my answers are even vaguer because we were walking quiet streets with no one around and then kissing in the grounds of an abandoned house.

But he keeps asking: about how well I knew Adam, where we were, what we were doing...I can't even give a good explanation for why I left when I did. And none of it helps.

There's a tap on the door and DC Norton gets up. He goes out of the room and closes the door behind him, leaving me alone with thoughts of gruesome triple murders and guilt and bloody Christmas cards—that stupid card looming large in my mind, like if only I'd opened the damned thing two months ago, there might have been something, some clue as to why the hell this was happening.

The detective comes back in and sits down, and I don't know how to read the look on his face.

"We've had local officers call at the address you gave us for your family." He pauses, that unreadable look still on his face.

I curl my hands into fists under the table. "And?"

"Your family isn't there. The house is empty." He pauses again. "The whole site is locked up. There's no furniture, nothing there. The local officers said your family moved out two months ago."

My breath hitches. I don't know what to say. It's a blank— last time I actually spoke to my father, did he say anything? No. No, he didn't. But did I let him? A two-minute conversation, me desperate to get off the phone before he said anything I didn't want to hear. Did he try? Did he even try to tell me? Or was the plan always to just leave and not tell me. Leave me behind properly, abandon even the pretense of contact in the form of those sporadic phone calls. Dump me at the side of the road like an unwanted dog.

But that's not true, is it? Maybe it wasn't entirely my decision to leave but I was the one who chose not to go back. Me. My decision to stay away, to leave them all behind. Even if it felt like the best way at the time, even if I knew they were glad I was gone, still it was my decision.

"The local PC said as far as she knew, they'd moved to West Wales. She didn't know where, but she's going to try to find out. There'll be records—at your sister's school, forwarding addresses, the estate agent even. Don't worry— we'll find them, make sure they're safe."

Is it pity? Is that the look on his face? Pity for the daughter whose family moved without telling her?

"And there's no evidence that...?"

He shakes his head. "No sign of anything wrong at the house, no break-in, nothing. No reports in the area of suspicious activity. It looks like they've just moved house. We are, of course, treating tracing your family as a priority— we need to know they're safe and we need to figure out the connection between yourself, them, and Mr. Webster."

My fists are still clenched, my nails digging into my palms. The small pain keeps my mind focused, keeps me from crying or screaming.

"Hanna, I'm going to ask again. Can you think of *anything* that connects you all?"

I want to say no. There's nothing. We're ordinary. An ordinary family with no secrets, no skeletons in the closet, no restless ghosts rattling the windows.

But. But...I don't want to expose myself or them to police scrutiny and I genuinely don't know what the elusive connection is, who hates one or all of us enough to have done this.

But I do need to know they are safe. So, I need to be honest and explain why my family has moved without me knowing, and why I left home in the first place.

I take a deep breath. "There's something...It's not a connection or anything like that, but it might be something that—" I stop. My voice is wobbling. I take another breath, press my nails harder into my palms.

"There's something I should tell you about my family."

Chapter 9

Saturday 3 p.m.

I walk away from the police station so fast I'm out of breath before I reach the corner, glancing back too many times. I'm not sure if I want to see Adam or if I'm more relieved I don't. Either way, I certainly don't want him driving me home. I want to know what the police said to him, if they told him anymore than they told me, but also...that PC's urgency as he took him back in, the way he held his arm, like he thought he might run; CID suddenly involved, the questions about those two women. I don't think I want to see him again until I've spoken to Dee and Seb, got my reassurances about him being *nice*.

And even more, I want to get distance from the humiliation of having to lay bare the disaster of my relationship with my family. What I need to do now is get home, to my safe space—and finally open that bloody Christmas card.

I should have got a taxi or taken the bus. My feet are killing me and I'm shivering by the time I get close to home. All I want to do is get in and wrap myself in a literal comfort blanket, but I freeze when I get to the end of my street—there's someone outside my house, looking up at my windows. Adam? I hover there, ready to turn and walk away when whoever it is moves on and keeps walking. I sag with relief. Okay. It's fine. Either Adam is still at the police station or he's gone home, probably with no intention of ever contacting me again, blaming *me* for bringing this ridiculous nightmare into his weekend. I let out a humorless laugh as I search my bag for my keys. Bet he wasn't expecting *this* aftermath from a blind date.

I head straight to the card as soon as I'm in, door locked behind me, but even with my newfound resolve, my hand is still shaking as I pick it up. I've given it such power over me in the months I've let it sit unopened—to the point where I almost believe it to be alive, as if when I finally open the bloody thing, my family will come bursting out of the envelope.

But I suppose in a way, they might: if there's an address in here, a phone number that gets answered. I rip open the envelope before I can begin prevaricating again and pull out the card, a glittery thing with a cheery robin and *Season's Greetings* in swirly text on the front. I draw in a shaky breath as I open it and see the message inside.

No address. No new telephone numbers, just a short paragraph scrawled in my stepmother's handwriting, not even my father's.

Dear Hanna,

I hope you're well. Your father said he has called and left messages which you haven't returned so I'm presuming you are either not listening to them or choosing to ignore them. So, I'm sending this as a last attempt— we are moving soon as your father has found another position in West Wales. Your father is, as I'm sure you understand, happy to be *finally leaving this village. We would like you to stay in touch so I'm asking—on behalf of your father and Sasha—to please call us over the Christmas holidays. If we do not hear from you, we will take that as your decision to cut all ties with your family and will not bother you again.*

Jen

Shit. It's an ultimatum that I'm faced with two months too late. I can read the annoyance in her words, picture her tight-lipped face as she wrote those words, the passive-aggressive bit about being happy to leave—yeah, she's *sure I understand*, because obviously their continued miserable existence there is my fault. Like they couldn't have left at any point in the last fourteen years. But my dad wouldn't, would he? He'd never let it show that he was bothered by being the subject of gossip and speculation. He'd have stayed and suffered there forever, making Jen and Sasha suffer alongside him. I wonder what finally changed his mind.

I look back down at the card. Did my father know she'd written this? Or had he already decided to cut off contact? I don't know what messages she's on about. It's possible I deleted them without listening and have forgotten. But it's also possible my dad lied to her about leaving messages. I never got on with my stepmother, but she was more patient than my dad ever was, and I can imagine her insisting he left me a message. And she really tried, I'll give her that. It was one of the biggest things that put me off her—she tried *so hard*. She might well have wanted to give me one last chance.

I think of Adam's website again, Jen relegated to nothing more than *the lonely wife*. Was she, really? I remember her as happy in our old house, fully embracing the house-wife role, baking and cooking and cleaning and decorating. There's nothing wrong with that and maybe if I'd been younger when Dad brought her home, with her arms stretched out, eager to become my stepmother, I'd have welcomed the stability she brought to our lives. *I don't have children of my own*, she said. *So, I'd love to be your mother if you would like that.* But I was all about the chaos then; I didn't want home-cooked food and my bed made for me. I can't remember exactly what I said in response to her, but I know it was something horrible. And then they had Sasha and they didn't need me anymore.

I've never really considered Jen beyond my teenage hostility and her Stepford ways, never stopped to wonder if she really was happy, stuck in the middle of nowhere, in a village that rejected us after what I did. I open the card and read her message again. She talks about *Dad* being happy to leave the village behind, but not her, not Sasha. The truth is, I have no idea. I made no real effort to get to know Jen and I rejected all her overtures, even after everything she did to help me. I have no idea if her life in Littledean was ecstatic or miserable, like I have no idea who Sasha's friends are, or if there could possibly be dark secrets hidden under the perfect teen exterior.

I thought it was odd when they stopped calling, but I left it, ignored it because in all honesty, it was a relief. Caught up in the mess of my relationship and breakup with Liam, I did not want the added turmoil of family guilt and regret.

I wonder—if I'd opened the card when it arrived, two weeks before Christmas—would I have called? I don't know. I honestly don't know. And I can't get away from that. That admission of my own failings.

The words on that website listing start their litany through my mind again—*gruesome triple killing, gruesome triple killing*—and I pull my knees up to my chest, let my head fall, arms wrapped around my legs, adopting the brace position, waiting for the crash.

Dee and Seb arrive within half an hour of my call, where I unloaded everything that's been going on. They come in bearing coffee and cakes for me, all hushed voices and grave faces like I've been bereaved. It's not what I want; what I want is for them to come in breezy and joking like usual, reassuring me that all is good, there's nothing wrong—that it's just some sick joke.

I don't show them the card—I don't want pity or questions from Dee about why I haven't opened it before now. She doesn't expect me to have any kind of loving reunion with my dad, but I know she has hopes for some kind of future relationship with Sasha, at the very least. As they sit down, I can see the card has dropped glitter all over the coffee table, an incongruous sparkle I have to look away from, praying they won't notice and question it, like it's blood spatter from a crime I've hastily hidden, like that Christmas card is a body I've stuffed behind the sofa and don't want them to find.

Dee asks to see the website and I bring it up on my laptop. She frowns as she clicks her way through it, even going so far as to get her credit card out to join the exclusive membership to get full access.

"How well do you really know Adam?" It's Seb I ask. I wonder again what he told Adam about me, if Adam approached him first expressing interest—Dee would have raved about me, but Seb? Did he warn him off? Did he tell him to be careful? Did he tell him I was trouble? I bite my lip. Did he tell him about Jacob, about my family and my past?

He sighs and runs a hand through his hair. "We've been talking about this since you called. I met him my first year of university—we were good mates, hung out in the same group the whole time."

"So, you knew him then as well?" I interrupt, looking at Dee. She used to visit Seb every three weeks—she was in the dorms in Bristol, but he had a shared student house in Cardiff, so it was better for her to go to him. That carried on until graduation when they moved in together.

I only know most of that through hearsay. Dee met Seb at sixth-form college and those and her university years were my lost years—she staged her intervention after she'd graduated and moved back to Cardiff. She turned up on the doorstep of the dive I was staying in, all shiny bright and furious. Furious with me for falling so far without calling her for help. She took me back to her flat that day and defended me to Seb, to the world, every time I made a mistake.

But Dee shakes her head, not looking up from the computer. "Not really—we tended to keep to ourselves on our weekends."

"Yeah," agrees Seb. "I had friends party weekends and quieter Dee weekends."

See? A bunch of nans from the age of eighteen. No wonder we were still such good friends. It just took me a bit longer to get there, that's all.

"But he was a good friend to you, Seb? You *really* know him?"

Seb hesitates. "We didn't see each other that much after

graduation. He moved to London, so we mostly kept in touch on Facebook and WhatsApp. Then he lost his job last year and we had work available at my place, so I invited him down. He moved here properly about six months ago."

I sit back. I'd been allowing myself to be reassured by the fact that Seb and Adam were best mates, like me and Dee, but Dee had obviously been exaggerating. Something I should have realized—wouldn't I have met him sooner if they'd been that close? But then...there were a few years when I barely saw Dee, that doesn't mean we're not the closest of friends.

"Hanna—I know this is freaking you out," Seb says, "but I swear—Adam can't have anything to do with this. I *know* him; he would *never* do anything to hurt anyone. His website—the abandoned house thing—that started as an art project, that's all, nothing creepy about it."

"Maybe that's how it started," I say. "But you didn't even see him for eight years—what if it did become creepy, some weird obsession in that time?"

"It's definitely not him," Dee says as she looks up from the laptop. "Look at these listings—you can tell. This is one of his...he talks about the crime sites completely differently to the new one."

I scan through the listings Dee has pointed out and she's right. The one about my family reads like a bunch of tabloid headlines, but all the others are matter-of-fact, detailing historic crimes with no sensationalism. I try to find the other new one, but it comes up "listing unavailable." I don't know why he's removed that one but not the one about my family.

I let out a shaky breath. "Yeah...I can see the difference, but why is it still up? He said he was going to take the site down, but all that's gone is the other new listing the police were asking him about."

"Have you tried calling him?" Dee asks.

I shake my head. "I think he's still at the police station."

"God, this is terrifying," Dee says. "I'm with Seb—it's not Adam, no way. But someone's doing this—someone who has to know you or Adam or both of you. And the other listing—you said it had something to do with the hit-and-run on the park road?"

"I don't know for sure—the name sounded familiar, that's all."

Dee taps a finger lightly on the laptop keyboard. "Let me do some research. Maybe it'll help us figure out the connection."

"That's the other thing I'm trying to work out," I say. "The connection when we only really met last night." I pause and look at Dee. "But Adam did say you've been trying to set the two of us up since New Year."

She sighs. "That's a bit of an exaggeration. I think what actually happened was he mentioned a while before Christmas that he fancied you, but you were seeing Liam. Then, when I was chatting to him at New Year, I just happened to mention you were now single..."

"And that's it?"

"Well. I *might* have mentioned it a couple more times?"

"But not to me."

"I knew it wasn't the right time for you. But I wanted to make sure he was still single when you were ready, so I was just...keeping him on the hook."

"Nice."

"But I was right, wasn't I? You did like him."

I shrug. "Problem is, now, with all *this*—whatever the

hell *this* is—I think your hopes of a hat-buying happy-ever-after are seriously ruined."

Dee frowns. "Well, that's just…that's just *crap*."

Seb shakes his head, then looks at me. "What do you want to do now, Han? Come back to ours? Or we can stay here and—"

"I have to go home," I say. I let out a sigh and the glitter from the hidden Christmas card floats up into the air between us. "Well, I guess it's not home anymore, is it? But I have to go back there just to see, just to check…I can't sit here waiting."

Chapter 10

thedarktourist.com
    Welcome to the Dark Tourist...
    \<search\> West Dean Holiday Park Murders
    sorry.
    this page is no longer available.
    please go \<home\> and choose another listing

Saturday 6 p.m.

"It feels so strange coming back here," Dee says, echoing my own thoughts as we turn off the main road. She didn't hesitate for a second when I asked her to come with me. Actually, I didn't even need to ask; as soon as I looked at her, she'd said yes, of course she'd come.

It's well over six months since I've been here—much longer for Dee, whose family moved away when she was at university. Dee used to live in Littledean itself, but I grew up a few miles outside, within the confines of the wrongly named West Dean Family Fun Park. Ha—the words *family* and *fun* did not go together in my experience.

The lane down to the holiday park twists and turns between high, overgrown hedgerows and trees that arch up and over us, dappling the road ahead with stripes of light and dark. It cuts off the noise of the main road, giving the impression we're entering some secret land. Especially now, out of season, when we're the only car on the road.

Dee laughs and shakes her head. "God—I used to be so jealous of you, living on a holiday camp—swimming pool, playgrounds, kids' club..."

"None of which I was allowed to use." I glance at her. "You probably used the pool and the playground more than I did."

"Yeah—okay, that was weird. I never got why your dad actually took the job when he clearly hated the place. It seems such a weird choice for someone so..." She pauses and laughs again. "When I first met him, I thought he was a vicar. Did I ever tell you that? He wasn't dressed like one, and I knew you all lived at the holiday camp and didn't hang around church, but he had that vibe, you know? I remember telling Mum all about the vicar who ran the holiday park and she was *very* confused."

"Ha, I'll bet."

"Vicar or cult leader, anyway."

"All of the strictness but none of the religious forgiveness—and hell no to cult leader: certainly none of the charisma needed to attract cult members there."

Dee's smile fades. "Yeah, he was just a shit, really, wasn't he? What did your mum and Jen ever see in him?"

"He mostly saved the horrible for me. And to be fair, he was at his worst after Mum had gone, when it was only me there to bear the brunt of it. He was almost amiable around Jen—and positively polite at work, despite his lip-curling contempt for everything about this place."

"Which again, leaves me wondering why take the job?"

I shrug. "Live-in accommodation? Plus, the camp was only open May to October, the rest of the time he could concentrate on his academic stuff and just be a caretaker without all the hideous tourists he hated. Not that I ever saw him actually write or do anything academic... Mostly he just sat at his desk in the spare room he liked to call his office."

I stop and shake my head. "I just realized I'm making him sound like Jack Torrance from *The Shining*, only without the alcoholism and supernatural shit." I pause. "And now I'm scaring myself thinking of the camp as The Overlook."

"Redrum, redrum?" Dee says, then winces. "Sorry, really bad taste in the circumstances."

I nearly miss the turn, the sign for the holiday park half-hidden by brambles. I frown as we turn in. The gates are shut and padlocked. Although the holiday park is seasonal, they never normally padlock the gates. Dad used to close them at night and run the bolt across from the inside, but he rarely bothered padlocking them—we were there as security over the winter months. The worst trouble we ever had was teenagers trying to sneak in to drink and smoke at the playground, soon frightened off by the glare of the motion-sensitive security light and a shout from my dad.

But tonight, the security light doesn't come on as I get out of the car and approach the gates and there are no other lights on inside. I can see what used to be our house—a crumbling coach house, all that remains of the old manor that used to be here.

I blink as I look beyond the house. Something is wrong. Lit by the headlights of the car, the field that should be full of static caravans is empty. The clubhouse is boarded up.

"Hanna—check this out."

I turn away from the padlocked gates. Dee is out of the car, standing a few feet away and staring at a sign on the fence. I shield my eyes from the glare of the headlights and crunch through the undergrowth to join her.

Land acquired by Thomson Homes, the sign says. What?

"I guess this is why they moved, then," Dee says.

Shit. All those un-listened-to messages Jen mentioned in the card, maybe Dad really did leave them. I've picked up voicemails from my dad in the past and deleted them without listening, saving my call-backs for when I know he won't be able to answer. It's possible he's been trying to tell me for months that they were moving, that the park was closing, and I just didn't listen. My throat tightens further as I remember the guarded message from Sasha way back before Christmas. She was telling me she'd got hold of a secret phone and must have waited and waited for me to text back, even just to acknowledge I'd received her message. Why didn't I? I don't mean answering Dad's calls, but why didn't I text Sasha back?

I turn in a circle, looking at the closed and locked-up camp, the sign on the fence. I don't know what to do. I suppose I thought the camp would still be here, even if my family wasn't. That even if the house was empty, it would be because the new caretaker family hadn't moved in yet. I thought *someone* would be around, so I could go in and check everything out, try to find some answers. And there's something else—something nagging at me...

Dee touches my arm. "Do you have the keys? For the gate—for the house?"

"What? Oh...yes. Yes, I do." I brought them as my excuse, in case there was a security guard or something here. I was going to say I'd made the trip to return the keys in the hope that I might get some information in exchange. I fumble in my bag and yes, they're all there—the gate, the house, the clubhouse. I had them from the days I'd help out with cleaning and maintenance, before I got the hell out of here, never looking back, and they've been gathering dust at the back of my junk drawer ever since.

"Then let's go and check it out."

I hesitate. Do I want to? We could get back in the car and drive home. We'd be there by eight, the roads quiet at this time. Back in time for a drink or dinner somewhere. Wait for the detective to call me, to tell me where my family has gone.

But. That website, the detail... The police said they'd found no evidence of a break-in, but whoever posted the listing has been to this house. Oh wait—*that's* what's nagging. I reach into my bag for a crumpled piece of paper— the printout of this house's listing on Adam's website.

"Look," I say to Dee. "This photo—the one on the website. You can see caravans in the background. But the camp's obviously been closed for *months*. This photo is old..."

"But what does that mean? Does it mean it's been on the website for months? But Adam would have noticed, surely? He only built the thing a few months ago; it's not like it's been sitting dormant for years."

"Or someone took the photo months ago and kept it until now..."

We look at each other. I'm afraid to use the keys to enter that creepy abandoned place—a place that holds nothing but bad memories for me. Is it irony that I stop to think how much Adam would love the possibility to explore here?

"Oh, sod it—let's do this." I unlock the main gate and struggle to push it open, managing to get it wide enough for me and Dee to squeeze through. The path to the house, without the camp lights on, is treacherous. Even leaving the car headlights on to light our way, we stumble up to the house, Dee cursing behind me. It's potholed and littered with debris from the trees. It was always a sod treacherous path, even with Dad keeping the potholes under control. Now, it looks like it hasn't been cleared or repaired in years. How long has the place been closed?

Unlike the clubhouse, the windows of my family home have not been boarded up, but it only takes a quick glance to see that behind the glass, the house has been emptied. But I knew that anyway, didn't I? I grit my teeth and unlock the front door.

The electricity is off when I try the light in the hall, so I open the torch app on my phone and hold it up. There's nothing. No furniture, no carpet, just a layer of dust that shows up my footprints when I shine the light on the bare floorboards. No other footprints in the dust, though; no sign anyone else has been here for a long time. I stride through empty room after empty room, leaving a trail of footprints in the dust.

I'm tempted to grab Dee and go once I've gone through all the downstairs rooms, but I'm here, we've made the journey, so I force myself to go up the stairs, instinctively avoiding the creaky stairs in the dance I'd perfected by the age of fourteen.

The spare room and Dad and Jen's rooms are as empty as downstairs, but I spot something the moment I enter my old room—or, more recently, Sasha's room. On the windowsill, lit by the pale moonlight from outside, is a little stack of photographs. I go over and pick them up, my hand surprisingly steady. I use my phone to shine a light on them. I recognize these: snapshots of a teenage me and my friends, the old gang I haven't seen in a very long time. Photos I used to keep hidden and left behind when I ran away. No photos of Jacob here, though. Those ones I did take with me.

Who found these and left them here? The movers? Dad? Sasha? My guess is my father. I think if Sasha found them, she would have kept them, reminders of a big sister who was never around for her. I used to feel so bad when I came back to visit. Sasha was such a quiet, shy girl, but it was always obvious she yearned to get to know me better, her attempts squashed and stifled all the time by my dad. Not that I ever reciprocated her efforts. Sasha was better off without me in her life. I believe that, no matter how many times Dee tries to persuade me otherwise.

"Shit—Hanna!" It's Dee's voice from downstairs, raised high in alarm.

I drop the photos and run back downstairs to the hall—someone is coming up to the house, a torch in their hand, blinding us and hiding whoever is holding it.

We're very much alone out here. It was still daylight when we set out from Cardiff and we both rolled our eyes when Seb offered to come along just in case we needed "help."

But now it's dark and I'm very aware we're a long way from the nearest inhabited house.

"Who's there?" I call. "Dad?"

"It's the police—come out where we can see you."

Double shit.

"Okay, okay." I walk out with my hands raised, one shielding my eyes from the glare of the torch.

"*Hanna Carter*?"

He lowers the torch and I recognize him. "Hey, Stephen."

Stephen Hayes—I went to school with him. Not that we hung out in the same gang—you can hear that in the cold way he says my name. Ah, the familiarity of that small-town disgust—such fun. How I've missed it.

"Nice uniform—suits you." The words don't come out as light and casual as I intended. My voice is shaking. Dee steps up next to me and I see Stephen visibly relax. I was always trouble—or that was my reputation, anyway—but everyone liked Dee.

"What are you two doing here? We had reports of a break-in."

That's when I see a second, female officer behind him. I don't recognize her, which is hardly surprising as I haven't been back here for longer than a day in thirteen years, and my visits were always confined to the holiday park—I never went into the village.

"I didn't think I was breaking in. I thought I was coming home."

There's a moment's silence from Stephen. "Home? Your family moved out of here months ago."

I look back at the empty house. "Yeah—I can see that."

"Didn't you know?" He glances at his colleague. "We were asked to do a welfare check on the place earlier. CID from Cardiff asking about them, where they were—we told them they'd gone, but they were really insistent we check the house."

I keep my face blank, not wanting to give anything away. "I kind of lost touch with them—just wanted to check they were okay."

"Okay..."

"So, as it's obviously a misunderstanding, can we maybe forget this ever happened?"

Stephen looks at his fellow officer, who shrugs. He nods. "I guess so. Come on, we'll escort you out." He turns away, then stops. "Hang on," he says. "How did you get in?"

My hand closes over the set of keys I'm still holding. Then I relax and open my hand. What's the point of keeping hold of them? My family is gone—I have nothing left to tie me to this place.

Stephen sighs and takes the keys out of my hand. "You shouldn't have used these." He hesitates. "Listen—I'll say I found you outside the gates, not on the property, okay? That you handed over the keys and left, end of story."

"Thanks," I mutter. It's a very reluctant thanks—I do not want to feel grateful to Stephen Hayes for anything.

He laughs. "Don't think I'm doing it as a favor. I just don't want the hassle of taking you into the station." He leads us back to my car, turning to go once we've both got in. His police car has us blocked in.

"Wait—Stephen?" I call, getting back out. "Who called about the break-in?" I look around—there are still no security cameras, no other houses in sight. We didn't pass a single car after we turned off the main road.

"It was an anonymous call."

Dee looks over at me, frowning. My flesh crawls. Was someone watching us as I unlocked the gate? Listening to our conversation? I'm suddenly glad the police car turned up.

Stephen is frowning at me. "We'll escort you as far as the main road. And Hanna—it might be better if you're not seen around here again. There's nothing for you to come back for anymore and it's a nice town, we don't want any trouble."

"*Trouble*?"

"You know what I mean," he says in a low voice, and my shoulders stiffen.

Stephen's partner, who never introduced herself, gets behind the wheel of the police car, but Stephen hovers, still looking at me. What, does he want me to pinky-swear not to be naughty in his lovely nice town?

"Funnily enough, Stephen, I don't really remember it as a *nice town*, but I can assure you I won't be visiting again."

Ah, Stephen Hayes, standing there in his shiny police uniform, representing the ninety-nine percent of this shithole village who viewed me as a waste of space, a troublemaker, worthy of disgusted looks, shaking heads, laughed at, sneered at, followed round the village shop by the suspicious owner, because I was already a lost cause, had to be a shoplifter as well, *right*? And now here stood spotty, skinny little Stephen, all ready to chase me out of town with a pitchfork, in case what happened to Jacob is catching, like I'm a fucking contagious disease.

I grit my teeth and get in the car, slamming the door so hard the car rocks. This *shitty* place. I watch in the rearview mirror as Stephen's colleague reverses and does a three-point turn, driving far enough to give us room to turn and then waiting. They really do intend to escort us out of town.

I wait until we're on the motorway, well away from Stephen and the village before I start a rant that lasts twenty minutes. Dee sits in silence and lets me vent until I run out of steam. This is why I visited less and less—if Stephen Hayes could make me feel like this, a visit with my family always left me feeling a million times worse. And on those visits I never had Dee with me offering her unwavering support.

I'm exhausted. Today seems to have gone on for a year and frankly, at the moment, I don't bloody *care* where my family is. They're going to be fine—I'll get a call tomorrow telling me the police have traced them and I'll have gone through all this trauma for *nothing*.

The Night They Vanished

I drop Dee off, turning down her offer to stay at hers. I just want to go home and sleep, forget today ever happened. I switch on the radio when the silence gets too loud and the local news comes on as I'm almost home.

"The body of a woman has been found in her home. Police say they are treating the death of Katie Bentley as suspicious and are appealing to the public to come forward with any information. This comes only months after her younger sister Gemma Bentley was killed in a hit-and-run in the city. The driver has not been found."

The car swerves as the names register—Gemma and Katie Bentley, the women that detective asked me about. Oh God—what does this mean?

There's someone outside my house again as I pull up. A man, head down, half hidden in darkness, sitting on the wall. He looks up as I get out of the car. It's Adam.

Chapter 11

SASHA—November, three months earlier

I'm so glad I had my meltdown on a Friday. The thought of going back in the next day after making such a fool of myself...I swear the burn of embarrassment covers me from head to toe. If today were a school day instead of a Saturday, I would have had to fake an illness, lie right to Dad's face. There's no way I would have gone in.

But hopefully, hopefully...It's Seren's party this weekend. Hopefully there'll be enough drama there so everyone will forget about what I did at school and be too busy talking about that. I'm good at being invisible and it's not even for two more years anymore, is it? We're moving after Christmas, so it's only a couple more months. Maybe I can fake a really bad illness, something non-life-threatening but bad enough to keep me off school until Christmas.

I lie in bed, staring at the ceiling. If I had a phone, I could google something: how to fake a temperature, how to fake an illness without your parents dragging you to the doctor or the emergency room. Maybe I should run away, do a Hanna, follow the family tradition. I could turn up on her doorstep and get her to Teach-Me-The-Ways to be a troublemaking rebel.

I sigh and sit up. It could be worse. At least the school didn't call home. They didn't even give me a detention. In light of my "exemplary school record," they let me off with a warning and talked to me about academic pressure and stress, like me scrapping with Seren Kent was the result of some tricky algebra. Miss Jennings even talked about moving me up to the top-set math class, so maybe I should have meltdowns more often.

I hear the sound of the lawnmower starting up and jump out of bed. From the window I can see Ethan on the other side of the path, weaving in and out of the trees with the rusty old lawnmower, wrestling the scrappy grass into submission. It's barely grown since the last time it was cut and I wonder if he's just making up stuff to do to fill the day. I didn't know they were working today—normally I hear Owen's van rattling past my window. Now this place is going to be sold, I wonder how long they'll still be working here. What's the point in the owners paying to keep the grounds looking all neat when they're selling it?

Ethan glances up at my window then. I leap away but he smiles, so I know he's seen me spying on him, still in my jammies, hair like a bird's nest. Damn it.

Mum and Dad have gone out shopping by the time I've showered and dressed. I usually go with them, but I couldn't face it today. I'm not hungry, so I don't bother with breakfast. I hover for a while outside Dad's office, the temptation to go and look for more messages huge. But…I don't know a great deal about computers, but I do know it would be too easy for Dad to find all my previous sneaky visits in his internet history if he ever felt the need—or if someone (*tut tut—what would your daddy say?*) suggested he look…I wonder if there's a way to delete the recent history? I look toward the kitchen. I can still glimpse Ethan slowly weaving in and out of sight with his lawnmower. I bet *he* knows.

Before I can chicken out, I shove my feet in shoes and slip out of the back door. I check for any sign of my parents' car returning before I call his name. He switches off the lawnmower as I approach, looking more than happy to take a break.

"Is Owen not here today?" I try to sound casual, but I don't think it works because Ethan smiles and shakes his head.

"Nah—he's taken his van to the garage for some repairs. You shouldn't let him get to you, though, Sasha—his bark's worse than his bite. He's just a grumpy sod sometimes."

Just a grumpy sod? He looks at us sometimes like he would murder us in our sleep given half the chance. Mum and Dad never seem to see it. Mum actually called him "*such* a polite young man" the other day. I guess Ethan could be right. I could be paranoid. Maybe he just hates teenagers. Can't say I blame him—I hate teenagers too. Still, I'm glad he's not here today.

"Do you know how to delete your internet search history?" I blurt it out without any other preamble.

Ethan looks surprised then laughs. "Oh dear—what have you been looking at? I never would have thought it of you, Sasha."

I frown. "Do you know how?"

He shrugs. "Course. It's easy. Hand us your phone and I'll show you."

"I haven't got a phone."

He raises his eyebrows but doesn't say anything. I glance back toward the house. "It's on my dad's computer."

He hesitates and stares at me. "Um…no. I don't think

your dad will be too impressed if he comes home and finds me in his house with his teenage daughter, fiddling with his computer. That might be taking his liberal tolerance for ex-cons a bit far."

"Please. There's time."

He shakes his head and reaches for the lawnmower again.

"*Please*, Ethan. I don't know who else to ask and I could get in so much trouble with my dad."

"You mean you don't know any other ex-cons who know their way round a computer," he says, but he doesn't start the lawnmower back up.

"Please?" I say again and he sighs but moves as if to follow me back to the house.

I do have the sense to pause at the back door. Yes, I want this done, but I am inviting a convicted criminal into my empty house in our deserted holiday park. My hesitation is only momentary, though. Mum and Dad have been gone an hour and he's known I'm here alone. If he had any nefarious thoughts about me, he's had plenty of time to act on them.

But my heart is still beating too fast as I lead him through the quiet house. I don't even know what he was sent to prison for. It can't be anything *too* bad. Dad wouldn't have him working here if he were violent or had done anything that would put his home or family at risk.

It becomes more of a thrill than fear as I open the door to Dad's office. Something so forbidden for me and here I am leading a strange man, a *criminal*, into Dad's inner sanctum. For a moment, I feel like Hanna, the big sister I don't know at all, the runaway, the bad seed, She Who Shall Not Be Named.

I kind of like it.

*

99

It takes Ethan about five minutes to delete the search history. He assures me Dad won't find that stupid Facebook account, that it would take a proper computer whiz to dig out my midnight internet feasts, but that I should change my password anyway, just in case. I stand behind him as he brings up Facebook and I tell him my login details. He hovers over it for a second and I can feel myself blushing as I read the last couple of things I posted through a stranger's eyes, as he brings up the anonymous threatening messages.

"Nice fake photo" is all he says, though, as he changes the security details and clicks off it. He smells of wet grass and damp earth, like he brought the outside into the house, clashing with the usual house smells of lavender air freshener and Mr. Sheen.

"All done," he says, closing down the computer and standing up.

"Thank you so much," I say as he heads back outside and I stand in the doorway, itching for him to be gone, so I can whip round with the polish and the vacuum, eradicating fingerprints and his smell, making sure there's no sign of mud and cut grass on the floors. Will Dad come in and sense someone's been in here?

"You should make sure the webcam's disabled before you use the computer again," he says.

"What do you mean?"

"The messages—about you in your pajamas. How did they know what pajamas you were wearing?"

I look at him, open-mouthed. I freaked out when I got the messages, but I didn't think…I didn't *stop* to think…I feel ill. Full-on ready-to-vomit-at-his-feet ill. What I'm picturing now is the idiots from school not only sending me vaguely threatening messages but actually *watching* me as I used the computer. Oh God.

He stares at me and sighs. "Do you not know anything about internet safety? I thought they taught that stuff in school these days?"

Maybe they did. But as I've never been allowed a phone or internet access, I always tuned those assemblies out.

"Oh, for God's sake," he mutters, shaking his head. "Look—I *might* be able to find out who's sending the messages."

"You can do that?"

"*Might* be able to, I said, but I do know someone who's good at tracing IP addresses on computers."

He means someone he was in prison with. I hesitate. Haven't I already taken too many risks?

"I don't need to," he continues. "Your dad's not going to find anything on his computer now. But it's obviously scared you."

I could say no. I'm safe from Dad finding out I used his computer, but whoever sent those messages is still out there. I can lie and deny, but if they *have* taken screenshots of my posts...yes, it's all fake details, but Dad would recognize the photo of Hanna. I was stupid to use it.

"Yes—please. Could you find out for me?"

He gets a phone out of his pocket. "Remind me of the login details to your account and I'll see what I can find out for you."

I don't know what I'll do when he does give me the details, how I'll scare off whoever is sending the messages, how I'll stop them going to Dad.

Maybe Ethan will have some ideas about that too.

Chapter 12

HANNA—Saturday 8 p.m.

I'm tempted to keep driving but Adam has seen me. And besides—that news report...I park and get out of the car, leaving the door open.

"Who's Katie Bentley?" I call, not walking any closer to Adam or my house. "What the hell is going on?"

He gets a piece of paper from his pocket and holds it out. I hesitate, then walk over and snatch it off him, before retreating back to the car. It's a printout of a webpage— from Adam's website, I recognize that right away. But it's not the listing about my family; it's the new listing I tried to find before.

About the murder of a thirty-one-year-old woman, the address given as Meadow Close, whose sister had been *tragically mown down three months earlier.* My chest gets tight and there's a roaring in my ears as I continue reading down as far as the date given for the murder—yesterday's date.

Adam is speaking and it takes me a moment to understand what he's saying.

"Katie Bentley was found murdered in her home late last night. It looked at first like a violent break-in gone wrong. Her door was kicked in, the place trashed. It looked like a break-in until it turned up on my website. The press weren't told until this afternoon—there's no way anyone not involved in this would have known these details."

My panic has escalated to the point where I want to scream at Adam sitting so damned calmly on the wall. A woman has been *murdered* and then details of that murder posted on his website. This is not a malicious prank, not a sick hacker making shit up. That woman was murdered for real. I have to find my family—the police *have* to find them. I look up from the printout at Adam. I was wrong to think he was calm. He looks ghostly pale under the streetlight and he's shivering. How long has he been sitting there?

"Were there really photos? On your website?" Jesus, no wonder they were so quick to take that one down.

He shakes his head. "It's a dead link. It doesn't go anywhere. There's nothing more than this."

"And what about the woman's sister? The hit-and-run? Are they saying it's a *coincidence*? Two violent deaths within three months of each other?" I'm remembering what Dee told me about the hit-and-run—how it looked deliberate, how the car mounted the pavement...

"They're not saying anything to me—but it can't be, can it?"

Wait...what did he say before? That there was no way anyone not involved in this would have known the details...

Jesus. *Jesus*. They can't really think he had anything to do with this, can they? And me—they asked *me* about Gemma and Katie Bentley.

But no—they wouldn't have let him go; he wouldn't be sitting outside my house if they really thought he'd done anything. Maybe it's stupid, but I'm reassured by the fact that they let him go—they haven't arrested him for anything and surely, if they thought he had anything to do with all this, they would have kept him there?

"They haven't arrested you for murder, then?"

He looks up at me, his face pale, hair all over the place. "They took my computer and my car," he says. "They took fingerprints and DNA samples. My *God*." He shakes his head. "I've never even been in a police station before."

"Lucky you," I mutter, but under my breath. I hover, not sure what I'm supposed to do now. The detective said to wait for news, that someone would call as soon as they'd traced my family, but am I supposed to just sit at home, staring at my phone? I've been back to the village, been chased out of town—what now?

"There was CCTV," Adam says, and I frown.

"What?"

"On the street—where I took you to that house last night. There was a building opposite that had CCTV. That's why they let us—me—go. Because I couldn't have been murdering a woman over the other side of town at the same time as showing you that house."

I can't help the tinge of relief. They won't have any reason to look closer at me now, no reason to go digging into any juvenile police records.

"What are you going to do now?" Adam asks, and he looks lost.

104

"I don't know, I really don't. I went home," I say. "To my family home. But they weren't there. They moved, apparently, months ago." I sound stupid, but I don't know what to say to him. Is he expecting me to invite him in? I live on a busy street, but right now, there's no one around and I don't want to have to go past him, don't want to turn my back on him to unlock my door.

Something occurs to me as I stand there. "Your website," I say. "When you look at the listings—you clicked through to another page with my family's listing, didn't you? It wasn't like this Bentley one . . . The hacker, could they have put all the details on that first page?"

He shakes his head. "It's a preview image—you have to login to see the details. There's only space for a couple of lines of text and one image on the listings page."

"But my family moved months ago—I would never have recognized their new house, because I have no idea where they moved to. God, even if I had the new address, I wouldn't recognize a picture of it."

He frowns as I run the idea past him, trying to figure it out. "So, whoever did this also knew you weren't aware they'd moved? Or at least knew you hadn't been to the new place—how?"

"No idea. But everyone else they knew would have known they'd moved."

"What about Dee and Seb?"

"They . . . Wait, you're right. Anyone who knows my *family* would have known they'd moved, but anyone who knows *me* wouldn't." I shake my head. "Dee's parents moved away years ago, and they were never friends with my dad and stepmother. So, whoever did this . . . did they actually murder those women? Or are they just some sick hacker who found out somehow and put it up on your site?"

"To be honest, I'd rather that than the alternative."

"But if it is a murderer and they somehow got that address from me or Dee or Seb and went there with the intention of murdering my family..."

"Didn't you say there was no sign of an intruder there?"

"But if they're working based on my bloody ignorance, they might still be lurking around the village, they might have been asking questions, trying to figure out where they've moved to." I stop to take a breath. "I'm going to have to go back there again. If I don't find out their new address, I'm going to go back to the village. I can't just sit around waiting for the police to contact me."

"Can I come with you?"

I stare at him, the silence stretching out, at his ruffled hair and beautiful arms, that smile now missing. I enjoyed our date so much—I would have said yes if he'd asked me out again.

But.

"I don't know."

But—he's a stranger. A stranger whose website, hacked or not, is now forcing me to look for the family I ran away from. A stranger who doesn't know me at all and has no idea what I ran away from. It's not Adam I need beside me if I'm going to do this.

"I'll call you, okay?"

"Tell your flatmate I'm sorry if I freaked him out," Adam calls after me as I walk past him to the front door.

I stop and turn back to look at him. "I'm sorry?"

"I saw him in the window when I knocked. But he just turned the light off and disappeared. I wanted to see you, so I waited... I didn't think. I'm sorry. He probably thinks I... Shit. He probably called the police, didn't he? Seeing me lurking outside." He stands up. "I'd better go."

"Wait," I say. "Flatmate? I don't have a flatmate."

Adam looks back at the house and points to my living-room window. "That's yours, isn't it?"

I nod and step away from the house. "I don't have a flat-mate," I repeat in a whisper. "Are you sure it was my window?" I point to Ben's window next door, the identical half-house, separated only by our two front doors. "Could it have been that one you saw the light in? My neighbor's window?"

Adam hesitates. "It could have been, I guess..."

There's no sign of lights from either window now. No sounds, nothing. I bite my lip.

"Should I call the police?" Adam asks, stepping up next to me and getting his phone out of his pocket.

"No," I say. "Do you really want to see the police again today?"

"Hanna—there was someone in your flat!"

"But you don't know that for sure." I take a step for-ward. "I'll just unlock the door and poke my head in."

"Are you kidding me? It could be whoever's hacked my site—it could be whoever killed those women."

I glance back at him. "Keep your phone handy—call 999 if I scream."

He shakes his head. "You're not going in there on your own."

"So, who's going to call the police if we're both in there screaming?"

"Just... unlock the door, will you? *I'll* look inside—*you* can be ready to call the police."

Chapter 13

Saturday 9 p.m.

I walk up to the front door, keys out ready; then I hesitate, take a hurried step back, bumping into Adam.

He steps up to me. "What is it?" he asks, keeping his own voice low.

"How long have you been here?"

"I dunno—about twenty minutes? I called Seb—he told me you and Dee were on your way back. Why?"

"My front door is open."

"Shit," he whispers. "I'll call the police."

"Wait." I put my hand over his as he gets his phone out. "I don't...I left the house in such a rush this afternoon... I wanted to go back home and find my family. I might not have locked it."

"But are you sure?"

"No. But look—it's ajar but there's no sign anyone's broken in."

"But if you left it open, anyone could have gone in while you were out. I told you I saw someone in there..."

I waver. I really don't want to have to face the police again. But...my family is still missing, and those women are dead. The hit-and-run was only a couple of streets from here.

"I'll just have a quick look—if it's obvious nothing's been touched, I probably just left the door open."

"Wait," Adam says. "We stick to the original plan—I'll go. Be ready to call the police."

My heart pounds as he goes through the door and the seconds he's gone seem to last forever.

I'm not reassured when he does reappear, gently pushing me away from the door.

"I'm sorry, Hanna—you do need to call the police. It doesn't look as though anything big is missing, but it's obvious someone has been in there."

"Oh God," I whisper, pressing a hand against my stomach. My flat, my home, my sanctuary. I shake off Adam's hand on my arm and rush inside. Sod preserving the crime scene, I need to see—

I stop dead in the doorway to the living room. Adam's right—the TV is still there, it doesn't look like I've been burgled. I had my laptop and phone with me, so I know they're safe. But the place has been ransacked. Books pulled off the shelves, letters and papers scattered everywhere, the coffee table tipped over. It doesn't look like anything's been broken, it just looks like someone came in and had a temper tantrum.

But then I think of what Adam said about the woman who'd been murdered—it looked like a violent break-in gone wrong. What if I'd been home when this happened? Would I be lying there dead as well?

"Hanna?" It's Adam's voice and I turn, tears in my eyes. He's standing in the doorway. "I've called the police— because of what's going on, I called DC Norton direct. He's asked if we can leave the property."

"Yeah," I say, my voice shaky. "Sure. Let's go."

*

Adam is back on his wall and I'm sitting next to him when the two cars pull up—one police car with two uniformed officers and a dark blue Toyota driven by DC Norton. He gets out and talks to the uniformed officers before coming over to us.

"Miss Carter, Mr. Webster," he says, standing in front of us, his hands in his pockets. "My uniformed colleagues are going to make sure there's no one still inside your house before forensics arrive, but I have a few questions if that's okay?"

I nod and shove my own hands deep in my jacket pockets. It's getting cold as it gets later. I think about correcting him on the name thing again—I don't like being a Carter again. That's a name I was happy to leave behind.

"Mr. Webster—you said you thought you saw someone on the property, before Miss Carter arrived home?"

"Yeah, but I was on my phone—it was out of the corner of my eye and I can't be sure it was definitely Hanna's house... I didn't realize the other window was her neighbor's."

"And how long were you here before...?"

"Before Hanna got home? About twenty minutes." He pauses and stares at the detective. "Not long enough to do the damage that's been done in there, if that's what you're implying."

DC Norton nods and turns to me.

"Mr. Webster said on the phone that the front door was open but there was no sign of damage to the lock or door?"

"Yes—I'm sorry, but I couldn't remember if I'd closed and locked it when I left earlier. I was a bit distracted."

He nods. "And if you did lock it, is there anyone else who has a key? Friends? Your landlord?"

"The flat's mine—I own it. Or the bank does until I pay the mortgage back, anyway. But no landlord." I pause, reluctant to say the next thing. "My ex had a key. I haven't thought to get it back from him."

"This would be the Liam Harrison you mentioned in your first interview? The ex you believed may have slashed your car tire?"

Shit, shit, shit. "Yes, him. But he wouldn't...Please don't go and see him."

DC Norton raises his eyebrows. "Is there a reason you're scared of us speaking to him?"

"I'm not scared. I just...He'll think I'm doing this deliberately. He'll think I've been accusing him because I'm a bitter ex-girlfriend." I can feel myself going red. "It wasn't the easiest of breakups."

"Well, I'm sorry, but if he's the only other person with a key, we will need to speak to him—if only to eliminate him from our inquiries."

I wince. Oh, bloody hell.

"Have you got somewhere you can stay tonight? I'll need to know where you are—I'll probably have more questions after we've finished here." He glances from me to Adam. "I'll probably have questions for both of you. I'm curious, Mr. Webster, as to why you're here. You must have come directly from the police station."

Adam doesn't show any nervousness as he responds to DC Norton. "I told you why—I wanted to talk to Hanna about those women."

He nods, then turns away from us as one of the uniformed officers appears in my doorway and calls to him. "Okay," he says to us as he walks away. "Make sure PC Morgan has full details of where you'll be tonight. I'll want to speak to both of you."

*

It feels weird walking away from my own flat, leaving it swarming with police who'll be poking through my drawers and cupboards. My cheeks warm as I try to remember if I put the washing in the basket or if a bunch of policemen are going to be tripping over my knickers.

"Do you want me to come with you to Dee and Seb's?" Adam asks as we stop by my car.

"No, I'm okay…" I pause. "Unless you want to come as well? I'm sure they won't mind if you don't want to go home alone. Or I could give you a lift home—you said the police had your car?" I wince as I realize why they're checking his car over. The hit-and-run. The woman who was hit so violently almost every bone in her body was broken. The car that hit her…there's no way it escaped unscathed.

Adam looks at me. "You know none of this is me, right? Whoever broke into your flat—I was at the police station when that was happening. And I wasn't even in Cardiff when that other woman was hit by the car. I was in London."

But they're still checking his car.

He shrugs and shakes his head. "Actually, I think I'm going to stop at the pub. I really feel the need for a cold pint in a noisy pub. Somewhere I can try to forget today ever happened."

I waver as he turns away. "Do you mind if I join you? I have a feeling it's going to be a long night waiting for the police to call me back and a noisy pub sounds quite soothing right about now. I'll just text Dee and let her know I'm taking a detour on the way to hers."

"So," Adam says as he puts a Coke in front of me and picks up his pint. "I guess this counts as our second date? That's a bit of a record for me—two dates, two nights in a row."

"And who knew? All you had to do was get your site hacked, kidnap my family, and murder two women to make it happen."

He shakes his head, downing a third of his pint in one go. "It's so crazy. Two days ago, everything was completely normal—I had a Friday-night date to look forward to, I was meant to be having a few drinks with some mates tonight, a new project in work to get stuck into..."

"I'm sorry. And I know it's stupid to even be saying sorry like there's anything I could have done—but I feel bad. Because if Dee and Seb hadn't set this up—set *us* up—you'd have been having that nice, normal weekend."

He shrugs. "Yeah, it is stupid. Because if we're thinking that way then *I'm* sorry for spotting you across the room at Seb's New Year party and asking him about you."

I smile, temporarily distracted. "Don't tell me—it was my spectacularly bad singing that did it."

"To be fair, I think I could beat you in a bad singing competition. I'd seen you before, but Dee told me you weren't single. Then—there you were again at New Year, wearing one of those sparkly cardboard party hats even though no one else was and you had the best laugh." He pauses. "I was coming out of a long-term relationship and you were the first girl I'd really wanted to ask out in a long time."

I look down into the melting ice in my glass. "What frightens me the most about all of this is not knowing who is doing it or when it started. Is it you or me they're targeting? Have they been watching us for months? Did someone overhear you asking Seb about me all the way back on New Year's Eve? But that would mean it's someone we know— Dee only invites friends to her parties."

Adam visibly shivers and I wonder who's walked across his grave.

"Bet you're wishing you'd stayed in London and never moved down here," I say.

He smiles. "Well, I'd lost my job and broken up with Natalie—I was ready for a change."

"Bit of a major change, though—London for Cardiff, a whole new life."

"Not completely—I lived here for three years at university. Seb's always been a good mate and I had as many friends still living here as in London. I always liked Cardiff, probably would have stayed here after graduating if I'd found a good enough job."

It's difficult to see anything sinister in his only having lived here a few months when I'm actually here in front of him. He's relaxed and open and—hate the word though I do—so damned *nice*. I can't sit here and believe him capable of anything bad.

"Do you want another drink?" I nod at his empty glass, but he shakes his head.

"Too tempting to get drunk. I think I'll head home. Do you want me to come with you to Dee and Seb's?"

I smile. "No, it's okay. It's only round the corner." I sigh as we stand up to leave. "I don't think I'll be getting any sleep, though."

"No. Me neither. What will you do now? Are you still planning to go back to your home town?"

I shrug. "I guess. I'll see what the police have to say—see if I can go back to my flat and clean up." I shiver as I put my jacket on but it's not from the cold air as we leave the pub. "To be honest, I'm not sure I'll feel comfortable there for a long time knowing someone's been in there."

"That's understandable—I'm sure I'd feel the same." Adam turns to face me as we both hover on the pavement.

114

It's so strange to think I only met him twenty-four hours ago. He hesitates then leans down and kisses me on the cheek. "Night, Hanna," he says before turning to walk away.

I unlock the car and stop to watch him. "Adam," I call after him.

He stops and turns back.

"Would you like to come with us tomorrow? If we go back to Littledean?"

He stares at me for a moment, then nods.

Dee has already made up the sofa-bed in their living room by the time I get there. She makes us tea and sits on the bed next to me as I tell her about the break-in. Seb hovers in the doorway. He's got that wary look on his face again, like he thinks I'm going to bring trouble into Dee's life.

"God," Dee says with an exaggerated shudder, "I'm so glad Adam was there waiting for you."

"Yeah, me too," I say, sipping my tea. "Although I did have a wobble at first, wondering if it was him who'd broken in."

"Han—come on," Seb says, stepping into the room. "He really likes you. This whole nightmare has really upset him. And you have to blame me for him being there. I was the one who gave him your address."

"I know, I know…We went for a drink. I asked him to come along when we go back to Littledean. I know it's not him. But I think this, however it turns out, has really screwed up any chances of a proper second date. He's going to run a mile, isn't he?"

"Adam? Nah." Seb sits on the bed, scooting behind Dee and wrapping his arms around her. "To be fair, even with all this going on, you're lower maintenance than Natalie."

"Ah, the ex? He mentioned her name."

"Yeah—he hasn't really had a serious girlfriend since they broke up. She was…He was a total mess after. But two years single is a long time. Murders and missing families aside, I have high hopes for you two."

I stare at Seb. "Two years? He told me he broke up with her just before he moved here. He made it sound like the breakup was one of the reasons for the move."

Seb shakes his head. "No, you've got the wrong end of the stick there. I know because he was totally screwed up after they split, and I've spent the last year and a half encouraging him to get out there and find someone else. You probably misheard him."

But I didn't. I know I didn't. He told me he was just coming out of a long-term relationship when he saw me at the party. He told me they'd just broken up before he moved here.

I'm about to ask him more when my phone rings. I answer and it's DC Norton.

"We've finished with your flat," he says. "We could do with getting your fingerprints along with everyone who's been there recently so we can eliminate them from our inquiries—but we can talk about that more in the morning. There was no sign of forced entry or major damage, but we'll need you to go through the place and see if anything is missing. We've made sure it's secure, but it would be a good idea to get the locks changed." He pauses. "We found a couple of things we'd like to talk to you about—can you come into the station tomorrow?"

"Of course, but what did you find?"

Another pause. "Nothing alarming. Just a couple of things we want to check belong to you."

My heart is now racing as I try to imagine what they

might have found. Did I have anything illegal or dodgy lying around the flat? Or is it something the intruder has left behind?

"There's another thing," DC Norton says. "We've traced your family's new address and—"

"Were they there? Are they okay?"

"We've ascertained it is their address, but they're not currently there."

"So where are they?"

"The holiday park owners believe they've gone on holiday, but as they're new to the area, we haven't found anyone yet who can tell us where they went or how long they are supposed to be gone."

Yes, it's the school half-term, isn't it? Dad always took his holidays early in the year because he worked all through the summer season. I allow myself a moment of relief. That's all it is, a week away before he starts his new job, his phone switched off because he's on holiday. He always was severely puritan about phones being off during meals or holidays. He would have been happier if none of us had ever had mobile phones if he hadn't needed one for work.

"So that's good, then?" I say, all the tentative hope obvious in my voice. "They're just on holiday and incommunicado."

"We hope so. But in light of what's been happening, we're still treating finding them safe and well as a priority."

Chapter 14

Dee stops me as I'm about to leave the next morning.

"You might want to have a look at this…" She holds out a piece of paper. She's frowning and I see her hesitate before handing it over. Ever keen to protect me, Dee couldn't make it more obvious that, whatever this is, it's bad news.

It's a bit much sometimes. Not that I'd ever say it to her, but Dee is definitely overprotective. And I know it's because she loves me, which is why I would never, ever say anything, but it also…

Like Seb and that hint of wariness. Like the way he hovers in front of Dee sometimes when I'm around.

They don't entirely trust me not to fall back into my bad old ways. That's what their behavior says. Dee is trying to protect me from anything bad, in case I instantly turn to drink and drugs and debauchery because I can't handle it. And Seb—hovering, wary Seb—is always waiting for me to turn back into old Hanna and hurt Dee.

I hold out my hand to take the paper. "What is it?"

"I did some more research—into the hit-and-run, like I said, remember? And I found this. It's an article in one of the local magazines. Written by the sister of the hit-and-run victim."

Katie Bentley. A stranger, but I won't ever forget her name now. I look at the date on the article: it was written just before Christmas. Only a couple of months before she also died.

"She says—she insists—that her sister's death wasn't an accident. That it wasn't even a spur-of-the-moment *deliberate* hit-and-run."

I stare at the paper but I can't take the words in.

"She says she knows who did it and that the *police* know who did it. She doesn't name them, but says the police had someone in for questioning and they let him go…"

I shake my head. "Whoever it is—they can't be a real suspect, can they? They would have brought them back in straight away."

Dee bites her lip. "Maybe they did. Maybe that's what they want to talk to you about today."

"Thanks for coming in, Miss Carter." DC Norton smiles as he leads me through the police station, but he looks tired and I wonder if he's been working all night. I doubt I look much better. I was okay when I was talking to Dee and Seb, but the demons came back with a vengeance after they went to bed and I don't feel like I've slept at all.

"Please—call me Hanna," I say as he shows me into his office. I'm glad it's not the same cold interview room I was in yesterday.

"Is this about the Bentley sisters?" I blurt it out before he can say anything.

"I'm sorry?"

"Dee found an article that said you knew who'd done the hit-and-run. Is it the same person who killed Katie Bentley? Have you brought them back in? Do they know where my family is?"

"Hold on, slow down," he says. "Gemma Bentley's death is still an open investigation, as is Katie Bentley's. No one has been arrested."

"But you questioned someone? Who?"

"We *talked* to a lot of people and no one was charged. We do not currently have any suspects."

"But..."

He sighs. "I know the article you're referring to. Katie Bentley was under the mistaken impression that someone deliberately targeted her sister, that it was more than a drunk driver or a joyrider. There was never any evidence..."

"What about now? Now Katie Bentley has been murdered? Now it's been added to Adam's website?"

"I can assure you all cases are being *thoroughly* investigated, but that is not why I've asked you to come in this morning.

"Have you been back to your flat yet?" he continues, pausing to thank the officer who comes in with two coffees.

"Not yet. Haven't been able to face it, to be honest."

He sighs. "Might be better to take someone with you. There didn't seem to be any major damage, but it is a bit of a mess. We'll have someone from Victim Support follow up with you as well."

"So, what did you find?" I say, not wanting to think anymore about the mess at my flat. "Why am I here?"

He reaches onto a shelf behind him and brings down two clear plastic evidence bags.

The back of my neck prickles and my throat feels tight as he lays the bags on the table in front of me.

"This is from home. Not my flat, my childhood home. It was always on the mantelpiece." I don't touch the plastic, I can't bear the thought of coming anywhere near that

picture. It's a photograph in a silver frame, of my father
and Jen with a baby Sasha nestled in Jen's arms. Dad and
Jen are both smiling. Sasha is only a couple of months old,
barely visible in the frilly monstrosity of a dress with matching headband they've put her in. That photo was always a
slap in the face to me. It was the only family photograph on
display—none of me anywhere and certainly none of my
dead mother, who wasn't even relegated to dusty albums
hidden in cupboards. No, my photos were banished to those,
my mother's photos were just banned as soon as she left us.

The photo used to be in a different frame, but I came in
drunk and raging one night and threw it across the room.
The glass created a spectacular mess, but the photo itself
was unharmed and was back in a brand-new frame by the
following day. It wasn't long after that that I left.

There's no way this could have ended up in my flat
accidentally.

When I turn to look at the second evidence bag, I think I
might actually be sick. I can taste the acid burn of vomit in
my throat.

It's another photograph, this one unframed. Unlike the
other one, I don't instantly recognize it. It's not a photo I've
taken or seen but it's familiar all the same, because it's a
photo of me. Me and Jacob and a group of teenagers I'm
not sure I could even name anymore, all crowded together,
clutching bottles of booze and cigarettes, all obviously drunk
out of our heads. Judging by the tragic haircut I remember
and the dodgy dye-job, I would have been about fifteen.

"Neither of these are mine. I mean, this is me in this
photo—me when I was a kid—but it's not my photo."
I'm surprised to hear my voice so steady. I look down at
them again and frown. Something about this second one is

nagging. "Wait…how did you know…? I mean, how did you pick these two out as odd? I've got photos all over my flat."

It's true. Not family photos—a couple of Sasha, that's all. Mostly my friends, but there are plenty of framed and unframed photos scattered around my flat.

DC Norton gets an envelope out of a drawer. "Ah yes—these two photographs weren't displayed like any of the others. They were…it was like the whole break-in—all the mess—was created and arranged around these two photographs."

He pulls two sheets of paper out of the envelope and I see they're printouts of photographs. Photographs of my flat. My bedroom, to be exact. In the first, the silver-framed photograph is sitting in the middle of my dressing table, but everything else on the dressing table has been swept off onto the floor. I can see my makeup, hairbrush, perfume bottles scattered on the floor. The photograph, upright in its frame, has been placed to face the bed.

And the bed—that's what is in the second printout, and there, in the middle, lies the photograph of teenage me. Unlike the chaos of the rest of the room, the bed is neatly made, the quilt smoothly laid over the pillows.

I have to swallow hard to stop the surge of bile rising higher. Because I didn't make my bed yesterday morning. I saw Adam's website, saw my home and family listed, and I left the flat in far too much of a hurry to think about making the bed. Frankly, I'm amazed I even managed to get dressed. Which means that whoever broke in to my flat to leave those photos made my bed, put their hands all over my sheets and pillows.

That's when it hits me, what's nagging me about this second photo. It's true I don't recognize it specifically but it's so like the photos I found back at the holiday park. Left on the windowsill in my old bedroom, I presumed they'd been forgotten, or even left behind deliberately by my father. I know those photos were mine. I used to keep them hidden when I lived there. I guessed one of my family must have found them when they packed everything up—but what if they didn't? What if whoever took the silver-framed family photo and left it in my flat also took those teenage snap-shots and left them in the empty house for me to find? All of this planned, all of this staged.

"This photo," I say, picking up the printout with the silver-framed photo in it. "This was in my family's home the last time I was there." I don't mention the other one. Stephen Hayes might have lied when he said he wouldn't tell about me and Dee being in the house, but just in case he kept it quiet, I don't want to sit here in a police station, confessing I broke into the holiday camp. I might have had a key, but it was still breaking and entering.

"We're continuing to work on the presumption that this is someone who knows you—either now or from your past. Do you remember the names of all the people in this photo?" he asks, nodding toward the teenage one.

I shake my head. Some of their first names, yes, but they were Jacob's friends, really, not mine. I was accepted because I was his girlfriend, that was all.

"It might be a good idea to continue staying with your friends while this investigation is going on," DC Norton says. "I'll have a uniformed officer run you back to collect whatever you need."

I look up at him. "You think I might be in danger?"

"Just as a precaution. Until we can be sure your family is safe and while we have an ongoing murder investigation."

*

The nausea is still there as I unlock my front door and step into the flat. The officer DC Norton sent to accompany me waits outside. I know he's being polite and giving me some privacy, but I actually wish he'd come inside. I know there's no one else here, but it doesn't feel like my home anymore.

I thought it might not look as bad in daylight, but it does. Like DC Norton said, there's no real damage done, just a lot of mess, but it looks awful. It's not only the mess, but knowing the intruder had their hands all over my stuff. In the bedroom, half my clothes have been pulled out of the drawers and wardrobe and I don't want to take any of those. I grab a couple of things that don't look as if they've been touched, add toiletries, and close my bag. I'll borrow anything else from Dee. Right now, all I want to do is leave, put the flat up for sale, and never come back.

I can't look at the bed, but the image from the printed photo is stuck in my head, the smoothed-down quilt, the plumped-up pillows, the bed made far more neatly than I ever do. DC Norton asked me to look around and confirm that nothing is missing, but my gaze flickers past everything and I can't stop flinching. It hurts, almost a physical pain, to really look. Nothing valuable is missing, but how can I be sure that someone who'd do this hasn't taken some tiny tokens, like a serial killer collecting trophies?

I close my eyes and take a deep breath. DC Norton told me they're going to speak to Liam, but I know this isn't him. In the months we were together, he didn't ask a single question about my family, my childhood. I did try, one night. I tried talking to him, telling him about some of the stuff from my past in the hope it would deepen our relationship somehow. I'm not sure if he was even listening. I don't think he'd have a clue if an officer asked him whether my parents were alive, whether I had any siblings. So those photographs—of my family, from my past—whoever's doing all this, it's not Liam. I almost wish it were—would it be so terrifying if I knew who was behind all this?

It's only as I'm walking back through the flat to leave that I realize there is something missing, something no one else would notice but should have been glaringly obvious to me the moment I walked through the door. It's the photograph of me and Jacob I used to keep on my wall just inside the front door. I took it down and out of its frame a few months ago, because I needed it for reference when I got my tattoo. I trace the black stars running up the inside of my wrist. I never got around to putting it back on the wall because I wanted to change the frame, but I'd propped the photograph on the shelf in my hallway to remind me. And now it's gone.

I sink down on the bottom stair and try to put all of it together. Whoever is messing with me ... is it someone who knows about Jacob? Who knows how and why he died? Or did they take the photograph because I was in it? The only people currently in my life who do know about Jacob are my father and Dee, and to a lesser extent Seb and possibly Liam, if he did actually listen to any of what I told him. Seb only knows what Dee has told him and Liam what I told him, which isn't much.

It could be a stranger—I kept the missing photo on display, so it's clearly important to me. The one left on my bed, I didn't recognize it, but it could have been among the set I found in the holiday park ... If the same person found those photos, then came here and saw the one I had on display, it would be an easy way to spook me—to take that one, and leave a different one featuring me and Jacob in its place. It doesn't mean they know the significance.

The other teenagers frozen in time in that photograph...
I didn't keep in touch with anyone after I left. Not even
Dee for a long time—she was the one who found me. My
plan was to go back to the village today to find out if any
suspicious strangers had been lurking about, but what if it
isn't a stranger at all? The rest of the gang I used to hang
out with—Jacob's friends, my party crowd—they dumped
me. After Jacob died, they closed ranks and shut me out.
Are any of them still there? Not in Littledean, none of them
were from my tiny village, but they all used to live in the
surrounding towns; some of them might still be there. And
it occurs to me as all this goes through my mind: there is
someone else who knows about Jacob, who was there then
and is there still. And although he obviously has nothing
to do with what's going on...he might well know who it
could be.

Chapter 15

Thedarktourist.com

    <EXCLUSIVE!> Photos from *inside* the murder victims' house...a creepy abandoned holiday park...inside info from those who knew the victims

Sunday 2 p.m.

"Welcome to the most conservative village in the UK," Dee says as we drive past the sign welcoming us to the village.

"Where the only newspapers for sale are the *Daily Mail* or the *Telegraph*," I add.

"Not the *Sun*?" Adam asks.

Dee shakes her head. "Too common. The *Express* at a push. The *Sun* readers were all forced out years ago, shunted off to the council estates in town or 'affordable housing' not found within ten miles."

"Shame—it's really pretty," Adam says, looking out the window at the village green and the cottages dotted around it.

"Don't be fooled. It's a cesspit. This village is made for a horror film."

"Where you're killed by tight-lipped disapproval," Dee says, grinning as we drive past the village shop.

"Slain by tutting pensioners," I add, smiling sweetly at

a woman peering out of her net-curtained window as we pull up.

"It's why Hanna had to leave," Dee says as we get out of the car. "She was moments from death, torn apart by laser beams of disgust at her shocking teenage behavior."

I raise my eyebrows at Dee, not wanting her to go into any kind of detail about the behavior that had me practically hounded out of town.

"I'm not even sure you could call it a separate village anymore," I say. "The new estates have got bigger and bigger, creeping further away from West Dean. Littledean is really just the tail end of West Dean now."

"Don't ever say that to anyone who lives here, though," Dee says with a shudder.

"So, monsters live in all these pretty cottages, then?" Adam asks, looking around.

"Yep," I say. "And the cottages are all made of sweets. You could go and take a bite of that blue one, and the old witch who lives there would lure you in, fatten you up, and eat the flesh off your bones."

"Nice."

Dee laughs. "Maybe it's not that bad—just your typical village. After all, Hanna and I came from here, so it can't be all bad."

"Really? You say that because you never experienced the real underbelly of this place," I say. "Plus, we've been back here all of five minutes and look—someone's called the police."

Sure enough, Stephen Hayes is walking toward us, all shiny in his uniform.

"For God's sake," Dee says, rolling her eyes.

"How nice," I say. "A welcome home party."

"What are you doing back here, Hanna?" He sounds irritated as he looks at all of us, his gaze pausing on Adam as he obviously tries to place him. It makes me realize that my idea of asking about any strangers hanging around is stupid: West Dean, maybe—it's big enough that a stranger might be able to sneak around unnoticed—but here? Dee and I didn't even manage ten minutes up at the holiday park the other night before the police were called.

"Last time I checked, I was free to go anywhere I please, Steve," I say. "Unless there are special rules for the amazing village of Littledean."

"Don't be facetious—and don't call me Steve. It's PC Hayes. And if I thought you were here just for a nice visit, it wouldn't be a problem. But it's never just a *nice* anything with you, is it, Hanna Carter?"

I shake my head. "What exactly do you think I'm going to do? I'm thirty now, *PC Hayes*, not fourteen. I'm not planning to get drunk in the woods and spray-paint tits on the pub walls."

Adam snorts behind me. "You did that?"

I glance back at him. "I was bored with the badly graffitied dick pics all over town. I thought we were due some equality in our dodgy spray-painted body parts." I turn back to Stephen. "Also, you weren't always so hostile toward me."

It's the wrong thing to say because he looks even more hostile. And it's not my graffiti skills he was referring to before. He looks at Adam again and frowns. "Do I *know* you?"

"No," Adam says, shaking his head. "I'm a friend of Hanna's, just here for moral support."

"A friend? You might want to rethink that."

"Look, I'm sorry," I say, before Stephen can lose his shit and say things I don't want aired in front of Adam. "We are honestly not here to cause any trouble." I pause and take a deep breath. "We're just here to visit an old friend."

Stephen folds his arms. "Which *old friend* is that? From what I remember, you don't have any *friends* left."

"Mr. Garner."

I hear Dee gasp behind me. Bugger. I really should have warned her.

"*Reverend* Garner?" she says.

"Not anymore," Stephen says. "Thanks to Hanna and her father."

I roll my eyes, reduced to the behavior of a fourteen-year-old just by being in his presence. "He retired, he wasn't hounded out of town."

"He was forced to retire early. Everyone knows why."

"No, *Steve*. The vicious gossip monsters in this town took a great deal of pleasure in making shit up. He was always going to retire early. I had nothing to do with it."

Stephen shakes his head. "You keep telling yourself that, if it helps you sleep at night. I'm sure the past is a right fairy tale in your head. But I don't think Mr. Garner is even in the country at the moment. He spends a lot of time abroad. He has an apartment in—"

"Spain. I know. We keep in contact occasionally. And I know he is here at the moment because I texted him last night."

I can feel Dee's gaze burning into me, but I don't turn to look at her. Ed Garner, the former Reverend Garner, got caught up in the mess that was my life purely by dint of his concern for me and Jacob. He tried to help and got caught in the maelstrom. Dee doesn't know all of the details; she

130

only knows that the sudden retirement of Reverend Garner was another crime laid at my door.

I can see, as we walk off toward Mr. Garner's house, that Stephen is desperately trying to find a reason to stop us. But there's nothing he can do—none of us are criminals, we've parked legally, and much as he'd like to, he can't rally the troops of Neighborhood Watch to hound us out of town with pitchforks. The collective disapproval of an entire village does seem to make the air thicker so it's harder to breathe but I know that's purely my imagination.

"*This* is what I always wanted to run away from," I say to Adam. "A life so small you can't breathe without some-one knowing."

Dee waits until we turn the corner and are out of sight of Stephen before she rounds on me. "What's going on, Han? Why the hell are we going to see *Reverend Garner*?"

I sigh. "Mr. Garner is literally the only person in the vil-lage who would talk to me. Even after everything...he kept in touch. He wanted to help. You and an ex-vicar, that's it, Dee. That's all I had." I pause. "For a long time...I was basically banished. My dad told me not to come back and he wouldn't take my calls. It was Mr. Garner who inter-vened, calmed Dad down after I was back on the straight and narrow, persuaded him to let me visit."

Dee's lips press together in a thin line and I smile. "Don't be jealous, Dee—I promise I never replaced you as my best friend with Mr. Garner."

She snorts and shakes her head. "God, Hanna—what are you *like*? Why didn't you tell me?"

Adam clears his throat and we both turn. I'd forgotten he was with us for a moment there. "I have no idea what either of you are talking about, but your overzealous policeman friend is still watching us. He popped his head around the corner and disappeared again. His covert following skills are pretty poor, but I think if we hang around here too long, he may decide to arrest us for loitering."

Mr. Garner had to leave the old vicarage when he retired, moving to a small cottage at the back of the village and investing the rest of his savings in an apartment in Spain where he spends half the year. He married young, but lost his wife to cancer when they were both in their late forties. I have vague but nice memories of Mrs. Garner—she ran the Sunday school that my dad of course made me attend. It stopped running after she died, but Mr. Garner still ran youth clubs with a group of volunteers. The one he had most involvement in was a group for what the village collectively called "troubled children"; I was sent to that one after my mum died. As a grieving child, I remember he was kind and patient and quiet and most of all sad, just like me. I became more "troubled" as I got older and stopped going, but Mr. Garner continued being kind and patient, and I'd sometimes hover at the edges of his group. He never judged, not even when I was at my most destructive. I used to wish he was my dad.

I've never visited the house he lives in now. After his retirement, our communication was purely by text or letter a couple of times a year. The cottage looks exactly how a retired vicar's cottage should look from the outside: crumbling stone, ivy, a blue-painted door, a pot of spring flowers next to it.

I'm guessing he must be in his early seventies by now, but to me, Mr. Garner doesn't look any different to how he looked back then. Maybe the gray hair is a bit thinner, maybe there are more lines on his face, but his smile is the same and it still soothes me like it always did. He remembers Dee, and I introduce him to Adam as he beckons us inside.

The rooms are small but not cluttered. It looks much as the vicarage used to, and I recognize most of the furniture although there's less here. Still lots of shelves loaded with books, still walls covered in framed photographs and paintings. It's like the vicarage in miniature, and it amuses me to imagine the rest of the old vicarage furniture now taking pride of place in some modern apartment in Spain.

"I was surprised to get your message," he says as we all settle in his living room. "Now that your family has moved, I wondered why you'd want to come back here."

I glance at Dee and Adam. I don't want to get into the whole story; it's not something Mr. Garner needs to be involved in. Despite my words to Stephen Hayes, I do still feel residual guilt over his retirement. Mr. Garner always insisted he was planning to retire, but I couldn't help but wonder at how sudden it seemed, I couldn't help but feel that my behavior and his involvement forced him into the decision sooner than he might have wished. I don't want to do that to him again. Bad enough that Stephen already knows we're here.

"I lost touch with them again," I say. "I'm hoping being back here will fill in some of the gaps."

Mr. Garner sighs and leans back. "You know your family very much kept themselves to themselves. I'd see your stepmother in the village sometimes, but your father and Sasha, very rarely."

"And you never noticed anyone...new hanging around town, or hanging around them? Or any of them acting oddly in any way?"

I wait. He's frowning, looking as if he's trying to find the right way to say something. He doesn't want to say anything negative about my father, that's clear.

"Not odd, exactly, but Sasha did come to see me," he says. "Just before Christmas."

That is definitely odd—Sasha would have no reason to visit Mr. Garner. It's a long time since he had any involvement in local kids' groups. "She came to see you? What for?"

He smiles. "To ask about you, funnily enough. To fill in gaps of her own."

My cheeks are hot. I don't need a mirror to know I'm blushing. I should have come to see him on my own. "What did you tell her?"

"Only that I knew you when you were young, that you were part of groups I ran." He pauses. "I think she wanted to know you better, and I hope I was able to give her an insight into the lovely girl you were."

Oh, this kind man. This kind, kind man. Only Reverend Garner would describe the messed-up kid I used to be as a lovely girl. Seeing the good in all of the troubled kids he helped is what ended up killing his career.

"She asked about some of your old friends, too. She said she'd found some photographs."

My skin is tingling. "How strange," I say, trying to sound casual. "I was going to ask you the same thing…if any of the old group were still around."

Mr. Garner sighs. He glances at Adam and Dee and lowers his voice, leans in closer to me. "The photograph she showed me—it was you, with Carrie and the others. But I'm afraid I said the same to her as I have to say to you— you're the only one who ever kept in touch."

"I'm sorry. I thought it was a bit of a long shot. I can't

even remember most of their surnames..." Except for Carrie, of course. I remember her surname.

"I have records of their names somewhere. I'd be happy to find them for you. I can't give you any contact information, obviously, and I doubt any of it would be any good now anyway, but I can give you their names at least."

"Thank you."

I half expect him to ask why I'm looking for them now, after all this time, but he doesn't. Maybe he assumes I'm trying to slay some old demons, like he was always encouraging me to do.

As soon as Mr. Garner leaves the room to find those names, I lean over to Dee. "You know who *will* have all the info about anything weird that happened when my family left town..."

I know who the local gossipmongers are, but there is no way on earth I would ever speak to any of them. Or that they would tell me anything even if I did. But Dee and Adam...They might speak to *them*.

Dee looks back at me and raises her eyebrows. She stands up and stretches. "You know what? I think I'll pop to the village shop and get some snacks for the drive home. Do you want to come with me, Adam?"

"Um..." He looks at me and I nod. He clearly has no idea what's going on, but Dee does. The village shop: hub of all the local news and gossip.

After he comes back through with the list of names, Mr. Garner waits until the front door closes, and we see Dee and Adam walking back down the hill before he speaks again.

"How are you, Hanna? Really? You look tired."

135

I smile. "I'm okay, Mr. Garner. There's some stuff going on at the moment, but I promise I haven't fallen back into my old ways. I don't even drink these days—I'm holding down a good job, I have a mortgage, a bank account in credit. I'm a positive saint compared to the bad old me."

He laughs. "You were never bad, Hanna."

"Try telling my dad that."

He sighs. "I'm sorry I could never help more. I'm sorry he never listened to me when I tried…"

I shake my head. "No—don't. None of what happened was your fault. *I'm* the one who's sorry. You should never have been caught up in it."

He smiles. "It was my job, Hanna. My vocation. Even if we hadn't been acquainted, I would have wanted to help you. You and Jacob."

I flinch as he says his name.

I think he sees my reluctance to talk about Jacob in my face, because he changes the subject back to more general topics until the door slams and Dee and Adam come back in. I can see from Dee's face they've found out something and it's agony to sit and make small talk when I'm desperate to ask. But I won't involve Mr. Garner, not again. Whatever he says, I am at least partly responsible for the way he was treated back then.

"Stephen Hayes is still hanging around," Dee says as soon as we've said goodbye to Mr. Garner and started back down the hill. "When did he get so creepy? He stood and watched us go into the shop, waiting outside, staring through the window like we were there to shoplift the place."

She sounds indignant. But Dee the good girl is tainted by association with me. She knows that. She was always outraged by it back then; you'd think she'd realize nothing will have changed, not here, not even all these years later. And besides, Stephen Hayes thinks he has good reason to treat me like trouble.

"Did you find out anything?" I ask.

"Not here," she says, shaking her head. "Let's get on the road and then I'll tell you. This place is giving me the major creeps."

"Still think it's a pretty place, Adam?" I ask.

We turn the corner and lo and behold, there's Stephen Hayes, standing in front of the village shop now, talking to Mrs. Thorpe. They both follow our progress as we walk back to the car, conversation on pause as we all get in and Dee does a three-point turn. I smile and wave as we pass them, blowing Stephen a kiss and getting a scowl in return.

Dee shakes her head. "You're such a juve," she says.

I shrug. "I would have given him the finger, but I thought he might use it as an excuse to arrest me. Bet he's dying to arrest me." I pause. "But don't head back to the motorway yet, Dee—there's a couple of other people I want to try to track down before we leave. Can we go into West Dean?" I get the list Mr. Garner gave me out of my pocket.

We drive in silence for a while and I only relax when we're out of the village, on the road leading to West Dean.

"So, go on, then," I say. "Hit me with it—what terrible scandal has someone in the Carter family been caught up in this time."

"Actually, Mrs. Thorpe seemed most put out that she didn't have the goss. But, *apparently*, they weren't supposed to move until January."

"And...?"

"In the end, they just...up and went. Overnight. Right

after Christmas—no notice, nothing. Your stepmum was meant to be hosting her book club New Year meet-up and the first anyone knew about them leaving was when people turned up and found the house empty."

"They did a midnight flit? Seriously? But why?"

The car has slowed down, and Dee is signaling, pulling off at the turn for West Dean. She stops in the station car park and turns to me. "You should call DC Norton. This could be nothing but village gossip, Mrs. Thorpe could be exaggerating, but…" She hesitates. "But if something happened to scare them off…"

They ran away. My family ran away. Something happened to make them run away…Or someone was chasing them.

Chapter 16

SASHA—November, three months earlier

They're waiting just inside the school gates. I was stupid to think the party might have made them forget about me and my Friday meltdown. They're all looking studiously away as I get out of the car, but I know they're waiting for me. I wish I could jump back in the car, beg Dad to take me away, but then I'd have to explain why, and he wouldn't care that Seren and Carly and their minions are potentially waiting to beat me up, he'd only care about the fact that I Got Into Trouble at school, that I got sent to the office. He'd look at me, but he'd see Hanna. He'd go into panic mode, haul me in, harangue Miss Jennings, either demanding more punishment to Teach Me A Lesson or going into full-on blame-the-school mode.

So, instead, I square my shoulders, force a smile, and step away from the car, hoping he'll wait and watch until I'm safely inside the building. But of course, he doesn't. He's delivered me to school and because I'm not Hanna, he doesn't need to check I actually enter the premises because I'm the good girl, I've never skipped school in my life.

The moment he drives off, Seren and the others move as a pack to block the gate.

"If you stop me going in and I'm late, they'll phone my

dad and he'll come straight back," I say, staring at Seren, summoning my inner Hanna, determined not to blink first, even if all I'm doing is threatening to tell my dad on them.

"You got me in trouble," Seren says. "My mum canceled my party because of *you*."

Oh crap.

She makes a move toward me and I can't help it, I step back. Carly and Dylan, henchman one and henchman two, laugh.

"I don't need to beat the shit out of you," Seren whispers, her face inches from mine so I can smell the mint from her gum on her breath. "I can think of much better ways to get you back."

She shoulder-shoves me and then spins and walks off, her gang trailing behind. I'm getting stared at as the other kids arrive, forced to walk around me as I stand frozen, right in front of the gate. I grit my teeth and carry on trying not to blink. I think if I blink I might cry and then they'll really stare.

I spend the day in full avoidance mode—even eating my sandwiches hiding in the toilets. Classes are easier, they don't dare try anything with the teachers there and I can tune out the whispered threats and insults. My biggest fear isn't whatever Seren's got in mind that's worse than beating me up; no, my biggest fear is that if it is one of them sending the Facebook messages, they'll go ahead and tell my dad. Yeah, my fear is that they'll get to the station and my dad's car before I do with a load of printed-out screenshots of my alter ego's Facebook timeline and webcam footage of me in my pajamas.

If I had a phone, I could call him or text to ask him to meet me somewhere else after school. If I had a phone, I could call Hanna. I know we're not close, but she's certainly got experience of being in trouble and I bet she could help. But I can't exactly call her from the landline at home, can I? We have one stupid phone that's a hundred years old—it still has a wire, it's not even cordless. And even if I could somehow get hold of Mum or Dad's mobiles, Hanna would never take a call if she saw their numbers come up.

I'm in such a state I feel genuinely ill by the time I go back to lessons after lunch, my cheese sandwiches sitting like a leaden lump in my stomach. I'll probably be sick. Chunks of cheese and bread spraying all over the class, probably all over Seren or Carly because of course I would, that's my current luck. I can feel sweat on my forehead, but I actually feel cold and my heart is pounding really hard. I'm clammy like I'm coming down with flu or something. I rest my head in my hands and try to focus on my work.

"Sasha—are you okay?" It sounds like Mr. Hillier is asking the question from a thousand miles away, but I manage to look up.

"Actually, I feel really sick. And faint."

There's a hiss from behind me—they think I'm faking to get away from them. I'm tempted to turn around and stop swallowing back the rising bile and just projectile vomit all over them.

By the time Dad arrives to pick me up, I'm already feeling better, the tightness in my chest looser, my stomach calmer. Not flu or a stomach bug, just panic and anxiety. I'm sent straight up to my room as soon as we get home. Dad doesn't even pretend it's because of concern for my health. He hates illness, sees it as weakness, and he's angry at me for missing lessons. He doesn't actually *say* that, of course, but it was pretty obvious by his silence on the drive home. I don't care, though. I spent the journey with my head resting against the window and my eyes closed, and I'm glad to be banished to my room. It doesn't even feel like a punishment; it's a relief. The only miserable thing about it is unless I really do physically throw up everywhere, I'll be straight back to school tomorrow morning.

I kick off my shoes and throw myself onto the bed. My stomach is still somersaulting, but I don't feel like I'm going to be sick anymore. But what about tomorrow? The door opens and Dad walks in. It's another subtle punishment, the lack of a courtesy knock. I wonder if he sees this as a different sort of illness—the start of me turning into Hanna, skipping school, faking illness.

"I'm taking your mother out to M&S to do some shopping and go for dinner," he says. "I'd planned for us all to go, but as you're ill, you'll have to stay at home. There's soup in the cupboard if your stomach settles."

I stay staring at the ceiling. Dad never goes with Mum to Marks & Spencer and we *never* go out to dinner. And it certainly wasn't planned—I could smell something cooking in the oven when I came in. But this additional punishment is even more of a relief. It would have been difficult to pretend all was fine, that it was just something physical, if I was sitting around a dinner table with him and Mum, here or out in a restaurant.

"We'll call you. From the restaurant. To check you're okay," he continues, and I hide a smile. Just making sure I don't sneak out. Even after fourteen years of me not once stepping out of line, he's still worried that any minute I'll turn into Hanna.

I lie on my bed, listening to them moving around downstairs, getting ready in a hurry. I hear the door slam, the key in the lock, Dad's car starting up and driving off. I count to one hundred, just to make sure, then I get up. I have homework, but I'm too restless to settle to that. It's ironic that my parents have gone out for the first time in forever and I have free access to Dad's computer just when going on the internet is the last thing in the world I want to do.

I'm not hungry but I drift down to the kitchen anyway, letting my restless feet pace the ground floor, stopping to stare out of the window. There's a tap at the back door and my stupid heart starts its galloping thing again. I can see through the textured glass that it's Ethan and my heart slows a bit. Has he found out who sent those messages already?

I unlock and open the door. "I've got a present for you," he says with a smile.

"You've found who's sending the messages?"

"Ah—no. Not yet. My friend's working on it, though. No, I got you this." He reaches into his pocket and pulls out a small mobile phone.

"It's a pay-as-you-go—cheap and cheerful, no good for anything but calling and texting, but something you can keep quiet from your dad." He pauses. "Every teenager should have a phone."

I stare at it, resting in his hand. Unexpected. Never thought my first ever phone would be a prison phone.

"Thank you," I say, taking it from him. "You didn't have to...I don't have much money to pay you back. I—"

He shakes his head. "It's nothing, seriously. I bought it on impulse for a few quid from my corner shop, that's all. Owen pays me a decent wage and there's not much I can spend it on while I'm on probation. There's only a tenner credit on it—you'll have to top that up if you want to make calls. And you can send texts and give the number to your mates."

I open my mouth to thank him again and embarrass myself completely by bursting into tears.

"Hey, what's up?"

"I'm sorry. I'm sorry. I've just had a really crappy day and then you gave me a phone and that's so nice and I just…I'm sorry." I wipe my eyes with my sleeve and take a deep, shuddering breath. *God, get it together, Sasha.*

He stares at me for a second, then sighs. "Listen, I've finished up and I've got a bit of time before Owen picks me up. Do you want to talk about it?"

He sounds horribly reluctant, but I don't even care. I swear I'm going to explode if I keep everything bottled up. "I can't leave the house, though—Dad's going to call to check on me. And I can't really…"

"Can't invite me in? I get it. But it's mild and dry enough outside—come and sit on the bench round the side. Leave the door open and you'll hear the phone if it rings."

I spill out the whole sorry mess to him sitting on the peeling wooden bench at the side of my house. It sounds small and ridiculous as I blurt it out to this grown man who's just got out of prison and facing a screwed-up future. But he doesn't laugh at me or act like I'm an idiot. He frowns and listens to the whole thing in silence, then waits a minute before responding.

"It seems like you just need a bit of time," he says. "Kids forget things, they move on. If you're out of sight for a few days, it all might settle down."

"My dad will never let me stay off school. Not unless I was really sick."

"Ring the school in the morning—put on a posh voice and pretend you're your mum calling in sick." He glances at me and grins. "I used to do it all the time."

I shake my head. "Dad drops me off and picks me up."

"Does he actually take you inside?"

I shake my head again and he shrugs. "So, wait till he's gone and then leave. Take a change of clothes, hang out in town a few hours, then be back by the end of the day."

He makes it sound easy, casual. Like it's nothing.

Maybe it is—that easy and that casual. It's not like I'm behind in school, it's not like a few days off would affect my grades in any way. Maybe it really could be nothing. Maybe there is a bit of Hanna in me after all because I'm even considering it.

"This is my last week on full time here," he says. "Owen should have other work for me, but I'll only be here part time. If things are still bad after this week, I could borrow a mate's car, take you out somewhere if you need more time away from school. Doesn't matter, really, does it? You'll be in a new school next year—this will just make the last few weeks of term easier for you."

Oh God, it's so tempting.

Chapter 17

HANNA—Sunday 3:30 p.m.

I look down at the list of names Mr. Garner gave me—it's not everyone I used to hang out with, just the three other kids I met in his youth group. Jacob's friends. Such a tight-knit group before I came along. The others I used to hang out with were just the local party-kids from town and the surrounding villages, the druggies, the drop-outs, the random older guys who'd latch on to our group to sell us drugs and drink as we were all too young to buy it for ourselves. I couldn't name any of them now, but the three names on Mr. Garner's list—Carrie Hayes, Owen King, Lee Brown—I remember them, a sudden flood of memories released on seeing their names. Along with Jacob, they became my inner circle in my bad old days. Actually, it was because of Jacob. They were his friends. All older than me, none of them still at school. Lee and Owen were seventeen and were friends with Jacob from way back and Carrie was sixteen. None of them worked, all of them except Jacob were from the dodgy estate at the edge of town. I liked to think me and Jacob were a bit different, both of us from what most people would consider to be stable homes, both of us bright but lost. Jacob was meant to stay on for sixth form but chose to leave at sixteen with his mates. They came as a set and I don't think the others liked me trying to wedge my way in. Owen and Lee, in particular, used to take the piss and call me posh, a rich kid on the lookout for a bit of rough. But that's not what I was. I was hurting and looking for oblivion just as much as they were, bored and destructive and always angry.

Poor Mr. Garner, desperately trying to help us, but by putting us together, he really just ended up creating a many-headed monster. If he'd never tried to help out us troubled youths, if Dad and Jen had never tried to help by sending me there, I'd never have met Jacob and the others, and my rebellion might have died a death much sooner. But maybe not. West Dean and Littledean were linked by more than just a B road and I think we would have ended up meeting somewhere. And it only took one meeting. It was like we recognized each other the moment we met in the old vicarage over tea and ginger biscuits, like something slotting into place, like we looked at each other and went, Oh, *there* you are. I've been waiting for you.

I think, sometimes, that Jacob's friends saw it too, particularly the boys, and that's why they were so quick to blame me for everything when he died. They severed all ties and by the time I left home, I hadn't seen them for months. I refused even to let myself think about them. But now... whoever is targeting me now knows me or someone from my family. It makes sense that it's someone from my bad old days. Perhaps even someone who might still be harboring enough hate for me to chase my family out of town...

I try googling them, but none of them have unusual enough names—I'd never find them in the dozens of results that pop up. If I want to find them, I'll have to go back to the beginning. And I know exactly who to ask. There's a reason Stephen Hayes hates me so much. Carrie was his big sister, the bad seed to his future model citizen. Even though I was his age, a year younger than Carrie, he decided, when everything went insane, that Jacob's friends were right: I was the ringleader, I was evil. I think it was because he asked me out once, in Year Nine, and I laughed in his spotty face. Like I said to Adam—I was the worst teenager.

"I made a mistake winding Stephen up like that," I say to Dee. "I could have asked him about Carrie."

"Why? Why would you want to see any of them again?" I can hear the edge of worry in her voice. Although I pretty much pushed Dee away back then, in the same way Jacob's friends rejected me, she still remembers the fallout from it all. And being my eternally loyal Dee, she blames them entirely.

"What if whoever is doing this is one of Jacob's old friends? Owen or Lee...what if one of them did something or said something to scare them away?"

"But why now, after all this time? And thinking about it, if there really was anything suspicious about your family leaving, wouldn't Stephen have said something? Not to you, but to Cardiff CID when they made their inquiries."

"His sister was one of that group. If it *is* one of them, he's going to want to protect her. You know that's why he hates me so much—he blames me for her going off the rails."

"I thought he hated you because you told him to get stuffed when he asked you out."

"Wait—that guy asked you out?" Adam interrupts.

"*Everyone* asked Hanna out at school, Adam," Dee says. "She told most of them to fuck off, so you should consider yourself very fortunate she said yes to you."

I scowl at Dee and glance back at Adam. "They asked

me out because they all thought I was a slut who'd have sex with them. Not because any of them actually liked me."

"There you go again," Dee says.

I shake my head. "I'm not putting myself down, Dee— you know it's true. Don't try to pretend I didn't have that reputation by the time I was halfway through Year Nine."

Dee folds her arms. "Stephen bloody Hayes is the main reason you had that reputation, spreading lies just because you turned him down. And how *dare* he try to make out everything was your fault? You were years younger than any of those others, for fuck's sake. They should have been arrested for corrupting a minor." She stops and goes red.

I sigh. "Take me to the estate, Dee. Let's go and take another trip down memory lane."

Instead of starting the car, Dee hesitates, then turns to Adam. "Will you pop over the road to Greggs and grab us some coffees? It's open until four. This is turning into a longer day than I expected, and I'd kill right about now for a latte."

It's an obvious and clumsy attempt to get rid of him, but bless him, he goes with it, strolling across the road to the little row of shops that make up West Dean's town center. I expect Dee to talk about Jacob, but that's not why she sent Adam away.

"Listen," she says, "it's probably nothing, but it's a bit odd, so I wanted to mention it while it's still sitting in my head being all odd…"

I smile. "What are you rambling on about?"

"When Adam and I were in the shop in Littledean… Adam sort of lurked around the shop while I was asking about your family, but he came over as I was ready to leave, and Mrs. Thorpe looked at him and said, 'Back again?'"

I look at her blankly.

"And I'd have thought nothing of it. I'd have assumed she was mixing him up with someone else, Seb even, although they look nothing alike, but his reaction..."

"What *was* his reaction?"

"He went red. And he looked guilty. He kind of mumbled something and nothing and left the shop."

"And did you ask Mrs. Thorpe about it?"

Dee rolls her eyes. "Of course I did. She said he'd been in before, a few months ago. That she could have been mistaken, but they don't get many strangers in, blah blah blah..."

"Yeah, right. She would have had a description of any stranger sent to everyone in the village." I pause. "So—was Adam here before?"

Dee sighs. "He says no. He says she must have been mistaken, but..."

I bite my lip, thinking of Stephen Hayes looking at Adam and saying, "Do I know you?" I think of that photo on Adam's website, taken months ago when the caravans were still there, of something or someone making my family do a moonlight flit...How long, exactly, was that listing about my family up on his website before I found it? Adam is coming back across the road balancing three coffees in his hands. He smiles when he sees me looking, the big smile that lights up his face.

He can't have anything to do with this, can he?

"I'll ask him," I say. "Later."

Stephen Hayes is not waiting at the outskirts of town with a flaming torch and a pitchfork this time, so we drive through unscathed. The estate the Hayes family used to live on is a couple of miles outside town, very much a halfway point between West Dean and Littledean, an ugly mix of terraced houses and blocks of flats. I can't imagine Stephen still living here, stepping outside his front door in his shiny police uniform every morning. They'd eat him alive. I'm not expecting Mrs. Hayes to tell me anything about Carrie, if she still lives in the same place, but I am expecting someone to call Stephen to tell him we're here, so I don't bother trying to be quiet or subtle as we walk up the alleyway onto the estate.

"Excuse me," I call, nice and loud, to the gang of kids hanging out on the bit of green in the middle of the estate. "Does Mrs. Hayes still live around here? PC Hayes' mum? Or his sister, Carrie?"

"What do you want them for?" one of the boys calls back, a little shit who looks no older than nine. "Want to tell her about God?"

Do I *look* like a Jehovah's Witness?

It's quite impressive, really. I'd forgotten what living around here is like. Within three minutes, four people have come out of their houses and we've gathered quite a crowd, not quite hostile, but definitely suspicious. And it works wonders, because only a couple of minutes after that, someone's coming out of a house, wiping wet hands on a tea towel.

I let out a breath as she steps closer and I recognize Carrie Hayes. She's cut her hair and it's blonder than it used to be, but she's still a sharp-featured, prettier version of her brother. She doesn't smile, but neither does she look surprised to see me.

"You shouldn't be here," she says. "You're going to piss everyone off if you keep nosing around, stirring everything up."

"That's not what I'm trying to do. I'm looking for my family, that's all. No one can find them and I'm worried."

"I haven't seen them." She frowns and glances back toward the house she came out of. "I can't hang about. My mum's not well and I'm looking after her."

"Please, Carrie—do you know if any of the others, Lee or Owen, might have seen them? Or—"

"Lee hasn't," she says, interrupting me. "And he's not here. He's working today. Putting in some overtime."

"How do you know?"

She smiles faintly. "We're married. Got married a few years ago and we've got two boys."

"Oh. I..."

She shakes her head. "Don't worry about offering fake congratulations. But seriously—we haven't seen your family. I'm a teaching assistant at the primary school and I help take care of my mum. Lee works at the garage—we've all grown up and moved on. Please don't try to open old wounds."

"What about Owen?"

She sighs. "Don't try to talk to Owen, okay? He's...still angry. He still..."

"Blames me?"

She nods, pressing her lips together in a thin line.

"You know I didn't—I *wouldn't*..."

She's torn. I can see it. She's not full of hostility like Stephen was, like Owen and Lee probably would be. Carrie was the first one I tried to talk to, back then, after Jacob died. It wasn't that we were particularly close, but because she was hanging out with Lee and I was with Jacob, we were often lumped together as "the girlfriends." Maybe that was why she listened, or seemed to be listening until

The Night They Vanished

Stephen stepped in, her twat of a little brother, spewing his venom, still smarting with rejection because I'd turned him down. The poisonous little shit called his mum, called Owen, called Lee. He called in the bloody Littledean army to see me off their land, to hound me out of town.

And here we are, and I can see it again—she's listening to me, and there's something she wants to say, or wants to tell me. I can see it in her face, see it in the way she glances back at her mum's house to check the door's shut, in the way she leans closer to me.

"Look, some things with Owen have got a bit out of hand…"

But again, again, again, here's Stephen Hayes, storming into shot, shouldering his way in front of his sister like he thinks I'm going to attack her. But it's not Carrie I'd like to punch in the face right about now.

I look past Stephen, trying to get Carrie's attention, but it's too late. Stephen's appearance has brought out more gawkers, and we've got an audience. The little brats are circling, but a few other people have popped out of their houses as well.

"She was looking for your mum, Steve," the boy who accused me of being a Jehovah's Witness calls out. "Wants to sell God to her."

Stephen raises his eyebrows but looks at me. "I don't think Hanna wants to sell God to anyone. But what is it you *do* want?"

"I came here to speak to Carrie, not you."

Stephen shakes his head. "Christ, Hanna, my sister can't help you find your family. She has nothing to say to you."

"Oh—what, you know that for a fact, do you? You speak for her?"

153

"Come on, Hanna. I'm not even sure why you're making such a thing about this. I heard your family just moved and didn't bother telling you." He pauses, folds his arms. "Can't say I blame them."

"Right. Great detective work there, *PC Hayes*. Of course, Cardiff CID got you checking out the old house because they just moved without telling me. *Yes*, they're missing and *yes*, I'm trying to find them and *yes*, I believe someone who knew me or knows me is involved."

"And you think that someone is my sister?"

He gets all hunched up and hostile but I refuse to back down. "No. But she might know who it is."

He's silent for an eternity and any second I'm expecting him to produce the flaming torch and pitchfork again, but in the end he sighs and tilts his head, beckoning us away from the estate, back down the alleyway.

I hesitate before following, scrabbling in my pocket for a bit of paper, an old receipt—anything.

"Can I give you my number?" I say to Carrie. "If you want to talk. About anything…"

Dee comes to my rescue, passing me both paper and a pen. I scribble down my number and pass it to Carrie, then turn to follow Stephen.

"Look," I say, before he can start speaking, "I promise, I'm not looking for trouble. But I'm worried about my family, and something weird happened to make them leave here in a hurry. I'm just trying to find out what, that's all."

"You've seen Carrie now. You know her and Lee don't know anything."

"What about Owen King? Does he still live around here?"

Again, that hostile stare as he shakes his head. "He left

years ago. No idea what happened to him. But you're wasting your time, Hanna. Everyone you used to hang out with has either moved on or grown up and settled down. You seem to be the only one who hasn't. You need to leave my family alone or I'll have you arrested for harassment."

"Oh, stop being such a sanctimonious little prick, Stephen bloody Hayes," Dee snaps. "Hanna's family is missing. Maybe you should be doing your job, as an officer of the law, instead of trying to score points because Hanna turned you down a million years ago."

Stephen stiffens and frowns at us. He snipes something back at Dee, but I don't hear because, for a moment, I'm right back in the corridors of school, walking past Stephen and his cronies, listening to one of the girls whisper *slag* and seeing Dee turn around to have a go like a mother tiger defending her cub, like she always did even then, when I was barely hanging out with her because I was so deeply involved with Jacob and my imploding party gang. I catch Adam's eye and see that he's trying to hide a smile. It never occurred to me to find it funny, this throwback to our teenage years, but I suppose it is. Ferocious Dee, all five foot two of her, standing there squabbling with a policeman like they're both twelve. I watch Adam and I'm tempted to ask him right then: *Have you been here before?* But I think I'm scared the answer will be *yes*, and then I'd have to ask why.

Instead, I grab Dee's arm and tug her away. "Come on, Dee. Your car was sounding pretty rough on the drive down here—let's call in the garage and get it checked out."

"Don't you dare," Stephen yells after us, but I don't bother turning around. Sod it. Let him arrest me. Let's see him try to make that one stick.

*

"Hey, hey, hey—little Hanna Carter." Lee Brown comes out of the dark workshop, wiping his hands on an oily rag. It's the way he always used to greet me, but back then it was never said in the flat, sour tone he uses today. There's no one else around, the garage office locked up for the weekend. Lee looks the same, except his dark hair is shorter and he's in oil-stained overalls rather than beaten-up leather. All that's missing is the big grin that was always on his face. Until that last time I saw him, of course.

"I take it you had a call from your wife—or was it from the law?" I say, getting out of the car, motioning to Dee and Adam to stay inside. I didn't expect a warm welcome—wouldn't have, even without the warnings from Carrie and Stephen Hayes—but I hadn't counted on the pang of loss I feel. We used to have fun. Me, Jacob, Carrie, Owen, and Lee. We used to have so much *fun*.

"What—from little Steve? That little prick," Lee says, shaking his head. "He's only got worse since he got the uniform. Carrie can't stand him. I take it she told you we got married?"

"Yeah, she said. Congratulations. I'm really happy for you both."

He stares at me. "Really? Why would you be? We weren't exactly nice to you back then."

"I...I understand why. I get it."

"Do you?" he asks, looking if anything more hostile.

"Yeah—you were looking for someone to blame and—"

"We didn't need to look for someone to blame—you were to blame. Jacob changed after he met you. And you know damned well he'd still be alive if you two had never met."

I flinch. "I wasn't entirely to blame. I *wasn't*."

"Yeah, you keep telling yourself that. So, what's brought you back here anyway? We never thought you'd come back after what happened."

I sigh. "I never wanted to come back, I can promise you that. But my family...there's been some trouble and I wondered if it had anything to do with...anyone from back then."

"Like what? Like who? Han, none of us would have gone within a million miles of your family after what happened."

"What about Owen?" My heart beats faster. "He was always getting in trouble with his temper." I can almost see it, almost picture it. Owen unleashing that temper on my family, scaring them into running away...

He frowns. "Owen? No, he hasn't been in trouble for years. He's got his own business now, landscaping and gardening. Funnily enough, I had his van in a while back for some repairs. First time I'd seen him in years."

He says the last oh so casually, but I don't believe it. There's something about the way his attention skitters away from me as he says it. And also, Stephen lied then, about Owen moving away years ago. They're closing ranks, just like they did after Jacob died.

Lee watches me. "Let's be honest, if anyone from those days was going to end up in trouble, we all would have expected it to be you. And maybe Jacob if you dragged him down far enough. Like Bonnie and Clyde."

I glance back at the car, at Adam, who doesn't know anything about my past, except about me leaving home at sixteen. Can he hear what we're saying? What is he thinking, listening to Stephen and now Lee? Is it enough to put him off? When all this is done, will he start avoiding my calls, making excuses? I won't blame him if he does.

I look back at Lee. "Look, I'm sorry. I needed to ask about my family and...I think I wanted to lay some ghosts of my own. Reassure myself I didn't leave total destruction in my wake when I left."

"What is this—a sudden pang of conscience after fifteen years? Come on, I'm not stupid." He shakes his head. "But, sod it—forget it. You were just a screwed-up little kid, Hanna. We all were. But the others...Don't stir it up again. Just go. Scuttle off back to Cardiff and stay away. You survived, we all survived."

All of us survived except Jacob.

Wait.

What did he just say? He's walking away, back into the shadows of the workshop.

"How do you know I live in Cardiff?"

He glances back. "You're not the only one keeping tabs on faces from the past."

Chapter 18

SASHA—Early December, two months earlier

I didn't take up Ethan's suggestion—the thought of Dad finding out was way scarier than the thought of facing Seren and Carly. And it turns out Ethan was right. Tuesday and Wednesday, I get a few snide comments, some hostile looks, and a couple of shoves in the corridor. But when I don't react, they seem to get bored and go back to ignoring me instead. I haven't seen Ethan to find out if he knows who sent me the messages yet, but as the days pass and Dad doesn't come roaring in, brandishing printouts of my stupid Facebook posts, the pool of dread in my stomach gets smaller.

I think Ethan's been avoiding me, actually. I don't really blame him as I keep freaking out and having meltdowns in front of him, but I can't be angry at him, not when he gave me a phone, not when he's the only person in the world helping me out.

So, instead of sneaking on the computer, I take a different sort of risk now. Dad's moved our leaving date forward, so we can go early January, just before the new term starts. Originally, it was going to be in the February half-term, but apparently, the current managers of the new holiday park are leaving before Christmas, and because the owners of this place are selling, they're not bothered about the notice period, so Dad sees no reason not to move early, even though it means packing over Christmas. This way we can be there before the start of term, too—heaven forbid I actually miss a day of learning.

I don't know—it all seems a bit weird and rushed. Dad's still agitated, and I don't think it's just about the stress of the move, because Mum's been a bit down as well. I don't think she wants to move. I think she was given about as much say in the matter as me.

And because they're selling the place, rather than sprucing it up for a new season, Owen has been given official notice of the end of his contract, and although Dad has told him he can stay on until Christmas, he and Ethan are going to be here less and less. So instead of sneaking into Dad's office to use the computer at night, I find myself sneaking out of the house after school to try to find Ethan when I'm meant to be in my room doing homework. Mum and Dad rarely check on me—one of the bonuses of having an exemplary good-daughter record—so it's actually pretty easy. Avoid the creaky stairs, carry my shoes until I'm outside, make sure Dad's tucked away in his office and Mum is prepping dinner and I'm free.

By Thursday, I've done enough sneaking and spying to have figured out where Ethan hides when he wants a break, so I don't even have to go looking for him. I'm glad Owen isn't here much anymore. There really wasn't enough work for two, so I'm extra glad it's Ethan who got to stay.

I smile when I look out of my window and see him disappearing behind the first row of caravans. Dad's in his office and Mum's at one of her church meetings, so I get to raid the biscuit jar before skipping off up the hill to find him.

The Night They Vanished

There's a row of caravans at the back of the site that don't get rented out—they're too old and dilapidated, moss-covered and leaky. It's like a caravan graveyard, and they're all too damp and bug-filled to actually go inside them, but the advantage is that no one ever goes up there and they can't be seen from the house, so this is where we meet.

I should have checked the car park before coming up here, though, because when I skip around the corner, it's not just Ethan hovering there, it's Owen too, sitting on the steps of one of the caravans. And he looks about as pleased to see me as I am to see him.

"What are you doing up here? Are you trying to get us in trouble?" he says.

"Of course not," I mutter. I hold up the bag I'm carrying. "I brought some biscuits."

Owen rolls his eyes and shakes his head. "Jesus—what the hell is wrong with you? Have you got the schoolgirl hots for older men and ex-cons? You know this could get us both fired, right? If your dad caught you here?"

"I'm sorry, I..." My voice trails off as he gets up off the step and stalks toward me.

"You're sorry for *what*? Does it give you a thrill going behind Daddy's back? Is this your little rebel moment—hanging out with us? Just like your damn sister?" His voice rises with every question and I hate how scared he makes me feel, how I'm standing here actually quaking in front of someone who works for my dad, so should be treating me with *respect*. Because he's right about one thing: I could get him fired. And hang on, what did he just say?

"Do you know Hanna?" I ask.

"For fuck's sake, Owen—leave the kid alone," Ethan says, shaking his head and pushing himself off the caravan

161

he's leaning against. "Look at her: you're scaring her to death. She's just brought us some biscuits, for Christ's sake."

"Oh, come on, Ethan, don't even try to pretend she's not—"

"Back off," Ethan says, and he gets between me and Owen and shoves him back, two hands on his boss's chest.

Owen staggers back a step and I cringe, expecting him to launch himself at Ethan, and I'm ready, poised on the balls of my feet, ready to run back down to the house to get Dad to stop them from fighting.

But Owen just shakes his head. His hands are clenched into fists, but he doesn't go to hit Ethan. "Get the fuck out of here," he says.

I don't know whether he's saying it to me or to Ethan, but we both walk away, in the same direction.

"I'm sorry, I'm really sorry," I say, all in a rush. My hands are still shaking. "Will he fire you? I can talk to my dad—I can get him to hire you direct."

Ethan looks at me and frowns. "Calm down, Sash—why would he fire me?"

"Because…he's your *boss*. And you *pushed* him…"

He laughs. "Don't worry about it. Maybe if I'd punched him…but me and Owen are fine. You caught him on a bad day, that's all; he's got a lot going on. It's probably best if you go home now, though."

"Can I see you later? I just wanted to ask…" I must sound so needy and pathetic, but it works because he gives that reluctant sigh again and nods.

"Come and find me tomorrow—Owen won't be around then."

I wonder, as I walk away, why Ethan is so confident Owen won't fire him. And I wonder again why he was in prison. Does it have something to do with why he's so sure Owen won't do anything?

It's cold and windy the next day when I head out after school, particularly bitter up on the exposed hill, so Ethan is sitting on the steps round the side of one of the caravans, collar up and a wooly hat on his head. He's frowning down at his phone and doesn't look up, even when I'm standing in front of him.

"Can't hang about too long today, Sash—we'll bloody freeze to death."

"That's fine," I say, all fake casual, like I haven't been watching the clock all day, waiting to meet him. "I've got loads to do anyway."

"Cool," he says and gets up as if to leave right away.

"Wait," I say. "I wanted to ask you..." I don't know what I want to ask. I just want to talk to someone. No one's talked to me at all today, other than a couple of questions from teachers and one remark about homework from Dad on the way home from school.

"What?" He sounds irritated.

"What were you in prison for?" I blurt it out and straightaway want to snatch the words back. He finally looks at me, but I can't tell if he's pissed off or offended at my question. He just looks sort of blank.

"Nothing exciting. Nothing cool enough for you to go bragging to your mates about your new crim friend, if that's what you're looking for."

I won't ask again. I'll let him evade the question same as I'll let him believe I have friends to brag to. "I'm sorry," I say. "I shouldn't have asked. It's none of my business."

"It's all a load of crap anyway. I didn't do it. I should never have gone to prison."

Is that true? Is he really innocent? Or is that just something all ex-prisoners say?

He finally glances up at me and drops the scowl. "Sorry I'm so grumpy. I'm not pissed off with you. Someone is hassling me." He holds up his phone and, as if on command, it dings with an incoming message. "There's a woman out there who just won't leave me alone."

He says it all lighthearted, like it's a joke, but when his phone dings again, then rings, he switches it off and practically throws it down onto the steps behind him. I chew on my lip. "You should go to the police. If someone's hassling you—it's like stalking."

He laughs. "Oh, yeah—they'd definitely believe me, wouldn't they? Forget it—it's nothing." His smile disappears and he sighs. "It's just I've got that, and Owen nagging at me for completely different reasons. Still," he says, shrugging, "it's not all bad. I've actually liked working here. I was lucky to have a mate like Owen prepared to give me a job. Your dad's promised me a good reference, so even if Owen doesn't keep me on, I'll probably get grounds work somewhere else."

"And is that…is that what you *want* to do?"

He raises his eyebrows at me. "Oh yeah, sure. It's all I've dreamed about since I was a kid. Being an odd-job man on a crappy holiday camp. But I haven't got a lot of choice."

All Dad's bitterness at being manager here when he wants to be something more academic sounds so petty now—Ethan's situation is way worse. "You deserve better. You should be able to get a job doing what you want."

He laughs. "You think companies will be lining up to employ an ex-offender?"

"But it's not fair. Especially if you're *innocent*. Even if they don't believe you, you've served your sentence. You wouldn't do anything wrong again, would you?"

"You're a good kid, Sasha." He says it with a smile, but I notice he doesn't answer my question, that one or the one about why he was sent to prison. But I answer it for him in my head. No, even if he's not telling the truth about being innocent, of course he wouldn't do it again—he made a mistake and got sent to prison. He wouldn't risk that again.

"My criminal connections are useful for some things, though," he says, picking his phone up again. "My mate has found out some info about your mysterious Facebook messages."

"You've found out who's sending them?" My heart sinks a bit. I haven't been back on Facebook; it's been nice just pretending the whole thing didn't happen, to be honest. I'd been kind of hoping Ethan had forgotten about it.

"Well, we can't exactly give you a name and address— he's not that good. But he got the IP address, so we know it's a mobile phone and he's working on getting hold of the number. If we know the number, we might be able to track down who it is." He pauses. "You should know—because I had to log in to your account for my mate to trace it, I noticed there were some more messages."

I want to put my hands over my ears and carry on pretending. "What did they say?"

"Do you really want to know?"

No, not really. But…"Yes. Otherwise I'll only imagine worse than they probably are."

He sighs. "I took screenshots. I've noticed that whoever it is, they're careful to delete the messages once they see that they've been read."

He gets out his phone and shows me the messages. They're similar to before, vaguely threatening. The last one makes me shiver: *Don't think by ignoring me you won't be punished for what you've been doing. I know where you live.*

"It's bullshit," Ethan says, watching my reaction. "They're just making shit up to scare you."

"Well, it's working."

"Don't worry. My friend will get the number, we'll find out who it is. If it's one of those kids from school, you can go straight to the head teacher, they'll get the parents in." He pauses. "You could probably even get the police involved—cyberbullying's officially a crime these days."

"But wouldn't you end up in trouble then for helping me?"

"You have a point there. Maybe it's something we'll have to sort out ourselves." He smiles and nudges me. "I have a few other friends who could have a word, scare the living shit out of them. Hell—I could get Owen to do it."

What am I getting into here? That's not what I want, some of Ethan's scary prison friends threatening someone. But I think of the sleepless nights those messages have given me, the near panic attack at school. Maybe it *is* what I want—for them to be as scared as they made me. Maybe if they think I've got a scary prison gang to back me up, they'll leave me alone.

"But what if we did that and *they* went to the police about *us*? Wouldn't it be enough to message them back and tell them I know who they are? Wouldn't threatening to go to the school or police be enough?"

"Sasha, calm down. I was joking. And I can't imagine they would go to the police anyway—they'll know they're in the wrong sending these messages."

166

I chew on my thumbnail. "But what if I get more messages and you're not here. Dad said they're cutting your hours right back." Urgh—I sound so whiny and needy.

"They're just messages—stay away from Facebook. They'll soon get bored when you stop posting."

"Can I call you?" I blurt out. "If anything happens, if I'm worried about anything?"

He's silent for *ages*. Long enough for me to just *die* of embarrassment. Oh God, could I be anymore pathetic? Why the hell would he want to give me his number?

"Look—forget it," I say. "I'm sorry, I..."

"Don't worry about it," he says. "It's fine. You can have my number. It's just..." There's another long pause. "I know I've been helping you out, but...I think you should be calling your friends if you're worried about anything, not me."

I pass him my phone to put his number in and wince as I see him hesitate when he goes into contacts. I should have thought, should have put his number in myself. Because how humiliating is it to have an ex-convict pitying me because there's only one other name and number in my contact list and it's my sister.

"I haven't got round to adding more contacts yet," I say, snatching the phone back. "That's why it's just you and my sister so far."

The silences are getting beyond awkward now. I need to make an excuse to leave so I can find a rock to crawl under.

"So, what's your sister like?" Ethan asks as I'm about to slink away.

I glance at him. "Did Owen used to know her?" I ask, not answering his question. "He mentioned her yesterday."

Ethan shrugs. "No idea. He grew up round here, though, so if they're a similar age, it's possible."

I picture Owen and try to work out how old he could be. "It's possible, I guess. I don't really know her that well—she's much older than me. She was already a teenager when I came along. She left home when she was really young. She was . . . she got in a lot of trouble. Went off the rails after her mum died."

"Maybe that's what Owen was on about. Is that why your dad's so strict with you? Because of what your sister did?"

My turn to shrug. "I guess. I've never known anything different." I pause. "But they do always bring up Hanna as an example of everything not to do, without ever going into detail of what she did that was so wrong. She's a proper mystery black sheep."

"Maybe you'll end up closer now that you've got your own phone and can keep in touch easier."

That's what I'd hoped too. I texted her as soon as Ethan gave me the phone. Sneaking a look at her number in Mum's address book, sending a text asking her to keep my secret phone hush hush but saying for her to text back so we could set up a time for a safe call. She hasn't replied yet.

I think of how when Hanna visits, she barely talks to me, doesn't even look at me. I'm always so shy around her, I sit in my own uncomfortable silence, but Hanna is anything but shy. Is it guilt? The way she avoids eye contact, the way she avoids *any* contact? Guilt because she's not around?

It stings. It always stings. Is it because she doesn't see me as her real sister? It's not like we grew up together. I get it's difficult on those visits because Mum and Dad are always around, but I've given her an opening now, with the text I sent. I look down at my shiny new phone, willing a text to appear, willing Hanna to be finally reading my text and happy to have a safe way to communicate with her little sister.

But there's nothing.

Chapter 19

I feel odd looking though the old photographs again, with my new perspective, my new sting of rejection. The stories I used to invent included me as part of this trapped-in-time gang: me and Hanna the same age, the best of mates.

But now when I imagine Hanna and her gang walking the corridors at school, the same age as me, they don't even look at me, unless it's to sneer or laugh. I'd be invisible to them, not even worth their notice. I'd be too intimidated to speak to any of them anyway, even if one of them tripped over me and was forced to see me. And that makes me kind of mad, because nothing ever changes, does it? Just because I'm quiet, just because I don't dye my hair, plaster myself in makeup, or pierce my face, that makes me unworthy, somehow? Because I work hard in school and don't get in trouble, that makes me boring and dull? How *dare* they make those judgments when they've never even bothered to speak to me?

I realize it's stupid. I realize it's bloody ridiculous to be railing against the people in those photographs because the photos are fifteen years old and the people in them must be in their thirties now. But would any of them have changed? Hanna hasn't, has she? She still looks impatient when I stutter shy answers to her questions. She still looks bored in my company without ever making any real effort to get to know me. No, people like them, new incarnations like

Carly and Seren, never change. I could leave town, come back a multi-millionaire at the top of whatever career I choose, and they'd still look at me the same way.

I carry on flipping through the snapshots, pausing as I get to the last one. This is the one I was looking for. It's another photo of Hanna and her dodgy-looking gang. And there's one particular boy there, standing behind her, all scowly and grumpy looking. He's a lot younger and his hair is longer in this photo, but I think—I'm almost positive—it's Owen King. I didn't make the connection before, because I wasn't looking for it. If he wasn't so horribly intimidating, I could ask him about Hanna...but from the tone of his voice, I'm not sure I want his memories of her.

But there's someone else I recognize in the same photo— Mr. Garner from the village. I squint closer to be sure. Yes, it's definitely him: Mr. Garner, who was Reverend Garner back then, smiling away in the background in his dog collar. I didn't really bother puzzling over it before, but now I'm wondering: why on earth would my troublemaker, rebellious sister have a photograph of herself with the *vicar*?

I return the photos to their hiding place and sit back on the bed with a frown. Does it matter? The thing is, it does. I can't rail against being pigeonholed myself while doing the same to Hanna—dismissing the photo because *Hanna* and the *vicar*? Plus, the photo was clearly taken in the garden of the vicarage in West Dean. Or what used to be the vicarage. The new vicar is stuck with a three-bed new-build on the outskirts of town now. The old vicarage was sold off years ago, but it's still one of the prettiest and most recognizable houses in town, so it's not just a case of him accidentally photobombing.

I chew on a loose nail, wondering what I want to do about this. Obviously, the easy answer is nothing, but...

Hanna has been a stranger to me my whole life. She exists in a mysterious mythical realm of the bad girl, my living lesson of what not to do and what not to be. We just don't talk about her. She's like a scandalous character out of a costume drama who's been shunned. And even when she does visit, we don't talk, we don't share anything. All I know is she was a troublemaker at my age, she left home very young, and now she lives a mystery life in Cardiff, in a house I've never seen, with friends I've never met, doing a job I know nothing about.

Every time she does visit, I have a million questions I want to ask, a million things I want to know that would make her less of a stranger and more like family. But I never do, because she *is* a stranger, and with all the hostility simmering in the air between her and Mum and Dad, there's never any room or space for those questions, even if I weren't usually intimidated into awkward silence around her.

So, if Dad won't tell me anything, and she won't tell me anything—and she won't even answer my text—maybe I should find out for myself exactly who Hanna used to be. Then it might give me an insight into who she is now. Maybe it'll give me something real to say, so I can text her again and this time she'll answer.

I'll treat it like an English or a History essay—I'll analyze the evidence and draw conclusions on character based on my findings. Breaking it down like that, into a project, helps it make sense to me, and I actually go so far as to get a new notebook off my shelf and start a list: what I know (very little), questions based on evidence presented (lots), tasks to do. And task one is to visit Mr. Garner, because that photograph presents the most questions and offers up the most possibilities of answers. Plus, it's either ask the nice ex-vicar or ask Owen King.

With my guise of this as a sort of school project, it's actually easy to get permission to go into the village after school the following Tuesday to go and see him—I tell Dad it's for Religious Studies, that we've been tasked to interview someone who is or used to be in the Church. Mr. Garner lives in Littledean now. Dad never says no to anything that involves schoolwork. He's surprisingly amenable to me going by myself as well; in fact, he seems almost eager not to have to pick me up at three. Instead of collecting me straight from school, he arranges to meet me in the village at five o'clock and gives me permission to get the bus from school to Littledean. The sense of freedom is dizzying. Obviously, I will go to Mr. Garner's house...but if I got the four o'clock bus rather than the three thirty...I'd have nearly an hour, alone and loose in the town. I could go to Greggs or the Spar with Emma, hang out on the benches by the rugby club like half the school do. I could stand on the edges and pretend to be one of them.

Of course, the problem with that is—why do they *want* to? Hang out in the freezing cold and do nothing? Fair enough in the summer, but now, at the beginning of December? All my daydreams of having a gang of friends and hanging out involve going to someone's house, someone who has central heating, books, a TV—maybe a phone or iPad I could have a sneaky go on.

But—if Mr. Garner isn't home, or my visit is done really quickly—there's not exactly much to do in Littledean, although the shop has one of those Costa Coffee vending machines. I could buy a hot chocolate or a cake, or *both*.

*

My plans get me through what is pretty much a crappy day at school. Seren and Carly and their idiot mates are only low-grade annoying in math, but it's the worst day of my schedule—double science, double math, and PE. Worst day known to man. Especially PE, because it's one of those gray, drizzly days but not rainy enough to keep us inside, so they still make us go out and play netball, which I'm horrible at. No one ever passes me the ball, so I spend forty minutes hovering and shivering at the edges of the court, flinching every time the ball comes near me. The only good thing about it is that it's last lesson, so I don't have to run the full gauntlet of the showers and changing room. It's not like I did anything to get sweaty, so I just put my school jumper over my polo shirt and leggings and I'm free to go.

I fight my way through the crowds at the door to find Emma, hoping she'll ask again about going into town. *I'm meeting a friend, but maybe for half an hour?* I'll say, cool and casual. *Where are you going?* But she doesn't ask today. To be honest, I'm not sure she even noticed me hovering behind her.

Doesn't matter, though, because today I have *plans*.

I have to walk past the rugby club and the crowds of teenagers queuing outside Greggs to get to the bus stop, but I don't feel as self-conscious as usual in leggings and trainers, and no one shouts anything or stares. It's a funny kind of invisibility, being the below-the-knee-skirted weirdo from the holiday park; most of the time, I'm beneath anyone's notice, but I'm also a target if one of them is in a vicious mood. I'm a full-on Schrödinger's cat experiment, both invisible and visible at the same time, all dependant on what side of the bed the school bitches get out of.

It's only a ten-minute ride on the rickety old town bus, and then a walk up the hill. Mr. Garner has moved to one of a row of cottages dotted up a hill on the outskirts of Littledean. It's a really pretty cottage, not as nice as the old vicarage, but proper picture-book pretty, with pots of flowers and roses and ivy climbing the walls. The gate squeaks when I open it and it must act like an alarm system, because he opens the door before I get chance to knock.

He gives me a smile, although I don't know if he really recognizes me. I've met him before; everyone knows Mr. Garner, but only in passing, like if he stops to chat to Mum when I'm out shopping with her.

"Hi, Mr. Garner," I say. "I'm Sasha Carter and I was hoping I could ask you a couple of questions?"

His smile widens in recognition. "Ah, Sasha, of course—hello. How are your parents? Is it a school thing you want to ask about?"

"Not exactly." I rummage in my bag for my Hanna project notebook. I've tucked the photograph inside for safekeeping and I take it out to show Mr. Garner. "I found this photograph of Hanna among her things and I recognized you as well. I was wondering if I could ask you about her."

His smile dims a bit as he takes the photo and looks at it, and I itch to get a pen and start making observational notes about his reaction.

"You'd better come in," Mr. Garner says.

He makes a pot of tea and puts chocolate biscuits on a plate. In his cluttered, cozy living room I feel way more comfortable than I would have sitting in a café in town.

"You looked sad when you saw that photo," I say, then hesitate, unsure how to word what I want to say next. "I

175

know Hanna got in a lot of trouble when she was my age... did she do something really bad?"

He smiles and shakes his head. "Hanna used to come to my wife's Sunday-school class, did you know that?"

I almost laugh. Hanna at Sunday school?

"I don't think she particularly *wanted* to come, but most of the local children did," Mr. Garner goes on. "We had another group, as the children got older. Nothing religious at all, more an opportunity for young people... often the more troubled young people... to spend time together away from their homes. It was my wife who set it up, and I'd help out. She'd get them to bake, or make things, sometimes sit and talk. After she died, I carried it on, but I was never as good at the baking and crafts." He pauses and smiles at me. "As you said, Hanna got into a lot of trouble when she was younger. Many of my little group did, but a lot of it was to do with troubled home lives, or simply the classic adolescent problem of clashes between parent and child. Hanna met several of her friends there."

He looks down at the photograph again. "Including Owen and Jacob. Sadly, they found gathering at the vicarage with tea and biscuits a bit boring after a while and stopped coming. But she used to call in to say hello if she was passing."

He sighs and leans back in his chair. "Hanna was a lovely girl," he says. "Too many people are quick to judge and won't look beyond what's on the surface. Miriam and I always tried to."

"And what about Owen?" I say, pointing to the boy in the picture. "Is that him? And the other name you mentioned—Jacob? What happened to him—does he still live around here?" I don't let on that I know the grown-up Owen. Well, sort of know him. I want to keep Mr. Garner reminiscing about the teenagers in the photo, about Hanna.

"Yes, that's Owen. There were a group of friends—Owen, Jacob, Lee, Carrie…Hanna joined later. She was younger but they let her in." Mr. Garner pours himself more tea and stirs milk in. "Owen and Jacob struggled the most, far more than Hanna," he says. "We tried very hard to help them, but sometimes people won't let themselves be helped. I'm sorry I can't tell you much. Besides the confidentiality issue, the group stopped coming to our gatherings very early. Hanna would be the best person to tell you about them."

I look down at my notebook. All I've written is *Sunday School* and *Church Youth Group*. I don't know what to think about everything Mr. Garner has said, or not said. I've grown up with Hanna as the villain in the family, someone I sometimes envy, sometimes hate. I fantasize about going to stay with her, becoming a whole new person hanging out with her and her friends in Cardiff. Other times, I think I'd be happy if she never visited again. But no one, ever, has said she was a *lovely girl*. And all the talk of troubled home lives and troubled teens…I don't like the way he made that sound. Like it was Mum and Dad who were the problem, not Hanna. I'm not sure if I'm glad or not that I came. I notice the time then, and jump up. "I'm sorry, I'd better go—my dad's picking me up soon."

Mr. Garner gets up to show me out, still talking as he walks me to the door. "Sometimes it's better to let things go," he says. "We all make mistakes—it's what we do with the rest of our lives that matters."

He shakes his head and sighs as we stand in the doorway, me on the outside, him on the inside. "And if you do find any of the others...you shouldn't necessarily believe everything they have to say. There was some trouble between the group and Hanna and they...Well, she certainly wasn't the first and won't be the last teenage girl to fall pregnant. I will never stop regretting what happened—to Hanna, and to you as well, Sasha—but I won't ever regret helping."

The goodbye smile I'd conjured up fades at his words and I can't think of anything to say, so I just turn and walk away. Hanna was *pregnant*? But...that makes no sense. Did Dad force her to have an abortion? Is that one of the regrets Mr. Garner was on about? Or is that why she left home? But she didn't have a baby, because if she did, that child would be about fourteen by now and—Oh.

Oh.

Chapter 20

HANNA—Sunday 6 p.m.

The journey back to Cardiff passes in silence. I know what's keeping me quiet—torturing myself over everything Carrie, Lee, and Stephen said, combined with an endless internal rehearsal of what I'm going to say to DC Norton when he gets my message and calls me back. And then there's Mrs. Thorpe's comment to Adam…*Back again?* I chose to sit in the back for the journey home and I'm staring at the back of Adam's head and he's turned into a stranger again.

It must be a mistaken identity thing. He would have said if he'd visited my home village before—it's not exactly a tourist hot spot. But his reaction was off enough for Dee to remark on it…Maybe it was years ago. He did say he'd heard of Littledean, and also that he stayed with Seb's family when he was at university. But no, that's ridiculous—I know Mrs. Thorpe is world class at gossip and spotting a stranger-in-town at a hundred paces, but even she wouldn't say "back again" if he once visited ten bloody years ago.

So, if she wasn't mistaken, then Adam has visited Littledean recently, and he's lied to me about it. Which brings us right back to it being Adam who put the story about my family on his website. Because why the hell else would he have gone there? Is he the reason my family fled town overnight?

No. It doesn't make sense. None of this does. I already feel guilty because I'm going to have to give DC Norton Stephen and Lee's names, as well as Carrie and Owen's, which means I'll be doing exactly what they expected me to do: bringing trouble into their lives. But I have to, don't I? Stephen lied about Owen still being around and Lee made it obvious he knew where I lived. And Carrie…She was about to say something when Stephen stormed in, I know she was. The police said to report anything suspicious that could connect all this. I close my eyes for a moment. I'm going to have to tell them about Adam as well, about that *back again?*

I wish I'd just texted Sasha back when she contacted me at the end of last year. If we'd started a proper line of communication, I'd have known they were moving, I'd have known where and when, and none of this would be happening. Why didn't I? She was taking so many risks just getting hold of a phone and contacting me and I didn't even bother texting her back. She must have hated me for that. And what's my excuse? That things between me and Liam were falling apart and I was distracted? Or was it that I believe the messages my father has drummed into me—that Sasha was better off without me? Has he done that good a job on me?

I glance over at Dee and think of all her lectures when I fall into one of my self-hate pits of despair. Yes, it's pathetic, but I do believe it. And that's all fine and dandy when it's only me I'm hurting, but I've become such a self-pitying stupid cow, so blindly selfish, I'm now hurting other people.

Well, not anymore. When they find my family, I'm going to insist on seeing Sasha regularly and I don't care what my father says. When all this is over, Sasha can come and stay with me, get a glimpse of a life away from the walls Dad has surrounded her with. And they will find them, and they will be safe. That woman's murder, the hit-and-run...they have *nothing* to do with this. It's just another way to mess with Adam or with me. And while I'm playing this game, I tell myself Adam cannot possibly have anything to do with this, it's just the hacker messing with us all...It's harder to convince myself, though, with Mrs. Thorpe's *back again* whispering in my head. But there must be an explanation— an innocent explanation—as to why he's lied. He's Seb's friend. Dee has known him for years as well. I'm going to try to believe he's just a pawn in this horrible game.

I'm buoyed by my new resolve as Dee turns the corner into her street. But that momentary high is instantly killed when I see a police car outside her building.

The doors of the police car open as we pull up. DC Norton gets out and stands at the entrance to Dee's building, with a female uniformed officer next to him. His face is solemn, and dread fills me, cementing my feet to the ground so I can't move and numbing my lips so I can't speak.

"Hanna? This is PC Conran, she's a family liaison officer. Can we come inside?"

Chapter 21

Sunday 6:30 p.m.

I think my legs have turned to stone. I can't move. But then Dee is there, and thank God for Dee, unlocking the front door, ushering them in and up the stairs, taking my arm and coaxing me to move. Seb is already in the doorway of the flat and he and Dee flank me, saying nothing but just being there, as I collapse on the sofa to wait for them to tell me my family is dead. Because why else would they be there? Why else would DC Norton have brought a family liaison officer? She's here to make tea, keep me company as a murder investigation happens around me. My father. Jen. Sasha...

"What is it? What have you found out?" It's Adam who speaks, who takes charge when I can't ask.

"We were able to gain access to your father's new house," DC Norton says. "To look for evidence as to where your family might be, or—"

"Are they dead?" I find my voice, but it comes out too loud, that brutal question. My attention goes from him to PC Conran, hovering awkwardly at the edge of the room. "Is that why you're here? Because you've found their bodies?"

My throat tightens and my eyes burn, but I swallow

down the rising hysteria. I will not lose it now. I will save that for later, when they've gone, when I'm alone.

But DC Norton is shaking his head. "No—Hanna, no, we haven't found them yet. That's not why we're here." He glances over at his colleague. "But we found...evidence of a disturbance."

Not dead. Oh. His words sink in slowly. A disturbance?

"We found the house in a similar state to your flat after the break-in."

"Do you think he's taken them?" I lean forward. "Whoever hacked Adam's site, whoever murdered those women? He has my family?"

"Hanna, please. The nearest neighbor lives on the road leading away from the holiday park. We spoke to her and she says she saw them leave in their car yesterday morning. Just the three of them. She heard a car driving along the lane late last night and thought they might have returned. But it was dark so she couldn't identify the car or who was in it."

My attention flutters to Adam and away again. Where was he last night?

"That was probably him, wasn't it? He's found out where they live and for whatever reason, he's still looking for them. Did he tear the place apart looking for them?"

"Hanna," Dee interrupts, touching my arm, "tell them what we found out—about how suddenly they left..."

I don't like the way DC Norton's shoulders stiffen as I tell the story, the way PC Conran draws closer and they both look at each other. I tell them about Lee and Stephen as well, give them Carrie and Owen's names, and feel the guilt pressing down on me. My attention flickers from Adam across to Dee. Do I mention the *back again*? Stephen

Hayes asking, *Do I know you?* Like he recognized him. Dee shakes her head. Is she reading my mind again? I bite my lip but sit back and don't mention Adam.

I'm restless after DC Norton leaves. PC Conran has been assigned to lurk outside in the police car and I know what I should do is sit tight and wait. But I can't. I jump up.

"I'm going to my flat. Tidy up a bit and see if there's anything I missed. I was in such a state after the break-in... there could be clues I missed."

"But the police will have found any evidence," Dee says.

"I don't mean evidence. I mean...they left those photos, didn't they? A message, a sign, I don't know. There could be something else, something the police wouldn't think was evidence, but I might."

"I'll come with you," Adam says. "You can't go alone."

I had actually assumed Dee might come with me. I glance at her and she smiles. "I think Adam might be more of a deterrent if someone's lurking about. I'll cook while you're gone. Some big, comfort-food feast. But come to the kitchen with me a sec—have a look and see what you fancy eating."

She practically drags me out to the kitchen and starts talking as soon as she closes the door behind us. "I must have been wrong. Mrs. Thorpe must have been wrong. I've been thinking about it the whole way back...None of this has anything to do with Adam; it can't. He and Seb have been friends since their first week at university. If there were anything dodgy about him, Seb would have picked up on it long before now."

I look at her. "Dee, if there's one person in this whole world I completely trust, it's you. And you, obviously, completely trust Seb. But…Adam only moved back here a few months ago. He and Seb were uni friends who've lived hundreds of miles from each other ever since. You only have to look at me to see how a person can change in almost ten years. I changed for the better…but what if Adam didn't?"

"Hanna, I—"

"I'm not saying that he's done all of this, that he's a murderer, or that he's kidnapped my family all by himself. God, I've been telling myself that just as you have, that he can't have anything to do this…But who are his friends— other than Seb, do you know? Who were his friends when he lived in London?" I pause, take a breath. "And when you set up our blind date…was that really all you? Or did Adam manipulate you and Seb into setting it up?"

"Of course not. Han, you know I would never try to set you up with anyone I thought was in any way dodgy. This is *Adam*. I know the Littledean thing is weird, but there has to be an explanation."

I glance at the closed kitchen door. Is Adam on the other side, listening?

"I'm trying. I'm trying really hard to believe you, that he's innocent in all this. But it's difficult when I know he's been lying. I will take up your suggestion, though. I will take Adam with me. I'll be safe enough with the police watching and it'll give me a chance to ask him about it."

Chapter 22

Sunday 7 p.m.

I tell PC Conran where we're going, and she insists on driving us over there in the police car. I lean closer to Adam as we drive, whispering right in his ear so there's no chance of being overheard. "It's years since I've been in one of these." I pause. "Not since I lived in Littledean."

Adam raises his eyebrows and mouths back, "In a *police car?*"

I nod and lean back, watching his reaction. Either he's a very good actor or his surprise is genuine. I catch PC Conran watching me in her rearview mirror and feel like a delinquent teenager again. I remember being sick in the back of a police car when I was fourteen, picked up when they found me semiconscious at the side of the road, attempting to find my way back home after a party where I'd lost all my friends.

I think Dad had given up on me by that point. He'd just moved Jen in without discussing it with me—I wasn't even aware, at the time, that he was seeing anyone. Of course, I found out later that Jen's predecessor was the reason my mum originally left. But Jen—I just came home from school and there she was, all smiley and Stepford, constantly cleaning and cooking and asking questions, like she thought she

186

could come into my life and be some kind of mother when she was a total stranger. I turn away from the police constable's eyes in the mirror. It wasn't Jen's fault, she didn't drive my mum away or cause her death, but I blamed her as much as I did my dad, and it wasn't her fault that the harder she tried, the more irritating I found her.

I reacted by acting up more than ever, not bothering to go home after school, so I didn't have to try to sneak out. Instead, I'd go and meet Jacob and the others, start partying by four in the afternoon. We'd stopped going to Reverend Garner's gatherings by then—they weren't the kind of parties we were looking for.

That night the police brought me home, a vomit-stained drunken mess, Dad didn't say a word. The curled-lip disgust and silent treatment were actually more effective than the screaming fury of the good old days. I remember I cried that night, anyway. I also remember when I got out of the shower, eyes red and throat raw from crying, Jen had left warm towels and freshly washed pajamas outside the bathroom and a cup of hot chocolate in my room. But I also remember the next day, I got up and did it all again. I never wanted that for Sasha, that misery disguised as rebellion. It's why I've always done what Dad asked and kept my distance from her. And it seemed to be working—Sasha never acted out, she had the stability of two parents at home, even if Dad was over-the-top strict. He seemed to have found, with Jen, whatever was missing in his relationship with my mother. And Jen—well, I might have always found her too much, but I can't deny she must be a pretty good mother to have in your life full time.

I glance across at Adam. My track record with men is pretty crap, but there's something...I *want* to trust him.

I want to trust that feeling deep in my gut that tells me he is genuinely clueless about how my family ended up on his website. But there's something he's not telling me...If I can get to the bottom of that, then maybe I'll be able to let go of the doubt.

"Here we are," PC Conran says, stopping the car. "I'll wait here, call in where we are. How long will you be?"

"Not long," I say. "No more than an hour." I'm already regretting it. We should have stayed at Dee's, helped her cook the comfort-food feast. My flat, my bizarre cut-in-half house, is no longer my sanctuary. I can't imagine ever feeling safe here again, even when this is all over. Maybe I'll sell it. Look for somewhere with two bedrooms, so I can have Sasha to stay.

I switch on all the lights as I walk through the flat, even in rooms I don't plan to enter. Without the shock of that first discovery, the flat isn't actually that bad. The bedroom is the worst when I reluctantly go upstairs. Not because it's been trashed, but because of that neatly made bed. It'll have to go. If I can ever bring myself to live here again, it'll all have to go, not just the bedding. I avoid looking at it as I open my wardrobe and take clothes off hangers, stuffing them into a bag. There's not much to take—most of my stuff has been pulled out and scattered across the room. I go to the drawers of my dresser, trying not to think of strange hands rummaging through them as I top up the bag with underwear and T-shirts. There's no sign any of it has been touched, but I know I'll be washing everything before I wear any of it.

My hands brush the corner of a box as I reach to the back of the top drawer for more socks. I reach further in and pull it out. It's a carved wooden box that Jacob gave me for my fifteenth birthday. I've always kept it tucked away, first from my dad, so I didn't have to explain where it came from, and later because it became the box I hid things in. Mostly hiding them from myself. Letters and photos and documents I don't want reminders of. This box is where Hanna between the ages of fifteen and twenty has been buried, the period of my life I'd like to forget.

The problem is, locking those years in a box doesn't banish them from existence, does it? I perch on the edge of my dressing-table stool and lift the lid of the box. It doesn't look as if anything has been disturbed, so I don't think either the burglar or the police have looked in here. Photos, letters, papers all still in their neat bundles tied with different color ribbons. I don't undo any of the ribbons. Opening the box is as far as I'm prepared to go. But I don't put the box back in the drawer—I add it to the pile of clothes in my bag.

I hear a noise from downstairs and whirl round, my heart thudding.

"It's only me," Adam calls and I calm down.

I pick up the bag and go back downstairs without looking back.

"So what number date is this?" Adam asks as we form a relay system—him picking up books from the floor and passing them to me, me putting them back on shelves.

"What?" I'm only half-listening to him as we tidy the books away—too busy trying to work out how to ask what I need to ask.

"What do you think—third, fourth date?" He raises an eyebrow and smiles.

"Let's see...we had first drinks plus bonus creepy abandoned house," I answer, playing along. "Then me screaming accusations at you in your flat..."

"Third date was our joint trip to the police station."

"Fourth was finding my flat broken into, followed by drinks," I say.

"Fifth was you taking me back to your charming home town."

"So, is this the sixth? Or a continuation of the fourth? The broken-into flat, part two?"

"Hmmm...I'm going to call this number six—same venue, but different vibe."

I nod. "There's certainly a bit of a theme going on, though, I think."

"It's definitely progressing along a different path to what I expected," Adam says.

"You mean, this isn't how all your relationships go?"

"I'm a bit out of practice, but I'm sure date six is usually when I pull out the big guns—cooking my finest Thai curry at home; wine, candles, the works."

I sigh. "I like Thai food."

He smiles. "I promise, when this is all over, when they've found your family safe and sound and caught whoever is doing this, I will cook it for you."

I frown and stare at him, searching his face for...what? Guilt? "Do you think they will? Find my family—safe, I mean?"

He nods. "I do. I really do. Even if our hacker killer had planned something awful, he seems to be out of sync with them. He was at your old house after they'd moved, at the new one after they'd gone away. I think the police will find them before he does."

He sounds so sure. So convincing.

"Adam," I say, "as this is our sixth date, if I ask you something, will you promise to tell me the truth?"

"Uh-oh, this sounds dangerous." He's smiling as he says it, because he thinks we're still playing the game, but that's a good thing. He hasn't got time to invent a lie.

"Have you been to Littledean before? Before today, I mean?"

I can see the answer on his face—he doesn't even need to say anything.

"Did I tell you how I originally got the idea for the website?" he says. "It was when I was visiting Seb's family when we were at uni. I was already getting into urban exploring and he told me about a local house that had lain empty for years, the Romeo and Juliet love story that ended in the tragic deaths of a whole family."

Oh, that stings. That Seb used my past as some story to impress his mate. We were hardly close then, Seb and I. I barely saw Dee in my lost years; I certainly hadn't had time to get to know her boyfriend then, but still. It stings.

"I didn't do anything for a long time," Adam says. "But the story stuck with me. I ended up writing an article about it, about urban exploration and dark tourism, to tie in with the launch of the website. That's when I went there. To Littledean. For research for an article, that's all."

I can't look at him as I walk out of the room, out of the flat, leaning against the wall outside on sagging knees.

I'm not surprised to hear someone approaching seconds later, not surprised to see Adam in front of me when I look up.

"Why didn't you tell me?" I say before he can speak.

"I'm sorry."

"Is that why you agreed to go out with me? Is that why you asked about me? More background for your fucking website? A follow-up to your bloody article?" I hunch over, clutching my stomach. "Oh God, I feel sick."

"No, I didn't know then. I swear. I had no idea at first who you were other than a friend of Dee's." He pauses. "It was only when Dee was trying to set up the blind date that Seb told me."

"And what exactly did he tell you?" My heart is pounding as I wait for him to answer.

"Nothing much, I promise. It was more of a caution than information. He just told me that you were the girl in the story he'd told me. About the house from near his home town."

"And when you knew—is that why you agreed to go out with me?"

His pause is too long. Heartbreakingly long.

"There was an element of curiosity so perhaps that's why I initially thought about it... because I knew your history. But I was attracted to you, before I knew, I wasn't lying about that. And within a few minutes of our date—none of it mattered anymore. I liked you. That was all that mattered."

I shake my head, pull away from him when he reaches out a hand toward me. "But you chose not to say anything to me? When you were telling me all about your creepy hobbies and your stupid website? Not even when we went back to the village—you *still* didn't say anything?"

"I should have, I know. I was going to come clean on that first date, when you were telling me where you grew up, but I didn't because I liked you. I liked you too much.

192

I didn't want you to think I was a total creep. You were never likely to come across the article I wrote—there was no reason for you ever to know. And when the website got hacked—I couldn't say anything after that. And none of it is on the current site. It was an earlier incarnation, more of an urban exploring site, that was where that original house was mentioned. Like an origin story."

"But *you knew*. When you launched that bloody website, every house and place you put on there is the site of someone's misery. Do you never stop to think about how the families of the victims might feel if they came across your website? And you went out with me, the—what?—the *tragic Juliet*...and you said nothing. The police asked about us, any connections between us, and you didn't say anything."

He's silent for a moment. "I told them. The second time I was questioned. I told them."

I want to cry. I want to curl up in a ball on the ground and cry. "So, you talked to the police about *my* past, *my* history, knowing none of what really happened, only what was public knowledge, but you didn't have the decency to mention it to me? When I talked about my family, my life, you said *nothing*." I look away from him and take a deep breath. "I'm going to go back in and carry on. I don't want you there. I don't want to be in the same room as you."

I turn back around as I get to the front door. "Did you tell me the truth about anything?"

"What?"

"Your ex-girlfriend—you told me you'd just broken up when you moved to Cardiff but Seb said something...Did you lie about that, too?"

He opens his mouth as if to answer then shakes his head and says nothing.

"Why?"

"Hanna..."

"Actually, forget it. I don't want to know. You are a stranger to me and everything you've said has been a lie. I should have stuck with my original instinct and not trusted you the moment I saw that bloody website."

Chapter 23

SASHA—December, two months earlier

"Sasha, what are you doing?"

I ignore her and carry on pulling drawers open and rummaging through them. And I know it's stupid. What—do I think they'll have hidden top-secret evidence of a fourteen-year-old lie in the kitchen drawer with the first-aid box and spare batteries? Of course not, but I have to *do* something, and slamming drawers feels *good*.

"Where is it?" I whirl around to face Mum when I've run out of drawers to slam. "*Where is it?*"

"Where is *what*?"

"My bloody birth certificate," I shout. "So that I can find out if you and Dad are actually my freaking *grandparents*." I take a deep, shaky breath. "Is it true? Is Hanna my mother?"

She doesn't even need to open her mouth to answer. I can see the truth in how pale she goes as she sinks into a chair.

Well then. Well. No wonder Dad freaks out so much if I do the slightest thing wrong. He's constantly waiting for history to repeat itself. Like mother, like daughter—that's what goes through his head, like he has no skin in the game, like his precious DNA is somehow apart and separate from the women in his family, like Hanna and me are only descended from the first wife who left him and nothing to do with him at all.

And the stupidest thing—the stupidest thing of all—all these years I've wished, wished, wished that I was more closely related to Hanna, not just a half sister, because maybe then she'd bother with me, maybe then she'd care a little, when all along, I'm actually her daughter? Which makes the rejection, the dismissal, the *abandonment* a million, billion times worse.

"Why didn't you tell me?" I say, slumping into a chair next to her.

She has her hands clasped together like she's about to pray, knuckles white. I could probably count on one hand the number of times I've seen Mum anything other than calm my entire life, but I can see she's on the edge today.

"Your father felt the break should be clean," she says.

I fold my arms and lean back. "So, you're saying it's Dad's fault you've lied to me my entire life."

She smiles at me very faintly. "No, we all agreed, Hanna included, to treat it as if it were a traditional adoption. I did suggest we talk to you about it earlier...but it was complicated because Hanna was still visiting. And your father said Hanna didn't want you to know. If we had adopted you from a stranger, you would have had to wait until you were eighteen to see if you could find out about your birth parents."

"So, you were going to tell me when I was eighteen?"

She nods. "I'm sorry you found out like this, Sasha. But I'm not going to apologize for bringing you up, for wanting to be your mother. I fell in love with you as soon as you were born, so I'm never going to apologize for that."

I can feel my eyes fill with tears and I have to force myself to stare straight ahead and not blink so she doesn't see. I'm not even mad at Mum, really. Because I know she loves me, that she sees me as her real daughter, of course I do. And if Hanna didn't want me…if it weren't for Mum and Dad, I would have gone to strangers or into care. But it's like…they've taken away my sister, who one day, when I was old enough, when I got brave enough, when I grew cool enough, would actually like me.

And what do I have now? Hanna, when she visits, avoids looking at me, she actually flinches if I speak sometimes. It's bad enough she was embarrassed by her half sister, but to find out I'm her daughter?

"So, how come…?" I have to pause and clear my throat. "How come Hanna let you keep me? If she didn't want me, how come she didn't just get rid of me when she was pregnant? And if she couldn't face that, wouldn't it have been better for her if a stranger had adopted me, then she wouldn't have to face me every time she visited?"

Mum reaches over to touch my shoulder, my face. "Because I asked. Because I *begged*. I begged her not to get an abortion. I promised to help, and I even promised to help with social services, with arranging for you to be adopted…We went away together, me and Hanna. We took her out of school for a few weeks before the summer holidays, so no one would know, no one would guess. Mr. Garner arranged it as a discrete way of avoiding village gossip and all the scandal of a teenage pregnancy. We were supposed to come back from our time away without a baby, but then you were born, and I loved you so much. I could see Hanna wasn't ready, wasn't capable of looking after a baby. But I could and I was so ready."

"And Dad?"

Her pause before answering is just a bit too long. "Of course he wanted to adopt you too."

"So, you and the vicar came up with some murky baby-swap plan and that's it?"

"Don't, Sasha. Mr. Garner helped us, that's all—he arranged for somewhere for Hanna and me to stay—away from the gossip of this town, away from all the horrible gossip about Hanna. It wasn't that difficult. At the time, neither your father nor I had particularly close ties to the village. By the time I first took you into the village, you were six months old and Hanna had already left."

"And my birth dad? He didn't have a say, I take it?"

"You'll have to ask Hanna about your birth father," she says after a pause. "It's not my place."

"Oh, great, so what does that mean? Hanna doesn't even know who my dad is?" Oh God—the photos. What if my birth dad is *Owen* and he doesn't know, he just hates us all because Hanna left him?

"*Daniel* is your father," Mum says. "He's the one who raised you."

"No wonder he's always been so strict, so bloody terrified I'm going to turn out like Hanna."

"Sasha, please…"

"Please *what*?"

Another one of those stupid damned pauses.

"Don't talk to your father about this. He's having a… difficult time. *We're* having a difficult time."

I shake my head. "You're kidding? I find out Hanna is my *mother*, that you've all been lying to me—and I have to keep quiet because Dad's having a *difficult time*? Fine. Okay. I'll do that, *Jen*."

I register her visible flinch as I call her Jen instead of Mum. Good. I'm glad. I am.

But tears are already blurring my vision as I turn to storm out.

Chapter 24

HANNA—Sunday 10 p.m.

I insert a coin to unlock the trolley and trundle up the first aisle of the supermarket, straight past the healthy fruit and veg, heading for the bakery section. I'm not the only one. The Spar is the only shop open at ten o'clock on a Sunday night and anyone here is not looking to fulfill their five-a-day quota. My trolley, by the time I'm on the final aisle, contains enough sugar to give an elephant diabetes, so I add a couple of tubes of Pringles and some Frazzles as counterbalance.

I spotted Adam round about the multipack of Dairy Milk, but I ignored him and his stupid basket that has nothing in it but six eggs and a loaf of wholemeal bread. Dee must have told him where I was going. I couldn't settle when I went back to hers after Adam's confession, couldn't eat any of the food she'd cooked. I didn't tell her or Seb what had happened, so I can't blame her for telling him. I like to think if she knew, she'd have kneed him in the balls instead.

I pick up a bar of Dee's favorite chocolate. But maybe she already knows. Even if Adam was telling the truth—that all Seb told him was that I was the girl in the doomed teenage relationship that set off the tragic chain of events that led to his morbid curiosity in an abandoned house—wouldn't Seb have told Dee before she set us up on that date? Of course he would—they tell each other everything. And he knows how protective she is of me. So, she knew. And Seb knew. And they all chose to say nothing to me about it.

I put the chocolate back on the shelf.

I can see Adam out of the corner of my eye, still following me around the shop. I don't really want to be removed from the Spar for braining someone with a two-liter bottle of Fanta, but I swear if he comes up and starts apologizing again, that's exactly what's going to happen.

He sidles up when I'm browsing the limited ice-cream selection, dithering between Chunky Monkey and Phish Food before chucking both in the trolley.

"I didn't lie when I said I'd recently broken up with my girlfriend. Not completely."

Fuck off.

"And I suppose I lied by omission by not telling you that Seb had...told me about you in the context of that house. And by not telling you I'd been to Littledean before."

No shit, Sherlock.

"The thing is...I was a mess when I broke up with Natalie. There was other stuff going on, I was beyond stressed and I had, well, I suppose I had a breakdown. Couldn't work, completely lost it. It took me a long time to get better. Seb knew that. He came to London to see me, saw what a mess I was. He planted the seed of me moving down here...but what he doesn't know is that Natalie came back. Tried to start things up again. And I...There were a couple of weeks when we tried. But I could see this time how destructive the relationship was, how damaging for both of us. So I ended it again. And I never told Seb because I know he'd think I was nuts for getting back with her. Moving to Cardiff was the turning point, but it was tough because I'd opened old wounds by seeing Nat again. I think building that website was something to focus on and that's why I became so obsessed with it for a while, visiting places I wanted to put on the website... And when I saw you—I didn't know, at first, who you were, I just liked you. When Seb told me, I figured it didn't matter, not really."

I raise my eyebrows.

"I don't mean what *happened* didn't matter," he says. "Shit. I'm saying this all wrong. It's just that... It was something that happened fifteen years before we met. I did wonder if I should mention it when we went on our date..."

I look at him in disbelief and swing my trolley round, only avoiding ramming him because he leaps out of the way.

"But I didn't want you to think I was a total weirdo."

Too fucking late, mate. I march down the aisle to the checkout. There's no queue, so I start unloading onto the counter. Adam comes up behind me and carries on talking.

"I'm not a hacker, or a murderer, or a stalker."

The woman on the checkout pauses in scanning my shopping. I smile at her. "He's just a creepy weirdo," I say. "Likes lurking in empty murder houses. Likes lying to women."

"Do I need to get security?"

I sigh and look at Adam still clutching his pathetic eggs and bread. It's tempting. I'd quite like to see him get dragged out by security, bundled into the back of a police car.

"No, it's okay. I can handle him."

It's no wonder I was attracted to him, I think as I pay and wheel my stuffed trolley away. I thought he was too nice, and I couldn't figure out what it was about him... But, of course, it was my built-in ability to attract losers and psychos. I'd thought for a second I'd broken the cycle, but it turns out that loser radar was working just fine, better than ever, in fact.

I don't look back again to see if he's following as I load up the car and get in. I don't even know if he's got his car back from the police or if he walked. But I'm so mad as I pull away that I drive on autopilot and only realize as I turn down my own street that I've come home instead of driving back to Dee and Seb's. Cursing myself, Adam, the world, I drive toward the end of the street to do a U-turn and slam on the brakes as I pass my flat because there's someone outside my front door. Someone *kicking* my front door.

The anger that's fueled my journey flares up and I'm out of the car, marching across the road before I can question the stupidity of my actions. It's nearly half past ten and I'm raging over to confront a man kicking in my front door. The fury doesn't get time to turn to fear, though, because the door-kicker turns and it's only Liam, not a psycho-murderer-stalker-burglar, and he looks as mad as I must do.

"What the *fuck*?" I keep my voice low, mindful of the neighbors. "What the hell are you doing here? What the hell are you trying to do to my door?"

"What are you going to do—call the police again?"

Oh, *that's* what this is about. "Oh, grow up, you self-pitying asshole," I say, folding my arms. "Stop acting like a wounded victim. So, what—you had to answer a few questions? Big deal. If you weren't such a dick, I never would have thought to give them your name."

"Are you *insane*? I've been questioned *twice*. They wouldn't tell me why, just kept asking where I was and what I was doing over the weekend. Asking me if I'd threatened you or slashed your tires."

He looks genuinely freaked out as I push past him and unlock my front door, marching inside and leaving the door open for him to follow. I wait in my still-destroyed living room, moving my hands to my hips.

He storms in and I watch him stop dead as he takes in the chaos.

"*This* is why you're being questioned. Because someone did this to my home. Because my family is missing, and two women have been murdered, and it all seems to be connected to me."

"What—wait...Two women have been murdered?" He goes pale. "And you told the police it was *me*?"

"For God's sake—*no, I didn't*." I yell the last words. I'm suddenly glad he's here, glad there's someone I can take my anger out on. "They just wanted to know about any assholes in my life capable of making trouble and you were top of the bloody list. Plus, you're the only other person with a key, so why you were trying to kick my door in, I've no idea."

He looks so taken aback by my raging fury that I realize it's the first time I've ever raised my voice to him. In the scant few months of our pathetic excuse for a relationship, I never shouted at him, never got angry even when he treated me like total crap.

And that realization makes me all the more mad, but it also makes me oh so sad, and the two battle for ascendency as I watch Liam gather himself up and settle himself back into poor-me affronted-outrage mode.

"God, you really are pathetic, Hanna—using all this as an opportunity to get back at me. I gave you that key back, you know I did."

I laugh. "Get back at you? Oh, get over yourself. And you did not give the key back, you bloody liar. Plus, I can assure you that you are *very* far down on the list of people I'm thinking about right now. I wouldn't waste the energy."

"You wasted enough weeping on my doorstep after we broke up. Sitting outside my girlfriend's flat in your car. Did you really think we couldn't see you?"

I take a breath at the contempt in his voice and sink back into a chair. I stare at Liam, this man who made me so miserable, standing there in his band T-shirt, with his scruffy long hair and tattoos, all self-righteous anger. I stare at him and finally realize the power he had over me is nothing to do with him at all. Liam is just the last in a line of overgrown Indie boys I've gone out with in the last decade. Boys and men who, really, are all just poor imitations of Jacob. All I've done since I was twenty, when I began the long climb out of the pit I was in, is go out with versions of my childhood boyfriend and let them treat me like shit. I've let them cheat on me, steal from me, gaslight me, verbally abuse me, hit me...I flinch at the memories of that one. And I've stood there, head bowed, and let them do it because I felt I deserved it.

Because of my guilt. Because Jacob died. Because it's my fault Jacob died. I'm not the "tragic Juliet" from Adam's story. I'm the fucking poison that killed poor Romeo.

Chapter 25

"I'm sorry," I say quietly to Liam and I can see I've wrong-footed him.

I'm not apologizing to him, of course. I'm apologizing to Jacob and once again I'm floored by that terrible mix of guilt and grief that sent me spiraling out of control all those years ago. It's not as raw, but I'll never stop being sorry. Still, I do want to stop punishing myself.

Liam shakes his head. "You're unbelievable, Hanna, you really are. Claire went nuts when the police turned up. But we told them the truth—how you're nothing but a desperate stalker, how you're obsessed and won't leave me alone." He pauses, smooths back his hair. His stupid, studenty, straggly hair that he's ten years too old for. "I told them you probably slashed the tire yourself."

Great. Bloody great. I stand up—he doesn't step back, carries on invading my space so I put my hands on his skinny sparrow chest and shove him away. "Just fuck off, Liam, you stupid shit. Stalker? You have to be kidding me— I do not want to ever see you again. Now give me back my key and *fuck off*." My voice rises to a shout and the living-room door flies open, Adam appearing in the doorway, out of breath with a plastic bag swinging from one hand.

"Are you okay? Your car's outside—you left your door open."

Looking at Adam standing next to Liam, I realize something else. I went out with Liam and all the previous Liams thinking they were all I deserved, thinking they were ghosts of Jacob, but they're not, not really. Not at all. Because yes, Jacob had long hair and tattoos, he was the pierced, scruffy rocker boy of my dad's nightmares, but he wasn't—never was—a loser, a cheater, an abuser. Beyond a bit of teenage drinking, a bit of drug experimentation, Jacob was *nice*. He was a nice boy.

He was more like Adam than Liam, and maybe that's why I've always run so far from the nice boys. Because I destroy nice boys.

"Did you follow me?" I say to Adam.

"I'd borrowed Seb's car to find you. And I wanted to make sure you got back to theirs safely," he says. "But then you drove the wrong way. I got caught by a red light, but I took a guess you were coming here and then when I got here and saw your car..."

I stare at Adam, who is doing a perfect impression of the nicest of nice boys. But is it real?

"And who the fuck is this?"

Oh, yes. Liam. I'd forgotten he was here for a second.

"Oh, I'm sorry, where are my manners?" I say, as if we were at a dinner party, rather than standing in my destroyed living room with the man who was just trying to kick my door in. "Adam, this is Liam. I caught him kicking my door in, hence the car abandoned in the street with the door open. Liam, I'm embarrassed to say, is my ex."

Adam raises his eyebrows and answers in the same calm, polite tone. "Ah. I see your relationship history is as flawed as mine."

He turns to Liam. "I think maybe you should leave before

I call the police. Unless…" He looks back at me. "Unless you think he has something to do with what's going on? In which case, I can make him stay until the police get here."

Liam lets out a short, ugly laugh. "Yeah? Like to see you try, mate." He steps up to Adam.

Adam stays calm. He doesn't back down or step back and I realize that Liam might look more intimidating with his tattoos and clenched fists, but Adam is taller and bigger with a zero-fucks-given look on his face. And in his dark hoodie and total calmness, he comes across as far more of a threat. Liam has no idea who he is, and I can see him hesitating, assessing. Adam doesn't give an inch, just continues to stare at Liam, and it's Liam in the end who backs down.

This Adam—the one standing there, facing down Liam—he could scare a family into a midnight flit.

I sigh and turn to Liam. "Don't be a twat, Liam. I know it's difficult as it's your default setting, but I'm betting Adam could kick your ass, so back the hell down and shut the hell up." I look at Adam again. "He's a dick, Adam, but I don't think he's a murderer or a kidnapper, and he hasn't got the brains to hack a website."

"Stay out of my life, Hanna," Liam says to me without taking his eyes off Adam. "Anymore visits from the police and I'll make sure that dirty little secret you confessed to me becomes public knowledge. Bet you haven't told your new boyfriend about that, have you?"

Adam takes one step closer to Liam. "If you come here again, or contact Hanna again, I will call the police. Or I could take on Hanna's bet and try kicking your ass. It's not my usual area of expertise, but I'm always willing to learn new skills."

I laugh out loud. Can't help it. Despite the awfulness of

everything, I laugh with joy at the sheer ridiculousness of Adam, this screwed-up liar, this *nice* man, fronting up to Liam the loser. I don't want to be his tragic Juliet or the poison; I want a whole new story with him, one with a happy ending.

And as Liam backs off, a tiny voice in my head, a new voice I've never heard before, says, *Maybe you can have that.*

But...

"Well," Adam says after the front door has slammed, "I'm glad to see your taste in men has greatly improved."

My laughter fades. I could smile at him now. I could smile at him and believe he's had nothing to do with any of this. I could believe Dee and Seb when they say he's one of the good guys.

But...

"You said you're not a hacker, or a stalker, or a murderer," I say. "Then who is doing this? Who else would know to use *your* website to get to *me*?"

He opens his mouth to answer, then closes it.

He doesn't have an answer.

Chapter 26

SASHA—December, two months earlier

My phone buzzing wakes me up. My head is throbbing, and my eyes still feel swollen and sore from crying myself to sleep. I sit up, fumbling inside the pillowcase where I've hidden the phone, freaking out at the thought that it'll keep buzzing and Dad will wake up and hear. I can't believe I forgot to turn it off. It's two in the morning. Who on earth is texting at two in the morning?

Hanna. It's got to be—she must have deliberately waited to make sure it was safe and—I open the message and it's from Ethan. There's nothing at all from Hanna.

have you got five mins? found something out about your FB messages.

I frown. *what??!*

too much to say on text. meet me?

now??? I look at the time again. Yep. Still two in the morning.

am outside the main gates. borrowed owens van

I get up and am halfway through pulling my trousers on when I stop. Am I insane? If Dad catches me, I am dead. If he catches me sneaking out to meet an ex-crim, carrying a forbidden phone, I am *beyond* dead.

So, don't get caught, a little voice whispers. The rest

of my mind is still shrieking alarm, but I carry on getting dressed. After all, the little devil voice is still whispering, *everyone* has been lying to me my entire life. Why should I care? Because *Dad*'s having a tough time?

Despite the security lights and the locks on the gates, it's not actually that hard to sneak out of the holiday park. Repairs that used to be done regularly have been let go since they announced they were closing the place. It was Ethan who pointed out the hole in the fence where several rotting boards have basically disintegrated. So long as I stay close to the hedges lining the entrance road, I should avoid setting off the security light.

The adrenaline rush as I make it out of the house without getting caught is like, wow...Is this how Hanna used to feel when she did it? It's not fear anymore, although I can feel it bubbling way below the surface. My mouth is dry, my heart is racing, I can hear my breath, fast and harsh as I sidle along next to the hedges. No, it's not fear, it's a buzz, it's...excitement. I want to laugh and cheer and whoop and dance around—look at me, badass Sasha Carter, sneaking out at two in the morning. I don't even need to be going anywhere—no party would give me the buzz I'm feeling right now.

Not that I'm really that much of a badass. I got the phone out to text Hanna after I spoke to Mum. I was going to tell her I knew...but I couldn't send it. I'm not sure I could bear it if she ignored that text as well.

Squeezing through the gap in the fence dampens the buzz a little—the rotting edges of the boards pull at my clothes and water drips down my neck from the trees. It's not a triumphant escape—I basically fall through and land on my hands and knees—but I make it through.

The van is parked fifty feet away, engine running but with the lights off. I walk slowly, and even though I know it's only Ethan in the van, I dip to check through the window before I open the passenger door.

"You made it—you escaped," he says, smiling as I get in.

I smile back, a hint of that reckless buzz, that pride back again. "I sure did. It was easy." I'm actually glad it's so dark in the van, so he can't see the mud all over my hands and knees.

"Shall we go for a ride? Get a bit farther away from the camp before we talk?"

My courage falters. It's one thing to escape, but I thought we'd have a chat and then I'd sneak back in and be back in bed within half an hour. Go for a drive?

"Come on," Ethan says. "You're more likely to get caught if we stay here—we won't go far."

Okay, now the fear level has risen, and the excitement has taken a dip. But he's right, if Dad were to wake up and look out, he might see Ethan's van parked here. Unlikely, with the lights off, but possible.

"Okay," I say. "But I can't be long. I can't go far."

"Trust me," Ethan says.

He drives down to the beach and pulls up in the car park, facing the sea. It's weird. I don't think I've ever been here at night before, certainly not this late when we are literally the only ones here. I can't see the water, there's not enough moon, so it's just empty blackness in front of the van after Ethan switches the engine and lights off, but I can hear it, the whoosh and drag of waves hitting the shore and sliding back.

I should probably be scared. Sitting in darkness in a van with a man who's just got out of prison at two in the morning. No one knows where I am. No one knows who I'm with. I could disappear and I would become one of those notorious unsolved mysteries.

Straight-A Student Vanishes In The Night.

Mum would cry at the press conference, pleading with me to come home; Dad would be all stiff upper lip. All the old stories about Hanna would come out again, but they'd never find a trace—I'd just have disappeared.

But it doesn't scare me. I mean, obviously, I don't want to disappear in a murdered-by-a-psychopath, left-in-a-shallow-grave way. I don't want Ethan to suddenly produce an ax.

But just to disappear. Leave it all behind. Start again somewhere else. *Be* someone else. Like Hanna did. She wasn't that much older than me when she left. I mean, obviously, I finally know *why* now. She had a baby she didn't want. She had me.

But I wouldn't be leaving behind a mess like she did, and I wouldn't do it like her. I wouldn't cut all ties. In fact, in reality, appealing though it might be, I wouldn't do it at all, would I? Because I care about my family. Even Dad when he's at his strictest and grumpiest. And Mum...what's she done wrong other than love me so much she couldn't bear for me to go to strangers? I wouldn't want to put them through that. And that's not a bad thing at all. Being the good girl is okay.

"I can't be long," I say to Ethan again.

"Neither can I," Ethan says. "I didn't exactly tell Owen I was borrowing his van." He stops and laughs. "I don't exactly still have a license."

I stare at him. "But...if you get caught...you could lose your job, for a start."

"Don't worry. We won't. It's not the first time I've borrowed it. I think he knows and turns a blind eye. Plus,

Owen thinks it's funny you and I have become friends." He glances at me. "I think he's hoping your dad will find out so he can watch the show."

See, there's all that hate toward my dad again. I think about asking Ethan about it—he might know if Owen and Hanna were ever...But what if it's true? What if creepy, permanently angry Owen King is actually my dad? I shudder at the thought. I can't ask.

"You shouldn't have taken the risk. Not for me."

He shakes his head. "You're a funny kid, Sasha. You're worrying about *me*?"

I shrug. "Well, if *I* get caught, I'll get grounded forever, but if *you* get caught—you could end up back in prison." He's frowning at me. "What?" I ask.

"I'm not used to having anyone worry about me, that's all. People always want something in return. Owen gave me a job, sure, but it's just another debt that needs to be repaid."

The silence gets awkward and I shift in my seat, wondering if he's going to say anything or if I should just ask him to drive me back. But when he does start talking, I kind of wish he'd stayed silent.

"So, I don't have a name, not yet," Ethan says. "But I found out the first message came from a computer in Cardiff, the others from a phone. I should be able to get the number soon. We know whoever it is knows you and where you go to school. Do you know anyone who lives in Cardiff?"

"No, everyone I know from school is local. Only..."

"What?"

"Only Hanna. She's the only person I know who lives in Cardiff."

There's a pause.

"And she knows where you go to school? She's probably

213

Vanessa Savage

even seen those pajamas that message mentioned. It might not have been a creepy webcam spying thing."

I shake my head. "No, it can't be her. That doesn't make any sense. Why would she *do* that? Why would she send such horrible anonymous messages?"

"Didn't you say the fake photo you used was of her?"

Oh God.

"Maybe she saw it, got angry, I don't know."

I knew it was stupid to use that photo. It wasn't my photo to use. Yes, Hanna left them behind, but they were hers. Private. Personal. And oh God, half of the "friends" fake Jules made were people who know Hanna. Even if Hanna's not on social media, Dee or someone could have told her and…But why would she send those messages? I say this again to Ethan and he sighs.

"Maybe it's some weird misguided way of warning you off?"

"But why do it anonymously? And she's got my number now, why not text me?"

He shrugs. "I don't know. But those first messages came before you had a phone. Listen, it might not be her at all. But give me her number and I'll cross-check. I'll find out for sure if it's her phone sending those messages."

214

Chapter 27

HANNA—Sunday 11 p.m.

I get back to Dee's with tears on my cheeks and three plastic bags full of junk food. Dee takes one look at me, then steers me into the living room, depositing me on the sofa with a melting tub of Ben & Jerry's and a spoon. There's no sign of Seb and I presume he's already gone to bed. She curls up next to me and puts her arm around my shoulder and I let her, because Christ knows, I need that comfort. I lean my head against her and close my eyes.

"What happened?" she asks. "Did Adam find you? Look, I'm sorry I told him where you were going, but..."

I shake my head and open my eyes, moving away from her to dig into the ice cream. "It's fine. It doesn't matter."

"It's clearly not fine," she says. "You sound angry."

I clench my teeth and drop the spoon on the coffee table. "It occurred to me...As my evening was getting worse and worse, it occurred to me to wonder if you knew: if you knew about Adam and his bloody website and the fact that my history with Jacob is what gave him the idea in the first place. Because Seb thought it was a good story to tell." My voice rises as I speak. I can't look at her.

"I didn't know," she says. "Until yesterday. Seb told me last night. Hanna, I promise, if I'd known, I would have told you. I might still have tried to set you up, but I would have told you."

I believe her. But the sting is still there, stuck under my skin and festering, because Seb told her last night and she didn't say anything. It's not that I think she was deliberately holding back, but I think she was waiting until *she* judged me ready to hear it. She thinks she's protecting me, I know that, but it still hurts. She stares at me, and I can't help but relent. This is Dee. I can't be mad at Dee.

"It's not just to do with Adam," I say. "Well, not entirely. I ran into Liam. He was an idiot. As usual. And it was just...too much. On top of everything that's happened."

"Okay. I get it. Do you want to talk about it? While we eat all the ice cream?"

I shake my head again, but this time with a smile. "No, really. The ice cream is enough. I do not want to waste a second of my time talking about Liam."

"Or Adam?"

"I think...I'm sorry, Dee. I know you and Seb trust him, but I just can't get past the knowledge that all of this has blown up since he came into my life. I know you're hoping for some kind of happy-ever-after for me, but I don't think it's going to be with him."

She sighs but nods. "Okay. Okay...I'll back off on that one." She grabs the spoon and pinches some ice cream before getting up. "I'm just going to put the frozen stuff away. You stay here.

"Listen, I've been thinking," Dee calls from the kitchen where she's stowing away the shopping. "Someone's got to know why your family left Littledean in such a hurry...if in some way it's related to what's happening. Other than Stephen bloody Hayes and Jacob's old friends. One of your stepmum's church friends, or someone from Sasha's school..."

"But they wouldn't tell me, would they? Thanks to Stephen Hayes, everyone in that bloody village knows who I am and that I'm bad news. And they're not going to speak to the police... Well, nosy sods like Mrs. Thorpe might, but she doesn't know anything. Anyone who does know something—"

"They might speak to me..." She comes into the room, her eyebrows raised, looking the epitome of goodness and respectability. Jen's church friends used to love Dee. They'd eye me with suspicion while at the same time beaming with approval at Dee. Yeah, she's right—even the kids from Sasha's school might speak to Dee. She has the schoolteacher vibe going on—one of the nice teachers that kids actually like.

"So, what are you suggesting?"

"We both pull sickies from work and we go back. Tomorrow. Without Adam, just me and you. Try again."

"You'd do that? For me?"

Dee laughs. "It's not exactly walking into a burning house, Han—it's being nosy in our old town. I think I can manage."

Monday 1 p.m.

"This is the third time I've been back here in three days," I say as Dee steers the car into the station car park. "That's more than I visited in the last two years my family was actually living here."

"I hear you—you're not the only one who was happy to leave this place behind." She fake shudders. "Well, let's make it third time lucky, then: the visit where we actually find out something of use and then never have to come back again."

217

I smile. "Oh, yes please. Let's do this thing."

"Right," says Dee, unplugging her seat belt and opening the car door. "You lurk here for a bit. I'll start in the café, with some loud questions to see if I get a bite. I'll save the church as a last resort—churchy types are more likely to close ranks, save the gossip for themselves."

She pokes her head back in the car before she leaves. "I'll text you if I find out anything. You can come in and be bad cop."

I close my eyes as soon as she leaves, hunching down in the passenger seat. Easier to pretend to be asleep than risk getting recognized by someone parking up to get the train or do their shopping in the precinct.

I think I do actually doze off, because it seems like only seconds before I'm jerked awake by my phone buzzing in my lap. I rub my eyes and glance down at the screen. Yeah, I definitely fell asleep because I've apparently been here half an hour and managed to miss six texts from Dee:

Scoping out greggs
No luck but got us steak bakes
And a latte
Trying the café
Nice cakes and full of teens and nosy looking types
Bingo! Get over here

I grin as I tap out a quick text reply and get out of the car. I jog across the road, skirting around Greggs and down past the Spar to the café that's been here forever. Dee's waiting outside with two girls who could be Sasha's age, or could be twenty-five. One of them is blonde, the other brunette, but other than that, they could be twins with their matching layers of makeup, thick, dark eyebrows, and straightened-to-within-an-inch-of-its-life hair. They're also both in matchy-

matchy clothes and it's like a teen uniform: ripped jeans, white trainers, tiny crop tops, and little puffy jackets.

It was a different teen uniform in my day, but the snotty look on their faces is the same as it ever was, as they take in my sad old-lady skinny jeans and crumpled still-half-asleep makeup-free face. Urgh—they're cool girls. I hate cool girls.

"Han, this is Seren and Carly. They used to go to school with Sasha."

One of them—Seren, the blonde one—looks me up and down, attention snagging on the tattoo on my wrist and my admittedly rather wildly tangled hair.

"You're Sasha Carter's sister?"

"That's right. And I'm a bit worried about her—I haven't been able to get hold of her and they left town so suddenly..."

The girls smirk at each other and I clench my fists at my side.

"Yeah, you might want to have a word with her boyfriend about that," Seren says.

"Boyfriend?"

"Older man—like, way older. Like your age older."

Oh, right. Ancient, then.

"And very dodgy," the other one chimes in.

I bite my lip. Sasha? It doesn't sound right. Sasha was the perfect daughter I never was. Perfect grades, perfect behavior. But then...aren't I living proof of how there's only so long you can suppress and repress someone before they rebel?

Here's another bucket load of guilt to add to my collection. I saw, particularly with Jen, love for Sasha. I believed, with her to counteract Dad's strictness, that Sasha was better off than I ever was, that Jen had mellowed Dad, that with Jen there, Dad would be so different with Sasha to how he was with me. I let Jen convince me of that—she even managed to persuade him to keep my choice of name, to keep her as Sasha when he wanted something more traditional and Welsh. Was I wrong? Was that just what I wanted to see so I could go off on my merry way assuming all was fine?

But Sasha with a way older, very dodgy *boyfriend*?

"Yeah—we saw them together," Seren says, and the smirk has given way to relishing-in-the-gossip full-on glee as she watches my reaction. "We were in the café a few days before Christmas and we saw him first. He came in and got coffees and started talking to Mrs. Brown—she's a teacher at my little sister's school—then he went outside, and along came Sasha."

Mrs. Brown? Oh—*oh*. That's Carrie, isn't it? Mrs. Brown now that she's married to Lee. A teaching assistant at the primary...I feel sick. It's Owen King, isn't it? It's got to be. But boyfriend? No, no, no.

Or...what if it was Adam they saw Sasha with? I think of him last night, facing up to Liam—a stranger in town would look *very dodgy* to these girls, wouldn't he?

But no. Adam was there when I spoke to Carrie. She would have said something if she recognized him...But. She *was* trying to say something to me, wasn't she? Before Stephen turned up?

Dee must be wondering the same, because she gets out her phone, scrolls through her photos until she finds one with Adam in it. But both the girls shake their heads when she asks if they recognize him.

"Nah, it's not him. I didn't put it together at first, but then we figured out who it was, didn't we, Ser?" Carly says. "It was the crim who was working up at the holiday park."

The blonde seems to find this hilarious as the brunette keeps talking.

"Yeah—not only was Sasha Carter shagging the gardener, he was an ex-con."

"What? Sasha and someone from prison?" I shake my head and actually laugh. Okay, at a push, I could picture Sasha talking to Owen or Adam, especially if they said they were friends of mine, but some stranger, an ex-offender? "No. No way—there is no way."

"I agree," Dee says, giving the sniggering girls one of her best cold looks. "I think this really is just gossip. But if the rumors were nasty enough, would it have been enough for your dad to have rushed them out of town?"

I frown. "Yes. Of course it would. Any hint, however outrageous, that Sasha was going off the rails like I did—"

"Hey, it's not just gossip," Seren interrupts, sounding all offended. "We saw them together. Draped all over each other. It's obvious they were together." She pauses. "That's what I told my mum, anyway." She folds her arms. "It's not my fault Mum decided to warn your dad..."

"You did that?" I say.

"Yeah, well—it was her fault my party got canceled, wasn't it? She attacked me in class, and I got the blame." She pushes her hair out of her face. "And it was for her own good, right? He's a psycho. He shoved me and threatened Carly."

"Yeah. Her new criminal old man boyfriend is obviously a bad influence," Carly says. "She was getting as violent as him."

They've both gone all hunched-shoulder, arms-folded defensive. And much as I'd like to have a go at them—God, these little bitches—I do not need to get myself arrested by Stephen bloody Hayes for fighting with two fifteen-year-olds, so I let Dee drag me away, back toward the car.

"Well," she says as we get back in the car, "at least we

know it's not Adam. He's definitely not been in prison or ever worked as a gardener."

"It can't be true," I mutter, as Dee hands me a lukewarm coffee and a steak bake in a paper bag.

"There must have been something, though, to fuel the rumors?"

My shoulders stiffen. "What—you seriously think Sasha is going out with someone from prison? And attacking other kids in school?"

"I'm not saying there's anything in it—but they must have been seen together or something? I don't think those girls were completely lying."

I shake my head again. "No. Not Sasha."

"We should tell DC Norton anyway," Dee says. "He'll be able to find out who was working at the holiday camp." She pauses. "Find out what they were in prison for."

She's thinking of those murdered women.

"Look—Sasha would never do that. She is not like me, not at all and—"

Dee turns her head to look at me. "That's not what I'm saying. I'm considering the possibility that if Sasha was seen with a prisoner, an ex-offender, whatever he is, she might not have been with him willingly."

I suck in a breath and hold it. No. No. If someone had... done something to Sasha, Dad would have gone to the police. He would have...Or would he? The scandal caused by his actions when I was barely older than Sasha...would he exercise more caution this time? Even if this time the crime was real? Surely he wouldn't risk doing to someone else what he once did to Jacob?

Chapter 28

Sasha—December, two months earlier

I sleep in on the first Saturday after the end of term, coming downstairs around ten. Mum has been busy—instead of decorating for Christmas, she's been packing everything up ready for our move in the New Year. We've never been a mad-about-Christmas family, more conventional and understated, but it's still strange to see empty shelves and gaps on walls rather than fairy lights and garlands on the nineteenth of December.

But I get a bigger shock when I walk into the kitchen in my flowery pajama trousers and baggy jumper, hair all over the place, to find Owen and Ethan sitting at the kitchen table across from Dad.

My first thought is panic. Ethan has come to tell! Owen must have found out that Ethan took his van. He's going to tell Dad about the phone, the Facebook messages, me sneaking out...I try to backtrack without Dad spotting me, but Ethan's face must have given me away because Dad turns and frowns when he sees me.

"Sasha, please go and get dressed."

"Sorry," I mutter, turning away with my face burning. Owen's grinning at me. He must have seen the panic on my face. I hate him so much. I look away, stupidly terrified

223

that I'll see something familiar in that annoying grin of his.

I pause in the hallway, wanting to hear what they're saying before I go back upstairs. Just to check neither of them is going to drop me in it. Just to check Owen isn't going to announce he's my dad and demand I go and live with him in his flat on the dodgy estate.

And also, because I haven't seen Ethan since that night in his van. He and Owen have hardly been here, and never when I'm in a position to sneak out to find him.

"I need you to repair the perimeter fence before your contract ends," I hear Dad say.

Shit. I cover my mouth like I said the word out loud.

"Security will be paramount when the premises are empty," Dad continues. "So I'd like you to make that a priority."

I wait, breath held, for Owen or Ethan's response.

"Sure. I'll check out what needs doing today, and Ethan will get it sorted for you," Owen says. There's a pause. "But I'll need supplies to fix it if there's nothing in the shed. I'll check it out today and drop a list in of what's needed, if that's okay? If you approve it, I'll pick up what we need over the weekend."

Ethan joins in then. "We can get the fence fixed Monday, so it's done before Christmas."

Is it my imagination or did Ethan say that last bit louder than the rest? I feel that surge of adrenaline rising again. Tonight, then. A last chance to sneak out, before the fence is fixed, before we leave here for good.

Sneaking out has become too easy. I have to force myself to stay cautious as I tiptoe down the stairs at a few minutes past two. I try not to think about the fact this is the last time I'll do it. I try to feel as casual about it as I did about my last day at school, when the teachers were the only ones to bother saying goodbye and to wish me good luck in my new school. Even Emma seemed to have forgotten. She came over to me at lunchtime and I thought she was going to say something. I even reached into my bag, ready to mention my secret phone and give her my number. But she just asked something about the English lesson we had that afternoon, then wandered back to her friends' table.

But it's difficult to stay casual with the realization—the acknowledgment—that Ethan, a twenty-six-year-old ex-prisoner, is my only friend.

He's waiting in a different car this time, a black one that's basically invisible under the trees. Much more stealth than Owen's white van. I don't ask if he has permission to "borrow" these cars. I don't think he'd be stupid enough to risk going back to prison, so I'm pretty sure he's not stealing them. And I tell myself he was joking about not actually having a driver's license.

He doesn't smile when I get in the car. Neither does he start the engine. And even though we're not *seeing* each other like that, not at all, it feels like he's about to break up with me.

"What's wrong? No one's found out, have they? About you meeting me?"

"It's not that." He sighs. "Look, I'm sorry, Sash, but I got the number of the person who's been sending you those messages."

I look down. My shoes are leaving mud in his friend's car. "It's Hanna, isn't it?"

"I'm sorry," he says again.

"I figured it had to be. She still hasn't texted me. I know that Mum and Dad have both tried to get hold of her as well and she hasn't returned their calls either. She doesn't even know we're moving."

"I'm sure one of your parents will have left her a message…"

I shake my head. "Dad said not to tell her and Mum would *never* go against his wishes. But this—I know she's got her issues with Dad, but I just don't get it…Why would she be so cruel to *me*? She *knows* what Dad's like, she *knows* how scared I would have been at the thought of him finding out."

"Maybe she's not the person you thought she was. She left you, didn't she? Went happily off to live her own life. What if she thinks it's funny? She catches you using her old photo and thinks it's a big joke to scare you like that."

His words are like needles under the skin. Especially now that I know she's my birth mother. "She wouldn't…"

"How do you know? She left when you were a kid, and she hasn't bothered spending any time with you since. She could actually be the total bitch she's rumored to be." He glances across at me. "What if your dad's the one in the right here? You told me she got into trouble, that she was forced to leave. What if she caused all that trouble herself?" He shrugs. "Your dad might be right to try cutting her out of your lives and keeping the move quiet."

I wouldn't know. Not for sure. Because no one ever told me why she really left. I was told she went off the rails, that she was a troublemaker. I know she had a reputation as a hellraiser, that she—how did Dad phrase it?—*brought the police and shame to his door more than once*—but the details? No one ever told me. Only the rumors, which were awful, which I chose to believe *were* only rumors.

But now...Did she only leave because of me? Give birth and then just walk away? What if Mum's sugarcoating it and actually, she didn't have to beg to keep me, because Hanna didn't care? Perhaps everything that was said about her was true and the sister I've alternated between resenting and hero-worshipping is just a total bitch who doesn't care one bit about me. Mr. Garner said she was a lovely girl, but he used to be a vicar, trained to see the good in people when sometimes there isn't any.

Now I just feel stupid for texting her. Now I just feel stupid for thinking one day, when I'm older, I'd be able to go and stay with her, maybe go and live with her and get to know her properly.

"I asked Owen. When I found out who was doing this to you. He told me he did used to know her, and he totally believed she would do something like that," Ethan says. "He said she was trouble, that she ruined more than one life when she was a teenager."

The ball of hurt that has formed a lump in my throat hardens to anger and I swallow it down, let it sit and fester in my gut. God, I really am stupid.

"I hate her." I say the words quietly but fiercely. "She's a *bitch*. She's worse than all the girls in school because she's meant to be *family*."

Ethan sighs again. "Go back now. Sleep on it. She probably won't do anything more now that she's had her fun. I'll talk to you again on Monday, okay? We'll sort something out before you leave."

*

Anger powers my walk back to the house, not even all anger at Hanna, but fury at my own stupidity forever thinking she might actually care. I'm so full of rage that I don't even notice there's a light on in the house until it's too late—I've already opened the front door and walked in.

Dad is waiting for me in the hall.

Oh God. Anger and fear do not mix well. I could probably write a whole chemistry essay on that really bad, explosive mix, right before I vomit all over my dad.

He doesn't look angry. He doesn't look anything. Doesn't stop me physically shaking in front of him. I have nothing, no possible excuse as to why I was out of the house at two in the morning. At least I'm not pulling a Hanna; at least I'm not coming back from a party drunk and stinking of smoke. Although that would probably be better than the truth: that I was sitting in a potentially stolen car with an ex-criminal twelve years older than me. I can't tell the truth. Ethan would be in way more trouble than me if Dad finds out. He'll make sure he's sent back to prison.

But oh, Christ—I have my forbidden phone in my pocket. If Ethan texts me now, if Dad somehow has X-ray vision and can see it in my pocket . . . I am so dead.

"Where were you?"

He says is so softly and that makes me shake more than if he'd screamed it in my face.

"I couldn't sleep."

"Where were you?" he asks again.

"Nowhere, I swear. I couldn't sleep so I went out for a walk, that's all. I haven't been anywhere."

"Liar."

"I'm *not* lying." The fear retreats a little and the anger surges like a snappy dog. "Where do you think I would have been? I don't have a group of friends to sneak off with. I don't *have* any friends—does that make you happy? I'm not Hanna, I'm nothing like Hanna—when will you stop expecting me to turn out like her?"

He shakes his head and the disgust on his face is like a punch to the gut. "You stand there at two in the morning when I've just caught you coming home, and you ask me that question?"

He turns to walk away, and I know my punishment is going to be this. Disappointment and heavy silence. He doesn't need to ground me as I don't go anywhere. He can't take anything away from me because I don't have anything. But that silence will grow. It'll fill the house over Christmas. It will become overwhelming and suffocating and by Boxing Day I'll be crying and begging for forgiveness. I know; I've been here before for far smaller crimes.

This is Hanna's fault.

I'm breaking every single rule by standing at the front fence talking to Ethan while he fixes new boards to cover the hole. Mum and Dad have gone to do the Christmas food shopping. Not being allowed to go with them is part of my punishment—the Christmas food shopping has always been one of my favorite traditions. God knows what Dad would do if he caught me out of the house again, but at least here, if I hear a car coming up the road, I can race back inside.

"I'm sorry you got caught, Sash—fucking nightmare getting punished this close to Christmas."

"It's okay. It's not your fault—it's Hanna's. She's the reason I was out talking to you." I want to tell him. About all of it. But the words won't come out. I'm afraid I might cry if I start talking about it. It's all just so awful at the moment—even Mum is barely speaking to Dad and she looks so miserable. That's probably my fault. I heard them—not arguing exactly—but there was a definite edge to their words. I don't know for sure what it was about, but it must have been about this, about me sneaking out and getting caught.

"Your dad won't have to worry about that anymore once I've finished this," he says, hauling another board into place.

"No. And today's your last day and in two weeks we'll be gone." I tuck my hands under my armpits, wishing I'd worn gloves.

"You can always call or text me."

"It won't be the same when I'm the other end of the country."

"Maybe I'll take a trip to West Wales in the New Year. Once you're settled."

The thought of the bleakness of the January ahead—in a new town, a new school, no friends, Dad still not speaking to me—is overwhelming.

"It's not fair." The words burst out of me. "If Hanna hadn't done all this, we could still have had a couple more weeks of meeting up. Over Christmas, at least."

Ethan puts his hammer down and looks at me. "Well, you'll just have to get revenge, won't you?"

He says it lightly, but I don't know if he's joking or not. I turn my head—was that a car engine? No, just the wind through the trees. It's a gray, cold day, the wind icy and bitter. I should be in the supermarket, filling the trolley with chocolate and nuts and choosing a turkey, not freezing my head off, with numb fingers and toes.

"And how do you suggest I do that when I'm not allowed to even leave the house?"

Ethan glances at me and grins. "Give me her address—tell

me where she works, where she hangs out. I'll arrange for a few anonymous messages of my own. See if we can scare her like she scared you."

The wind seems to get colder. "I'm not sure I want to..."

"Don't worry—I'm not planning anything nasty," Ethan says. "Just a little warning." He pauses. "Not even a warning, really. More just letting her know that you know what she's up to."

I sigh. "I don't know. I still don't see how it can be her."

"But can you say for sure there aren't people living around here who are still in touch with her?"

"What—*spying* on me?" It sounds ridiculous.

He shrugs. "I dunno. I'm just thinking aloud. Someone sent those messages, didn't they?"

"I could just send her a message, tell her I know what she did. Or you could send the message for me."

"I'd rather not use my phone for that. An anonymous letter would be less traceable."

It doesn't sit right with me, but when I really do hear a car engine and have to run full pelt back to the house, the anger comes back. Because of Hanna, I can't even leave my own *house*. I take off my boots and coat and run upstairs. As I sit at my desk, getting my breath back, I send a text to Ethan with Hanna's address and where she works. Sod her. She *deserves* to feel a bit of what I'm feeling.

Chapter 29

Western Vale News

A Dark House for a Dark Tourist
article by Adam Webster

There's always a sadness about an abandoned house, knowing it was once a home, even without knowing who lived there and why it was abandoned.

But when you do know the history, when you know the tragic Romeo and Juliet story that led to a home being abandoned, when you feel you know the people involved...

HANNA—Monday 6 p.m.

I ask Dee to drop me at Adam's. I've left messages for DC Norton about everything we learned from those girls. It could well be gossip, exaggeration, or bitchy lies, but if it's true...I sigh. I still can't believe Sasha would ever do something so out of character and I worry I'm sending the police off chasing village gossip like it's a lead, and by doing that, something else will get missed. But Dee's right. The timing—the rumors, my family's sudden move, their disappearance—it's too much to be a coincidence.

But Adam...he might be able to fill in the missing puzzle pieces. If, through his website, or elsewhere, it turns out he knows someone who used to be in prison...I press the buzzer for his flat and wait for an answer. I didn't phone in advance. Maybe I should have asked Dee to wait until I found out if he was in...

But then the door buzzes and I'm in, and when I get to his floor, Adam is waiting at his door, and I see him visibly tense as I walk toward him.

"Hanna. This is a..."

"Surprise? Yeah. Well, I have a question for you."

He moves aside, beckons me into his flat. "Of course. Anything. You know I'll do anything I can to help. Come in."

He offers me tea and I follow him into his kitchen. It's actually easier to ask my questions when he has his back to me.

"Do you know anyone who used to be in prison?"

He freezes, milk carton in hand. "What?"

"Dee and I went back to Littledean. It seems Sasha was seen hanging around with an ex-offender. Someone who was working at the holiday park."

Adam turns to look at me, shaking his head. "No, I swear. I don't know anyone who's ever been in trouble with the police."

I think of our ride in the police car, all the time we've spent in police stations in the last few days, and I want to laugh. Look at me, so suspicious of Adam, when it's me with the troubled past, me who's somehow dragged him into all this mess because of my family.

And, I suppose, if anything good has come out of that visit to Littledean—I know it's not Adam who forced my family out of town. I let myself look at him, really look at him, and I can't believe he's that good an actor, that he's hiding something dodgy. It's a relief to let the suspicion go, to choose to believe Dee and Seb; to believe, once and for all, that Adam is one of the good guys. That whatever is going on, he's an innocent victim or unwitting pawn.

He hands me a mug of tea and we take it through to his living room, settling onto the sofa together. It's not exactly cozy and comfortable, but it's not horribly tense and awkward anymore, either. From the outside, it probably looks completely normal.

Although I wouldn't be doing any of this if things were normal. I've only known Adam a few days; we should be a long way off from cozy nights in on the sofa. And to be honest, if things were normal, I wouldn't be here at all, I'd be with another Jacob imitation, letting him treat me like shit, still caught in that never-ending self-destructive spiral.

I decide, after a few minutes of not quite comfortable silence, to go straight for the jugular and destroy the pretend normal. "I'm guessing you'd like to know how I ended up as that *tragic Juliet*?"

Adam shrugs. "Only if you want to tell me. It's none of my business, really, is it?"

"But you are curious."

"Of course. Not because of that stupid article I wrote a million years ago, but because I want to get to know you."

"So how much do you already know?" I ask, without looking at him. "From your story, your little visit to my home town."

There's a long pause, but I resist the urge to look over.

"I know you had an older boyfriend. I know he died, and that his parents also died."

"Jacob. His name was Jacob." I pause. "And when you visited Littledean—did everyone you spoke to tell you it was my fault? That I lied to the police and got him arrested, that I caused his death?"

He doesn't answer and I nod. "Of course they did." I answer my own question.

"Well, I don't believe that for a second," he says. "You were a kid, I know that much—how the hell was it supposed to be your fault?" He shakes his head. "That's what I wrote, in my article. It was about how a town ganged up on a . . . a *child*. Because that's what you were."

"You might have written it differently if you'd known me back then."

"I don't think so. Your mum had died and then—"

"Then what?" I interrupt. "You think I went off the rails because my mum died, because Dad was ridiculously strict then brought a new wife into my life?"

"That's not what happened?" he asks.

"No. Because my mum buggered off and left us years before she died. My parents were the quintessential odd couple. He was studying for his Ph.D., and he took a part-time bar job at the holiday park to fund it. Mum was one of the entertainers who worked there regularly. She was a singer, not an especially good one, but good enough for local gigs. It was the usual clichéd opposites-attract romance that should have fizzled out over a summer, but of course she got pregnant with me. They married, were miserable. Mum couldn't travel to sing anymore; Dad got his qualification but wasn't ever good enough to get a decent paid academic post, so he ended up working full time at the holiday park, worked his way up—or sideways, whatever—ending up as a manager/caretaker for a crappy, second-rate holiday park. So far, so predictable, right?"

Adam leans forward to put his empty mug down on the table.

"So, they trundled along, she got bored and just upped

and left one day. Didn't take me with her because she wanted to keep working the entertainment circuit and I barely saw her. She died in a car accident a couple of years later. And honestly? I was sad, of course I was, but she wasn't really in our lives. I did my grieving when she left, so I'd run out of tears by the time she died."

"So, you didn't go all Hulk-smash out of grief?"

"I think...she left when I was ten and died just as I was starting secondary school, which was a bad time. I acted out a bit. I was grieving and sore as well as feeling rejected and unloved. I kind of acted out enough to get a reputation as a bit of a troublemaker. I wasn't *bad* then, more loud and disruptive in class, pretending I was bored, not bothering with homework. It got me attention and I liked that."

It still hurts looking back. Yes, the other kids at school loved it and egged me on when I disrupted lessons, but the teachers would give me the same I'm-so-disappointed-you've-let-me-down vibe as Dad, so I built this horrible don't-give-a-shit shell that was only ever the most fragile of shells and felt rejected over and over again when no one bothered to try to break it.

Except Reverend Garner. I'd long since stopped going to Sunday school and church kids' clubs, but Jen encouraged Dad to send me to his troubled teens group when she moved in. At first I saw it as another punishment. Then, for a while, it really helped because Reverend Garner actually *listened*. But I was a teenager and partying became my priority—he was fighting a losing battle then.

"Dad was just...I think he looked at me and saw her. He always expected me to be as flaky as her, so he was over-the-top strict, always disapproving, always expecting the worst of me. He'd say nothing if I did well at school, but go nuts if I did badly. So I just gave up on trying to impress him and started doing exactly what he'd expected of me all along." I stop and sigh. "Maybe that's all it ever would have been—a mini rebellion, I don't know. Problem was, a couple of years after she died, I found out my mum didn't leave because she was bored. Turns out, she left because my dad had an affair. My holier-than-thou, sanctimonious father. And he let me blame her."

I look over at him and shake my head at the sympathy on his face. "Don't feel sorry for me—I became a total little shit. I really was. The worst teenager you could ever hope to meet. I found myself an older gang who had access to drink and drugs. I'd go off with boys four or five years older than me. I'd steal money off Dad and Jen. I wanted to *punish* them. I thought they *deserved* it. I thought I was some punk, rebellious badass." I pause, leaning forward to put my own mug down.

"I thought Jacob was more of the same when I met him. But he wasn't. He was different. He was *good*. I don't mean in some saint-like way—he partied as hard as anyone, but he was...I'd shut everyone else out by that point, even Dee. I think it was only Jacob who stopped me from going completely evil."

"I think *evil* is pushing it a bit..."

I stare up at the ceiling, remembering those bad old days. "Jen—my stepmother—tried to stop me from storming off to some crappy party once, and I hit her. Pushed her over. I walked out and left her lying on the floor. What if she'd hit her head? I didn't even check. I didn't even stop to check if she was alive or dead. And what had *she* ever done to me? I was just...I remember just being so angry all the time."

I look at Adam and he smiles at me. "Okay, so you were pretty evil. But not now. That's not who you are now."

"But does that make it okay? All the shitty things I said, all the terrible things I did…Does it make it okay that I'm not like that now? You have Nazi war criminals who lived model lives after the Second World War—does that make what they did okay?"

Adam leans forward and kisses me, whispering as he pulls away, "You are not a Nazi war criminal."

I waver, a part of me wanting to run away, but the rest of me…I sigh and let my forehead lean against his. "My dad still thinks I am."

"I think your dad should stop punishing you for your past behavior for a moment and see who you are now and what you've achieved. And see the part *he* played in it all."

Yeah, the rest of me wants more of that. I smile. "You sound like Dee. Are you going to join my fan club? You and Dee against the rest of the world."

"Clubs with exclusive memberships are the best kind of club," he says.

I bite my lip to stop the automatic need to put myself down, to tell him worse things, to list all the bad things I've done. I suppose I don't need him to recoil in horror at my past misdemeanors. I punish myself enough. I lift my head and kiss him this time, pulling him closer, closing my eyes as his hand curls into my hair.

I'll allow myself this. I'll allow myself one night.

And then I'll tell him the rest.

Chapter 30

Sasha—December, two months earlier

It's two days before Christmas and I'm still under virtual house arrest. No punishment has been given out, but I know the rules. Still. It's two days before Christmas, so I summon my courage and go downstairs. Mum is in the kitchen finishing off icing the Christmas cake and Dad's reading the paper at the table. I can smell mince pies cooking in the oven and if it weren't for the packing boxes everywhere, it would feel like a normal Christmas. Except for the fact that none of us are really talking.

"Um...I was wondering if I could go into town and do my Christmas shopping?" I say it to Mum, but it's Dad's permission I'm asking. Even Mum knows that because she looks at him rather than at me.

"Emma asked if I wanted to meet for a Christmas coffee and exchange presents and I still need to get you guys something." I can feel myself going red at the enormity of my subterfuge, but as they don't ever ask about my friends, or lack of them, it's not a glaringly obvious lie.

"Do you really think you can be trusted to—" Dad begins but Mum interrupts.

"I think that will be fine, don't you, Daniel?" she says,

and there's that edge to her voice again, the one I heard the other night.

Dad looks at her over the top of his newspaper, and it's like there's some kind of silent war going on. I expect Mum to back down as usual, but then Dad sighs and puts his paper down. "Okay. For two hours—that's all. I'll take you in—I have some things I need to get myself."

I blink and my attention swivels between them. What did I miss there? Maybe he's just realized he needs to get Mum a present. That must be it. Ha. Result. It also means I know exactly where he'll be so I can avoid him—the jeweler's and the chemist. Earrings and perfume, standard Dad gifts. Mum doesn't look particularly happy she got her way, though.

"Brilliant—thank you! I'll go and get my coat and bag." I run upstairs before he can change his mind, closing my door before pulling my phone out of its hiding place. I send a quick text to Ethan. I don't know if he'll be able to meet me at such short notice, but if not, I'll use some of my credit and call him when I'm safely away from the house.

Dad parks at the station in West Dean and we go our separate ways. Ethan texted me back straight away and agreed to meet me. I'd suggested the café in the old part of town—it's well away from all the shops so we should be safely hidden from Dad there.

I'm practically skipping down the street like some stupid idiot, giddy with the thrill of doing something so forbidden, and, of course, it smacks me in the face when I turn the corner and see Ethan waiting. But not just Ethan, Ethan with a *girl*, standing next to the black car Ethan met me in the other night.

I slow down, not wanting to interrupt if this is Ethan's girlfriend and not sure how to feel if it is. I don't like him like that. Not at all. He's way too old. So, I think mostly what I'm feeling is awkward—because if it is his girlfriend, what's she going to think when I skip into the picture? What would I say? What would *Ethan* say to explain me?

But I can't go any slower and it's too late anyway, because they've seen me and both of them are looking at me. Ethan's a bit scowly, but his girlfriend is smiling. Closer up, though, I can't really call her a girl. She's older than Ethan, obviously so, not nana old, but more like Hanna's age or a bit older.

"Hiya," she says to me, big smile, very friendly. "Don't mind me—I was just off. I'll see you later," she says, turning to Ethan, kissing him on the cheek before getting in the car.

"Sorry if I interrupted something," I say into the sudden heavy silence. Ethan isn't looking at me, he's frowning after the disappearing woman.

"You weren't interrupting. It's just Carrie," he mutters, still looking in her direction.

"Is she…is she your girlfriend?" I ask. "Or the woman you mentioned—the one who's been hassling you?"

He finally turns to look at me, but the frown is still there. "Who, Carrie? No, of course not. She's a friend of a friend, that's all. She had a message for me."

"Sorry. I just thought…you looked angry about something and it looked a bit intense and—"

"Stop fishing, for God's sake. It's personal, private business, okay? Not some stupid playground gossip."

"Sorry," I mutter again, and he sighs.

"Forget it," he says. He turns to pick up two cardboard

cups from the wall behind him, handing one to me. "It's pretty full inside, so I got takeaways—are you okay out here? Not too cold?"

"It's fine," I say. And it is. It's cold, but bright and sunny and tucked away out of the wind, with a coat and scarf on, it's nicer out than in.

There's a silence that's getting beyond awkward, so I flounder for something to say. "So, what are you doing for Christmas? Spending it with family?" I realize, as I ask, that I have no idea how Ethan is living, where, with who... He's just been someone associated with the holiday camp.

He shrugs and takes a sip of his coffee. "I don't have family, so I guess it'll just be a quiet one. Me, the TV, my four walls. Or I'm sure I can cadge an invite off Owen—he owes me one."

"No family? That's awful. You should..." What? What am I about to do—invite him to Christmas with us? Oh, yeah, *that* would go down well with Dad.

He smiles as my voice trails off. "You don't have to feel sorry for me, Sash. I was in care from when I was younger than you and I've spent the last few years in prison, so a Christmas in my own place, with my own TV, a bottle of something, and a takeaway sounds pretty damned fine."

But it's not, though, is it? How is any of that fine? When I got old enough to wonder about it, I used to worry that Hanna was spending Christmases alone. The thought became an obsession that manifested as almost full-blown panic attacks when I was around ten. I used to wake up sobbing, with this weight on my chest that had me gasping for breath.

It totally freaked Mum and Dad out and they even took me to a doctor about it, but I could never say why I was panicking because we weren't supposed to talk about Hanna, so I'd pretend I was having nightmares. It stopped a few months later—Hanna came on one of her mini-visits and mentioned her Christmas with Dee and Dee's family, so the panic attacks stopped. But I still remember that weird crushing weight and the awful, well, *grief* I felt. It's a faint echo, but that same feeling is there as I think of Ethan in some scummy bedsit on his own watching the depressing *EastEnders* special, eating a takeaway Chinese, no tree, no presents.

"Wait here a minute," I say on impulse, and jump down off the wall we're sitting on. I run up the hill and around the corner before he can say anything, into the Spar. I've got a couple of pounds left out of the money Mum gave me to buy presents and I spend it on a Cadbury's selection pack and a tube of Jelly Tots, scrabbling around in my purse for enough for a fifty-pence gift bag to go with it. I shove the sweets in the bag as I walk back to Ethan, handing it over with a smile.

"Merry Christmas, Ethan. It's to go with the takeaway on Christmas Day."

He looks inside the bag and smiles. "You're a good kid, Sasha," he says as I pull myself back up onto the wall. He puts an arm around my shoulders and pulls me in for a hug.

It's nothing more than that, nothing more than a quick hug, but I pull away fast when I hear a familiar voice saying, "Oh my *God*!"

Too late. Caught. Seen. Totally screwed. There's six of them, coming out of the little tucked-away café I thought would be safe because the kids from school normally go to Greggs on the high street—Carly, Seren, and their gang of boys. Carly and Seren both look gleefully horrified.

"Sasha Carter—is this your *boyfriend*?" Seren calls out, way too loud.

I jump down off the wall, trying to think what to say, when Carly, who's been looking at Ethan and frowning, suddenly gasps and recoils. "Holy shit," she says, even louder than Seren. "I know who that is—it's that crim who's been working up at the holiday park."

"*Jesus*, Sasha—how desperate are you?" Seren says.

Ethan jumps down from the wall and stalks over to Seren, and as they all back off, even the boys, even though there's six of them, I'm reminded how big and actually quite intimidating Ethan can be.

"Ethan, I don't think…" I start to say but let the words trail off as Ethan glares back at me. He looks angry. Like, really, *really* mad.

"Yeah, that's it, call your *boyfriend* off," Seren calls in a mocking voice, then gasps as Ethan reaches out and shoves her, like *really* hard, sending her stumbling back into Dylan and Finn. Carly lets out a little scream and Ethan spins round toward her.

"Why don't you piss off, little girl," he says, "before I decide to show you what I was in prison for?"

For a second, I think he's going to do it—he's going to launch himself at a bunch of fourteen- and fifteen-year-olds and beat the crap out of them. I don't even feel relieved when they all make a hasty retreat. I'm too busy wetting myself in fear. Because I am *dead*. My life is over—there is no coming back from this. And Ethan, by scaring them to death like that, has actually made things *worse*.

"Stupid assholes," Ethan mutters, before turning to frown at me. "You okay?"

I flinch away from him and regret it when I see the anger

on his face. Oh God, he never answered me that time I asked what he went to prison for, and his threat to Carly just now...

"Christ, Sash—don't look at me like that. I was just trying to scare them, that's all. Come on—you know me...Do you really think I'd have a go at a bunch of kids?"

Oh God, he looks so hurt. But...

"Of course. I know you wouldn't have done anything. It's not just that, though..." I shake my head and take another step away from him. "Dad's going to find out," I say, panic making my voice high and shaky. "They're going to tell *everyone* and Dad's going to find out." The awfulness of it hits me again. "And they're going to say they saw us together. Like *together* together. They'll lie and exaggerate. He's never going to believe me when I say we're just friends. Not after Hanna, not after what she did."

"Calm down, Sash. Keep it together. All you have to do is deny it."

"*Deny* it?"

"Play it down. Tell him they're the school bullies. Tell him you ran into me outside a shop, and we were just saying hello and they're stirring up shit."

I stare at him. He doesn't get it. He doesn't understand what Dad is like now, what he's been like since Hanna left. Like, even if what he was saying were true, that I just ran into him and said hello...it wouldn't matter. Not to Dad.

"Why did you have to *do* that?" The words burst out of me. "You were terrifying—and you pushed Seren. She's *fifteen*, for God's sake, a *girl*. And you threatened Carly!"

I'm shaking but I can't stop berating him. "They could go to the *police*—don't you get that? Or tell their parents and they'll ring my dad."

"Jesus fucking *Christ*—will you *shut up*?" he shouts—roars—at me, and I freeze.

"I was helping you out, you ungrateful little—I should never have listened to Owen."

"What?" It comes out as a whisper.

"I know how to piss off the old man, he says. Chat up the kid, he says. An ex-con and his precious kid, that'll do it, he says. Bloody Owen. I should have stuck to ignoring you."

"I have to go," I mutter, already walking away, my eyes stinging. Oh, why did I come here? Why, why, why? I won't think about what Ethan just said. I need to find Dad before Carly and Seren spot him. Not that it matters—if he doesn't find out today, he's going to find out at some point over Christmas, as soon as he goes into town again, into a shop. And even if he doesn't, I know what this town is like: someone will find a reason to search him out to tell him. This gossip is too juicy to go unheard.

I get back to the car before him and spend the ten-minute wait in a paranoid hell of imagining all the people he might bump into who will tell him that his daughter was all over his ex-offender groundskeeper. He'll put two and two together, remember me sneaking out, think of all the times and all the places I could have been meeting Ethan when he was working at the holiday park.

I can't remember, right now, a single sensible reason I had for any of it.

Chapter 31

It takes five days. I know this is only because it's Christmas. Any other time of the year, Dad would have found out within forty-eight hours. Village gossip is *good*, especially when it's teenagers spreading it. It starts on social media, but it only takes one parent policing their kid's Snapchat or Instagram for the gossip to spread wider. Then as soon as it hits one of the gossip hubs—the shop or the pub—boom, everybody knows. And if it's killer gossip like this, someone will be desperate for the inside intel. Someone will go straight to Dad.

Ethan keeps texting. I read the first and it was an apology, but I didn't read past *I'm sorry*. I got home and hid my phone under my mattress, and I don't take it out, but I keep hearing the thing buzzing as messages come in. It's my very own beating heart under the floorboards, like in that Edgar Allen Poe story we read in school. I don't fool myself that it could be Hanna, the only other person with the number, finally responding to me. I no longer hold any illusions that she will come riding in to save me any time soon. Not when it's her that started this whole thing.

The worst—the absolute worst—is on Christmas morning. We've opened our presents and Mum turns to me with a smile. "I know you wanted a phone, honey, and I know I said no, but your father and I have been talking and we've decided if you settle in well to your new school and continue to do well, we'll consider letting you have a phone for your birthday."

I know this is a guilt thing—Mum still trying to smooth things over. Dad looks sour-faced, so I'm guessing it's another argument that Mum's won. I wonder for a second what he's done wrong to have to give in—twice now.

And I nearly laugh at the sheer bloody irony even as my forbidden phone-heart beats from its hiding place upstairs. I manage to smile and act thrilled, because that's what they're expecting. A phone of my very own, a reward for being the good daughter, for doing so well, for always toeing the line, for never breaking the rules.

Dad watches me as Mum makes the announcement. This promise of a reward, along with the silent treatment received for my misdemeanor of sneaking out...He thinks this will be enough to keep me on the straight and narrow. Too late, Dad. Too bloody late. I fell off the path, I plunged into the pit, I am doomed, I am just what he never wanted me to be, I am just like Hanna.

Five days I wait, in limbo, in purgatory. I expect the ax to fall when Dad or Mum have to go into town, when we've run out of bread or milk, but in the end, the gossipmongers can't wait.

The phone rings at ten thirty in the morning, three days after Christmas. I leap up to answer it, but Dad gets there first. I hear him making small talk and sounding confused at first. But then he goes quiet and he's only listening, but he's looking at me and, oh God, the expression on his face...

He ends the call without saying goodbye and there's a silence so heavy I can barely breathe. I feel it sitting on me, pushing me down, pushing all the air from my lungs, from the room, from the world, and as he finally opens his mouth to speak, I am literally gasping for air.

"Is it true?" He takes a step closer and his voice rises to a roar. "*Is it true?*"

"I don't... I don't know..." The words come out between gasps and there are tears in my eyes as I sit before him, shaking.

Mum comes running out of the kitchen. "What's wrong? What's going on?"

Dad turns to her. "Your daughter has been sneaking around with the... *criminal*, the *prisoner*, who's been working here." He looks back at me. "She was seen with her arms all over him in town before Christmas. When she told us she was shopping, when she told us she was meeting a school friend, she was with *him*. A man nearly twice her age, who has only just been released from *prison*."

"Oh no—oh, *Sasha*. You wouldn't—you couldn't..."

"Dad, *please*. It's not like that, it's not. We're friends, that's all."

"*Friends*? With a man nearly twice your age? A *violent criminal*?"

"He's not violent. He said he was *innocent*. And even if he isn't, he made a mistake, that's all. But he's been released now, he's been rehabilitated. Isn't that why you employed him? You said it was good to give him this chance."

Dad is quiet for a long minute. A minute that lasts a millennium. "Is that what he told you? That's he's innocent?" He pauses and shakes his head. "You have no idea. You foolish little girl, you have no idea."

"He wouldn't have lied, why would he? And there's no way you would have employed him if he was violent, no way. Why would you do that when me and Mum were here on our own sometimes when he was working?"

He ignores me and goes back out to the hall and picks up the phone. "I'm going to contact Owen and then the probation service—inform them what one of their ex-prisoners has been up to with my underage daughter."

"No, Dad, you can't. It's not true—none of it is true! You'll get him fired, or sent back to prison, when all he's ever done is talk to me, all he's ever done is be my friend."

"Why on earth would I believe you'd want to be friends with *him*?"

"Because I don't have any other friends." I shout it and the tears spill over. "Because I'm the weird girl with the skirt that's too long, who doesn't wear makeup, who's never allowed out, who doesn't have a phone, who never does anything wrong. *Nobody likes me.* Nobody."

"That is not an excuse."

Oh, he says it so coldly and something curls up inside me and dies.

"Fuck. You," I say as coldly as him.

Mum gasps at my words, but Dad's expression doesn't change. He starts punching a number into the phone. "Get upstairs. Get upstairs *now*. I don't want to see your face anymore."

I run upstairs and lift the corner of my mattress to pull out my phone. I dive across the landing and lock myself in the bathroom, my hands trembling as I look at the string of texts from Ethan. *I'm sorry I lost my temper. R u ok? Hope you didn't get in trouble. Text me back when you can.* I take a massive risk and call Ethan instead of texting, talking in a fast and frantic whisper as soon as he answers.

"Ethan—stop, listen. My dad found us out and he's got it all wrong. I *told* you he would. He thinks we're together and he's calling Owen and the probation service. He's going to get you in trouble. I had to warn you."

"Sash—calm down. It's okay. It'll be fine. We haven't done anything wrong—there's nothing for me to get in trouble for."

"But he's going to lie. He's going to say we're together and I'm underage and—"

He laughs. "Christ—history repeating, or what?"

"What do you mean?"

"Nothing. It's okay. Seriously, Sash. Don't worry about me. Worry about yourself. I'll sort this out; I'll put them all straight. Stay safe, hunker down. I'll contact you soon, okay? Keep your phone safe and hidden and I'll—"

"No, don't. I don't think...I don't think we should speak anymore." I hear a creak on the stairs and almost wet myself in panic. "I have to go. Someone's coming." I end the call and turn off the phone. I put it in my pocket, pulling my jumper down, checking in the mirror to make sure it can't be seen.

I flush the toilet and run the tap, taking a moment to try to calm down before unlocking the door to find Dad waiting outside. Did he hear me talking?

"Pack a bag," he says. "I've spoken to the head office of the new holiday park. They've agreed we can settle in early. I'll drive you and your mother there today and then come back and organize the full move alone."

"*Today?*"

"We're leaving in an hour."

An *hour*? I'm supposed to pack up my life, say goodbye to the house that's been my home for my entire life, in an *hour*?

But actually...what do I have to take? What do I have to say goodbye to? I pack some clothes and toiletries, making sure my phone is carefully hidden, packed at the bottom. My school books, some favorite novels...I hesitate when I take out the hidden photos, the ones of Hanna when she was my age. They've been my hidden lifeline to a sister I've never really known for so long, but she cut that line with what she did on my Facebook account. So, instead of putting the photos in my bag, I put them on the windowsill and leave them there. So what if Dad finds them and realizes I had them? I'm already in all the trouble. And if they were photos she kept hidden too, those images of her drinking and smoking and kissing, well, what does it matter to me if Dad thinks even worse of her? I don't care.

I zip up the bag and turn away with my teeth clenched. I don't look back as I leave the room and close the door behind me.

I come downstairs with my bag; the whole thing still seeming unreal. Mum's in the kitchen, putting the kettle, cups, and bits of food in a box. I don't know where Dad is.

"Are you really going to do this?" I say.

Mum carries on filling the box. "Do what?"

"Just...*leave*. No notice, no goodbyes. Just because Dad says so."

She stops filling the box and looks at me. "Sasha, this is about more than just your actions. I don't expect you to understand." She sighs and shakes her head. "What do you expect me to do?"

What do I *expect* her to do? I guess I expect her to do exactly what she's doing—follow orders, do what Dad says with a smile and no complaints. What she's always done, like we're still living in the 1950s. What I *want* her to do, though, is quite different... There was a girl in Year Eleven, on the last non-uniform day, who got sent home for wearing a T-shirt that said "F*** the Patriarchy." So, I guess what I want Mum to do is say exactly that to Dad, only without the asterisks, and refuse to leave.

I can't do anything—I'm fourteen, I don't want to do a Hanna and run away. Where would I go and what would I do? No—university is my escape, but that's four years away. But Mum, she's a grown woman. She has a *say*.

"What about your New Year get-together with your book group?" I ask. "It's your turn to host—you've been planning it for ages."

Something flickers across her face for a moment, but then Dad walks into the room and it's gone.

"They'll understand," she says quietly to me.

"Are you both ready?" Dad says.

Mum nods and smiles at me. "It'll be great," she says. "To have the opportunity to get settled in early. We'll be all ready when your father gets there with the moving van."

I turn and walk out without saying another word. The patriarchy is very much alive and well in our house. I don't even know why I'm so angry about it. I'm not leaving behind an unfinished life here; I don't have a boyfriend or a group of friends to miss. I don't have a job or anything really tying me to this place. But Mum *does*. If she won't stick up for me, I wish she'd at least stick up for herself.

Chapter 32

HANNA—Tuesday 8 a.m.

I wake up the next morning to the sound of my phone buzzing. I'm warm and still wrapped in Adam's arms and I try to extricate myself without waking him, but he wakes up with a jerk, sitting up, his hair sticking up everywhere.

"Sorry," I say, smiling, as I reach down and pull out my phone from my hoodie pocket. My smile vanishes when I answer and it's DC Norton on the other end.

"We have the name of the ex-offender your sister was linked with. Can you come in so we can try to establish any links between you?" There's a pause. "And we've found another connection from that list of names you gave us."

I get out of bed after the call ends, talking over my shoulder and telling Adam what the detective said as I pull on my jeans. He's already up and getting dressed himself by the time I turn around.

"I'll come with you. Let me make you some tea. Or coffee? I have travel cups if you don't want to wait."

I don't even want to wait that long, so we're out of his flat within ten minutes but I stop dead and swear as we hit the pavement.

"Fuck. My car is at Dee's."

"The police have still got mine."

254

I waver for a second, trying to decide if it would be quicker to pick up my car or try to find a taxi. I start walking in the direction of Dee's flat. Adam catches up with me and as he does, his hand reaches over and grabs mine and we walk the rest of the way like that, hand in hand, still half-fogged with sleep, my insides full of butterflies.

"Let me drive," he says, holding out a hand for the keys as we get to Dee's street. "You're too distracted."

"I'm not going to know him," I say as Adam starts the car. "Whoever this guy is, I'm not going to know him. I don't know anyone who's been to prison."

Adam taps the steering wheel as we wait at a red light. "But…did you used to? Know anyone who might have ended up in prison?"

I look out of the window as we turn left, rather than at Adam, thinking of the older boys and girls I hung out with in my bad old days. I already know it's not Carrie, and I'm guessing it's not Stephen—I don't think ex-convicts can join the police force. It could be Lee or Owen—I have no clue if they've been in trouble in the years since I left home. And what about the others, the ones on the periphery, who were already supplying the drugs and feeding us underage kids alcohol? Any one of them could have ended up in trouble with the police—beyond the minor trouble we *did* get into. Hell, if I hadn't left, if Dee hadn't helped me drag myself out of my pit, *I* could have ended up in prison. The drugs could have become more than recreational, the shoplifting could have become a bigger crime, the graffiti could have turned to serious criminal damage. Who knows where I could have ended up? I left them all behind with my old life, but it's certainly possible—more likely *probable* with some of them—that one or more of my old party-going friends could have ended up with a prison sentence.

But why would they do all this? That's the sticking point. Yes, I can imagine some of them ending up in prison, but none of us knew much about each other beyond what we liked to drink and who we liked to dance to. None of them cared enough about me to go on some weird revenge trip, fifteen years later. Christ—would any of them even remember my name? And as for hanging out with Sasha? A fourteen-year-old girl? No, it doesn't make sense.

I've talked myself out of the possibility of it being anyone I know, but it doesn't stop me being nervous as we pull up at the police station. Adam takes my hand again as we walk across the road and I'm glad of the comfort.

We're shown to the same interview room we were initially seen in and offered coffee, which we both gratefully accept. Under the table, our hands stay gripped together.

DC Norton comes in clutching his own cup of coffee in one hand and a folder in the other which he puts on the table.

"Thanks for coming in, Hanna. You too, Mr. Webster—it will be good to share the information with you as well, in case you have any connections we're not aware of." He pauses to open a folder. "The first connection—and one you've already flagged with the names you gave us before—is Owen King. He owns a small landscaping and property maintenance company and the owners of the holiday park awarded him the contract for the upkeep of the site."

I lean back and let out a shaky breath. Back then, Lee and Carrie were friendly enough with me as Jacob's girlfriend, but Owen never got beyond grumpy or hostile with me. He didn't even try to pretend in front of Jacob. It was

256

one of the things me and Jacob used to argue about—he wanted to spend what I thought was too much time with his friends. They were *so* tight-knit, particularly the three boys...Lee was okay, but I *never* wanted to spend time with Owen. And if he disliked me, he *hated* my dad after Jacob died. And now he's *working* for him?

"It's him—it's got to be him," I say. "He hates me, and my family. And he's been there for months...it *has* to be him."

"We're bringing him in," DC Norton says. "We're looking at his van and we have a warrant to search his house."

"But what about the ex-offender? That's not Owen, is it?"

DC Norton shakes his head. "It's someone who works for him."

He takes a photograph out of the folder—it's a man in his mid-twenties, short fair hair and a lean face. There's a small scar cutting through one of his eyebrows, and his eyes are dark, a startling contrast to the light hair. If I saw this man in a pub, I'd definitely look twice, because he looks dangerous, and dangerous—until now, until Adam—has always been my Kryptonite. But mostly, what I feel as I look at the photograph is relief. I don't know him. I've never seen this man before, so he can't have any connection to me—this ex-offender who's been seen with Sasha is not the one who's doing all this.

Although I probably shouldn't feel relief, should I? Because if it's not this man, who the hell is it? Owen King? Really?

"His name is Ethan Taylor," DC Norton says. "Recently released from prison after a four-year sentence for various fraudulent computer crimes. He was working part time as a groundskeeper at the holiday park under the employ of Owen King."

Adam frowns. "If he was in prison for computer crime, could he be involved? Working with Owen King?"

"We'll be speaking to both of them."

I frown, looking at the photograph again.

"What about the other murders? The Bentley sisters?"

There's too long a pause. "There are connections we are...investigating."

I look at Adam and he shrugs. What the hell does that mean? Who the hell is Ethan Taylor and why would he be helping Owen?

Chapter 33

SASHA—December, two months earlier

The new house is crap. A horrible modern box on a huge, unfamiliar holiday park. It's smaller than our old house, still three bedrooms but all the rooms are smaller. Dad's going to hate working here. Unlike home, because I can't think of this new place as home, the holiday park is open from March right through until November, and whatever Dad says about it being bigger and having more staff, he's still going to be working more and harder here than he was before. Why would he do this only a few years before he wants to retire?

And Mum...How is she going to be happy here in these square rooms with their perfectly straight magnolia walls and wall-to-wall beige carpet? Mum likes original features and polished wood, built-in storage and our old range cooker. None of our furniture goes. It's going to look weird here. This is a house made for Ikea furniture, not antiques.

Dad dropped us off with our hastily packed bags, turned straight round, and went back to supervise the real move. There's already some furniture here, left by the old tenants: a cheap pine table and chairs in the kitchen, a couple of beds, a hideous cream leather sofa in the living room.

"Why did you agree to this?" I ask it again after Dad has left, watching Mum potter about, looking in the boxes and bags she brought with us for the kettle and teabags. I'm still carrying around that anger and frustration. She looks at me with her eyebrows raised.

"I don't just mean the suddenness of it. Why did you agree to move here in the first place?" I say. "You loved the old house. We all did."

"Your father didn't," she says, filling the kettle with water. "He hasn't been happy there in a long time."

"But what about you? Don't you get a say?" I don't mention myself. I can't pretend I was really happy before. I can't say this new place looks like any kind of improvement, but still. "What was it—adopting me was your thing and now you owe him forever? You don't ever get a say anymore?"

Mum sighs, pouring milk in our cups before putting it away in the gleaming, empty fridge. "That's not how it is. Not at *all*. It's just a house, four walls and a roof. We can make this place a home."

"What, this ugly, cold box?"

"Yes. The old house was full of too many bad memories."

"Bad memories for *Dad*. Ancient memories. *You* loved it there."

"No, Sasha. Not just bad memories for your father, for me. *Me*." She looks at me and shakes her head. "I liked the house, yes, but I care more about our family's happiness than I do about a house. You don't remember—you were only a baby when Hanna left. But I remember everything that happened, how it tainted what should have been a happy home. And I've watched it eat away at your father over the years. I've watched it change him. I think—I hope—he'll be happier here. He'll learn to relax again. A fresh start is what we *all* need—including you, Sasha. This is an opportunity, not a punishment."

Is she telling me or telling herself? Because it wasn't just a house. She had friends there, a nice little group from the church who'd meet for book group nights and regular monthly lunches. But Dad said, *Pack a bag, we're going now*, and she did it. Walked away from all of them. It's okay for me, I didn't have a group of friends, neither did Dad. But Mum...If there was ever a time to bring out the "F*** the Patriarchy" T-shirt...

"I think you should have fought harder to stay," I say quietly, and for a fleeting second, I see sadness on her face, but then her expression hardens.

"This is not a war. This is not a battle we are fighting against your father," she says. "You have to realize— your father acts out of fear and love. What you're rebelling against...he's not acting this way to punish you. He's scared for you—he already lost one daughter. He loves you and wants to protect you."

"But he didn't *lose* a daughter. Hanna's still alive."

"You know what I mean."

Yes, I know what she means, but that doesn't mean I accept it. What—I'm supposed to be happy to be basically locked in my room until I'm eighteen, only let out for school, because Mum says it's about love, not punishment? I feel another surge of anger—this is another thing to lay at Hanna's door, isn't it? Dad's doing all this because of what Hanna did, because he's terrified I'm going to go the same way.

I look away. "Can I go out for a walk? Or has Dad alarmed the house so it goes off if I leave?"

"Don't do this, Sasha."

"I'm not doing *anything*," I say as I pull the front door open. "I didn't do anything before, either, that's the point. You'd think Dad would know better than to listen to gossip

261

and lies, rather than believe me when I say I didn't do anything. And don't tell me this isn't a punishment."

I feel guilty as soon as I slam the door behind me. Mum's only doing what she always does: trying to keep the peace, trying to make the best of things. My anger isn't at her. I just get frustrated. And maybe, for once, I'd like her to be honest and say, *Yes this is shit, isn't it?* Maybe I'd like to sit and have a good cry with her, and then I'd feel like we're in it together and that, actually, we could make the best of things, and make this new life work. Maybe then we'd both feel a bit less lonely.

I walk around the back of the house, climbing a hill toward the rows of caravans that will soon be filled with tourists. It's exposed and windy at the top of the hill, but the views over the coast are beautiful. The sea seems bluer. From up here, I can see all of my new kingdom, bigger but basically the same as my old one. A playground. A pool. A clubhouse. All those enticements I won't get to use. And even when this place is filled with people, I won't be any less lonely, because they'll be fleeting strangers passing through and I'll be stuck here permanently, still the weirdo, just in a different holiday park in a different town.

I pull my phone out of my pocket and switch it on. There are four more messages from Ethan. I haven't texted him back. I can't get past that look on his face when he faced up to Seren and the others, how for a minute there, I genuinely thought he was going to hit one of them. Or me. I can't be friends with someone I'm scared of.

I hear someone coming up behind me and manage to get my phone back in my pocket before they come around the corner. And thank God I do, because it's Mum. She's breathing heavily after walking up the hill as she stands next to me, looking at the view.

"You should know..." she says when she gets her breath back. "You should know it was my decision to leave Little-dean and move here."

"What?"

"I don't want you to think I don't care, that I wouldn't fight if it was something important...So if you're going to be angry with anyone about the move, be angry with me. But God knows, that's not what any of us should be angry about."

Her words burst out and I'm not sure I've ever heard that tone from her before. She pauses, wraps her arms around herself. "I gave him an ultimatum: we all had to move or I would have taken you and left him."

"I don't...I don't understand..."

"You father was having an affair. He ended it but I refused to stay in the same village, knowing that woman was still around."

I stare at her. No *way*. "But...I don't...Who is it?"

I can't get my words out properly, because I don't know what to say. Dad—an affair? I can't—I really cannot—for a second imagine it.

"One of my *friends* from the church group turned out not to be such a friend after all." She shakes her head. "All the times I thought she was visiting *me* to talk about books or flowers..."

I bet it was Marianne. She was always such a sneery, snooty cow. But still—*Dad*, seeing another woman? *Kissing* another woman? I refuse to let my mind go beyond the kissing part because I'd definitely be sick. Possibly explode in disgust.

"I found out in the summer and that's when I gave him his ultimatum," Mum says. "He started looking for a new position then, even before they announced they were closing the holiday park. But that's not important now, *She*'s not important. I know Daniel is sorry and that he regrets it. I also know it wasn't about the affair; it was a symptom of other issues going back years. His ridiculous need for some kind of validation in life, for something *more*."

She pauses and takes a deep breath. "For some reason, it's never been enough for him, the life we have. The life we've made together as a family. I couldn't stay there any longer. It was making me miserable, worrying he was seeing her again every time he left the house or made a phone call…God, the hell I went through that afternoon you were late home because you had an after-school meeting…"

I force myself not to react. The day Dad was late picking me up and he made me lie…Oh bloody hell, was he seeing his other woman?

"I didn't want to have to tell you," Mum says. "But I don't want you believing all of this is down to your father punishing you and blaming him forever. Or thinking I don't care. And I don't want your father to pretend this is all your fault either."

She looks at me and smiles. "I know you don't see any similarities, but I see it. There's a line of stubborn that passes down, from Daniel to Hanna to you. It drives me crazy, but I have loved all of you in spite of it."

Oh, blimey bloody squared. I can't tell her now, can I? That Dad was the one late that day, not me. I can't tell her now because she'll think he's with the other woman now, that he never ended it…

Maybe he didn't. Because just before Christmas—when he relented and took me into town—was he seeing her then? When he had the actual nerve to go off at me for meeting Ethan?

And now he's parked me and Mum here, pretending it's all my fault, pretending to Mum he's ended it with the other woman, when really, he—what? Was just getting us out of the way for one last hurrah? How *dare* he? How bloody dare he?

Chapter 34

February, one week earlier

I get off the bus and start walking home, head down and shoulders hunched, ignoring the banging on the windows, the words called out as the bus starts moving again. I never thought I'd long for the days when my dad would drop me at the school gates and always pick me up at the end of the day, but getting the bus... That bus is like a zoo, Full of the worst animals, the nastiest, man-eating ones.

School hasn't actually been that bad. Not bad as in no one has really spoken to me, but at least no one has bullied me. But the bus is like a free-for-all, and my anonymity is picked up on like a red flag. No one gets to be invisible on the school bus and in the month and a half I've been riding it, I've had to wash spit out of my hair a million times, had to ignore having my seat kicked, had to duck to avoid things chucked at my head, had to listen to obscene songs sung with my name in them and, on one memorable occasion, had to ignore it when some total, utter *dick* from Year Nine thought it would be hilarious to shove his arse in my face and fart as he was getting off the bus.

Something smacks into the back of my head and I cry out, my hands flying up to my hair to find it wet. The bus is driving past me and there are laughing faces pressed against the windows. An open water bottle rolls to a stop next to me, clearly the missile thrown by someone with good aim.

Could have been worse, I suppose. It could have been a glass bottle and the wetness trickling down my neck could have been blood.

It would do me no good telling Mum or Dad about any of this, because Dad isn't speaking to me. And that was fine at first, because after Mum told me he'd had an affair...I couldn't even *look* at him when he arrived with all our stuff. For that first week, I was glad he wasn't speaking to me, because if he had...I would have had to say something. And Mum begged me not to. It was done, it was over, she'd forgiven him, that's what she said to me. Don't talk to him about it.

Another thing not to talk to him about. So yeah, for a week or so, him not speaking to me was a relief. And it's not full-on silence, he'll answer my questions with one-word answers, but he hasn't engaged me in conversation since we moved here. Mum referees between us, all anxious awkwardness, ready, I think, to jump in if I look like I'm going to talk about his affair, or my adoption, or Hanna, or anything of importance. We're basically living like polite strangers. We talk about school and the weather and the latest news, and I am just so lonely. So, so lonely.

And in that time, my bitterness has festered. It's a weeping, pus-filled wound and it *hurts*. It's like Dad's given up on me. I alternate between being really mad and wanting to cry. It's not even a punishment anymore; it's like he just doesn't care what I do. He never asks how I'm doing in school. Mum does, but he doesn't. I tested it, two weeks into term. They gave us a math skills test, to see where we were, and I sat there for the hour-long lesson and didn't answer a single question, fueled by my...*fury*. I handed in my blank paper and waited for the explosion. When the teacher confronted me, I chickened out and pretended I'd had a headache. She phoned home while I was sitting across from her in the main office to tell Dad I had to stay after school to make up the test. I know it was Dad she spoke to, I could hear his voice, if not what he said.

I stayed after school and did the test properly, and because the bus had long gone, Dad had to pick me up. And he said nothing, literally not a word the whole way home. Not about me failing the first test. Not about me having to stay after school, my first ever detention. Not a word. He couldn't have made it any clearer that he no longer cares. I'm tarnished now, even though I've done nothing wrong, nothing but made friends with someone he doesn't approve of. And that fully dampened the fury. Drowned it, in fact.

But then I got home, and he still didn't speak, and I stopped being sad and miserable and got *so mad*. Because how *dare* he? How dare he take the moral high ground here? First he lies about my adoption. Then he cheats on Mum. He had an *affair*, for God's sake. A dirty affair with one of Mum's friends. All I did was make the wrong friend—wrong in his eyes, anyway.

So really, why am I bothering? It's exhausting, this whole rollercoaster. Why am I still trying to be the good daughter? The revelation stops me in my tracks fifty yards from the gate to the new holiday park, adorned with the big OPENING EASTER WEEKEND! sign.

Why *am* I still doing this? Still putting up with all the crap when Dad doesn't even care? Next time someone hassles me on the bus, I should just punch them in the face. Dad won't care. He won't do anything. No, scrap that, why am I even getting the bus at all?

The forbidden idea sets my heart racing, but that's nothing to the overwhelming cold spill of relief at the thought of not having to get on that bus tomorrow morning.

It's easier, in the end, to miss the bus than I thought it would be. I mean, of course I know it's *physically* easy to miss the bus. If you're deliberately trying to miss a bus, you just get there late, or don't go to the stop at all. But I thought I'd have to wrestle with my conscience a bit, or a lot. That I'd have to fight the panic at the thought of the school ringing home when I don't turn up. But it's easy. Maybe I'm more Hanna than I thought. I stroll right past the bus stop just before eight, stopping around the corner to use up some of my precious credit, leaving a message on the school answerphone, pretending I'm Mum calling in sick, just like Ethan advised me to way back when all I had to worry about was a few anonymous Facebook messages and those stupid girls at school. It might not work, it'll probably be obvious it's me and not Mum, but actually, right now—who cares?

I step under the cover of the trees at the side of the road as the bus comes around the corner, raising a hidden middle finger to all the idiots inside. I watch it disappear into the distance. Well. That's it. Bus well and truly missed.

Now what?

I ask myself that question, but I already know the answer. I knew what I was going to do as I lay awake last night thinking about this. I text Ethan. I haven't spoken to him since we moved here. I didn't even answer his texts for a long time, but I caved a couple of weeks ago. All I sent was a message saying keeping in touch wasn't worth the risk, but it opened the line of communication again like I knew it would, and as soon as I switched my phone on to make that call to the school, there was a string of new texts from him.

Im sorry.

How many times do I have to keep saying it?

Look—heres the truth. Remember that woman I said wouldn't leave me alone? Shes been giving me so much hassle. It made me lose my temper that day.

I shouldn't have taken it out on you and those kids.

Its not an excuse I know, but im getting it sorted now.

I chew on my lip as I read through the messages. I don't—I *won't*—believe Dad is right about him being a violent criminal. And I could forgive him for losing his temper. I've been so damned lonely here I think I would forgive him even if he'd shoved me rather than Seren. It's not that that's making me hesitate...

Was it the truth—what you said about Owen? About just talking to me to wind up my dad?

I type it quickly and press send before I can chicken out and watch the dots that tell me he's typing a reply...

At first. Not now.

I *knew* Owen hated us—it was so obvious, even if Mum and Dad never saw it. I've spent ages looking at that picture of him when he was a teenager, but I can't see any familiarity there. He can't be my birth dad, he just can't. And he's a long way out of our lives now. I can leave Ethan behind as well... or I can believe that "not now."

I don't want to see him again, I'm not ready for that, but I still have credit left on my phone. I could call him. I could go into this new town, find a takeaway hot chocolate, and call him if he's not working. I could walk brazenly around town in my school uniform when I should obviously be in school and dare anyone to call me out on it. *Go on*, I'll say, in this imaginary confrontation. *Do your worst—my dad won't care. Even the school won't care that much.* I'm the unproven new girl who's bumping along in the middle because I can't be bothered to try for straight As anymore. I'm no longer the great Oxbridge hope.

I'm not in school today, I text Ethan. *Want to talk?*

I keep walking toward town, staring at my phone, waiting for his reply. When it comes, I stop.

Hey. I've got a better idea. I'm not working tomorrow. Let's meet.

Oh God. Oh no. That's not what I wanted. Not at all. I text back.

No. you can't. I'll be in school tomorrow. Will text instead.

And then I switch off my phone before he can text me back.

Chapter 35

It's actually a relief to go to school the next day. After all my bravado in missing the bus, all I ended up doing was hiding in the town library, doing homework and cringing every time someone walked in in case they asked why I wasn't in school. I waited in dread when I got home for a call from the school asking why I hadn't been in that day, but there was nothing. When I got on the bus this morning, it was easy to ignore the idiots at the back. Maybe because I was too worried about Ethan knocking on the door, or maybe I was past caring, but the dicks on the bus were suddenly nothing. I didn't even try to keep my head down, I responded to the verbal crap with an unflinching cold glare that seemed to work as I was subjected to nothing worse than a couple of kicks to my seat. Perhaps they're getting bored. I get a week off for half-term after today and when we're back, maybe if I carry on ignoring it and giving them Paddington Bear Hard Stares, it will get easier. Dad will start speaking to me again eventually and things can get back to normal.

But when I'm waiting for the bus at the end of the day, I hear someone calling my name and realize I've just been kidding myself. Ethan is walking across the car park toward me. The bus still hasn't arrived, so I can't escape unless I go diving back into the school building and how will that look? People are already watching, probably wondering who the sketchy-looking guy shouting my name is. I feel bad then, because Ethan doesn't really look like a dodgy ex-offender, he just looks like a normal twenty-something. It's my imagination, at peak freak-out after yesterday, painting him as suddenly sinister.

The easiest thing to do is to go over to him, away from the others waiting for the bus, far enough away that they can't overhear our conversation.

"What are you doing here?"

He grins. "You said you were in school, so I waited until the end of the day. I did text to tell you, but I think your phone's off."

"I said I'd text. I said not to come..." I pause and frown. "Wait—how did you even know this was my school?"

He raises an eyebrow. "It wasn't hard to figure out. There's not exactly a million schools in this area, you know."

But it's not actually the nearest school to the holiday park. Dad got me in this one, a few miles farther away, because it had better exam results.

"Look," he says, running a hand through his hair, "I wanted to say sorry. Again. Properly and in person, not by text. I know I lost it at Christmas, and I wanted to explain."

The bus goes past, trundling round the turning circle to the pickup point.

"Let me give you a ride home, and we can talk," Ethan says.

I don't want to. I'd actually rather get on the hell-bus.

"Please?" he says. "Come on, Sash. I don't want to have to turn up at your house to get you to talk to me."

He says it all casual, but it comes across as a threat. The thought makes me want to vomit. Turn up at the house? Dear God, no.

"Okay. But you'll have to take me straight home—Mum and Dad need to believe I got the bus, so I can't be late."

"Sure, no problem," he says, smiling. "Come on—the car's over here."

We're two miles out of town, me sitting with my hands tucked under my thighs, so Ethan doesn't see the clenched fists I can't seem to relax, when I realize I haven't given him any directions.

"So, I guess you figured out where I live as well?"

He glances across at me. "I used to work in computers, before I got sent down. A stint in prison hasn't got rid of all my skills."

I know he's right—it would be easy for someone techy to find out where I was at school, which holiday park had new management. It doesn't make it less unnerving.

"Look," he says with a sigh, "I just wanted a chance to explain why I got so angry. It's not you, okay? The woman giving me hassle...she's been accusing me of stuff that could get me in trouble. I've been trying—working, saving, following the rules—and she's threatening to ruin it all for me."

I think of him "borrowing" cars to meet me, finding out who was sending me those messages, offering to "scare" Hanna. Even this, turning up here today...does he really believe he's been "following the rules," whatever that means?

I wait, but he doesn't say anything else. He says he wants to explain but telling me some random woman is giving him hassle isn't explaining anything.

"Dad said...he said you were violent. A violent criminal."

He shakes his head. "Is that why you've been giving me

the silent treatment? Sash, he's just trying to get you to stay away. I went to prison for computer fraud. A white-collar crime I didn't even do. No violence—I swear."

I should feel relieved. I suppose I do, a bit. But him turning up, knowing all this *stuff* about me that I haven't told him...

"And what about Owen? Why does he hate my dad so much?" I ask.

Ethan sighs. "It's nothing personal. Not really. I don't think he was keen on the way your dad talked to him like he was a servant, when he's probably more successful and earns way more money."

"My dad treats everyone like that."

"I noticed." He pauses. "Plus, he never liked your sister when they were kids."

I bite my lip. "It's not because they went out and she dumped him or something, is it? An angry ex thing?"

Ethan frowns and gives me an odd look. "Don't think so. He said she caused trouble between him and his mates. It was nothing, though. We used to spot you, following us round the holiday park—he just said I should chat you up because it would wind up your dad. He said it as a joke, really. I didn't do it, obviously. But I liked you. We got chatting and I liked you. And it's like I said in my texts: I was angry with someone else and I took it out on you. I made it sound worse than it was." He stops and looks over at me. "So, what's the new town like, then? Is everything else the same? Better? Worse?"

"Worse," I say, looking away from him, out of the window. "Starting a new school midway through the year is a nightmare. I hate everyone there and they all hate me. And my dad's not speaking to me."

"And you still haven't heard from your sister? She still doesn't know you've moved?"

I shake my head.

He sighs. "Your sister's caused you a lot of shit, hasn't she?"

Why does he keep bringing it back to Hanna? And is it really all her fault? We were moving anyway. Because of Dad and what he did. *Hanna* didn't make him have an affair, did she? Even if we hadn't done that ridiculous moonlight flit, I'd still be here, wouldn't I? I still don't know one hundred percent that it was her sending those messages, but...

"Well, you'll be pleased to know I've been a busy boy," Ethan says.

I look back at him. "Are you still working for Owen?" I'm pleased Dad didn't get him into trouble.

"Well, yeah, but that's not what I meant. I meant I was busy with our plan."

I wince. I'd forgotten my angry agreement to his suggestions.

"I've been in full-on stealth mode, spending some time in Cardiff over the holidays and in the last few weeks. I'll tell you what, Sash, your sister's friends are *very* gullible. I even managed to swing an invite to the New Year party she was at."

"You went to a party with Hanna?"

"Don't worry—she didn't see me." He pauses. "But I saw her."

I think of my own New Year, spent alone in my room in our crappy new house, and how many times I've dreamed about spending Christmas or New Year with Hanna and how I didn't even get a text from her, but Ethan was in the same *room*. But... It's kind of creepy, actually, isn't it?

Not something to be jealous about at all—Ethan being in the same room as Hanna, watching her without her even knowing...

"Listen, Ethan, I was angry before, when I agreed we should get Hanna back, but I kind of...I don't want to anymore. I don't want to be that person. I don't want anyone to be as scared of some anonymous messages as I was. It just makes me as bad as her, doesn't it? And also, she's not bad, she's *not*. Will you leave it? Please?"

My heart is pounding so hard as I wait an eternity for him to answer. We're well out of town, on a quiet country road. This is the quickest way to the holiday park, but it's not the same route the school bus takes, so if he stopped and kicked me out of the car, or I jumped out when he slowed, I'd be stuck in the middle of nowhere.

"I don't think you know her at all," he says.

"What does that mean?"

"Owen told me all about her. She used to be with a friend of his and she treated him very badly."

He looks at me again and is it my imagination or has the car slowed down? There are dark wooded areas on both sides of the road, huge trees stretching up and over the car.

"She ruined his life," he says.

"Who was it? *When* did this happen? Why didn't you ever say anything? And how do you know it's true, anyway? Owen could have been messing with you."

Oh God, Owen's got some decades-old resentment against Hanna and I gave Ethan her phone number. I told him where she lived and where she worked. He's even hanging round at the same parties, getting Owen's revenge for him. Whatever he's done, I'm an accomplice.

"What happened to Owen's friend? How did she ruin his

life?" I ask again. Maybe it's not Owen who's my birth dad, maybe it's Owen's friend and that's why Owen is still mad at Hanna.

There's another silence, but the car speeds up again, so I'm able to relax the tiniest bit.

"He's dead."

I let out a shaky breath. "But that's not Hanna's fault, right? She wouldn't have—"

"Oh, she is entirely responsible. Owen told me the whole story. She may not have physically killed him, but she is one hundred percent responsible for his death."

We turn the corner and there's the main gates for the holiday park. Ethan pulls up at the side of the road, not driving close enough to be spotted from the house.

"You asked me to leave it," he says, putting the handbrake on but not turning the engine off. "You asked me to leave your sister alone, but I'm sorry...I can't."

My insides turn to liquid.

"I won't ask you to be involved, but I will remind you that it was you who set this in motion, so don't even think about telling your parents or the police or anyone. Because you'd be in as much trouble as me."

I think I might be sick, really, really sick. All over him, all over his car. "What have you done?"

"Don't think she's the innocent in this—I've met her most recent ex, and she's basically been stalking him." He smiles. "Don't look so scared, Sash. I haven't done anything. I'm a computer guy, not a murderer. I'm just planning on messing with her a bit, that's all." He pauses and laughs. "I've got an idea that will really mess with her head, though. More so now that you've told me she doesn't even know you've moved...It's what she deserves. Owen's done a lot for me and I owe him this."

I'm not reassured, not at all, especially not when the two extremes he mentioned were messing with her on a computer or murder. Everything that's happened to me in the last couple of months was the result of someone messing with me via a computer. And I'm no longer sure that it ever was Hanna sending me those messages. I only have Ethan's word that they could be traced back to her phone number, the number I gave him in the first place.

And I don't know enough about all this tech stuff—if I texted Hanna to warn her, if she even read my message, would he be able to see that, somehow?

Oh God, what have I *done*?

"You'd better go," Ethan says. "Before your dad catches you with me. I'll text you. You're on half-term now, aren't you? I might want to see you again."

I go to get out of the car. We're going away tomorrow for a few days—should I tell him or keep quiet? I don't want to annoy him when he's in this weird mood...maybe I'll wait and tell him after we've left. But if me not being around makes him angry...he knows where I live, where I go to school. He could get me in so much trouble. I chew on my lip. Maybe if I tell him...He said he liked me. He went against Owen over that, over me, didn't he?

"Ethan, please..." I say. "Please leave her alone. I don't know what she did—or what she's supposed to have done—but she's...she's more than just my sister."

I pause and take a deep, shaky breath. "She's my mother."

The silence stretches out so long, I wish I could take the words back. When I risk a glance at him, it's like he's frozen, his hands white-knuckled on the steering wheel, staring straight ahead.

"I never knew Hanna was my mother, not until recently," I say, the words tumbling out to fill the horrible silence. "I thought she was my sister, that's all. And...I'm still mad at her, but I don't want her hurt..."

"Who's your father?" he says eventually.

"I don't know," I mutter and risk another glance. He's staring at me now and the look on his face...the *rage*...

"Give me your phone."

I fumble the phone out of my pocket and hand it to him. It's almost a relief to be rid of it.

"Get out. Get the fuck out," he says.

When I walk into the house, everything must be showing on my face, because Mum looks instantly concerned when she comes out of the kitchen to greet me.

"Honey, are you okay?" she says, putting her hand on my forehead. "You look really pale."

"I've got a terrible headache," I say, and I can't stop the tears coming to my eyes as she puts her arm around my shoulders and leads me into the kitchen, rummaging in a drawer for a box of pain reliever.

"Oh, I hope you're not coming down with anything so close to our holiday," she says, filling a glass with water and putting a pill in my hand. "There's so many horrible bugs around at this time of year."

"I'm okay," I manage to say. The pill sticks for a moment as I struggle to swallow past the lump in my throat. "I might just go and lie down for a bit until the painkillers kick in."

I lie on my bed and close my eyes when I get upstairs, but

I can't close off the thoughts that are whirling around in my head. I've made things worse. I shouldn't have said anything. The look on his face... And he can't be right. Owen must have been lying to him. There's no way Hanna could have caused anyone's death, is there? He didn't answer my questions about who or when—is he talking recently, or years ago? And what could have happened? Did she give him drugs and make him overdose? Run him over? Feed him peanut butter when he was allergic?

As I try to process it all, I realize how much I don't know. I have no idea how long Ethan has been in prison for. I have no idea who Hanna went out with, who the candidates are for my father other than horrible Owen King—I couldn't name a single one of her boyfriends. I don't even know the real reasons she left home and left me behind. All I know is she got into a lot of trouble, that she used to drink and smoke and sneak out. But no one's ever told me if there was a definitive reason for her leaving and not really being welcome back... like someone dying?

There's a knock at my door and I sit up, just as Dad walks in.

"Your mother said you were ill."

It's the first time he's initiated conversation with me since Christmas.

"It's a headache, that's all."

He nods and turns as if to leave but I call him back.

"Dad? I really am sorry. For everything. But I promise— I really didn't do anything with Ethan. I *wouldn't*."

He sighs and answers without turning back to look at me. "I realize that. You're not like Hanna."

"Why didn't you ever tell me... that you adopted me from Hanna?" I can't call her my mother in front of Dad.

"It would have been too complicated," he says after a long silence. "Adopted children don't have their birth mothers walking in and out of their lives on a regular basis. They need stability and security. *You* needed stability and security."

"What did she do? What did she do that was so bad? Was it just because she got pregnant and had me? It can't have just been sneaking out and drinking...God, half the kids in my year have been doing that since they were thirteen."

Dad has his hand on the door, but he lets it drop and turns back to face me. "Of course it was more than that. It wasn't just drinking. It was drugs. Even while she was pregnant. When she knew she was pregnant. She stole money from us—she was violent toward your mother. She never accepted Jen, she was constantly hostile. It was a relief when she left. I'm sorry to have to say that about my own daughter, but it was. We gave her money, so we knew she wasn't living on the streets."

"She was violent to Mum?"

"Your mother tried to stop her leaving the house once and yes, she lashed out. Pushed your mother over, left her bruised and, frankly, scared."

Oh God, *this* is the rebellious, cool Hanna I used to hero-worship? Someone worse than all those bitchy girls from my old school, someone worse than all the dicks on the school bus.

"If she hadn't left, we would have asked social services to have her removed." He pauses. "And it worked. She turned her own life around, it seems. She has a job, a home, a life. Would she have done that if she'd stayed here? I don't know."

He looks down at me. "We will try to be a little less strict

The Night They Vanished

with you. But remember this conversation, remember why we do this—to keep you from making the same mistakes. To protect you."

I do understand, I do, but there's still that little voice that keeps piping up, asking, wondering: if they'd been less strict with Hanna, would she have ever rebelled in such a spectacular way?

But it doesn't matter now. Everything Dad has told me, everything Ethan told me, everything he's *done*—I'm not going to be doing any kind of rebelling.

I don't want to be anything like Hanna.

Chapter 36

Thedarktourist.com
  <One New Listing!>

HANNA—Tuesday 1 p.m.

We don't even make it halfway home before DC Norton calls. "Can you come back? He's put something new up on the Dark Tourist website."

I turn to Adam, but he obviously heard as he's already moving into the right-hand lane as we approach a roundabout, ready to go back toward the police station. The volume of traffic makes our progress through the city agonizingly slow and I'm ready to scream by the time we find a parking space that's not too many millions of miles from the police station.

I'm half-running down the street, two paces behind Adam, when my blast from the past literally plows into me. I stagger, a very British apology already on my lips even though *he* ran into *me*, but the words die before they come out when I look up and it's Owen King in front of me, walking away from the police station as fast as I'm walking toward it.

I recognize him straight away, just as I did Lee. It bothers me, how little we've all changed, when so much in our lives has. We should look different too. I shouldn't see that flood of shocked recognition in his face, even when I know it's reflected in my own.

And I shouldn't have to see the way shock dissolves into disgust and anger, when it's him doing all this, not me.

"You should be in handcuffs," he says, and I stare at him in disbelief.

"*Me* in handcuffs? Where is my family, Owen? What the hell have you done? Where's Sasha?"

"I have no idea. You should try keeping better track of your family rather than getting me hauled in here for no reason. But then you never gave a shit about family or friends, did you?"

Adam looks ready to step in as Owen moves closer to me, but I don't look anywhere but at Owen as I put my hand on his chest and push him away.

"It's been fifteen years, Owen, for God's sake. *Fifteen years.*"

"What—you think I've wasted a second thinking about you all these years? You think I *want* to be here? Questioned by the police, my van taken away, letting clients down, losing business because of you?" He glances back at Adam before turning to me again. "You and your friend here, his little article. The fucking *lies* about Jacob. If you want to know what's got me so fucking pissed off, then maybe reread that dirty lying *crap*. And know that whatever happens, it's all *your* fault, you and your new boyfriend."

I frown, looking between them. I didn't want to read the article Adam wrote, didn't want to read a version of my past laid bare for some voyeuristic dark tourism thing… but what did Adam say last night? About what he wrote? He said he wrote it with me as the victim. A child blamed by the town…He didn't mention what he wrote about Jacob. But no. It's rubbish. It's Owen just being Owen.

"Do you know what, Owen King? Jacob used to say you were jealous, that's why you were such a bastard to me. Because he used to be your best friend and you never wanted to share."

"I was never jealous," Owen says, cold and calm and loud. "You never stood a chance of coming between me, Lee, and Jacob by being his girlfriend. But I could see how destructive you were. And I was right, wasn't I? You couldn't have him all to yourself so you destroyed him. You destroyed his family. And then you got to just walk away." He glances past me. "And there's my ride, so I need to go and get my bloody van back."

I turn and see Carrie behind the wheel of a black Mazda, double-parked a few yards away. It's impulse that has me pushing past Owen, running toward the car, talking through her half-open window. "Carrie—please. Does he have them? Has he got Sasha?"

She ignores me, pushing the button to close her window.

"Please, Carrie. Sasha is *fourteen*. She's a *child*."

"Fuck off, Hanna," Owen says as he gets into the passenger seat. "We haven't done anything to your damned family."

Carrie starts driving as soon as he's in, leaving me a breathless mess on the pavement.

Adam comes over, touches my shoulder. Has it really been less than a week since our blind date? It feels more like a year and I feel ten years older. I stand next to him, shoulders hunched as I wait for the questions. He thinks he already knows. But he has to be wondering—all that hostility from Owen, from Lee and Stephen.

"I know it wasn't your fault," Adam says. "Jacob's death."

I look down at the pavement and in my mind, all I can

hear is Jacob's voice the last time I spoke to him: his one call and he made it to me...the *anguish*, the *desperation*. I can't...I can't bear it. Even now, it's so raw. I should have done more. I should have done *something*.

"Yes, it was," I say, shrugging away the hand on my shoulder and turning to walk back toward the police station. "Owen's right. It was my fault."

"Why the hell have you let him go?" I ask DC Norton, the moment I see him.

He sighs. "He has alibis for both the hit-and-run and the murder of Katie Bentley. We've gone over his van, inch by inch. There's no evidence—nothing—to suggest he's done anything to your family. The only link is him working for them. That's not enough, Hanna." He pauses. "We will, of course, be keeping an eye on his movements."

I have to resist the urge to scream. I'm glad Adam is here, glad he's here to be the calm one.

"You said he put something new on the Dark Tourist website?" he asks, and he curls one of own hands around my clenched fist.

"We've had an alert set up for any changes on the site," DC Norton says as he leads us down the corridor. "We didn't want to shut it down in case the Digital Investigations Unit had any luck tracking him down. This is the first new traffic to the site since you came in."

Instead of an interview room, he takes us into an open-plan office, full of desks and computers. He turns a monitor around so we can both see the screen.

WELCOME TO THE DARK TOURIST—ONE NEW LISTING!

Underneath there are two photographs and one line of text.

I don't recognize the house in the first picture—it's a new-build, obviously not even lived in, part of a building site, a new housing development. The second photograph, though...it's Sasha. Not an old photo, obviously recent. I haven't seen her since last summer, and in this photo she looks older. She's all wrapped up in a coat and scarf, leaning against a wall, looking away at something, caught unawares. My heart stutters as I read the text underneath.

INSIDE INFO ON THE TERRIBLE MURDER OF SOUTH WALES SCHOOLGIRL

I reach for the mouse, but DC Norton stops me. "That's all there is. It doesn't link to a page—it's just this, on the home page."

"There must be more," I say, and I can hear the panic in my voice. "We have to find her, we have to find her *now*. You need to bring Owen back in. If he has her...if he hurts her..." My breath hitches and I know I'm on the verge of losing it. He thinks I killed Jacob and now he has Sasha. "There must be something we can do—we can't just sit here and wait for him to murder her."

"We're not sitting doing nothing, Hanna—we have a whole team on this." He frowns as another plainclothes officer comes over and beckons DC Norton away. They carry on a quiet conversation as I watch Adam going through the Dark Tourist website, searching every page for clues.

I can see something's wrong as soon as DC Norton comes back.

"What is it?" I say.

"We got a hit—a connection between the listings. Gemma Bentley—the hit-and-run victim. I spoke to the team working that case. She was a key witness in the trial that got Ethan Taylor sent to prison. They worked together." He shakes his head. "Damn it. They questioned him, but he had alibis for the night of the hit-and-run, doesn't own a car..."

"Don't tell me—his alibi was Owen King?"

DC Norton winces. "Close: Lee and Carrie Brown."

"Shit...So why, what—are they all working together? Giving each other alibis?"

"We have people checking out his last known addresses, his known associates," DC Norton says. "All forces have been alerted and sent his photograph as well as your family's. We might need you to do a media appeal."

"That will all take too long—we need to find him *now.*" I know I'm not helping, I know what I'm saying isn't logical. What am I expecting them to do—find him by magic? But my mind is screaming in panic and DC Norton and Adam are standing there so damned calmly and—

"What about a date?" Adam asks. "The other listings put dates."

DC Norton shakes his head. "There's nothing. Do either of you recognize the house?"

I lean in to look closer at the photograph, taking in every detail, desperate to find something familiar. But it's just an empty shell of a house, there's nothing familiar to find. I look at Adam, but he shakes his head.

"We're analyzing everything we can about the photograph—we have software and an expert digital team. We're seeing if we can find enough information to figure out where it is, if not the exact address. If we know the area, it might ring some bells for you." He hesitates and looks at me. "We hope he doesn't have your family. We hope this is just intended to frighten you. But…you have your family's mobile numbers. We'd like you to sit with a member of our team and call their numbers again. If your family is with him and he has their phones…We're applying for communications data in relation to the mobile phones, so we may be able to trace their location that way."

I take a deep breath as we all stare at my phone. DC Norton thinks he has them. He doesn't want me to leave another message for Dad or Jen or Sasha. He wants me to leave a message for the man who has taken my family.

My phone rings then, and the serendipity of it ringing just as we're staring at it makes us all jump.

The number on the screen is not one I recognize. My heart starts pounding as I look at DC Norton and he nods.

Oh God. I connect the call.

"Hanna? It's…it's Carrie."

My heart rate doesn't slow. Carrie Hayes or Brown or whatever name she's using is not going to be ringing me for a nice, cozy catch-up.

"I'm sorry about earlier," she says.

I let out a shaky breath. "Is it Owen? Does he have my family?"

Silence on the line.

"Please, Carrie. If you're scared…if he's threatening you—"

"It's not what you think. It got out of hand, that's all. And now Owen has roped Lee into it—using him as an alibi. I could lose my job. We both could. He made us lie to the police and—"

"Carrie, please. I'm at the police station now—will you talk to them? Will you tell me what you mean? Help me."

"I can't. I'm sorry. But I never realized...We thought we were covering the fact that Ethan had broken a probation rule, that's all. That's what Owen said." There's another long pause. "It's Ethan. Owen started things, but he got Ethan all riled up and...I tried to talk Ethan out of doing anything when I last saw him, before Christmas, but he wouldn't listen..."

I shake my head, even though I know she can't see me. "I don't—Carrie, I don't know Ethan. Neither does Adam. It has to be Owen. Ethan is a stranger—why would he do this?"

I can hear Carrie breathing. "Ethan is not a stranger. I know he took a different name when he was fostered, but...Hanna, Ethan is Jacob's brother."

She ends the call without another word, and when I try to call back, it goes straight to voicemail. I try to unravel her words as I look at Adam and DC Norton and the world shrinks a little bit more as I process it. Oh. I see. I see now.

Ethan Saunders.

He thinks I killed his brother and now he has my family.

Chapter 37

SASHA—Tuesday 3 p.m.

I was looking forward to half-term so much. A week without having to get the bus or go to school. Although, to be fair, other than Ethan showing up, yesterday wasn't that bad, and I'm not dreading going back after half-term quite so much. I'm not the weird new girl anymore, I'm just another girl. I've even started talking to a couple of the girls who sit near me in class. Nice, normal girls who, in nice, normal times, could end up becoming friends. Moving here, starting this new school, could have been the happy-ever-after to a really boring YA novel, where I end up with some friends, I pass my exams, and go off to a good university.

But instead of half-term being this lovely much looked forward to break, I spend every second in a state of heightened anxiety. Because after I told him about Hanna, there's been no sign of Ethan. It's what I thought I wanted. He's gone, and so is the phone he gave me. He didn't call the house or turn up again, thank God, but I jumped every time the house phone rang, or Mum or Dad's mobiles. Every time I heard a car driving past, I froze, waiting for it to stop, pull in, for Ethan to climb out.

But in the very long day between me telling him and us going away, there was nothing. And I don't feel reassured, not in the slightest. The look on his face when I told him about Hanna... I don't know what to do.

If I still had the phone, I could take it to the police, but when I think about it, even if I did, what could I prove? Yes, there's a whole history of my contact with Ethan on there, but he's never said anything incriminating on text— nothing police-worthy, anyway.

I can't tell Mum or Dad, because then I'd have to explain that I'd actually had a forbidden phone for months, that Ethan gave it to me, and I've been lying to them the whole time.

And if I *did* tell someone? I don't know where Ethan is living, where he's working, if anywhere. I suppose he's meant to keep the authorities informed as he's just got out of prison, but I don't know that for sure. And worst of all—he knows where *I* live. He knows where I go to school, where I get on and off the bus.

The only other thing I could think to do was go back to Littledean. Find Owen King. Get him to speak to Ethan for me. But he wouldn't. He'd see my worry and misery as a victory—a point against my dad, against Hanna. Plus, I'd basically have to run away from home, even if it was just for a day—there's no way I'd actually get permission to go back there.

My head constantly aches and I'm struggling to act in any way normal because I'm so distracted all the time.

And I don't... I don't know what to do.

It's half-term and we're away for a few days. Dad booked it ages ago and it's the last chance before the holiday park opens at Easter. Because it's a much bigger, busier park than the old one, it's going to be frantic right through until

October. Dad said—and the irony of all this is enough to make me cry—he said if I carry on with the good behavior, there might even be a part-time job for me. A chance to actually be part of the holiday camp I live in, a chance to actually earn some money of my own. He said this as I was desperately contemplating running off, taking a bus to *beg* Owen King to help me.

So, with this half-term, with this last chance, we've headed back to southeast Wales, traveling along the Heritage Coast before moving west to the Gower, staying in B & B's with sea views and full English breakfasts. Bracing walks on the beach, and afternoon teas. I didn't want to go; it's harder to pretend everything's fine when the three of us are together all day. But I didn't want to stay either. Staying meant my every last nerve getting shredded each time a phone rang or a car passed.

And it's not like I had a choice, so here we are, ten in the morning on the Tuesday of half-term, driving the coastal roads toward our second stop. We spent the first weekend in Porthcawl, and even though hardly anything was open, I spent almost the whole two days by the fair, because I knew Mum and Dad wouldn't want to waste their time there. So, while they walked the coastal path or relaxed at the hotel, I lurked around the amusement arcades, ate too much ice cream, watched people mindlessly shoving money and tokens in machines. For two whole days.

We've moved on now and it's actually sunny today, and with the windows closed and the car heating on, I could almost pretend it was summer. It's weird, being back this side of Wales. Like coming home rather than going away. The new part of Wales we're living in is very pretty, the sea a lovely deep blue. Back here, it's very much a stormy gray.

But still, two months in, this feels like coming home and West Wales feels like the holiday.

That's stupid, I know. I was *miserable* back in Littledean. Miserable at school, bored stupid at home. Mum was right that the move could be a proper fresh start. This week could be the start of it—for the first time, I can fully appreciate Dad's no-phones-on-holiday rule, so his and Mum's mobiles have stayed switched off at the bottom of Mum's handbag since Saturday, there just for emergencies. Ethan doesn't know we're on holiday. Maybe if he has reappeared over the weekend, he'll get bored and give up when we don't come home. I mean, it's true what he said—he's just a computer guy. How much damage can he do?

And when we get home—I'll *beg* Dad to start picking me up from school again. I'll tell him all the horror stories about the bus, and I'll beg and plead. I'll bloody beg him to go back to the old ways, where I'm never free to meet or get calls off *anyone*. And I'll stay locked up like Rapunzel in her tower until I'm eighteen. The thought is actually a relief.

Another thought pops into my head as we drive down a steep, winding lane toward our next destination. Maybe Dad *should* find out about the phone, and all of the meetings. I wouldn't say anything about Ethan's scary revenge thing with Hanna, but if I played stupid and cried and said Ethan gave me the phone ages ago and I'd felt so *guilty*, but I didn't know what to *do*...

Dad would go back to the police or probation service again, probably. This time, it might really get Ethan into trouble...But if it was Dad who did it, if Ethan was watching and saw that I'd been grounded again, that I wasn't going on the school bus anymore, that I was basically under house arrest—if he was already in trouble and he saw all that, he'd give up, wouldn't he? He'd step back and leave me alone. And he'd leave Hanna alone.

I'll risk being locked in the tower forever for that. For things to just go back to normal, or whatever passed for normal before I made that stupid Facebook account. I don't even care if the promises of my own phone and a part-time job are taken away. It'll be like my own prison sentence for computer fraud, but with better food. I'll be out in four years—maybe less for good behavior.

I duck my head down to hide a smile, as Dad parks in the car park behind a small hotel on the seafront. I feel like I've been in limbo for weeks and even though it's hell I'm on my way to, because the fallout will be horrific, it's definitely relief I'm feeling in the pit of my stomach. Relief at making a decision to actually *do* something.

The hotel at our second stop is old, all chintz and dark wood. It's clean, but there's a definite musty smell as we walk through the door. A smiling woman with the most hideous pink lipstick checks us in and I'm happy when we're given two rooms. I was worried we'd all be in a family room like in the last hotel, and I wouldn't get a second alone, but I'm given a single room on the same floor as my parents and we all troop up the creaky stairs together before going our separate ways.

The relief disappears when I step into my tiny room, though, because there's a brown paper parcel sitting in the middle of the single bed. I freeze and quickly close the door behind me, in case Mum or Dad decide to come and check on me.

This is a small, seaside hotel in a small, seaside town.

There's no room service, so no convenient phone next to the bed for me to phone down and find out where the parcel came from. There's not even a key card to open the door. The door was unlocked and open when we came up the creaky stairs, the key for the door sitting on the table next to the bed in a china dish. I'm guessing the room has been unlocked since it was cleaned earlier in the day, so even if I asked at reception, they might have no idea how the parcel got here.

There was no one behind the desk when we first walked in—we had to ring the little brass bell and wait an age before the pink-lipsticked receptionist appeared. Which means if the desk isn't manned all the time, anyone could have walked in at any time, checked the reservations, found out which room I was going to be staying in... Two rooms booked under the name of Carter, mine was obviously going to be the single.

I crouch down and look under the bed, then open the wardrobe to check for lurkers in there. It's not an en-suite room, so I don't have to worry about a madman with an ax hiding behind the shower curtain. I pull the curtains closed and lock myself in the room before sitting on the edge of the bed to look more closely at the parcel.

There's no name on it, so it can't have been sent up via reception. It has to have been hand-delivered to my room. I pick it up. It's about the size of a hardback book, but lighter in weight. I'm tempted to open the window or door and hurl the thing away, but I'd end up feeling mighty foolish if it turns out to be some cute welcome thing from the hotel. I can imagine the scene if I chuck it out like an unexploded bomb, and it turns out to be complementary toiletries.

But I passed Mum and Dad's room down the corridor

on the way to my room, and I saw inside and there was no parcel on their bed. I try to handle it as little as possible as I tug at the tape, just in case it contains some severed body part and I have to call the police. I'm trying to joke to myself, but now I'm picturing Hanna's hand, with that tattoo I spotted last time she visited, seven tiny black stars dotted across her wrist. *Yes, Officer, I recognize my sister's hand, I recognize this star just by where it was severed.*

I pull the brown paper off and am left with a white box. Not leaking blood, not smelling like death, but that doesn't ease the way my entire insides are somersaulting.

I lift the lid off the box and frown. It's a photograph in a frame, that's all. A plain, cheap wooden frame, a snapshot-size photograph. I don't get it. I recognize Hanna in the photograph—Hanna at the age she was in the photos I found of her, or perhaps a little older—but this is a new one. She's facing the camera, arm in arm with a boy who looks a few years older than her, both of them smiling, both of them looking happy. The boy has bleached-blond hair, long at the front and hanging over his face. He has his ears and nose pierced and he's wearing almost as much black eyeliner as Hanna. I don't recognize him; I don't think he was in any of the other photos I found.

I just don't get it. Why would Ethan—because it has to be Ethan—leave this here? Is this Owen's friend—the one who died? I drop the framed photograph back in the box and that's when I spot it. The arm the unknown boy has slung around Hanna's shoulder—there's a tattoo. A dozen tiny black stars on the back of his hand.

I lean back and blink, trying to remember how Hanna's tattoo was arranged. *It's a constellation,* she said when she caught me looking at it—the only words she spoke directly to me on that visit. I grab the pen and tiny notebook that's on the bedside table and draw what I remember of her tattoo. It's not the same as the boy's in this photo, but they're clearly both constellations, there's clearly a connection.

And Hanna's tattoo was new. Not something she got way back then.

This must be the friend Owen told Ethan about, the one whose death he claims Hanna had something to do with. I chew on my lip, staring at the door. How long do I have before Mum or Dad come knocking? I have some school books at the bottom of my bag, because it's me, so of course I do. We're doing space and the planets as a topic in physics and one of the books has diagrams of some of the constellations...I look from the book to my scribbled drawing of Hanna's remembered tattoo to the one on the boy's hand in the photograph. I'm not even sure, in the end, I've found the right ones. There are no numbers on this dot-to-dot puzzle, so I can't be sure I've joined them up right, but I think, I'm almost sure, that Hanna has a tattoo of the constellation *Andromeda*, and the boy in the photo, *Perseus*. A bit more searching, and I have a meaning.

Andromeda, the chained maiden, and *Perseus*, the boy who rescued her.

I look at the photograph again, this time more carefully at the boy. Looking for some resemblance to me.

Chapter 38

Tuesday 5 p.m.

That's it. That. Is. It. I cannot do this anymore. Not on my own. Is Ethan here? Waiting outside the hotel? Is he *in* the hotel? Oh God, he could be in the next room. I'm finding it difficult to breathe and my hands are shaking as I walk down the corridor to Mum and Dad's room. I knock and start talking as soon as Dad opens the door.

"I need your help. I've done something stupid and I really need your help."

He *will* help, won't he? However much trouble I end up in, however appalled he is at what I've done, even if I'm grounded until I turn eighteen, he'll help... He's my dad, he has to.

But he didn't help Hanna when she got into trouble, a little voice in my head says, and I swallow as he closes the door and waits for me to speak.

I tell them everything. I don't look directly at either of them as I talk, but from the corner of my eye, I see Mum sinking down to sit on the bed as I tell them about fake Facebook accounts, making friends with Ethan, him giving me the phone... I don't dare look at Dad's face. I tell them everything, right up to skipping school and my fear about Ethan being here, now, and then I wait. I cross all my fingers behind my back, and I wait for Dad to go nuts, but then take control and make everything all right again, because that's what dads do. I wait for him to promise to sort all of this out for me, so I don't have to worry anymore.

I wait. And I wait.

"I should have expected this" is what he eventually says, and there's no reassurance in his voice, only disappointment. His words are heavy with it, saturated. I could write an English essay in metaphor and simile on the weight of disappointment in those five words.

"Dad, please..." I finally manage to look up, but he's not looking at me. His gaze is averted, like he can't bear to look at me.

"Enough, Sasha. I don't want to hear another word from you. Jen? Will you go downstairs and book a table for dinner? Just for two people, I think."

Mum stands up and looks from me to him. "I don't think—"

"Please," he says. "I need to have a little talk with Sasha—I know you don't like confrontation, but there are some hard truths she needs to hear. I think it will be easier for all of us if it's just Sasha and me."

I don't think it will be easier. I don't think it will be easier at all, but Mum's already moving toward the door, because this is the way it always goes. If I'm due a telling-off or a grounding, Mum leaves the room.

"Mum—please..."

She wavers at the door; I can see the indecision in her face as she looks from me to Dad. *Stand up for me*, I think, willing her to hear my thoughts. *Stand up to him. Fuck the Patriarchy.* Dad must see her indecision, because he's frowning at her now, rather than at me.

"Jen," he says, "we've talked about this... *This* is what happens when you begin to give children more freedoms... Trust me on this, okay?"

Mum's shoulders sag and she turns away from me. I think she used up all her newfound girl power on forcing him to move away. It seems to have gone back to business as usual. I really should stop expecting things to be different. I only ever end up disappointed. I don't think I've ever greeted that quiet click of a door as she leaves with quite so much dread before, though.

He doesn't shout. That's rarely his way. He doesn't actually say anything for ages. He walks past me to the window and stands there looking out at the sea.

I break first. I usually do. I wonder if Hanna did too, or if they'd stand in epic silence until one of them fell asleep? Maybe that's what got to her in the end, what made her leave: the endless silence.

"Dad, I'm sorry."

He finally turns to look at me. "Well, of course you are. You're sorry now, because you've been caught out. Because you've got yourself in trouble."

"That's not what I mean."

"Isn't it? Would you have been sorry about creating that Facebook account if you'd never received those messages? Or would you have blithely carried on? Would you still be sneaking into my office to use my computer?"

Is he right? His words throw me because is he right? If I'd never got that first private message on Facebook, would I have carried on with my fake life online, stalking my sister's friends, pretending to be someone else, someone *with* a life?

I'm sorry all this has happened, but really, is what

Dad's saying right? That I'm not sorry for doing something wrong—I'm not sorry for sneaking around and lying and breaking rules—I'm only sorry because I got caught. That's not...I don't like that idea. I don't think that's the person I want to be.

Dad smiles but it's not a happy smile. "I suppose I should be grateful you're showing any regret for your actions. Hanna never did. When she got caught she only ever showed defiance. And she certainly never came to me and confessed her wrongdoings. Not until it was too late."

I grab on to that thread. "Will you help me sort this out? Because I've learned my lesson, I really have. This has taught me what happens when I break the rules. I'll never do anything like this again; I'll work hard at school and I won't ever do anything wrong. I don't..." I pause. "I don't want to be like Hanna."

There's another silence as he returns his attention to the view out of the window.

"The thing is, Sasha...when Hanna went too far, when her actions had consequences, I made the decision to step in. To do what I thought was the right thing, for her and for the family. But my decisions, and my actions, led to things happening that I couldn't have foreseen, that led to her leaving and a fracture within the family we've never been able to mend."

I want to be sick. Is he talking about me? Am I the *consequence* of Hanna's actions? He turns, then, to look at me. And this time, there is emotion on his face. I don't know if it's sadness or regret, but it's there and gone in a second.

"I'm not going to do anything this time. I've often wondered—if I'd left Hanna to sort out her own mess, would things have turned out differently? After all, what she has managed to achieve since leaving, she's done on her own. You say you don't want to be like Hanna. Well, this is your chance to prove it. This is your chance to prove you're mature enough to sort out your own mess."

"What? But, Dad—I told you the things Ethan has said, the things he said he's going to do...I have no idea what he's done to Hanna. I thought you could ring her and—"

Dad shakes his head. "Enough. You've brought this on yourself, and so, in a way, has Hanna. I know Ethan and I know Owen King. I spoke to them many times and I don't believe either of them is dangerous, not in a physically violent way, so I don't believe anyone has any intention of harming either of you. It seems Owen is another person damaged by Hanna's past—Lord knows, there were plenty of them."

"But...but *you* said Ethan was a violent criminal. *You* said that."

"I said that in the hope you would stay away from him. Clearly it didn't work. It seems to me Owen is using you and Ethan for some petty revenge, and you were foolish enough to fall for it. But I won't call the police and have Ethan rearrested for a series of messes *you* caused, that *you* asked him to get involved in. He's taken the phone back, I'm sure he'll leave you alone now. I should have let Hanna deal with the consequences of her own actions instead of stepping in. I won't make the same mistake with you."

I stare at him with tears in my eyes, but he doesn't say anything else. That's it. String cut. Hopes shattered. I feel...I feel...What do I feel? What is this sharp stabbing?

Betrayal. I feel betrayed. I'm Julius Caesar and I'm Othello, I'm Harry Potter's parents; Dad is Brutus, Iago, and Peter Pettigrew all rolled into one, standing there with a bloody knife.

The Night They Vanished

"Well, maybe…" My words come out as a whisper and I hate that. I clear my throat and make myself speak louder. "Maybe if that's the way you feel, I should go and live with Hanna. Maybe I should try to be more like her, not less."

"Good luck with that. She doesn't even call you or visit. Has there been a single second in your entire life where she's shown any inclination to step up and be your mother?" Dad sighs and shakes his head. "If Jen hadn't stepped in, if she hadn't insisted we adopt you, do you really think Hanna would ever have kept you with her? No. Of course not. If it weren't for us, if it were only down to Hanna, you would have ended up in care, taken away by social services."

"And what about my father? My *real* father?" I hold out the photograph I brought with me to the room.

Dad goes pale as he looks down at the photo, white other than two growing red spots on his cheeks.

"Go to your room," he says between clenched teeth.

"What about—"

"*Now.* Not another word. Go."

Chapter 39

Dad has gone downstairs to join Mum for an early dinner and I'm lying on the bed in my room. Although, why should I just stay here, a kid sent to bed with no supper? My stomach's rumbling, Dad's made it very clear I'm a disappointment and that I'm on my own. He basically said he's washed his hands of me, so why should I stay here and starve in misery? I've still got the holiday money Mum gave me—I can go and get chips. Doesn't matter if I get caught, doesn't matter if they come back up and find me gone. I'll just throw Dad's words back at him—I was out sorting out my own mess, I'll say. And for that, I need chips.

My hair is one big tangle, so I pick up my brush and attack it until it's smooth, tying it back in my usual low ponytail. I pull a face at myself in the mirror. There's none of Hanna in the face that looks back at me, none of Dad either that I can see. He and Hanna do look alike, same blue eyes and wavy dark hair. My hair is boring light brown and dead straight and my eyes are a sludgy hazel. It's no wonder I never guessed about Hanna.

I pick up the framed photograph of Hanna and the mystery boy again. I know nothing about my real father, not his name or anything, but from looking at my face and knowing basic

306

genetics from school, I've worked out he must have straight hair, blond or brown, and brown or green eyes. It's difficult to tell from this photo. His hair is dyed, so I've no idea of the natural color, and I can't really tell the eye color behind all that eyeliner. Am I imagining a similarity in face shape?

I look at my own reflection again and the plain, unmade-up face, the neat hair—it bothers me today. It doesn't feel like me anymore. I have makeup at the bottom of my toiletries bag, makeup I've bought but never had the courage to wear. That annoys me today as well. I prop the photo of Hanna and mystery boy up against the mirror and attempt to re-create their eye makeup with black eyeliner. I go across the hall to the bathroom and grab one of the complementary toiletries packs, bringing it back to my room. There's a sewing kit in there, with a tiny pair of scissors. Without allowing myself time to have second thoughts, I grab my ponytail and start cutting through it, right above where the bobble holds it at the nape of my neck.

I realize I've made a mistake the moment the first chunk falls, but it's too late then. The scissors are pretty crap and by the time I've finished sawing through my hair, my hand has cramped up and the scissors are all bent and mangled. I drop the scissors and let my hair fall free to swing round my face. I lean forward to inspect my work in the mirror.

"Oh, God," I mutter to my horrified reflection. When they do this in books or films, it's always some big cathartic moment, and the newly shorn hair always looks cool. Mine looks...my lips twitch. It looks...absolutely *terrible*. I let the building laughter go, collapsing into absolute hysterics at the sight of my handiwork. It's all completely uneven, the left side longer than the right, with a massive clump at the back a full two inches shorter than the rest.

Even if Mum and Dad took me to an emergency hair-dresser appointment to fix it, they'd have to cut it horribly short to even it out. And they wouldn't anyway, Dad at least. He'll make me wear this hair until it grows out to *learn my lesson*. I picture myself getting on the school bus next week looking like this and I start laughing again. I look *unhinged*. It looks as if I've had a mental meltdown with my stupid smudgy panda eyes and this hair. Which, I suppose, I have. That's what all of this is. But seriously... I ruffle my new short hair, hoping it'll fall into some kind of—*any* kind of—shape...Oh, books and films, you *lie*.

I look at the severed pile of hair on the dressing table and wait to feel sad. Or regretful. But I don't. I look hideous, but the laughter has made me feel better. I'm going to own this foul haircut. No. More than that. I'm going to *rock* this haircut. It hasn't made me look anymore like Hanna or mystery boy, but it certainly feels like a Hanna thing to do.

And maybe, I think as I walk down the stairs, if any shops are open, I'll buy bleach for my hair. Miss Pink-lipstick is behind the desk as I walk through the entrance hall. She's bashing the keyboard of her computer and scowling at the screen.

I go to walk past, but hesitate as she swears out loud. "Are you okay?" I ask.

She sighs and shakes her head. "No, this damned computer has frozen—I can't get to the bookings system, I can't get anything up. It's frozen on a website, and it's not even a website I've gone on to."

She looks on the verge of tears, so I change direction and go over to the desk. "Do you want me to see if I can do anything? I'm not great with computers but..."

"Please do—I can't get hold of my manager, but I'm

screwed if I can't sort this out. I can't prepare bills or check bookings or anything." She looks up from the screen at that point and takes in my new look. Her eyes get *really* big.

I swallow down another surge of hysterical laughter. I'm really going to struggle to be invisible now.

I join her behind the desk and look at the screen. She's probably been looking at some dodgy website and crashed her computer. I don't know anything about computers, but I can offer the wise advice of if in doubt, switch it off and on again, but as I reach for the mouse I freeze.

Welcome to The Dark Tourist, the website says.

And right underneath is a picture of a house I don't recognize. And a picture of a girl that I *do* recognize, because the girl is me, and according to the headline, I'm the victim of a terrible murder.

Chapter 40

Thedarktourist.com
   <One New Listing!>
   <EXCLUSIVE for members—Inside info on the terrible murder of South Wales schoolgirl.
   Who was she and why was she brutally killed? >

I reach down and yank the computer's plug out of the socket. Miss Pink-lipstick gasps as everything goes off.

"I think you've been hacked," I say. "All sorts of malware could be being dumped on your system. Switching it off is the best way to stop it." I have no idea what I'm talking about. Pulling the plug was a panicked instinct—I just wanted those pictures, that headline, *gone*. This isn't a vaguely threatening anonymous Facebook message, this is…horrible. This isn't Hanna messing around—was it ever Hanna? Oh God, I only have Ethan's word that it was. This is Ethan. This is *all* Ethan.

I've been so stupid.

And now I'm thinking I was stupid to panic and unplug the computer. I should have looked further, clicked on the link.

Before I can even think about plugging it back in, though, the phone on the front desk rings and the receptionist answers, but not before taking a wary step away from me.

"Good evening, Seaview Hotel, how can I help...?" Her voice trails off and she stares at me. She holds out the receiver. "It's for you."

I hold the phone to my ear. I already know who it's going to be.

"Did you get my present?"

I swallow, my heart thumping. He sounds so damned cheerful.

"What's wrong, Sasha? Surprised to hear from me? You know, you really shouldn't have given me access to your dad's computer. I found out a lot of things while you were keeping lookout. Passwords, where you were moving, your new school—everything. It was easy, even remotely, for me to find out all your plans for this week. To be fair, it wasn't all you—I *may* have had to sneak into the house to use the computer a few times when you were all out, before we were *friends*. Your dad's security is pretty crap. It's how I got the original idea for the Facebook messages—it was easy to figure out who had the Facebook account when I went through your internet history. You and your parents went skipping off shopping and there it was. To be honest, I did you a favor. If your dad had opened the computer rather than me and was tech savvy enough to check the history..."

Bizarrely, it actually makes me feel better knowing he basically broke into our house to sneak around on the computer. Because it means not *everything* is my fault.

"Where are you?" It comes out as a whisper.

There's a pause before he answers. "I'm outside."

I take a shaky breath.

"Meet me at the harbor."

"No. *No*, I won't. I..."

"You will if you don't want me to lose my temper and take it out on Hanna. On your *mother*."

My throat closes up as he ends the call. Of course, I could call his bluff and just run back upstairs, lock my door, and hide…but he's *here*. He's *outside*. And if I don't go and meet him…I don't know him. I thought I did but I don't. I don't know what he'll do to Hanna if I don't go out there now.

I hand the phone back to the receptionist, apologizing again about the computer before asking if I can borrow a pen and paper. I scribble a note, addressing it to Mum, telling her I've gone for a walk. I hesitate, then write down the time and that I'd be back within the hour. I hesitate again. I want to write something about Ethan, but…if I write that I'm meeting him in this note and Dad reads it before I get back and calls the police, that would make Ethan really mad. Mad at them as well as mad at me and Hanna.

No. I'll leave it like that. The fact that I've left will be enough of an alert.

Just in case.

Ethan has his back to me, leaning on the harbor wall, looking out to sea. I glance back toward the hotel, wondering if we can be seen, but the road twists enough that we can't be spotted from any of the windows.

I go to stand next to him and he turns to look at me. He doesn't even seem to notice my hair or the crap makeup. "I should have seen it," he says.

"Seen what?" I ask, but he shakes his head.

"Not here," he says. "We can't talk here." He takes my arm and pulls me toward a van parked on the side of the road.

"No way," I say, trying to pull away from him. "I'm not getting in a car with you."

"Don't be stupid," he says as the van's driver door opens, and Owen King gets out.

The panic proper kicks in then and I go to scream, but Ethan has his hand over my mouth, and he shoves me into the back of the van, climbing in after me as Owen slams the doors shut.

"Calm the fuck down," Ethan mutters as the van starts moving.

Calm down? *Calm down*? My breath is coming out in gasps, I'm shaking and crying, and I think I'm going to wet myself, I really, really do.

"No one's going to hurt you. It got…it got out of hand, that's all. I thought I was doing Owen a favor—he gave me a job, I do a bit of computer work, check up on some old acquaintances." He stares at me. "And then you told me Hanna was your mother…" He stops and shakes his head.

"It wasn't ever about you, but then you told me, and I was so angry…so *fucking angry*…and that stupid Katie Bentley constantly harassing me, blaming me for a stupid accident…" He pauses, takes a deep breath. "I tried to tell her it wasn't me, and it *wasn't*. Gemma set me up, got me sent to prison, when I didn't know what I was doing—it was her. I thought I was helping her, I didn't know she was using me to siphon off funds…and Owen…he said he'd talk to her. Get her to confess so I'd be exonerated, be able to get my life back—some compensation for wrongful conviction, even. But he found her out running, and he tried to talk to her…It was a bloody accident, that's all." He stops again. "I had to keep it quiet, but then her sister was *ranting* at me. *Blaming* me. Threatening to get me sent down again for something else I didn't do."

I've no idea what he's talking about. Who is it about if not me?

Hanna, of course. Whatever the hell is going on, it's about Hanna and the boy in the photograph.

"Who is he—the boy in the photograph? Is it Owen's friend? The one who died? Is he...is he my father?"

Ethan doesn't answer for a long time.

"His name was Jacob. And yes, he was your father. He was also my brother."

Chapter 41

HANNA—Tuesday 6 p.m.

DC Norton tells me what to say. I leave three separate messages, one each on Sasha, Jen, and Dad's phone, all saying the same thing: *This is a message for Ethan. The police know who you are. Please call me and we can talk. Please call me and let me know my family is safe.* I'm careful not to let slip that *I* know who he is—who he really is. I'm frustrated leaving these begging messages when I want to be actually doing something, but DC Norton believes the temptation to speak to me, now that we know one hundred percent all of this is aimed at me and why, will get him to open communications. And if he calls me, we can try to trace that call, or get him to give something away to help us find him.

I'm sitting in the corridor with Adam, staring down at my phone and willing it to ring, when Dee and Seb come out of one of the rooms. I stand up and Dee comes over and hugs me.

"God, I'm so sorry. The police said they think he's been hanging around us." She shudders and steps back. She looks freaked out and even Seb looks shaken. Bad enough when some anonymous stranger was doing this, but knowing he's been watching us, maybe for *months*... That's what

315

the police said. He got out of prison in October. Gemma Bentley was killed in a hit-and-run two minutes from my flat in November. Was I next on his list?

"It's Jacob's brother," I say in a low voice to Dee. I look over toward Adam, but he and Seb are talking and not listening to us, so I draw Dee further away. "Ethan," I say. "The guy that's doing this, he's Jacob's brother."

Dee visibly pales. "Shit. The officer that was talking to us, he wanted to know about Owen, and he showed us photos, wanting to know if we recognized this guy... He kept asking questions. We didn't know, couldn't even remember... but then, after we'd gone through every possible social event he could have been at in the last couple of months since he was released from prison, we figured it out. Or Seb did, anyway."

"It was Liam."

I jump. I hadn't heard Seb coming up behind me until he spoke. I turn to look at him. "What was Liam?"

"It was Liam who brought him in. Right before you two split up... or it could have been just after. It was some time just before or over Christmas, anyway. There was that weird night me and Dee were out, and Liam came over with a couple of other guys and started chatting like nothing had happened." He stops and looks at Dee. "I think it was then. I think that was the night. Do you remember? Between Christmas and New Year? They all just joined our table."

"Oh God, you're right," Dee says. "I don't specifically remember this Ethan, because I was too focused on wanting to escape from Liam the loser," Dee says. "The police think that's how he got into your flat, that connection with Liam. You didn't leave the door open—either Liam gave him the key or he stole it from him."

I remember the shock on Liam's face when he saw the state of my flat after the break-in. And how pale he went when I told him about those two women who were murdered and how *adamant* he was that he gave me my key back...

I don't think Ethan stole the key. I think Liam gave it to him for some reason, probably petty revenge for what he believes I did, and that's why he is panicking so much about those visits from the police. He probably thought Ethan was just... Actually, what the fuck *was* he thinking? He gave a stranger a key to my flat—what did he think he wanted it for? Oh, that absolute *shit*. I turn away from the sympathy on all their faces. This must be how he found out about Adam's website. Liam gave him a way into my life, into Dee, Seb, and Adam's lives, and with his computer background... he must have seen it as the perfect way to mess with me.

"But why go after my family? If he knew where I was—if he knew where I lived—why not just come after me?"

"I think..." Dee pauses.

"Just say it, Dee."

"He thinks you took his family away from him. I think he's doing the same to you."

"I need some fresh air," I say, but as I get up to leave, my phone rings—and it's my dad's number that flashes up on the screen. I suck in a breath and stare at Dee. Adam rushes off, calling for DC Norton as I pick the phone up. Will it be him? Ethan?

I answer with a wobbly hello.

"Hanna?"

Oh God. Oh, thank God—it's my dad.

"Dad? Where are you? Where have you been? I've been so worried, I—"

"Yes. I just got your message. We're away and my phone's been off for a few days." There's a pause. "I don't understand. Why are the police involved? Why are you leaving messages for Ethan on my phone? Is that Ethan Taylor? The man working for Owen—for us?"

He sounds rattled. I frown. "There's been some stuff going on..." I look up as Adam and DC Norton come running toward us and put the phone on speaker so they can hear. "This guy, this Ethan...we think he's dangerous. And when no one could find you...But it's okay. You're safe. You need to tell us where you are; we'll get the police to come and get you. Keep Jen and Sasha close and—"

"Hanna," Dad interrupts me.

"What?"

"Sasha went out. There was an...argument. She told us about Ethan—she said they've been friends. That he gave her a phone and that they've been meeting up. We...I sent her to her room. Jen and I went to dinner. I thought I'd check for messages while we were waiting. When we went back up, Sasha wasn't in her room. She left a note saying she was going out for a walk..."

DC Norton comes striding over. He takes the phone off speaker and starts asking Dad questions—what the argument was about, what time they went down to dinner, how long they were gone. The moment he comes off the line, he's calling out orders, beckoning me to follow him out of the station.

"They're only half an hour away. I've got local officers heading straight to the scene—to make sure your parents are safe, to see if we can find Sasha. It's possible she's just sneaked out after a family argument."

"Possible, but you don't think so," I say.

318

He doesn't answer that. "Let's just get there as soon as possible."

"Wait!" We both turn to face Adam as he comes running down the steps after us. "Hanna, I..."

DC Norton stares at him. "We have to go, Mr. Webster."

Adam nods and steps back. "I'll follow you," he calls as I climb in the back of the police car. "I'll bring Dee and Seb."

By the time we get to the hotel my family is staying in, DC Norton has been able to get a rough time when Sasha left the hotel, and that she left alone. The receptionist, when he repeats the questions in person, tells us about a girl I wouldn't have recognized from her description, a girl with punky hair and too much eyeliner, who wrecked the hotel computer before taking a phone call and leaving the hotel. Her note said she'd be back in an hour, but there's been no sign of her in the town or on the beach since and that hour deadline has long gone.

Adam, Dee, and Seb arrive as DC Norton is questioning the receptionist. He frowns but doesn't say anything. In fact, he hesitates as he's leading me to where Dad and Jen are and beckons to Adam. "You come as well, Mr. Webster, in case we need to ask more about your website."

Dad and Jen are waiting for us in the office behind reception. Jen looks as if she's been crying, but Dad doesn't. He jumps up the moment I walk in and he looks, if anything, *furious*.

"Mr. Carter? DC Norton." The detective holds out a hand to shake, but Dad ignores him, keeping that angry face aimed in my direction.

"What on earth is going on? What have you done, Hanna?"

I recoil. "What have *I* done? Jesus fucking Christ—what have *I* done?" I have to stop, take a deep breath, because otherwise I think I might launch myself at my father and try to beat the crap out of him.

"Ethan," I say through gritted teeth, "is Jacob's brother. Jacob Saunders."

I see the name register, watch his face go pale, then flood with color. Oh, yes, he knows that name. Didn't he ever check? Before he hired an ex-offender to work on the site, so close to his wife and daughter—didn't he do any bloody background checks? Adam and DC Norton are standing to my right. DC Norton looks solemn, Adam just looks confused.

"Sasha isn't my sister," I say to him. Words I meant to say after we spent the night together, but never got the chance.

"What?"

"She's my daughter."

His turn to take a deep breath. He opens his mouth as though to speak, but then stops, closes it, and shakes his head before trying again. "And Jacob? I'm guessing he was—"

"Sasha's father, yes."

"I don't...I don't understand. I researched it, the history of his house, his family...I read that he was arrested, before he died, and people told me that..."

"What? That it was my fault? He committed suicide. I didn't do anything. I was fifteen, for God's sake. He was my boyfriend and I loved him, I really did. But I got pregnant and it all...it all went so wrong."

Oh, that moment. That awful moment when I sat in the toilets in school with a positive pregnancy test clutched in my hand. Every stupid thing I thought was so important— the parties, the drinking, the freedom, Jacob—all shrank to insignificance when faced with that brutal reality check.

"He was arrested for sexual activity with a child," DC Norton says.

"I didn't get him arrested. It wasn't me," I whisper, looking up to meet Adam's eyes. I want him to see the truth there. I want him to believe me. "I would *never* have—"

"No, she didn't." It's Dad who speaks up and I freeze. *No, don't*, I want to scream, but Dad's still talking.

"Hanna was *fifteen*. She was underage and legally unable to consent. Jacob had just turned eighteen—a legal adult. *I* had him arrested for rape."

And there it is, the dirty truth, out there at last.

I thought Dad would help me. When I found out I was pregnant, I panicked. I didn't know what to do. Instead of going to Jacob, I went to Dad. I thought, despite the nightmare of our relationship the last year, I thought he'd help me over this. I didn't want a baby. I was fifteen, for God's sake. Of course I didn't want a baby. And I thought Dad, with his strict codes of always needing to appear in a positive light, I thought he'd quietly organize an abortion and make all this go away.

Stupid, stupid fifteen-year-old Hanna thought it would be that easy, thought having an abortion would be a nothing moment I could get past and then carry on as before.

But that's not what happened.

I told Dad and Dad called the police.

I was essentially locked in the house, not allowed to contact Jacob.

Dad told no one I was pregnant, but made it known throughout the damned county why Jacob had been arrested.

Oh, the *scandal*, in such a small town...Didn't matter that eventually the charges were dropped. It was too late then; the damage was done. Not just to Jacob, but to his whole family. And to Reverend Garner, who spoke up in Jacob's defense because he knew him, he knew *us*. And then, after the charges were dropped and Jacob committed suicide...the blame turned to me. The gossip started, spread by his friends and family, that I was a liar, that I'd lied about everything.

"I was wrong," Dad says, and I take a deep breath and hold it. Those are words I thought I'd never hear my father say.

"I was wrong," he continues. "I should not have interfered. I should have let Hanna deal with her own mess. And I said as much to Sasha."

I recoil. Oh. *Oh.*

"Is that what you told her?" I ask.

He doesn't answer.

"She came to you for help and you told her to sort it out herself?"

"Daniel—you didn't...?" Jen finally stirs and I want to turn and scream at her. Where the hell was she when this was going on? Oh, let me guess, doing fuck all, exactly as she always did.

Dad glances at her. "You know my feelings, Jen. I told you after the fiasco with Hanna we should have left her to deal with it. Children have to learn to take responsibility— but oh no, you insisted that if we *nurture* Sasha, *protect* her, everything would be fine. And look where we've ended up."

"*No*," Jen interrupts. "I won't listen to that...that *nonsense* anymore. Sasha is *fourteen*. Hanna was fifteen— she *was* your responsibility. She was a child. *You* were the adult. You were the responsible parent. Yes, you were wrong. But you were wrong in what you *did*. Because it was all about punishment. It wasn't about helping your daughter and it should have been."

"Jennifer—"

"I've always believed that, but I've never said it, because Hanna was your child, not mine. I didn't believe it was my place to criticize. But now you've repeated the same mistake with Sasha and she's *missing. You're* the one who needs to take responsibility. This is down to you."

"It is *not*. Did I force Sasha to disobey all the rules? Did I force Hanna to sneak out, to skip school, to drink and take drugs? To have an underage relationship?"

"Stop it, Daniel. Stop it now. I have kept quiet over many things in our marriage, but I swear to you now—if anything happens to Sasha, I will *never* forgive you."

Chapter 42

Tuesday 7:30 p.m.

I walk across the road and lean against the sea wall. DC Norton had stopped Dad and Jen arguing before it turned into a full-blown fight, getting back to asking them about Sasha, but I had to get out of that room, had to get away from my father and Jen. I'm not surprised when Adam follows me out. I don't know how to feel. I was glad Dee and Seb weren't still waiting in reception. I don't know where they've gone, but I don't think I could stand sympathy or pity at the moment. Adam is easier to be around. He doesn't seem to mind just standing in silence while I take great gulps of sea air.

My phone buzzes and I jump. The relief when I see Sasha's name on the screen is so great I actually feel faint. I forget everything in that second, and just for that one moment everything is fine and this last week has been nothing but a bad dream... "Oh, thank God!" I say, holding up the phone so Adam can see Sasha's name. Adam puts his hand over mine before I accept the call.

"It might not be her."

I swallow and nod before accepting the call. "Sasha?"

"This isn't Sasha."

The shock is a punch to the stomach, and the bad dream

is reality again. I almost drop the phone and have to fumble for a moment before I press it to my ear.

"Ethan?" I turn to start walking back toward the hotel, thinking, *Keep him talking, keep him talking.* DC Norton said they'd be able to locate the phone if it's switched on. If I can just keep him talking... "Where's Sasha?"

There's a pause and I stop moving. "She can't come to the phone at the moment."

Get the police, I mouth to Adam. He nods and starts back across the road, but freezes as the stranger on Sasha's phone speaks again, loud enough for him to hear.

"Tell Adam to stay where he is. It won't be good for Sasha if he takes one more step toward the hotel."

My insides turn to liquid and Adam and I stare at each other, both frozen in place. He's watching us. We're *so close.* DC Norton is less than a hundred feet away and I daren't move, daren't move from the spot we're standing in. It's like we're both standing on live mines, but Sasha is the one who could get blown up if we move. I shouldn't have come outside... But then, he wouldn't have called otherwise, would he? If he's watching, he's been waiting for me to leave the hotel.

"Where are you?" I ask again, turning my head, trying to figure out where he's watching from. Does he have Sasha with him now? He could be anywhere, in any of the buildings on this street, hiding in the shadows of the rocks on the beach, sitting in a stationary car.

"What do we do?" Adam mutters, his hand moving toward the phone in his pocket.

"Uh-uh," the man on the phone says. "Hands away from your pockets, Adam."

"Okay," I say. "We won't go back to the hotel, we won't call the police. What do you want?"

"I want Adam to put his phone on the ground and then I want the two of you to get in your car and go home."

"Home? What?"

"You know what home I mean, Hanna. Go home and stay on the line. If you disconnect this call, I'll assume you're calling the police and that will be very bad for Sasha. Same thing goes if you mute the call. I want to know you're still on the line. You have thirty minutes. No police. No stopping on the way. I'll be with you the whole time."

"Wait—please. I don't have enough charge on my phone. It'll die before we get there and—"

He laughs. "Come on, Hanna. Don't play with me— one or both of you will have a charger. You can charge the phone as you drive."

"What do we do?" Adam says again, keeping his voice low.

"We do what he says," I say, my voice calm, covering the phone so we can't be heard, but careful not to disconnect. "He's watching, he has to be. I can't risk Sasha."

"Hanna..." Adam pauses and takes a deep breath. He looks back toward the hotel. "The police think this man has murdered two women. We can't just dump my phone here and drive off to the middle of nowhere. No one will know where we've gone. Look where we are. I'll run. I'll run back to the hotel, raise the alarm. He's close enough to see us—they can find him before he gets away and—"

"*No*. You heard him—if we tell DC Norton and they all come storming out, he could hurt Sasha. And it's not going to be instant, is it? Even if you run in there screaming, they'll stop you, ask you questions. And he'll be gone and so will Sasha."

"But—"

"No," I say again, shaking my head. There are tears in

my eyes. "Sasha is fourteen, she's a baby. I refuse to risk her life for mine."

"Hanna, I know she's your family, but this is stupid. You have to see that. He's a *murderer*," Adam says.

"You don't understand." My voice is a whisper. "Sasha is…I walked away from her before. All I've done her entire life is walk away from her. I can't do it again." I step closer to him and let my hair fall in front of my face as I whisper the next few words. "They can trace him while the phone's on. They're monitoring Sasha's phone. The police will be able to find him…and Sasha."

He presses his lips together, looks back toward the hotel again, then back to me. He nods, then gets his phone out of his pocket, holds it up, then puts it on the sea wall behind us.

"Let's go," he says. "I'll drive."

"I'm sorry," I say as we run toward my car. "I'm so sorry you've been dragged into this."

"It's fine," he says, unlocking the car and getting into the driver's seat.

It's not fine, not at all. The worst part is, I can't even talk to him about it. Not with the third passenger in the car. Ethan hasn't said anything since giving his instructions, but I can hear him breathing. I plug my phone into the car charger and pray we don't lose signal at any point on our journey.

"Where are we going?" Adam asks as we pull out and drive away from the hotel.

"Back to Littledean," I say.

"Very good, Hanna," Ethan says, sounding amused. "I think you've figured out who I am, haven't you?"

"No," I say, but I don't even sound convincing to myself.

"Liar," he says. "But then, you always were a liar, weren't

you?" There's a silence, some background noise on the line. I take it off speaker and put it to my ear again, desperate to hear signs of Sasha in the background, some proof she's still alive and well. I look back at all the cars behind us—are they in one of them?

"It doesn't matter, anyway," Ethan says. "If you know who I am, if the police know. We're almost at the end now."

"The end?"

"You'll find out." Another pause. "Tell Adam to speed up, will you? The clock's ticking."

Chapter 43

SASHA—Tuesday 6:30 p.m.

I don't know how long we've been driving. Not long, I don't think. I tried, at first, to count. I thought, like they do in films, if I knew how long we'd been traveling and I got the chance (somehow) to call for help, I'd be able to give some clue. The van is windowless, so I can't gather any visual clues. We could be driving inland or further along the coast, west or east. So yeah, I started counting but lost track, because how am I supposed to keep an accurate count in the situation I'm currently in? Ethan dropped that bombshell that apparently he's my fudging uncle and hasn't said another word. But it was enough, for a bit, to stop the fear of wetting myself. Beyond the shock of it, there's also that thing—he won't hurt me, will he? If I'm family?

I try to remember, then, what Ethan has told me about his family. But there's nothing—he said he was in care, that's all. Other than that, he's never mentioned family and it never occurred to me to ask. And even though I'm currently locked in the back of a van having been actually, literally *kidnapped*, I still feel bad for not having asked.

I stare at him across the van. He's looking the other way, a frown on his face. "You never..." It comes out croaky, so

I stop and clear my throat. "You never told me you had a brother."

He looks over at me. "He died when I was a kid. Younger than you."

"But Hanna couldn't have...I mean, she was a kid as well, wasn't she? I worked it out. When I realized she was my mother. She was only a year older than me when she got pregnant."

"She's responsible for his death. Owen told me..." He stops, shakes his head. "Owen told me what she did. And then she just walked away, like she walked away from you. It killed my parents as well. The shock of it. They wouldn't have had that accident if their lives hadn't been ripped apart by Jacob's death."

I open my mouth to ask more, but the van comes to a halt.

I thought, when the doors opened, I'd find myself back at the old holiday park. Back home. But we're not. Instead, we're parked by a building site, what looks like a new housing estate. It's at that creepy stage where half the houses are finished, but the place is too much of a building site for anyone to have moved in yet, so it's an eerie modern ghost town, empty shells of houses with churned-up mud-pits for gardens.

I wonder if I could make a run for it, but Owen keeps hold of my arm after helping me out of the van, holding on tight as he waits for Ethan to follow. The fear is back, because Owen isn't family. He hates Hanna and my whole family for whatever he thinks they did to his friend. But after he basically hands me over to Ethan, he gets back in the van.

"That's it now," he says in a low voice to Ethan. "No more. We're done."

Ethan nods, fingers digging into my arm. "Agreed. We're even. Just...keep quiet."

Owen doesn't look at me as he starts the engine and drives off, leaving me here, alone with Ethan. I wonder if he will keep quiet. Or if this—being a party to *kidnapping*—will be a step too far for old-boy loyalty.

There's a tall, padlocked gate barring our entry to the site, but Ethan walks us past the main gates, large enough for all the construction traffic to pass through, to a place around the corner where the fence is lower.

"Over we go," he says, his tone light, like we're out on a jaunt. He makes me go first. The gaps in the wire fence are large enough for me to get my feet in, so it's a fairly easy climb, with a bit of a wobble as I go over the top. I don't try to run as he follows me over—what am I going to do, play hide-and-seek on a building site? He could have a knife. God—he could have a *gun*.

I wonder if there's CCTV on the site. I hope so. Whatever happens tonight, I want him to get caught. He doesn't make any attempt to keep to the shadows, though, as he leads me through the site, and it makes me think he's already been here, already sabotaged the CCTV. And shouldn't there be security lights? Alarms? There are diggers and vans and tools everywhere—there should be a lot of security. It shouldn't be this easy to break in.

It's like he reads my mind, or maybe he just looks back as I'm eyeing up the lights that haven't come on. "Don't worry, Sash. Or is it don't get your hopes up? No one knows we're here." He pauses. "Other than Owen, and he won't say anything."

We walk up what will eventually be a road, but for now is just a muddy track. It twists and comes out by one of the shell-houses, a large detached one with a garage that doesn't yet have a door. It's the end house, and looks almost finished other than the windows. Ethan leads us through the mud, right to the front door. It isn't locked. At first I think that's so, so wrong, but as we walk in, I realize the house isn't as finished as it looks from the outside. He leads me to a room at the back, the only one with a door. It has bare plaster walls, wires hanging from holes where I guess electrical sockets will end up. Bare floorboards covered in plastic sheeting to protect them from the mud on builders' boots. In this room, the window is boarded up rather than just being covered in plastic like the ones at the front.

"Take the frown off, Sash. I can see you trying to figure out where we are, but you won't. You haven't been here before, but I have," Ethan says, turning slowly in a circle, hands held out. "It didn't look like this then, of course. There wasn't a whole housing estate. It was just one row of houses." He looks back at me. "Anyway, make yourself at home. I've got to pick up our special guest. I bet *she'll* know where we are."

He walks out and shuts the door behind him, leaving me in darkness. I hear a key in the lock and run over to the door, trying to pull it open before he can lock it, but I'm too late. I look around, my eyes blinking as they try to adjust to the dark. There are gaps in the boards nailed across the window, enough for me to make out the edges of the room, enough for me to see there is no other way out.

Enough for me to see I'm trapped.

Chapter 44

Thedarktourist.com

<What about the forgotten victims?>

What about those left behind—the sisters, the brothers, the children, the parents?

HANNA—Tuesday 8:15 p.m.

Do I expect him to be at the holiday park, waiting for me with Sasha? Not expect, no. The person who's gone to such lengths to torture me through Adam's website, stalking me and my friends, breaking into my flat, this phone call, this race across Wales—of course he's not going to make it easy. So, no, I don't expect to find him waiting, but I still hope.

But, of course, the gates are still padlocked. The construction company who've bought the site have now added huge boards all the way round, so I can't even see in anymore. I test the padlocks, walk all the way round, looking for a way in, while he stays silent on the line. Will anyone have realized we've gone yet? Is anyone tracing Ethan's call or my phone?

"I'm here," I say, when Adam and I have finished our circuit and get back to the car. "Where are you? Where's Sasha?"

"So impatient, Hanna. Isn't it nice to have this time to get to know one another?"

"Please—just tell me Sasha's okay. Can I speak to her?"

He ignores my question. "It was your tattoo. The thing that made me agree to Owen's plan to mess with you—the straw that broke the camel's back, as it were. Before that, I was just going to mess about on the computer—freak out your family. Maybe send you a few messages."

My tattoo? I look down at my arm, the black stars that disappear under my sleeve.

"I was so angry. I saw you—laughing with your friends over Christmas, not a care in the world—I saw you with that tattoo. How *dare* you? How dare you carve that reminder of my brother into your arm?"

I grit my teeth. "If I have it lasered off, will you let Sasha go?"

He laughs. "Perhaps if you sliced it off your own skin with a knife."

"Then give me a knife. I'll do it. I'll do it right now." I ignore Adam's gasp. Because I would. If Ethan promised to let Sasha go, I'd gouge the damned thing off my arm with a blunt, rusty knife.

"You almost sound convincing there, Hanna. But it doesn't matter. The tattoo made me angry and when I told them, it mattered to Owen and the others too. And they thought they could use me in their little revenge plan. Especially after they found out your new boyfriend had turned up in town asking questions." There's a pause. "Especially after the hatchet job he did on Jacob."

"What?" I turn to look at Adam, remembering Owen's... *fury* outside the police station.

"Did you ever read the story he wrote? Surely you did— it is all about you, after all. What a *tragic* heroine you were, what a *terrible* villain Jacob was... It's his fault that Katie

334

Bentley girl died. His article set me on a path where I got so *fucking angry...*"

"And Gemma, the hit-and-run? Are you blaming that on Adam too?"

There's a long pause. "That wasn't me. You can tell that to the police. I didn't do it. And I didn't do the crime I got sent down for either. But this—all this? Your fault. And Adam's fault. *You* caused all this."

I close my eyes, thinking of the hit-and-run—the girl who turned him in—I can't stop thinking of the details Dee told me, about how hard the car hit, how it mounted the pavement to mow her down...Of course it was him. Who else could it have been? I need to give him reason not to hurt Sasha. He would do it to hurt me, that's clear. "Please...Ethan." I take a deep breath. "She's not my sister. She's my daughter."

I can hear him breathing on the line and the silence lasts an eternity. "I know. Sasha told me. Why do you think we are where we are?"

"Ethan...She's your niece. Please, let her go. She's your *family.*"

Nothing. No response. And then he ends the call. No, no, no! I call him back, but it goes to voicemail. As soon as I cut the automated message off, my phone rings again.

"Ethan?"

"No—it's Dee. Where are you? Where did you go? The police are going nuts here and I couldn't get through to you—"

"Dee—I can't talk. He's got Sasha and—"

"Oh God, oh fuck. Han, I'm so sorry. Where are you? I'm going to come and get you," Dee says.

"I have my car."

"I don't care. You shouldn't be on your own."

"I'm not. I'm with Adam." I take a breath. "He said he didn't do the hit-and-run. But he basically admitted killing the other sister. And now he's got Sasha. Oh God, Dee..."

There's a pause. "There's something else."

I frown. "What is it? What's wrong?"

There's a too long silence.

"They arrested Liam."

My heart thuds. "What?"

"We were right. He gave him his key to your flat. Ethan—Liam gave him the key. Ethan turned up at his work's Christmas party; he told Liam he worked there and Liam was stupid enough to believe him, to start inviting him out with his friends. That's why he was in the pub that night Seb and I saw Liam. He worked his way in with Liam's friends, with our friends in the weeks leading up to Christmas and New Year..." She pauses, takes a breath. "He told Liam he knew you. He told him it was you who scratched his girlfriend's car, that you...that you had a history of stalking. He told him all sorts of things...I told the police it couldn't be true. But Liam believed it. He told him everything about you and gave him the key."

I swallow down the hurt and the dread. "I'm at the old house, the old holiday park. I can't leave. He might call back. I have to go; I need to keep the phone free."

I end the call and try Sasha's number again, over and over, but it keeps going to voicemail. I don't know what to do.

"This is all my fault," I whisper.

"No," Adam says. "Don't you dare say that—do not think that for a second."

"But it is. Everything he's done—even hacking your website. My fault."

336

The Night They Vanished

I never thought about—never considered for a second—Jacob's family, particularly his kid brother. I never met him. Jacob vaguely mentioned a brother a couple of times, but I don't even think he gave me his name. I knew Jacob's parents had died, one more tragedy to add to the list, but did I even remember he *had* a brother then? It was only when DC Norton mentioned his surname that I remembered.

God. What happened to him in the years between Jacob's death and now? He must have been younger than Sasha when his parents died, so he'd lost his entire family in the space of two years. Didn't he have other relatives? Carrie said he was fostered, so he must have ended up in the care system. What happened to him in his life to lead him to where he is now—just out of prison, a murderer and now a kidnapper? Is this really all down to me?

I close my eyes. No. I have to stop this. I was a kid myself when I met Jacob. I was fourteen, for God's sake; I couldn't possibly have foreseen the consequences. I met an older boy, already hell-bent on the type of self-destructive nihilistic path that seems impossibly, seedily glamourous to a teenager. The doomed rock star, the tortured, angst-ridden hero. God, he was beautiful. Of course I fell in love, full, headlong first love for the boy who introduced me to parties and sex and drink and drugs. I thought I was finally living. After a stifled, shut-away life with Dad, I thought I'd finally found the life I wanted to live.

He was sixteen when we met. Just turned eighteen when he died.

I open my eyes again. I can't go down that spiral of guilt and regret again. Not now. I need to stay focused. For Sasha. I call her number again.

"Ethan? I hope you're listening to these messages. If you

let Sasha go, I'll come to you. I'll come alone. I won't tell the police. I'll get Adam to tell them you didn't kill Gemma Bentley, that you're innocent of that…I'll come alone and we can talk—I'll tell you everything that happened with Jacob. But, *please*. Let Sasha go. It's not her you want." I pause, hoping he'll come on the line. "Call me."

We get in the car and I chew on a nail, trying to work out what to do, where to go, staring down at my phone, willing it to ring, willing Ethan to call me back.

"Hanna, you can't," Adam says.

"Yes, I *can*. And I will. Sasha is my daughter. I'm going to get him to let her go in exchange for me. That's who he wants—not her. That's who all this has been aimed at. Maybe he never intended it to end this way, I don't know. But that's what I'm going to do." I stop and take a shaky breath. "But you don't need to be involved in this anymore. When he calls back—give me my car keys. I'll go alone. I don't want you to get hurt."

"You know I won't let you go to him alone, even if he calls back and agrees," Adam says, and I look across at him.

I open my mouth to answer, but then the back door of the car opens, and someone gets in.

"Hello Hanna," Ethan says.

Chapter 45

I jump when my phone rings again, but hesitate before reaching for it.

"Who is it?" Ethan asks.

"It's Dee."

"Answer it, put it on speaker, but don't say a word about me."

I put the phone on speaker, and Dee starts talking before I can even say hello. "Hanna? The police have figured out where they think the house in the picture on the website is. They managed to see the edge of one of the hoardings, the edge of a logo. They think it's on that new housing development, a few miles from Littledean, between West Dean and Barry. The police are on their way there now."

"End the call," Ethan whispers and I do.

I take a breath and hold it. Ethan's in the car with us...If he does have Sasha at the housing estate, the police can go in and get her out and...I frown. Why would he have taken her there?

Behind us Ethan laughs, and I shiver. "Oh dear," he says. "They're all racing in the wrong direction, to the wrong site." He sighs and reaches out a hand. "Switch off your phone and give it to me, Hanna. And Adam, drive around the back of the holiday park, down the lane. You know the way."

I hear Adam gasp and when I look, he's staring over at me.

"Ah," Ethan says. "I think Adam's just figured out what his connection is in all this."

"What—what is it?"

"Why don't you tell her, Adam? But start driving."

"It's the story I wrote," Adam says, going pale. "The article I wrote when I built the website. The one I came here to research ... the one about you and Jacob. I called my stupid article 'A dark house for a dark tourist.'"

"Ty Tywyll," I say at the same time as him. Dark House, that's what it translates as. It is—it was—Jacob's house. Where he grew up. Where he died. Named Dark House because of the way it was hidden away among all the trees, it became the dark house for different reasons after Jacob died.

"It was derelict when I first found it and wrote my article," Adam says, starting the engine. "When I went back, when I'd built the website and went back to take a photograph of the house that started it all, the building company's sign was already up. The houses were already gone."

"And was it worth it?" Ethan says. "Wallowing in the misery of all the victims' families, parading their pain all over the internet—was it worth it?"

I flinch at his words—I said almost the same thing to Adam. I don't want to be anywhere near on the same side as Ethan, but I guess, in a way, I am. He blames me and he put my family and my family's home up on Adam's website as part of his revenge, but when Adam told me about it ... I felt the same as him, that Adam's site was exploiting others' misery.

"And you get to slant it any way you want. Oh sure, the facts were there—Jacob's arrest, his death, my parents' death—but you made it sound like Jacob was some seedy, junkie pedophile, preying on little, innocent Hanna here…"

"It was never meant to be—"

"What?" Ethan interrupts him. "Never meant to be what?"

"It was never meant to hurt anyone. It was…urban exploration, dark tourism. It's a hobby. And the website was just a way to make some money."

"Never meant to hurt anyone? Oh, I get you, Adam, I really, really do. Owen never *meant* to hurt anyone when he saw that *bitch* that set me up and got me sent down out running. I never *meant* to hurt anyone when I went to see her fucking sister, because she would not leave me alone."

Owen? The hit-and-run was *Owen*? Oh God, it's so much worse…Does Owen have Sasha now? Owen with his anger issues and his festering hatred of me and my family?

Ethan's in the back seat, sitting in the middle behind us both, not wearing a seat belt. I watch Adam's knuckles whiten on the steering wheel and wonder if he's planning to swerve off the road, deliberately crash the car. But we're not wearing seat belts either, and he's just as likely to kill himself and me, leaving Ethan to escape and go after Sasha. Plus, I'm not sure I could find my way there on my own, on foot, if Adam and Ethan were injured. If I leave Ethan dead or unconscious and he's got Sasha locked up somewhere, if he's still lying to us, she could die before the police find her.

I'm tempted, though. Tempted to try for the wheel myself—particularly when Ethan starts talking again.

"Did she tell you she was stalking her ex-boyfriend?" he says to Adam.

I clench my fists.

"Pull over here," Ethan says, pointing between us to a lay-by that's tucked away among towering trees.

341

"Yes," he says, in the most casual tone as Adam stops the car. "She found out he was cheating on her, and for *revenge*, she decided to become a psycho stalker." He leans right over, takes the keys out of the ignition, and puts them in his pocket. "Our dear Hanna deliberately keyed his new girlfriend's car, and she badmouthed him to his boss, nearly got him fired by pretending he was abusive." He laughs. "It was actually funny—there I was, following her and she was stalking her ex. We were like a stalker chain. Her ex was *very* happy to share all this with me."

Oh, he makes it sound so much worse than it was. The damage to Liam's new girlfriend's car, okay, that was temper, spur of the moment. I'd just caught them together, for God's sake, and that cow was so smug about it, and her car was right outside...

As to the rest—I was not lying about him being abusive. He had his hands around my throat. I was outside his flat and he came storming down, dragged me out of my car...

I don't like that part of myself. It was a darker, out-of-control Hanna. It reminded me of the girl I used to be. And I stopped myself, after that. I realized, as I got home that night with bruises around my throat, what I was in danger of becoming. I phoned Dee. I used Dee as my twelve-step program, I confessed my sins and sorted myself out.

I was lucky, I know I was, that Liam didn't go to the police. Maybe his burst of temper, when he pulled me from the car, prevented him, because I had as much reason to go to the police as he did.

But this is not the time or the place to try to explain myself to Adam. That's what Ethan wants, him condemning me, me condemning him. For now, we need to stay calm. We need to save Sasha. I swallow. And I need to make sure Adam gets out of this alive. It's the first time I acknowledge that I might not.

But again—now is not the time to think about that, or I'll spiral into panic.

"Get out of the car," Ethan says. Both Adam and I obey. My muscles feel stiff, like I've been in the car for hours. I think it's just that every part of me was tense the entire time we were on the road.

He leads us through a gate into a field. We skirt the edges, walking across to another gate that lets out onto a narrow lane. There is no sign of traffic as we turn left and start walking again. I know where we are now. Where we left the car, the field, it threw me for a while, but I know this lane, I've walked this lane many times. It's the lane that's barely more than a track that leads from the back of the holiday park down to the beach. It's a public road, but so narrow and treacherous with potholes that no one ever uses it except for the occasional tractor. Dee and I used to think of it as our private road to the beach. None of the tourists from the caravans ever came this way. And later, I'd walk this way to meet Jacob.

"Look what they've done to it," Ethan says as we reach the building site.

I don't recognize it at all. Jacob's old house was one of four crumbling old cottages on a couple of acres at the top of the hill, surrounded by trees with panoramic sea-views down through the valley. They've torn them and all the trees down for this: a tiny development of a couple of dozen houses, all big, all detached. I can see why the police are currently haring off to the wrong place. I know the development Dee was talking about—the massive one on the other side of town, the two- and three-beds.

It's the same construction company. I guess that's where the confusion has arisen. This one is small, top-of-the-range, sea-view palaces, separated from the herd by about five miles.

"The police are on their way to the wrong place," Ethan says. He pulls my phone out of his pocket and smiles. "They can't trace it while it's off, but just in case..." He drops my phone and stamps on it.

"This place was beautiful," Ethan says. "And look what they've done. The only legacy left is Adam's fucking story where he took my family's personal tragedy and made it public. Of course, no one wanted to buy such a tragic house, did they? Doubly so after your article, Adam. It got picked up and quoted by the local paper and that was enough. No one wanted to live next to it, so all the cottages emptied, and no one would buy them, so we all had to accept crappy offers from a construction company. Your fault again, Adam. And yours, of course, Hanna, for starting it all in the first place. So many lives ruined because of you two."

It is sad. Jacob's cottage and its neighbors always looked like they were part of the landscape, tucked in a huddle three-quarters of the way down the hill. They fitted. This small group of new-builds is going to look all wrong.

Ethan stops outside one of the unfinished houses and turns to face us. It's the first time I've actually looked at him since he got into Adam's car. He stands in the doorway of the house with a big smile on his face, like a host greeting guests arriving for a dinner party. I stare at him, this stranger who's been doing his best to destroy my life. I stare and I try to find some of Jacob in the bones of his face. All those years I spent going out with Jacob replacements, and it never occurred to me there was a real one out there in the world.

There is something there. Ethan has different coloring, but close up there's something familiar in the shape of his face, in his smile. Maybe it was more visible when he was younger, but Jacob got frozen permanently at eighteen so I can only speculate how his face might have changed in the last fifteen years. Would my angsty indie boy have polished himself up, cut his hair, worn a suit? Would he have developed frown lines or laughter lines? Let the bleach grow out of his hair and maybe a first gray hair grow in? His dad's hair had been almost entirely silver the couple of times I met him and he was only in his late thirties.

"Please, both of you, come on in." He turns and gestures up the hallway.

I take a deep breath, step past him, and let the house swallow me up.

Chapter 46

Sasha is sitting huddled in the corner of what will eventually be the living room when the house is finished. It's difficult to see when the only light is from the small flashlight Ethan is holding, but she doesn't seem hurt in any way.

She starts to get up when I walk in ahead of Ethan, but stops and freezes when he enters.

"Well, this is nice, isn't it?" Ethan says, putting the torch down on the ground. "A family reunion."

I flinch and Ethan must notice because he turns to me. "Yes, Sasha seemed as ignorant as me about that *family connection* when she told me you were her mother." He glances at Sasha and pulls a knife out of his pocket. I gasp as he goes over to her, and Adam grabs me as I lunge forward. But Ethan just leans down and hauls her to her feet with the hand not holding the knife.

He turns his back on me to face Sasha. I tense, thinking I could throw myself at him, try to tackle him to the ground to give the others a chance to get out. I'm on the balls of my feet when Ethan moves slightly, and I see he still has that knife in his hand. I hesitate and the moment is lost because Ethan shifts so I am in his eyeline as well.

"All these years. All those fucking awful, lonely years. Turns out I did have family left after all. Turns out I didn't have to be alone at all." He stops and shakes his head. "It's not your fault, of course, Sasha. You didn't know either. Hanna has been lying to you her whole life. About being your mother, about who your father is and what happened to him. I guess the reason she doesn't want you to know is because then she'd have to confess that she killed him, and that's not something any mother wants to tell their child."

"He's lying," I say, looking only at Sasha as I say it. "I'm sorry, Sasha—and Ethan, I'm sorry, I really am, but Jacob killed *himself*. You know this, Ethan. He committed suicide."

"Because of *you*. Because of what *you* did. You had him arrested," Ethan screams at me and my stomach lurches. "You had him arrested for *rape*."

I hear a noise and from the corner of my eye, I see Adam sidling across, behind and out of sight of Ethan.

"What do you think that did to him? To our family?" Ethan says. "And you say you *loved* him? The police came to our door and dragged him off, put him in handcuffs and in the back of a police car in full view of everyone."

"I'm sorry," I say, not taking my eyes off the knife in his hand. What does Adam think he's doing? He knows Ethan has a knife. "I never—"

"You never what? Never lied to the police? But you *did*. It wasn't rape. Don't you dare try to tell me it was. He was your boyfriend."

"I didn't go to the police." I take a deep breath. "It was my dad."

Sasha gasps and I wince. I know the truth is going to hurt her, but I have to try to deflect Ethan's rage—just long enough for the police to get here, just long enough to take his attention away from my daughter.

"I told my father I was pregnant, and he went to the

347

police, because I was still underage and Jacob had just turned eighteen."

"*Enough*," Ethan yells and I jump. "Get over there. You too, Adam," he adds, swinging around to where Adam is hovering in the shadows.

"I don't think you've met Adam, have you, Sasha?" he says, when we're all gathered together. "Hanna's latest candidate for your new stepfather. Adam here is like the worst of tabloid journalists, exploiting people's misery for his own financial gain."

"That's not true," Adam says.

"Really? Your oh-so-charming website—do you think the surviving family members of the murders you describe like having their homes and the crimes that happened there plastered all over the internet for *entertainment*?"

Adam says nothing and Ethan laughs. "Do you know how I felt when I came across that article you wrote— about my brother? My parents' deaths? How do you think I felt when you were congratulating yourself on exploiting my family's deaths to make money?"

"It's—"

"It's what? Already a *thing*? Already an *industry*? Oh, it's okay for me to photograph the murder victim and stick it online because everyone else is doing it? Fuck the family, right? Fuck the shell-shocked, grieving survivors; let's make some *money*."

He turns to me. "I suppose he told you he liked you? Told you it was your smile or your pretty blue eyes that attracted him?" He steps closer to me and my attention flickers from his face to the knife in his hand.

"Did he tell you about the *new* article he wrote about you after his last little visit to your home town? The guest post he did, all ready to post on the anniversary of my brother's death, celebrating the story that started it all?"

I shake my head and glance at Adam. No—he wouldn't have...

"I never posted it," Adam says, and I want to sink down to the floor and curl up in a ball. "After Dee set up our date and then I met you properly—I never would have posted it."

"But you wrote it, didn't you? You didn't delete it, either," Ethan says. "It's still on your computer. I've read it." Ethan smiles. "But don't worry, Adam. Hanna can't exactly claim the moral high ground here. Oh, the things she's done. All there, so easy to find out. The lies, the cheating, the stealing. Her life's been like a soap opera—you really should include some of it in your article. It's a far truer picture than the one you painted, where she's some poor, innocent schoolgirl caught up in a tragedy." He pauses. "Actually, maybe the two of you are perfectly suited. Shame I'm not going to let it happen."

He turns and smiles at Sasha. "Don't you have anything to say to your daughter, Hanna? The girl you were so desperate to save? The girl who actually hates you because of what you did?"

"Yes," I say. "I do." Because it might be my last chance.

"I'm sorry, Sasha. I should have fought harder for you. It's not an excuse, but I was barely older than you are now. And I was destroyed by everything that happened. And Dad said... he said I wasn't fit to look after you. That if I tried, I'd be in the care of social services and if I messed up, they'd take you into care. So I agreed to let them keep you, and I left."

"You could have stayed," Sasha says and her voice breaks. "You could have been in my life, even if you weren't the one looking after me day to day."

"Dad told me to leave. The moment I turned sixteen, he

told me to leave. He kicked me out." It still hurts to remember. To remember how I begged. I begged him to help me, to let me stay. I promised to give up drinking, give up drugs, if he would just help me. It still hurts to remember his rejection.

After Adam told me about his website, I went home and looked up dark tourism, interested enough to find out more. *Tourism that involves traveling to places associated with death and suffering*, that was what I found. Traveling to places associated with death and suffering. I close my eyes. For me, I don't need to travel to an actual place to become a dark tourist. My past is a place of death and suffering. I just have to close my eyes and remember.

But my future doesn't have to be. I open my eyes and look straight at Ethan.

"So, what are you going to do?" I say to him. "Kill us all? Murder Sasha, the only family you have left, just when you've found her?"

I hear Sasha gasp, but I ignore it. I want Ethan's attention focused solely on me. "Or is your plan to kill me and Adam and let Sasha live? You think she'll want to be related to you after watching you murder us in front of her?"

I sigh and shake my head. "I don't think you've thought at all, have you? Were you thinking when you murdered Katie Bentley? I don't get it. And you say you didn't commit the crime that got you sent to prison, that you didn't run Gemma Bentley down... You could have just got on with your life. Even what you did with Adam's website—everything you've found out, everything you did to mess with me, using Liam...that was *clever*. Really damned clever. And you could have kept yourself hidden in all that—left it at that. But this—Katie Bentley, kidnapping Sasha, us—all of this—is anything but clever."

The hand holding the knife moves, and I take a step back. But Ethan just cocks his head and smiles. "I wasn't planning on killing anyone, just...*confronting* the one who got me sent down. I wanted her to admit what she'd done. But Owen convinced me it was a bad idea, said *he* would do it. And the other woman...she was so convinced it was me that ran her sister down, because she knew. She *knew* her sister set me up. She was so sure I did it out of revenge. But she could hardly tell the police why she was so sure it was me, could she? Not without tarnishing her precious sister's reputation. Even after the police cleared me and I had an alibi. She wouldn't leave me alone. She made me so angry." He looks at Adam and Sasha huddled against the unplastered wall. "Why don't you two leave? Let me and Hanna talk."

I want to collapse with relief, but I force myself not to react. Adam starts to protest, but I shake my head at him, pleading in my mind for him to get Sasha to safety. *Please*, I mouth.

I sag with relief when they leave. Whatever happens to me now, it doesn't matter. Sasha and Adam are safe.

Chapter 47

SASHA

Adam takes my arm as soon as we're out of the house, steering me toward the muddy track that leads away from the building site.

"Stop," I say and turn to look at him. He looks so unlike any of the boys in those old photos of Hanna, so unlike anyone I ever pictured Hanna being with. He looks so... normal. Nice. He looks nice.

"Please, Sasha," he says. "Let me get you away from here. Let's get to a phone, call the police..."

"What about Hanna?"

I looked at Ethan as we left and I knew, I *knew*...He's going to kill her. He's going to kill Hanna, my mother or my sister—whatever the hell she is—he's going to kill her. I can't let him do that.

"The police will get here too late," I say. "You heard him—you saw him. He's going to kill her."

"It's okay." He looks at me and smiles. He has a really nice smile and I wish I could get to know him properly, as Hanna's boyfriend. He came here with her, into certain danger, doing more than me or Dad have ever done for her.

"I'm going back in," Adam says. "I'm going in and I'm going to get her out." He looks at me again. "Don't worry,

352

I'll make sure she's okay. But I need to make sure you're safe, that you're away from here and safe."

I shake my head. "I can't. I can't just run away."

"This is why Hanna is here—why we're both here. To make sure you're safe. Let her do this for you. She needs to. You go—get back to the road. Try to flag someone down or get to a phone."

My throat goes tight, but I nod and step away from him, watching as he lopes back toward the house. Oh God, I need to get help, or Ethan's going to kill them both. I start running back toward the road. Which way do I go? I don't know where we are . . . I could start running the wrong way, away from help rather than toward it. I get to the edge of the road and stand there wavering, my breath coming in gasps. A flash of light catches my attention and I turn to see headlights approaching on the lane. My heart starts racing and I launch into a sprint, skidding and stumbling down the muddy road. Help is here. Help is here. I can save them both.

It's not just help, it's the bloody cavalry. An unmarked police car with a detective in the front, Mum and Dad in the back seat; two proper police cars with flashing lights. I almost die, throwing myself in the path of the unmarked car, but it skids to a halt and just manages to stop before it squashes me. Mum's out of the car before it even comes to a proper stop, flinging her arms around me and squeezing all the air out of my body.

"Oh, thank God, thank God," she keeps muttering, and she's pulling me toward the car.

"Wait," I gasp. "Help. Ethan's in there—he's got Hanna. And Adam. He's going to kill them."

*

They won't let us go anywhere near the site while the detective in charge coordinates his rescue plan or attack plan or whatever the hell it is they do when there's a man with a knife hell-bent on killing his hostages. They make me wait in one of the police cars with Mum and Dad, sitting in between them, unable to stop shaking. I hate this. It's only been minutes, but it feels like hours. Sod that, it feels like *years* since Ethan sent me and Adam out.

"Don't worry," Mum says, squeezing my hand. "They'll get in there in time. She'll be fine."

I burst into tears and bury my head in her shoulder. "This is all my fault. I should never have made friends with Ethan. Never have told him Hanna was my mother. If he kills her, it will be my fault."

"No—enough," Dad says. "It is not your fault. You were foolish, yes, but he manipulated you and he did it because of what *Hanna* did. This is her own fault, all down to—"

"All down to *what*?" I say, shaking now with anger rather than fear. "I know everything now—I know what you did. I know what you did to Jacob and I know what you did to Hanna. You kicked her out. Is that what you'd do to me if I messed up?"

Mum looks up. "Sasha, no honey, that's not true. Hanna ran away. She—" Mum stops talking and stares at Dad. "Oh, Daniel, please tell me you didn't..."

"It was the right thing to do," Dad says, still so cold. Even now, even with all this happening, still so bloody cold. "She was still drinking, still bringing drugs into my house, even with a baby there."

"She needed help," I say, my own voice breaking, "like I needed help, and you threw her out."

"You told me she chose to leave. When I came home with

Sasha that day, you told me Hanna had packed her bags and run away, that it was *her* decision," Mum says.

"She would have destroyed us all if she'd stayed," he says. "This all comes down to Hanna, and the choices she made. I could see the direction she was going in when I made the decisions I did. And everything I did was to protect the family."

He looks at Mum. "You think it would ever have worked out if she'd stayed? You wanted Sasha as your daughter, not a step-granddaughter. I just made sure that happened."

"I *never*, for one second, suggested me wanting to adopt Sasha was at the expense of Hanna," Mum says.

"You didn't need to. For heaven's sake, Jen—I was tired, after sixteen years of struggle with Hanna—sick and tired of it all. And you wanted to start again with another baby. There was no way that was going to happen with Hanna still on the scene."

I feel sick and Mum looks like she's going to either cry or punch Dad in the face.

"*Get out*," she shouts. "Get out of this car. I've let you control and bulldoze me for our entire marriage. But not anymore. I'm not letting you control any part of my life anymore."

Mum squeezes my hand as Dad gets out of the car, stiff-backed as he marches away toward the other cars. Despite the howling loss I feel and however scared I am, however scared she is, the fact that she finally, finally stood up for me, for Hanna and said no to Dad...that loosens something inside. I look back toward the silent building site.

Now we just have to wait.

Chapter 48

HANNA

Ethan turns to me after they've left. "Let's sit," he says.

I sink down on to the cold floor.

"I didn't know to hate you when Jacob died," he says. "I was too young, and my parents didn't tell me the details. They didn't tell me about you or why he was arrested."

He sounds so calm; it's difficult to believe he's already killed one woman. Maybe two, if he's lying about Owen. Well, it would be difficult to believe if he weren't still carrying that knife. And I don't really know how much involvement Owen has had in all this.

"To be honest, he was almost six years older than me. We weren't close in any way. It was weird when he died, but it was my parents dying that was the real fucker." There's a long pause. "Owen came to see me when I was in prison. He was pretty much my only visitor. And he liked to tell a lot of stories about Jacob. And about you."

I bet he did. I picture the horrible stories—not all of them lies—Owen could have told Ethan.

"I never realized Jacob was struggling mentally," Ethan says. "Before his arrest, and especially after."

"I didn't know either," I say. "I was fifteen, and troubled enough myself. I thought he was like me, just another

356

angsty teenager. To me, we were Cathy and Heathcliff, tortured, troubled souls, eternally romantic." I pause and sigh. "When I got pregnant, reality intruded in a big way, and I reverted to what I really was—a frightened kid who ran to her dad for help."

"That's not an excuse."

"I'm not offering it as an excuse. I'm offering it as an explanation. I know what I did—or rather, I know what I didn't do. I should have insisted on speaking to the police myself, making them know our relationship was consensual. I should have found a way to get out of the house, to go and see Jacob. Maybe if he'd known I was pregnant, he never would have done it. But I didn't. I was a frightened, selfish kid, too caught up in freaking out over my own situation. I let Jen drag me off to hide out halfway across the country like some shamed unmarried mother from Victorian times, and then I let them take my baby away from me. I've regretted it and punished myself for it every day since. You could stab me now and it wouldn't be more of a punishment than what I've done to myself over the years."

"That was the plan at first," he says. "Just mess with you a bit. Especially as I got to know Sasha and found myself liking the kid. I didn't want to mess with her anymore. I just wanted to get you thinking, get you remembering, get you torturing yourself a bit more. You and Adam, especially after I read that article he wrote about Jacob." Ethan looks at the knife in his hand, then twists around and throws it across to the other side of the room. I feel the faintest fluttering of hope. If I can keep him talking… Sasha and Adam will be racing back to the car, back to the road. But—oh God—Ethan still has the keys. No, it's okay. They might find someone, another car to flag down even sooner.

"The thing is..." Ethan says, softly, turning back to face me. "The *problem* is, you're not punishing yourself anymore, are you?"

"What do you mean?"

"Maybe if Owen had come to see me a few years earlier, maybe if I hadn't been sent down, I would have found you and seen the miserable, tortured woman you tell me you were. Maybe I would have seen that, and it would have been enough." He pauses. "But now...now I see a woman with friends, a home, a job. A woman on the verge of a new relationship. I see a woman who's *happy*. And we can't have that." He gets up as he says that and drags me to my feet, fingers biting into my upper arms as he pushes me toward the wall.

"That," he says, "was the problem with Gemma *fucking* Bentley. She got me sent down, ruined my *fucking* life, and there she is, living her best life, while I'm forced to mow *fucking* lawns while your *fucking* father lords it over me. Owen did me a favor there, and this is how I'm going to repay it."

The breath is forced out of me as my head and back slam against the wall, but I don't get a chance to take another one to fill my lungs, because Ethan has his hands around my neck, squeezing, choking. I try to pull his hands away, but he's too strong.

There are black spots in front of my eyes and the strength has gone out of my legs, when the pressure around my neck is released and someone hauls Ethan off me, *Adam* pulls Ethan off me, dragging him away as I sink, gasping and coughing, to the floor.

No, get out. You were out, I saved you, I think—I scream—in my head, no breath to say it out loud. I fight to stay conscious as I lie there, watching Adam and Ethan fight, because I know the knife is over there somewhere, and Ethan knows, but Adam doesn't, and I see Ethan crawling toward it.

I scream a warning, ignoring the pain in my throat, and I struggle to my feet as Ethan picks up the knife and turns toward Adam, ready to turn this place into another site worthy of The Dark Tourist, making me and Adam today's tragic Romeo and Juliet.

But no. Not this time. I reach down, pushing tarpaulin and rubbish aside until my hand closes on a piece of wood. Ethan still has his back to me as I grab it and swing it, my whole strength behind it as I smash it into Ethan's back. He collapses and I stagger over to where Adam lies unmoving on the floor.

I slide back to the ground next to him. Everything is whirling and the world is turning black but finally, finally, I can hear sirens in the distance.

Chapter 49

I wake up in the hospital. My throat feels like someone is still squeezing the life out of me and shoots needle-like jabs of pain into me when I move my head. Dee is huddled in the chair next to the bed and she flies to her feet when she sees my eyes open.

"Don't try to talk," she says, reaching above my head for the call button.

I look at her, blinking back tears. I open my mouth because I need to try to ask, but she does her special Dee thing and reads my mind.

"Adam's alive. He's going to be okay." She smiles at me. "Your family is all okay. Sasha is here, outside. Your dad tried to make her go home when he took your stepmother, but she refused to leave." Her smile dims and dies. "Ethan got away. They're looking for him now. It's only a matter of time before they find him."

"What about Owen?" I whisper it and it still hurts.

She shakes her head. "He claims he had no idea what Ethan was up to. He's got alibis for all of it—when Gemma Bentley was killed, and her sister, when your flat was broken into. All of it."

"But Ethan said it was him who did the hit-and-run. He took Sasha, he was the one driving the van and..."

"He claims Sasha went willingly. Or he believed she

360

was willing. He claims he thought he was helping them be together, that Ethan told him they were family, that they wanted to get to know each other and your dad was keeping them apart."

"That's bullshit. That's bollocks."

She nods. "You know it, I know it—the *police* know it. But until they catch Ethan, they have little chance of proving it."

"Sasha is *fourteen*. She was bloody *kidnapped*."

"But she's told the police that they were friends to start with, her and Ethan. That they were meeting up and messaging. Owen says he doesn't believe Ethan killed Katie Bentley either. And, Hanna...he's also claiming Ethan never intended to hurt you, or Adam. That he just arranged to meet you to talk."

"He had a knife."

"That wasn't found at the scene. And only you saw it: neither Sasha nor Adam saw him with a knife."

I stare at her as the door opens and a nurse and doctor come in. I'm afraid if I look away, I'll wake up for real and this time, they'll all be dead. Or Ethan will be next to my bed, not Dee. Or Owen fucking King.

"They are all fine, I promise you," Dee says. "And they will catch Ethan. And they'll find a way to get Owen, too. You deserve a happy ending. It's time to stop punishing yourself."

That's all very well, but when they *do* catch him—is he just going to stop? And Owen—Lee and Carrie, Stephen Hayes, even—were they all involved in this plan for some kind of revenge for what they believed I did to Jacob? Are they all just going to stop?

That bloody article and that stupid website—why did Adam have to come up with that idea?

*

Dad is sitting where Dee was the next time I wake up.

"Hey," I whisper. It's hard to resist the urge to sit up straight and check my hair is tidy. Even fourteen years after leaving home, one look from him makes me a kid all over again.

He doesn't respond to my greeting. He just talks like we were in mid-conversation when all this happened. "I tried to explain, to Jen and to Sasha, why I did everything I did, but they won't listen. Jen is talking about leaving me, taking Sasha." He shakes his head. "They just need to look at you, though, to realize what I did was *right*. I need you to explain that to them."

Explain *what*—that he was right to call the police, to kick me out, to make me feel I wasn't capable of looking after my own child?

"You never showed any interest in Sasha when you visited. You never gave me any indication that you wanted to be more involved in her life. I took from that that the decisions I made were, in the end, the right ones."

It's always been hard to look at Sasha when I've visited because she looks so much like Jacob. Hard, as well, to get past the guilt of leaving her. But that doesn't make what Dad did *right*. It doesn't matter that I believed, and still believe, it was the best thing to do for Sasha at the time. I went on a very steep downward spiral after Jacob died, after Sasha was born. There was no way sixteen-year-old me was in any way capable of looking after a baby. But I could have been. If I'd been given the support I needed. If Dad had tried to help me rather than kick me out.

It's funny—as I was getting myself together, clawing my way up from the pit in my twenties to a position where I had a stable job, a proper home, where I'd given up drinking and drugs, I always said I was doing it for Sasha, so I could be a proper mother to her, but every time I visited home, every time I saw her, I wanted to run away again. I never felt *worthy*, and that's just crap, isn't it? Sasha never wanted worthy—she probably didn't even need me to be a proper mother, she had Jen for that. I should have been the sister everyone's pretended I was.

And if my father had really done the right thing, that's what would have happened.

"No," I say. "You were not *right*. None of what you did was *right*. I should have stood up and said that a long time ago, but you destroyed my confidence and my self-worth. If Jen and Sasha are angry with you, then that is down to you to fix. I hope Jen *does* leave you. She and Sasha will be better off."

"Don't you dare—"

"No—don't *you* dare. I do not have to listen to you anymore. You are not part of my life and I will not listen to your crap anymore. I will speak to Jen about seeing Sasha, and it will be on *my* terms and in *my* home."

That look—the cold, disapproving anger—is taking over his face and I turn my head away. I will not let him do this to me anymore.

"I'd like you to leave," I say.

Chapter 50

SASHA

I take a detour to the toilets before I go in and see Hanna. Mum had a go at sorting my hair out for me before we came to the hospital. There hasn't been time to go to a proper hairdresser, but it looks almost normal now, more a choppy chin-length bob than an attacked-by-a-hedge-clipper mess. I kind of like it. I think it suits the new "kidnapped by a psychotic serial killer and lived to tell the tale" me.

I close my eyes for a moment. Oh God. Maybe I do like the new hair, but I can't carry off cocky bravado. That will never be me. I don't know how to *feel*. I had a complete meltdown when I was speaking to the police. I honestly thought I was going to pee myself when I was sitting in that police station. Even though Mum was with me, and they told me I wasn't in trouble, the questions they asked...I sounded stupid. I sounded gullible and reckless and *stupid*. They got a really nice policewoman in to speak to me after I got full-on hysterical and she was brilliant at calming me down, but it didn't make me feel less stupid. Or guilty. Doesn't matter what they told me about how Ethan had all this planned, that it wasn't my fault, I made it easy for him to do what he did. Hanna could have died. Her boy-friend could have died. At any point, he could have killed

Mum or Dad or me or all of us. He'd already killed one woman.

I start shaking again. Crap. I need to pull myself together or Mum is going to come in looking for me and if she sees me all hysterical again, she won't let me go and see Hanna. And I need to see Hanna. Now that I know the whole story, I need to see Hanna.

I cried when the detective told me what happened to Jacob. Ethan's brother. Hanna's old boyfriend. My real dad. I don't know how to process all that yet. Or the fact that Mum's not sure if we're going to go home with Dad at all, that she's finally having her "F*** the Patriarchy" moment. She's not sure if she can forgive him for everything he's done, even though he keeps saying he's really, really sorry. I'm not sure if I can forgive him either and even if I did, I'm not sure I could ever forget how he let me down. I'm hoping Hanna will help with all that too.

I stand straighter, push my shoulders back.

Mum hovers behind me when I enter the room. Hanna looks at me and smiles, then her gaze flickers to Mum.

"I'm sorry," Mum says to her. "I'm sorry I didn't do more."

Tears shine in Hanna's eyes. "I'm sorry too," she says. "For everything."

I hear the click of the door as Mum leaves and I take a deep breath.

"I like your hair," Hanna says.

I put a hand up and smooth my hair down. "Yeah, well, you wouldn't have liked it if you'd seen it yesterday. Turns out Mum's a bit of a genius with a pair of scissors."

"It suits you like that—shorter."

I stare at her. "Is this what we're going to do? Talk about my hair and that's it?"

She shakes her head. "No, I...I don't know what to say. How do I say everything I should have said to you in the last fourteen years? If I start apologizing, I'll never stop. I almost got you killed..." She takes a deep, shaky breath. "And I don't know how to be a mother. I don't know..."

"I don't want you to be my mother," I say. "I've already got a mother. What I'd like is for you to be my sister."

She's quiet for ages. "I can do that."

"I'd like you to be there at the end of a phone when things are crap and I need someone to talk to."

She nods but I keep talking before she can answer.

"I don't know what's going to happen next, whether we'll go back to West Wales with Dad or not. Mr. Garner called Mum. He's thinking of moving to Spain full time and offered to rent us his cottage. He's still trying to save us Carter women," I add as I see tears come to her eyes.

"I'd like to come and stay with you. I'd like you to take me shopping and let me buy stuff that Dad would never let me wear in a million years. I'd like you to teach me how to do makeup. I'd like to stay in with you and watch crappy Netflix films. Everyone talks about Netflix and I've never seen anything."

"I can do all of that. I can take you out with my friends and take you to the cinema. I'll order all the takeaways because I remember how rare a decent takeaway was under Dad's rule."

"Pizza. Can we get pizza?"

"*All* the pizza."

"And Adam. I'd like to get to know Adam. He saved your life. He's a hero."

"He is a bit, isn't he? Him and Jen—heroes of the hour."

I smile. "Does he have any friends as nice as him?"

"Oh, I don't think so. You are not going to be hanging around with anymore men twice your age. Not on my watch."

My smile gets bigger. "See—you're getting the hang of this already. Before you know it, you'll be encouraging me to eat healthily and lecturing me about the length of my skirts."

She smiles back at me. "I think we'll be fine. I think we'll be better than fine."

I sit on the chair next to her bed. I don't mention the note that was waiting for me when I finally got home yesterday. The note that was in my bedroom, in the drawer of my desk. The note that just said:

Sorry
  E   x

I don't mention it and I didn't mention it then because it would have meant more police and Mum and Dad freaking out and searches and Hanna panicking and...maybe he really is sorry. He said he never committed the first crime, that it was Owen not him who ran over that woman. And the rest...I think Owen manipulated him. And I did like him. I thought he was my friend. And now it turns out he's my uncle. The police will catch him, of course they will. I don't have to tell them about the note, it won't help.

Besides, me and Hanna...We only have an hour until Mum comes back for me and fourteen years to catch up on. Time to get started.

Chapter 51

HANNA

They let me out of bed the next day and I shuffle down the corridor to Adam's room. It'll be a few days before they let him up and about, but he looks remarkably well considering he was beaten half to death by a psychopath.

"So," I say, my voice coming out a bit croaky with nerves, "what number date is this?" I cross my fingers behind my back.

He laughs, then winces. "Well, I've met your dad and your stepmother, I've met your daughter. We've been kidnapped, faced death together...I think we've skipped the dating stage and we're actually five years into a long-term relationship."

"Yeah." I sigh, uncrossing my fingers and reaching for his hand. "Do you think, for our next date, we could just order pizza and watch a film on Netflix?"

He squeezes my hand and smiles. "Sounds like a good plan."

"I don't want you to think I always need saving," I say, rushing the words out before I can overthink them. "That's not who I am and not who I want to be."

"Don't worry. I've given up being a hero. Turns out it hurts." He pauses. "Besides, it was you who saved me in the end. Have they caught him yet?"

I shake my head, a flutter of fear making me shiver. "Not yet. But they will."

They haven't caught Ethan yet, but I've told DC Norton to speak to Carrie. Owen and Lee won't ever give Ethan up, because he's Jacob's brother, and the bond between the three of them back then...I always hated it, resented it. Selfish teenager that I was, I wanted Jacob all to myself. But he was never all mine. I don't think I ever even came first. No, Carrie and I were always outside that little band of brothers.

And Carrie knows it too. Knows her husband would go to prison himself for lying to the police before he'd give up Ethan or Owen. But Carrie...I think she'll tell. I think she'll tell for the sake of her family.

There's a long pause and I wonder if everything that's happened has killed all the possibilities between me and Adam. Old Hanna would nod and accept that, *expect* that, and walk away.

I'm bored of old Hanna.

"I want you to take your website down."

"Okay." He says it without hesitation.

"I want you to completely delete it and I want you to take down that original article you wrote as well." I pause to take a breath. "And I can't...I can't keep being with you if this dark tourism, or even the urban exploring, is something you still want to do. It's not right. What you write, what you post—it exploits people. Ethan was right about that. You're exploiting people's misery."

"Okay," he says again. "You're right. I'm sorry. I just... No. I'm not going to offer excuses. I'll just say yes, Hanna. The site will go. I swear."

"Good. But first..." Another pause, another deep breath

needed. I hold out two pieces of paper, covered both sides in my handwriting. "I need to make amends. *You* need to make amends. To Jacob's friends, to the people who knew and loved him. I want you to publish this article, about the real Jacob."

I watch as Adam takes the paper and starts to read. Maybe when it's published, Ethan will stop running and Owen and the others will stop hating.

And maybe I can stop hating myself.

Want to know what really happened the night they vanished?

You do, don't you?

Then **Sign up here:**

...

<New post: updated by Adam Webster>

This is not what you came here to find. I know that. You wanted to know **why, who, what happened...** You wanted the **secrets,** the **shocking truth,** the **true and terrible facts behind the headlines.**

The thing is—I didn't write that original listing. My site was hacked. That's not an excuse, though. I didn't write it, but I *could* have, because isn't that what my site promises—an understanding of the darker side of life?

But the night they vanished is not where the story began, it's not where the story ends and, more importantly, it's not my story to tell and it's not your story to hear.

There's only one story left for me to tell and that's why this one new listing is going to be the last listing on **The Dark Tourist.**

Welcome to **The Dark Tourist:**

<One new listing....>

The real story of the boy from the dark house,

Not a hero, a prince or a knight in shining armor,

Not a villain, a criminal or a bad influence,

But a nice boy, who deserved better, who deserved more.

Acknowledgments

I began writing *The Night They Vanished* in a pre-COVID time, and have chosen to allow my characters to remain in a COVID-free bubble for the duration of the story—it seemed cruel to put them through a global pandemic as well as everything else...

In such difficult times, the help and support I've received has been wonderful and I am incredibly grateful to so many people.

A massive thank-you to Juliet Mushens, best agent in the world, for her continued faith in me and her enthusiasm for this book. Thanks to all at Mushens Entertainment, Liza, Kiya, and Silé—you are a dream team to work with.

I want to thank the whole amazing team at Sphere and Little, Brown; from editorial manager Thalia through to everyone in sales, marketing, and publicity, with an extra-special thank-you to my wonderful editors, Rosanna Forte in the UK and Alex Logan at Grand Central Publishing in the U.S. Your enthusiasm for this book has made the publishing process a total joy!

Thanks to former DCI Stuart Gibbon of GIB Consultancy for the advice on police procedures—his books, *The Crime Writer's Casebook* and *Being A Detective*, were also invaluable. Thanks to Savage and Gray Design Ltd. for the wonderful website and book trailers.

Acknowledgments

All the thanks to my fabulous writing friends, the Romaniacs and the Cowbridge Cursors.

And, of course, to all my family and friends for their continued and fantastic support with a special shout-out to the Thompsons, the Savages, the Griffith-Joneses, and the Ryder-Grays.

About the Author

Vanessa Savage is a graphic designer and illustrator and the author of two thrillers. She has twice been awarded a Writers' Bursary by Literature Wales, most recently for her debut novel, *The Woman in the Dark*. She won the Myriad Editions First Crimes competition in 2016 and her work has been highly commended in the Yeovil International Fiction Prize, shortlisted for the Harry Bowling Prize, and the Caledonia Fiction Prize. She was on the longlist for the Bath Novel Award.

Vanessa lives by the sea in South Wales with her husband and two daughters.